N. C. SCRIMGEOUR

MISTS OF MEMORY

Contents

SILVECKAN
THE DRIFT
THE STRAIT OF SILVECKAN
ARBURGH
EILEANAN SELCH
(THE SELKIE ISLES)
THE SOUTHERN REACHES
CAIM

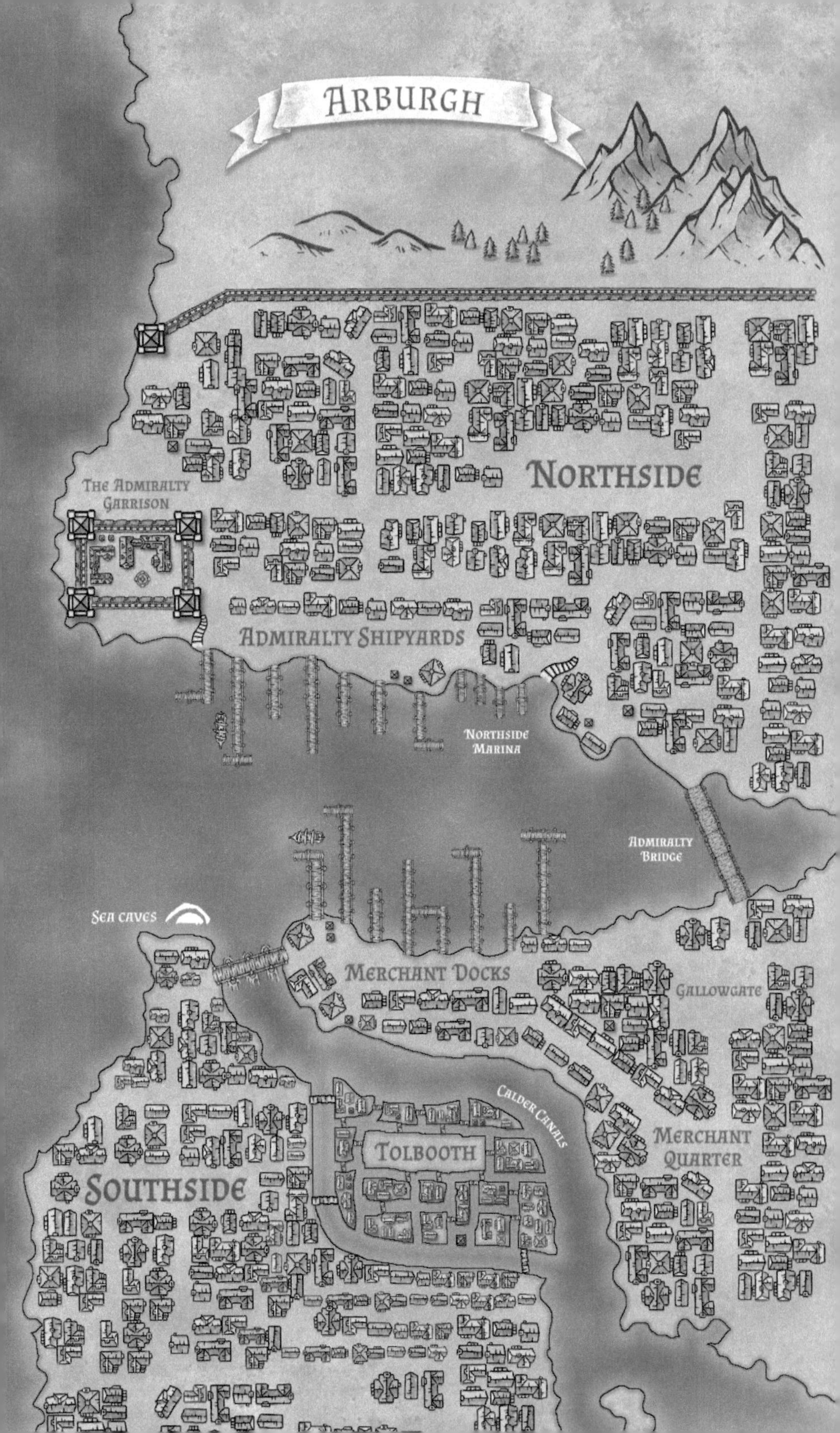

ARBURGH
NORTHSIDE
The Admiralty Garrison
Admiralty Shipyards
Northside Marina
Admiralty Bridge
Sea caves
Merchant Docks
Gallowgate
Calder Canals
Tolbooth
Merchant Quarter
Southside

Gun-anam (noun): Soulless. A selkie who loses their pelt and surrenders themselves to the sea, becoming one with the salt and spray to return as a mist-like wraith

Pronunciation Guide and Glossary

Persons of note

Isla Blackwood [EYE-lah]

Alasdair Cunningham [ALLA-stir]

Darce Galbraith [darss gahl-BRAYTHE]

Eimhir [AE-veer – 'ae' rhymes with 'stay']

Lachlan Blackwood [LOCH-linn – soft 'ch' sound, known as a voiceless velar fricative]

Mhairi [VAH-ree]

Nathair Quinn [NAH-hir]

Nishi [NIH-shee]

Rhona [ROE-nah]

Locations of note

Arburgh [ARR-bruh]

Caim [KAIM – like 'eye']

Caolaig [cull-AEG - 'ae' rhymes with 'stay']

Eileanan Selch [ill-ANN-inn SELCH – soft 'ch' sound]

Loch Mòr [LOCH MORE]

Silveckan [sill-VECK-an]

Animals and creatures

Cirein-cròin [KEE-rin CROW-inn] – a legendary sea monster once rumoured to roam the Silvish coast

Gun-anam [GOON-ann-AHM] – soulless spirits of slain selkies

Kelpie [KELL-pay] – an undead water horse made from salt and spray

Selkie [SELL-kay] – a seal shapeshifter which can shed its pelt and take the form of a human

General terms

Aineol [ANN-yoll] – stranger, outsider

Anam-long [ANN-am-long] - soulship

Auld [AWL-d] – old

Bairn [bay-rne] – a young child

Caraid [CARR-itch] – friend

Close [as in 'close by'] – a small alley or street

Crabbit [CRAB-bit] – grouchy, ill-tempered

Dreich [DREE-ch – soft 'ch'] – dreary, grey weather

Firth [firth] – an inlet or estuary leading to the sea

Gobby [GOBB-ee – hard 'g'] – mouthy, brash

Haar [harr] – a cold sea fog

Ken [ken] - know

Laird [LAY-rd] – lord

Loch [soft 'ch'] – lake or sea inlet

Màthair [MAH-herr] - mother

Nae [nay] - no

Nighean [NEE-inn] - daughter

Skerry – [SKERR-ee] – a small, rocky island

Sgian dubh [SKEE-an DOO] – a small ceremonial blade or knife

Wee [wee] – small

Wynd [wine-d] – a small alley or street

A letter, unsent

Read on for a recap of Sea of Souls...

Dearest Lachlan,

I don't know if this letter will ever reach your hands, but if by some chance it does, I beg you not to be too hasty in throwing it aside. I know your first instinct will be to crumple this parchment and feed it into the fire, but if you have any love left in your heart for me, please keep reading. Whatever has happened between us, you are still my brother. You are still my family.

Sometimes I wonder what might have happened if Mother's letter hadn't called me back from sea. Maybe it would have been simpler if I'd stayed away, if none of this had happened. But I so desperately wanted to see her one last time before the sickness took her. I had so much I wanted to say to her, so much I needed to hear. But... Well, you know I didn't make it in time. That was the first time I disappointed you since coming back to Silveckan. I wish I could say it was the last.

The truth is, I never felt like I belonged. Even when I came back to Blackwood Estate, I felt like I was intruding in the home of a stranger. It wasn't your fault, or Father's. You both tried your best after we buried Mother, and I so desperately wished that things might change. Perhaps I even believed they could. But we never had the chance to find out.

I still dream about what happened that night. Sergeant Galbraith...

Darce. The way he burst through my bedroom door, sword drawn. The fear on his face as he dragged me from my bed to your quarters. Seeing your door ajar, not knowing what we'd find inside...

Tides, I thought you were dead. The room was freezing cold, thick with salt and mist. Then that wraith appeared, drawing a ghostly blade from the shadows and sending it towards your heart. If I hadn't screamed, if you hadn't rolled away...

I don't like to think about the things we saw on our way out of the estate. The blood, the flayed bodies... Believe me, brother, I hated the selkies as much as you that night. Those raiders attacked our home. They summoned those wraiths from the mist. They butchered the people of our village. They killed our father. They'd have killed us too, if Darce hadn't been there to get us out. Even then, he was looking out for us. *Both* of us, Lachlan.

You know I didn't want to flee to Arburgh. The capital held too many rotten memories for me, and it holds even more now. But you asked me, and I've never been able to refuse you anything.

So we left, didn't we? The three of us, the only ones who survived that wretched night. But we weren't alone for long.

Sometimes I wonder if that was the moment I lost you. The moment I decided to trust a selkie. But Eimhir and Finlay weren't among the raiders who attacked our home. Eimhir, at least, was different. She wanted to end the violence between our people. I believed the awful truth she told us: every time a human steals a selkie's pelt, that selkie withers with salt and sorrow, until they are faced with no other choice but to drown themselves in the sea and become one of the soulless—one of the gun-anam. The gun-anam are the cause of the haar, that awful sea mist, and the mist drives the selkies to bloodlust, causing them to attack humans.

The violence is a cycle, brother. Do you still not understand why we had to try to end it?

You didn't like it when I agreed to help Eimhir find her aunt's stolen pelt. You didn't believe Eimhir's claim that it held an old selkie magic capable of stopping the gun-anam. But you went along with it, at least for a while. I don't think I realised how much that hurt you, how much you resented me for it. You were grieving. We all were. But I was so focused on finding a way to ease my own pain, I didn't stop to consider that I might be making yours worse.

Sailing to Arburgh only widened the rift between us. I hated the capital, hated how you turned to Nathair Quinn for help, and I didn't see how deep he'd ensnared you into his schemes until it was too late. I wish I could say that was the only thing I'm to blame for. But I turned to Darce for comfort, starting something I could never take back. I grew close with Eimhir, becoming friends with a selkie who should have been my enemy.

All my misgivings about Arburgh seemed to come true when Eimhir's pelt was stolen. I admit, I did some terrible things to help her try to get it back, but in the end, it only made things worse, like you said it would. But she was dying, and I couldn't find a way to save her. I wish you could understand how desperate I was in that moment.

Finlay blamed me, of course. He fled the city and came back with selkie raiders to take revenge. He tried to kill me that night at the docks, but you saved me with your sgian dubh. Our parents gave you that blade to protect me, and that's what you did. But I couldn't protect you when Finlay dragged you beneath the waves, and when you came back up, your leg was rotting with poison.

I'm sorry, Lachlan. I truly am. But Eimhir said it was the only way to save you. I couldn't let you die. Even if you hate me for it, even if you never forgive me for letting her axe fall on your leg, I couldn't let you die.

By then, I knew I'd failed you. But I still had a chance to save Eimhir.

Everything happened so quickly after that. There was no time to think. I broke into the Grand Admiral's office to find his charts. I discovered where he was keeping the pelt he'd stolen from Eimhir's aunt. I ran off with the Sea Kith to take it back.

You weren't there on the crossing, and I'm glad of it. The gun-anam attacked the ship. Perhaps you still don't truly believe they exist, but you would if you'd seen what happened. We'd never have survived if it weren't for Nishi. She's a fine captain. They call her a pirate, but the Sea Kith are so much more than that.

One of the wraiths tried to kill Darce. I don't know what happened, all I know is I couldn't let him die. I stepped in front of him and took the wraith's blade to my belly. That should have been my end, but sentinel magic is powerful. Darce spilled his own blood to save me, tethering his soul to mine even though I begged him not to. Believe me, Lachlan, I never wanted him in chains. I never wanted him to have to choose between us.

When at last we found what we were searching for, it was not what Eimhir or I expected. The Grand Admiral was waiting for us. He looked at me like I was a ghost and called me a name I had heard only from Eimhir's lips—the name of her aunt.

Mara.

This is the most painful part to recall, for I know now I am not truly your sister, at least not by blood. I am the Grand Admiral's bastard child, a half-blooded human. The other half... Well, you know the truth now.

I am Eimhir's cousin. I am one of the creatures that killed our family. I am a selkie.

That alone should see me hang, but I have committed enough treason in the Admiralty's eyes to meet the noose a dozen times. I shot the man who claimed he was my father, though it was not enough to kill him. I took my selkie mother's pelt and claimed it for myself. I swam to the Grand Admiral's ship and stole back Eimhir's pelt to save her life.

That was the last time I saw you, the last memory I have of you. You held your sgian dubh against my throat. The blade trembled in your hand as you decided not to kill me, but to let me go.

Do you regret it, brother?

As for the rest, well, I'm sure you know by now. Word from across the

waves says you joined the Admiralty. I only hope that if our paths cross…
But no, I don't have the right to ask anything of you anymore.

I didn't want to leave Darce behind, but he gave me no choice. He brought the Admiralty down on himself to give me the chance to escape. Please remember he's not to blame for any of this. Don't let them hurt him. If not for my sake, for your own. I fear you'll need him in the days to come.

I'm still trying to find my place in this world—the home that was stolen from me, the family I never got the chance to know. But I'll never stop being your sister, Lachlan. If tides be kind, you'll realise that before it's too late for us both. I write this letter in the hopes that one day, you'll forgive me. That one day, we'll be family again.

Until then, wee brother.

Isla

CHAPTER ONE
DARCE

A dying, bloody glow danced off the sea's surface as the sun slipped beneath the waves, and Darce Galbraith gritted his teeth against the ache of his fractured soul as part of it followed.

The gentle wash of water soaked the sand at his feet as the tide lapped at his boots, picking at the flecks of dirt and blood splattering the leather. Part of him knew that he should move, that he should do something—*anything*—to make it harder for the Admiralty to find him. But another part of him pulled further away with each passing second, straining at the frayed line connecting him to Isla Blackwood.

Tides take him if he was the one to let it snap.

A bitter wind stung his cheeks, but the pistol he held—*her* pistol—still pulsed warm in his hand. He could almost feel the echo of the shot he'd fired into the orange-streaked sky. The shot that had finally convinced Isla to leave, to dive beneath the surf and escape with her life—a life he wasn't meant to be part of.

The shot that had brought the Admiralty running, just as he'd intended.

He listened for them coming. Boots crunched against the brittle stems of beachgrass as they scrambled over the dunes. Raised voices barked out directions. Muskets clicked in formation, waiting for the order to end it, to end *him*.

Darce stared at the horizon. Despite the threat of violence, there was something peaceful about the shore. A gannet preened its white feathers, watching him with suspicious blue-rimmed eyes. Waves washed against the sand with a hushed sigh. The sound was like a whispered promise, reassuring him Isla was out of reach, lost below the surface to the world she belonged in. He couldn't follow her there, but neither could the Admiralty. For the moment, at least, she was safe.

Which was more than he could say for himself.

His boots shifted against the damp sand as he presented himself to the advancing officers. They stood in a line, muskets pointed squarely at his chest. Around their shoulders hung cloaks of teal and sapphire. The fleet's finest captains and commodores, all here for him.

His gaze fell on the familiar features of Blair Cunningham, the young lieutenant stone faced at the forefront. The steel in his expression sat at odds with his boyish curls, but Darce knew how dangerous it was to trust in appearances. Lad or not, this was the Grand Admiral's nephew. He'd be a fool to take that lightly.

"Sergeant Galbraith." Blair's voice was clipped, his capital accent sharp at the edges. "By order of the Admiralty, you are under arrest for aiding and abetting Isla Blackwood's escape from custody. I'm here to take you back to Arburgh, where the courts will decide your fate." He glanced down the shoreline, narrowing his eyes. "Where is she?"

Darce gave a pained smile. "Long gone."

"You expect me to believe that?" An angry flush reddened the lieutenant's cheeks. "Your Sea Kith friends are halfway to Breçhon. You have no other ship. I know she's somewhere on this island. Tell me where she's hiding, and you might yet be spared the gallows."

"Wherever she is, it's far out of your reach." Darce shrugged. "Nothing I say will change that."

"Sergeant, I'm warning you—"

"He's telling the truth." A familiar voice cut through the air, and the rest of the Admiralty officers drew back in their jewel-toned cloaks, like the tide from shore. Through their midst came a lone figure, hobbling across the shifting sand with a rosewood crutch tucked under his arm and the empty folds of his breeches pinned around the stump of his left leg.

Lachlan Blackwood lifted his chin and met Darce's gaze with a humourless smile. "Galbraith. Ever the loyal soldier, until it truly mattered."

The words were spoken to wound, and Darce struggled to keep the sting from showing. It wasn't right that a lad he'd known all his life should have become so much of a stranger in a matter of weeks. A shadow had crept across the younger Blackwood's tawny eyes. Gone was the aura of nobility that had once clung to him, haughty and cocksure in equal measure. What remained was the sullen grief of a man who'd lost more than he wanted to admit. Darce understood that only too well.

"My loyalty remains where it always has," he said flatly. "With your sister. And with you."

It was the wrong thing to say. Lachlan's expression darkened, and he muttered something in Blair's ear. Darce didn't need to hear what was spoken; it was clear in the pall settling over Blair's face. He knew what Isla was. Which meant *Lachlan* knew.

And he'd never forgive her for it.

"There's nothing more we can do," Lachlan said. "The sergeant is right. My *sister*"—his voice caught on the word, the edges of his mouth curling—"isn't here. You know we cannot track a selkie through these waters. The best we can hope for is to return your uncle to the capital alive."

"She shot him, nearly *killed* him. That's high treason, even before taking into account what she is." Blair tightened his grip around his musket. "Your sergeant here helped her escape. I should shoot him where he stands, courts be damned."

The composure on Lachlan's face flickered, yielding to the temper

Darce had come to recognise over the years. The slip was fleeting, the mask settling back into place before Blair or anyone else noticed. But Darce had seen it. It was a promise, however faint, that something of their old friendship had survived. A hope that whatever damage they'd wrought could be navigated, if not undone.

"Shooting me would be a mistake," Darce said. "Your uncle would tell you so himself, if he could. Those with the auld blood are difficult to come by these days. Do you really want to lose a sentinel?"

Lachlan's head jerked towards him, irritation flashing across his face. "Galbraith, I suggest you—"

"If the Grand Admiral is alive, then the young lieutenant here still answers to him." Darce surveyed Blair with a cool glance. "Family or not, I don't think he would appreciate you ridding the Admiralty of a valuable resource."

"A valuable resource?" Blair scoffed. "You place rather too much importance on yourself, Sergeant. Sentinels can only unlock the magic of their auld blood *after* making an oath to a captain. Do you expect me to believe you'd swear loyalty to the Admiralty after what you've done?"

The silence lasted for little more than a heartbeat. Then Lachlan laughed quietly. "He doesn't need to." His eyes drifted to the pistol Darce was clutching, and he twisted his lips in wry amusement. "He's already made his oath."

Of course Lachlan knew. The lad had always been sharp—usually too sharp for his own good. He'd recognised the polished mahogany stock in Darce's hand, the mother-of-pearl plating glinting under the glow of sunset. It was a fine pistol. More importantly, it was Isla's pistol, and that was all Lachlan needed to understand.

Darce lifted his gaze to meet Lachlan's, expecting to find the old resentment there, an accusation he could not answer. Instead, all he found was the shape of a mocking smile, hiding whatever bitterness might have been behind it.

"A blood oath made to a selkie?" Blair glanced at Lachlan. "That's impossible. Sentinels are supposed to *protect* us from the skinchangers. They can't make a damn oath to them. He's bluffing, trying to save his skin. Auld blood or not, your old swordmaster here has no more magic at his disposal than I do."

Darce closed his eyes. Everything disappeared but the sounds of the coast. The yawn and crash against the shore. The rustling fronds of beachgrass, disturbed by the breeze. The piping cheeps from an oyster-catcher in the distance. They anchored him to something he couldn't see, something he could only reach for and hope to grasp.

Tides be kind, he thought. *I might not have asked for this, but I could use the help.*

The first sign was the cold, as though all the blood in his body turned to ice water, threatening to drown him from the inside out. He gulped down air, trying to breathe, but tasted only salt and spray.

Don't fight it. The whisper came from the depths. *You called for us, after all.*

Aye, he had. Deep-water currents hidden far below the surface. Streams of bubbles rising from clefts in the seabed. They rippled through slick ribbons of kelp. They shifted across sand and shells. Through his blood, the spirits of the sea itself sang to him.

Help me, he urged.

All he felt was the numbness of his lips and the squeeze of his heart straining. The whispers fell silent in his ears, drowned by the crash of the waves. Kerr had told him back on the *Jade Dawn* that the sea did not answer to sentinels; it only listened, then decided for itself. Perhaps the tides had found him unworthy. Perhaps they were not on his side.

A raucous caw tore through his thoughts, and Darce opened his eyes to find the gannet from earlier watching him. The seabird had a baleful look that seemed at odds with the elegance of its white wings and curved neck. It cocked its head and released another rattling cry, shooting him a glare almost humanlike in how much contempt it held.

Before Darce could make sense of it, something washed over his feet.

He found the waves lapping at the worn leather of his boots—the same waves that only moments ago had been retreating from shore. Now, the water surged around his ankles as if he'd summoned it.

Tides, he *had*.

The waves came faster, crashing against him with more urgency. Their restless ebb and flow rushed through his body. Their salt saturated his blood. He shivered, then reached out a hand and bade the water to rise.

A blue-green pillar leapt beside him, stretching towards the sky. Currents roiled and raged in a spiral, spitting out seafoam as they churned. The sea spirits brushed his mind. They danced in every droplet of water scattering the sand. They whistled in the wind whipping around his neck. They sang along with the fierce cackle that escaped the gannet's throat as it ruffled its feathers and circled the watery tower he'd created.

Blair stood on the shore, transfixed by the pillar. The spray soaked his hair, leaving it clinging to his forehead in wet coils. It made him look more like the lad he was, not the shadow of his uncle.

Darce met his eyes. "Your choice, Lieutenant. What will it be?"

Blair lowered his musket, motioning for the rest of the Admiralty officers to do the same. "You've shown enough to buy yourself some time. I don't have the authority to execute a sentinel, no matter what you might have done. That decision lies with the Grand Admiral. But I warn you, my uncle has no use for a sentinel he cannot trust. You might have magic, but you made your blood oath to our enemy. To a tides-damned *selkie*."

Darce released his hand and the sea pillar collapsed, sending a surge of foam crashing onto the sand. It raced to Blair's feet, and he quickly retreated from its reach. Beside him, Lachlan remained still as the water pooled around the single boot beside his crutch.

"I made my oath to Isla Blackwood," Darce said. "But that is not the only promise I am beholden to." He waited until Lachlan lifted his chin, ready to meet the defiance there. "Your father died asking me to protect you. I've not forgotten that, no matter what you might think of me. I'm willing to keep my word to him, if you'll allow it."

This time, he saw through Lachlan's rigid composure. The tightness of his jaw wasn't enough to hide the war raging beneath his expression, the traces of pain and resentment resurfacing at the mention of Isla's name. There was jealousy there—there always had been. Grief, too, though Lachlan would never admit it. Grief for the way his sister had been ripped from him as cruelly and irrevocably as his own leg. For her making the choice for him, both times.

Then the look was gone, covered by a shrug that carried more weight than Lachlan's shoulders seemed capable of bearing. "Your word is no longer mine to accept," he said stiffly. "The Grand Admiral will decide what it's worth when we're back in Arburgh. Until then, I suggest you cooperate with the lieutenant."

"As you wish." Darce offered the pistol to Lachlan. "Best you keep hold of this for the time being, then."

Lachlan took it, wrapping his hand around the polished mahogany stock. He stared at the barrel, a muscle in his jaw twitching, then slipped it into his belt with a pained expression.

Darce turned to Blair and held out his wrists. "Go on, Lieutenant. You'll have no trouble from me between here and Arburgh."

He barely felt the bite of iron against his skin as the Admiralty officers clamped shackles on him. The sun slipped below the horizon, leaving the water dark and glittering. Something pulled tight in his chest, the part of him lost, leaving behind only an ache that burrowed to the bone.

Maybe you are made for waters I cannot follow you to, he'd told Isla.

He closed his eyes as the sea breeze nipped at his dry lips, promising a taste of the wind that would carry them to Silveckan's capital city and all that awaited them there. That was the path he'd chosen, for both of them.

A croak broke through his thoughts, and he opened his eyes to find the gannet back on the shore, staring at him expectantly. When he made no move, the seabird ruffled its white feathers and let out another derisive screech from its long beak.

Darce shuffled between two Admiralty officers as they trudged across the dunes. Ahead of him, Lachlan pulled himself across the shifting sands on one leg, cheeks flushed and crutch sliding as he climbed. When Blair moved across to help, Lachlan shrugged him off, readjusting the crutch under his arm to scramble to the summit.

As if he sensed Darce's gaze on him, Lachlan looked back, eyes fierce with defiance. When Darce said nothing, he turned away again, shoulders stiff and unyielding as he vanished over the dune, leaving only the rustling of beachgrass behind.

As stubborn as your sister, little laird, Darce thought, unable to keep the faint smile from his lips, bittersweet as it was. He knew better than most how fickle the tides were. He answered to them now. He could only go where they took him, and if that meant Arburgh, so be it.

Isla might have been out of his reach, but there was still a Blackwood he could save.

CHAPTER TWO

ISLA

Three months later...

Isla was running out of air, and the surface was too far to breach.

It wasn't the first time she'd cut it close. Eimhir often spoke about the dangers of being reckless on a dive, but the ringing of her warnings slipped from Isla's mind the moment she left behind the light of the surface. There was something thrilling about the way the sea closed in, its weight pressing on her bones like a crushing embrace. It promised a world kept from her for too long, a world she didn't want to return from, even when the precious air stored in her blood dwindled to its last reserves.

If she'd been human, her lungs would have burned from the effort of holding her breath. But she wasn't human, not anymore. Her heart slowed, each beat a muffled thump a dozen seconds apart. The thick layer of blubber under her skin shielded her from the water's icy chill. Her hind flippers thrust her forward as she climbed towards the surface. She was close enough to see the glitter of the sun breaking through the waves.

All she had to do was reach it.

Isla pushed harder, muscles straining as she forced them to carry her through the water. A distant part of her seal brain wanted to surrender to the fatigue and sink to the comforting depths below. The animal inside her knew the sea would claim her one day, after all—why not this one?

Because then it would have all been for nothing, she reminded herself. She'd lost too much to let that happen.

Desperation flooded her aching body as she propelled herself the last few metres and crashed through the swell. The salty air never tasted so sweet, even to her selkie senses. She filled her lungs, bobbing against the waves as her heart picked up pace in a frantic thrum.

She'd made it.

Barely. A pulsing call floated up from beneath the surface, muffled by the water. Isla didn't need to see Eimhir to know it was her. She'd learned to recognise the whistles and clicks and rumbling wails that formed into words whenever they communicated in selkie form. It was like listening to a language she'd never been taught, but somehow understood.

You were under for almost an hour this time, Eimhir continued, disapproval puncturing every note. *We'll never find a way to stop the gun-anam if you get yourself killed.*

Isla expelled the air from her lungs and slipped below the waves again, circling until she found the familiar shape of Eimhir's selkie form. *We'll never find a way to stop them unless I learn how to dreamwalk*, she countered. *You were right about coming out here to sleep instead of back at the crannog. It's different. When I close my eyes, something calls to me. Something in the deep. Every time I dive, I'm drawn closer to it.*

That doesn't reassure me, Eimhir said. *I told you once before, we selkies are far from the most dangerous creatures lurking in these waters. If you sense something, that's reason enough for us to stay away.*

Isla released an impatient stream of bubbles from her snout. *But—*

The memories in your pelt will come to you eventually. That's your best hope of learning to dreamwalk. It won't do you or our people any good if you drown in the meantime. Eimhir whirled around, muscles rippling under her pelt as she flexed her flippers. *Come, cousin. Let's go home.*

Home. The word rang in Isla's ears as she swam. Every rolling wave, every ripple in the current brushing her whiskers, reminded her of all that single word held. Even through the greyscale vision of her selkie eyes, the water never seemed so bright. Down here, she'd found the part of herself that was missing. Her pelt had given her the sea. It had granted her passage to Eileanan Selch—the Selkie Isles. It had carried her to where she was meant to be.

And yet...

There it was: the persistent ache that never subsided. Over the last few months in Eileanan Selch, she'd learned to push it aside, banishing it to a distance she could endure. But she'd never be fully free from it. She'd left too much of herself behind, lost in the tattered remains of the blood oath Darce had made to save her life. The oath he'd all but broken when he fired her pistol into the air and brought the Admiralty running.

You have my soul, he'd told her. *No matter where you go, there is no stretch of water vast enough to keep me from you.*

Isla pushed the memory from her head as a familiar underwater cavern bled into view. It took her eyes a moment to adjust as she slipped through its gaping mouth, barnacle-encrusted stone jutting out on all sides. It was the only way to access Caim, the heart of the isles. Any approaching ship would be cut to pieces on the fierce teeth of the rocks above. Only a selkie could make the dive through the submerged cave. It was a sacred place out of the Admiralty's reach. A safe haven for selkies.

At least, for those who had a pelt.

The reminder filled her with a chill that burrowed far deeper than the surrounding water. She knew the terror of the gun-anam—selkies whose pelts had been stolen from them, who'd withered and returned with the mists to reap bloody vengeance on those who had wronged them. More than once, their icy touch had crept across her skin, freezing the hair on her arms. She'd tasted their brackish breath from behind their seal-skull masks. They were the soulless—monsters of the Admiralty's making.

Monsters that would soon bring the end of the selkie people if they weren't stopped.

The surface glittered above, and Isla followed Eimhir out of the water. Colour crept back into her vision as she began the transformation from selkie to human. The dark green of the water lapping at the rocks, the grey-brown volcanic columns stretching towards a cleft in the cavern roof above. Pale yellow sunlight glinted through, casting shadows on the stone steps leading out of the cave.

They were home again.

Eimhir grinned as the speckled, fawn-coloured fur of her pelt settled into shape across her shoulders. To anyone who didn't know better, it looked nothing more than a fur tunic, the damp folds cascading across her chest and down her thighs. It didn't seem possible for it to contain a selkie's soul. Yet Isla knew how true it was, now she had her own. It was the comfort of knowing who she was, wrapped around her like an embrace.

"It's good to be back." Eimhir stretched until her shoulders popped loudly. "Float-sleep isn't the same as a proper bed with warm furs. Hopefully the chieftains won't detain us for long."

"We're heading straight into a gathering, then?" Isla asked, trying not to sound disappointed.

Eimhir's lips quirked as she climbed the steps. "The chieftains will expect a report. Do you want to keep them waiting?"

Isla bit her tongue as she followed. The cold stone beneath her bare feet wasn't as much of a discomfort as it had been only a few short months ago. She was used to the gritty bite of rock against her skin. After suffering the bleeding and calluses, her feet had hardened against her new home.

If only her nerves had, too.

Aineol, the chieftains called her. A stranger. Someone who didn't belong to Eileanan Selch.

Bile rose at the back of her throat. Even now, the shadow of the Grand Admiral loomed over the sea, heralded by the sails of his fleet. No matter how deep she dived, she couldn't escape that—couldn't escape *him*. She was half-selkie, but the other half of her shared his blood.

"It's like my skin is peeling back whenever they look at me," she said. "Like they can see through this pelt to what I really am. *Who* I really am."

"You are Mara's daughter," Eimhir said firmly. "You might not have known her, but she is part of you in a way the Grand Admiral will never be. Her pelt is yours now. You carry what is left of her."

"The chieftains—"

"Sent me to find my aunt's pelt, and I did as they asked." Eimhir's grey eyes glinted in the dim light. "They might have preferred me to claim it as my own, but I could never have taken it from you. Not after I realised what you were."

Isla snorted. "The half-breed bastard child of your worst enemy?"

"Family," Eimhir said softly.

The word stirred something in Isla's chest. She regretted her glib response, the bitter aftertaste it left on her tongue. Eimhir was right. Whatever else she'd lost, all the pain and grief from the bones of a truth laid bare, she had this. She had Eimhir.

"I..." Isla swallowed the lump in her throat. "I only wish they trusted me more. That they saw Mara when they looked at me, and not...him."

"It's difficult for them to accept. Half-selkies are not something known well among my people. It's rare for one of us to take a human as a mate." A stony look fell over Eimhir's face. "I'm not sure I believe the poison that came from the Grand Admiral's mouth. That Mara would willingly—" She broke off, cheeks paling. "I'm sorry, I didn't think. I didn't mean to—"

Isla pressed her lips together, trying to quell the churning in the pit of her stomach. Eimhir's words were only an echo of the dark thoughts that whispered at her ears ever since her encounter with the Grand Admiral all those months ago.

I loved her, he'd said. *And she loved me.*

The memory left Isla cold. It was difficult to know what frightened her more—that the words might be a lie, or that they might hold a sliver of truth.

"It doesn't matter," she said, voice weak to her own ears. "I can't change who I am, or how I came to be. All I can do is make sure Mara's sacrifice meant something in the end."

Eimhir placed a hand on her shoulder, squeezing through the fur of her pelt. "You will, caraid. I know it already. It's only a matter of time before the chieftains realise it too."

The faint warmth of the sun caressed Isla's skin as she climbed out of the narrow cleft and gazed over Caim's terrain. The cliffs fell sharply away to the barrier of rocks and sea stacks surrounding the island. Waves threw themselves against the stone as if they'd been scorned. They were hungry, ready to gorge themselves on wood and sail if any ship dared draw near.

Her eyes fell across the winding shingle path cutting through the overgrowth. Countless times over the last few months she'd trudged its length to Loch Mòr, where the clan's crannogs sat on stilts over the water. Countless times she'd been met with wary glances and mutterings of disappointment from the chieftains. It was difficult to believe this time would be any different. Unless...

She looked at Eimhir, her cousin's ragged blonde hair spilling across her wiry shoulders as she scrambled down the overgrown trail. *We selkies are far from the most dangerous creatures lurking in these waters*, she'd said. *If you sense something, that's reason enough for us to stay away.*

Perhaps, Isla thought, drawing her pelt close as an icy gust of wind swept over her skin.

Or perhaps it was all the more reason to go down there.

Loch Mòr lay at the foot of a craggy ridge, its calm blue waters cast in shadow. The surrounding hills rose in steep slopes of green, only shedding their colour at their rocky summits. Isla often imagined the peaks as towering guardians, watching over them with ancient, crumbling faces of limestone and grass.

On the loch itself stood the crannogs—wooden settlements built on stilts rising from the water. They were like floating islands, linked with chains of bridges. It was where the selkie clans came to gather in times of threat from the Admiralty.

There had been too many gatherings of late.

Isla followed Eimhir across one of the bridges, feet half-submerged under the icy loch water spilling across the wooden struts. The knot in the pit of her stomach tightened when she caught sight of a red-haired selkie outside the chieftains' enclave. He stood taller than Eimhir, with piercing blue eyes and pale skin smattered with freckles the same colour as his shaggy crop of hair.

Angus. The younger brother of Caim's chieftain.

His mouth pinched in disapproval as they approached. "They expected you back a day ago. I hope you're bringing good news this time—for your sake, if no one else's."

Eimhir grimaced. "More trouble?"

"Aye, you could say that." A shadow fell across Angus's pale features. "The mist sickness is spreading faster than we realised. We lost another three this week."

Isla's neck prickled. *Mist sickness.* The true horror of the gun-anam, more than their deathly chill and rotting armour of blackened bone. Every time the gun-anam appeared, so did the haar—the damp, salt-thick fog between the world they knew and the soulless realm. The more a selkie came into contact with the gun-anam, the more the haar infected them, until they could do nothing but succumb to mindless bloodlust.

"Sorry bastards set themselves on an Admiralty man-o'-war before we could stop them. They never stood a chance." Angus swallowed. "We arrived in time to see them thrown into the wake, throats slit and pelts stripped from them."

"Better a slit throat and a race to the depths than to be left alive without a pelt." Eimhir's voice was steady on the surface, but Isla couldn't mistake the grief rippling through each word. Eimhir knew better than most what it was to be separated from her pelt. For weeks, she'd shrunk and withered, scars of salt encrusting her skin as her body wasted away. If it had taken any longer to get it back...

Eimhir was right. No selkie should have to bear such torture.

"There's more." Angus flicked his gaze to Isla. "The Grand Admiral is getting bolder. His patrols skirt closer to the isles each passing month. It doesn't look like he's giving up on his hunt anytime soon."

Heat rushed to Isla's face. Her pelt rippled in the pale winter sun, its dappled patches of blue-black like inkblots scattered across the grey fur. She knew too well what the Grand Admiral was hunting. Not just her pelt, her soul, but *her*. She was the last surviving part of Mara, and he would never let that go. He'd scour the sea until he found her, even if it meant turning all Silveckan's waters to blood in his quest.

"This is my fault," she murmured. "I thought I'd killed him. I *should* have killed him."

"You saved my life," Eimhir said. "You returned my pelt to me. Whatever else happened that day doesn't matter. We'll have the chance to make things right soon enough." She glanced at the wisps of smoke rising from the pointed roof. "Come, we better not keep the chieftains waiting. Duncan is difficult to deal with at the best of times. I can't imagine he's taken this latest news well."

She pushed open the enclave's thick oak doors, and Isla followed her. The six chieftains sat in a half-circle around one side of the room, stone faced and wary eyed. Each of them represented one of the Selkie Isles, and every voice carried as much weight as the next. But it was Duncan's uncompromising gaze Isla was most afraid of meeting. From his place at the end of the row, his presence filled the room in a way none of the others' did.

He fixed her with an even stare, umber-coloured eyes glittering in the dim light. "I fear from your expression we're still no closer to unlocking Mara's dreamwalking gifts."

There was no malice in his words, but the bluntness of them rocked Isla all the same. *Mara's* dreamwalking gifts. Not hers. The pelt around her shoulders—*her* pelt—suddenly felt like a stranger's skin. A remnant of the selkie mother she never knew, stolen by the man who claimed to be her father. The man threatening the existence of the people she was now part of. How could she blame them for looking at her like she was the enemy?

"We're doing all we can," Eimhir said, voice ringing sharply against the walls. "Mara was the last dreamwalker among the clans, and nobody understood how her gifts worked. Isla has only been among our people—*her* people—for a few short months. You need to give us more time."

Her words disappeared into silence. The orange glow from the firepit in the centre of the room cast shadows across the chieftains' faces. Everywhere Isla looked, she only saw distrust and disappointment.

She pulled her pelt closer, its sodden fur heavy against her skin. It was their only hope of ending the mist sickness. The only way to banish the gun-anam beyond the haar. But the soul memories contained within the ripples of fur remained out of reach, lost behind a veil she hadn't been able to pierce.

"You think we have the luxury of time?" Duncan asked, voice hollow. "The Admiralty has made Silveckan's waters its hunting ground. Every month, patrols creep closer to Eileanan Selch. It's only a matter of time before they find our shores." He turned to Isla. "But this should come as no surprise to you, aineol. After all, your own brother sails with them, does he not?"

Isla flinched. Though Duncan hadn't spoken Lachlan's name, she still heard it. She felt it, buried between her ribs. The wound was as raw as ever and showed no hope of healing.

Your own brother... It was all Isla could do not to let out a bitter laugh.

If only he knew. If only any of them knew. When she closed her eyes, she could still see the hurt on Lachlan's face when he realised what she was.

A low growl rumbled from Eimhir's throat. "You want to bring up family? Don't forget this is Mara's daughter. My cousin."

"Be that as it may, she is not one of us." Duncan's dark eyes settled on Isla, and she tried not to squirm at how they bored into her. He looked different from Angus, with tightly coiled black hair and golden-brown skin the colour of sand under a sunset. Clan-brothers, Eimhir explained. Not connected by blood, but by choice.

Only now, with the way Duncan was staring at her, did Isla realise how much of a stranger she was to them. She might have been Mara's daughter by birth, but that didn't mean she had a place here, no matter how much she yearned for it.

"Not one of us?" Eimhir repeated. "Even if that were true, it's not her fault. Mara left her pelt behind to escape the Grand Admiral. She gave up her soul so Isla could be born free of his clutches. She must have known her sacrifice would extend beyond her own life." She turned to Isla fiercely, reaching for her hand. "You would live, aye. But with no pelt, you would live only as a human, separated from your people. That was Mara's choice, not yours. You made your choice by coming here. Coming *home*."

Isla squeezed Eimhir's fingers, her rough skin a familiar comfort. Her mind flooded with the echo of Darce's gunshot on the shore, Lachlan's face when she lost him, the lingering pain of everything that had brought her here. It hadn't felt like a choice at the time, just the cruel will of the tides. But the moment she'd followed Eimhir into the waves, she'd found where she was meant to be.

The sea had called to her, and she'd answered.

She lifted her chin and looked at the rest of the chieftains. "I'm not what you asked for. You wanted Eimhir to claim Mara's pelt. But she gave it to me, and I cannot be sorry for it. She gave me the one thing I never had—a place where I belonged. A home. And whether you see me as one of you or not, I'll do everything I can to protect that home from whatever storm the Admiralty brings. I swear it on Mara's memory." She burrowed her fingers into the soft fur of the pelt across her shoulders. "I swear it on her soul."

A low murmur rippled between the chieftains. One of the older women scrutinised Isla, her weathered hands twisting together. "Those are commendable words, lass, but we cannot defend Eileanan Selch while the mist sickness ravages our people. Only a dreamwalker can navigate the haar to find a way to the soulless realm. Only a dreamwalker can stop the gun-anam from crossing over. I fear our hopes for that died when Mara did."

"The float-sleep is helping," Isla insisted. "I'm getting glimpses of memories. It's not enough to make sense of yet—only fragments and fleeting impressions—but..." The rest of her words dried up on her tongue, leaving behind the stale taste of trepidation. She risked a glance at Eimhir, who gave her an almost-imperceptible shake of the head. "There's something else..."

"Isla—"

"Let her speak," Duncan said. "I want to hear what she has to say."

Isla steadied herself with a breath. "The depths call to me whenever I'm in selkie form. I may not have harnessed the ability to dreamwalk, but something out there is drawing me to it, drawing my soul to it. If I find it, perhaps the memories will follow."

"Or perhaps you'll misjudge how long your lungs can hold out, and you and your pelt will be lost to us for good." Eimhir glared at Duncan. "We're not meant to dive to such depths. She's pushing herself too hard, and it's on your account."

Duncan pursed his lips, eyes glittering as he watched the flames dance in the firepit. "We're not meant to wither to salt either, but such is the fate we are faced with. Every time a human steals a pelt, another one of us is lost to the gun-anam. And the more gun-anam, the more the mist sickness spreads. More raids, more blood spilled, more pelts stripped from the bodies of our people. Unless we end the cycle, it will be the end of us."

He turned to the other chieftains, addressing them in a low burr. Clicks and whistles interspersed the rumble of their voices as they conferred. Even if they spoke louder, Isla wouldn't be able to understand more than a word or two. The selkie tongue was one thing to comprehend in the water, but the spoken dialect was still too elusive for her human ears to unpick, no matter how she'd fought to learn it.

Just another thing stolen from her without ever knowing it existed.

Duncan rose from his wolfskin-clad chair, the black folds of his pelt spilling to the floor. He surveyed Isla with an expression that could have been carved from stone. There was no warmth there, no fondness. But, for the first time, she thought she might have imagined something more than distrust and suspicion.

It felt like a chance.

"Take Angus with you when you dive again," Duncan said. "He's the best scout across all Eileanan Selch when it comes to navigating deeper waters. If there is something out there, he'll help you reach it."

Eimhir bristled. "This isn't the answer. I know you're desperate, but—"

"Desperate?" A guttural laugh tore from Duncan's throat. "Do not speak to me of desperation, Eimhir. Not when the Admiralty's bloody wake draws ever closer. Not when they trade the souls of our people for coin. Not when they force us to return our bairns to the water with scars of salt and empty lungs. You know the cost of their cruelty as well as I do."

A pall fell over Eimhir, her skin taking on a sickly sheen. Her lips parted, half forming a word. Then she pressed them shut again, eyes bright and furious.

Duncan fixed Isla with a measured stare. "I don't know what you think you'll find in the depths, but if there's a chance it could help banish the gun-anam, it's worth the risk." He nodded, and the other chieftains rose around him in pelts of rich cream and soft brown and speckled grey. "You say you want to protect your home, aineol. Prove it, and there may yet be a place for you here."

Isla nestled his parting words to her chest as she followed Eimhir out the enclave, the half-promise burning fiercely against her ribs. Eileanan Selch *was* her home. She'd find a way to protect it, even if it meant diving to places a selkie was never meant for. She'd prove to Duncan and the rest of the chieftains that she was one of them.

No matter what she had left behind, this was where her soul belonged.

CHAPTER THREE

DARCE

The grey morning light crept across every tired line on Darce's face, darkening the shadows under his eyes as he stared at the stranger in the mirror. The cool relief of the water he'd splashed across his forehead faded quickly. Every droplet trickled away at his command, even without drawing on his sentinel magic. They loosened themselves from strands of hair, evaporated from his cheeks, until he questioned whether he'd imagined twisting the damned tap at all.

Aye, it was going to be one of those days.

He released his grip on the edge of the sink and redressed the bandage around his left hand, wincing as the wound began to bleed again. Everything hurt these days. Here he was, barely a year past thirty, with an ache in his shoulders and stiffness in his spine as he reached to tie his hair in a knot. It was longer than it had been at Blackwood Estate, the tousled lengths tangling more wildly the longer he neglected them. He didn't look anything like the man he was only a few short months ago. Perhaps he wasn't.

He rubbed a hand over the rough stubble on his jaw and eyed the doublet hanging in the corner of the room. Every time he pulled the teal-trimmed fabric around his shoulders, it felt like a betrayal. Donning the Admiralty's colours instead of the muted greys and blacks of his old

Galbraith tartan was another reminder of how much had changed. He was one of *them* now, tides take him for it. He'd sworn his loyalty through gritted teeth and a clenched fist, and every morning, he tried to convince himself it meant something.

This one would be no different.

A drizzle clung to the air as he trudged down the barracks' stone steps into the garrison courtyard. Arburgh was dreich at the best of times, but on mornings like this, the grim walls and gloomy canopy of low-hanging clouds closed in, reminding him of the prison he'd chosen for himself.

"I seem to recall you bloodying my knuckles any time I was late to a sparring session back home, Galbraith." Lachlan's voice drifted across the courtyard, light and airy. "Is it time for me to return the favour?"

Darce gave a begrudging smile. "I suppose you could try."

"I'll do more than try. I have an excellent teacher, after all." Lachlan gestured to the whalebone claymore propped against the fence, then shuffled to the centre of training yard, twirling his cutlass in one hand. The rosewood crutch under his arm left a trail across the sand packed underfoot as he took up a defensive stance, waiting with gleaming eyes and a grin.

Darce wrapped his hands around the hilt of the training sword. Whalebone didn't bite like steel, but it could still make a man bleed. Back at Blackwood Estate, Lachlan would have used every excuse in his considerable repertoire to get out of the cuts and bruises that came with a morning sparring session. He'd preferred the comforts of his bedsheets and the company of whatever noble he'd charmed into them the night before.

Things were different here. *Lachlan* was different here. Every day, the traces of the lad he knew grew fainter, whittled away like the whetstone that sharpens the blade. It might have made Darce proud, if it didn't make him so damn afraid.

Without warning, Lachlan swung on his crutch to hurl himself forward. He brought his sword down in a fierce movement, forcing Darce to step back as he warded off the blow with the broad side of his claymore. The whalebone blades met with a crack, echoing off the garrison walls.

Lachlan's grin widened. "Apologies, Sergeant. Didn't realise you were still getting ready."

Cocky wee shite, Darce thought. Not everything had changed.

He lifted his sword, noting with satisfaction the way Lachlan reset his stance, his crutch and cutlass perfectly balanced in each hand. When they'd first started training, Lachlan had barely managed to parry a single blow without falling into the dirt. The crutch was a hindrance—too unfamiliar, too much of a reminder of all that was wrong. Since then, he'd learned to trust it. He knew how to shift his weight to swivel and skirt blows. Tucked in the crook of his armpit, the crutch had become an extension of his own body.

Lachlan tightened his fingers around the handle and braced himself as he aimed a kick at Darce's knee with his good leg. The attempt was a cheap one and missed its mark, but that wasn't enough to temper Lachlan's amusement. "You're awfully quiet, Galbraith. That would have earned me a cutting remark about sloppy footwork back in the old days."

As light as the barb was, it still twisted Darce's stomach. He couldn't shake the guilt for the things he no longer said out of fear or regret or worst of all, pity. And Lachlan knew. Of *course* he knew; the lad was too canny not to. That was why he was goading him.

Darce swung the claymore in a heavy arc, forcing Lachlan to hop backwards. *Bloody Blackwoods.* Isla had known how to needle him too. He pictured her at the estate: pale cheeks flushed pink, sable hair swept into a braid, the previous night's whisky on her breath. He'd pushed her until she retched, and even then she'd had the gall to—

Something struck the side of his head and he stumbled, dazed. All he could do was blink away the blurriness and frown at the new, violent throbbing against his skull. It wasn't until he pressed his fingers to his temple and they came away bloody that he realised Lachlan had caught him with the tip of his cutlass.

He smiled, despite himself. "A fine blow, little laird."

"Was it?" There was no satisfaction in Lachlan's eyes. "You were distracted, and it's not difficult to surmise why."

He started forward again, but Darce was ready for him this time. The whalebone blades rattled as he pushed back with more bite than before, forcing Lachlan to retreat.

"I can tell when you're thinking about her," Lachlan continued, hanging out of reach. "There's a part of you that goes distant. Like you're adrift, not really here."

Darce ignored him and swung his claymore in a scything blow. Lachlan dropped his crutch and ducked as the blade swept through the air above him.

"She's gone, Galbraith." Perspiration beaded across Lachlan's forehead, dampening the strands of golden hair falling loose. His breaths were more ragged, but that did nothing to dispel the challenging glint in his eye. "She made her choice, and you made yours. It would be nice if a day passed when you didn't make me feel like you regretted it."

Darce stiffened. "That's not—"

"Don't deny it." Lachlan regathered himself and sprang, slashing at Darce's face. "You need to let it go—let *her* go. You could make a difference here, if you'd only let yourself."

"Make a difference *here?*" Darce wheeled around, neatly stepping out of the way. The rain pelted down more tenaciously now. If it were anyone else standing across from him, he might have used that to his advantage. But drawing on his sentinel magic against Lachlan felt wrong, somehow. Another betrayal on top of all he'd suffered already.

Instead, he drew back, fixing Lachlan with a frown. "I thought your intention was to gather ships and resources so you might one day restore Blackwood Estate. Is that still the case, or have you set your ambitions higher now you've had a taste of the capital?"

Lachlan scowled. "The best I can do to honour those we lost at Blackwood Estate is to help rid Silveckan of the monsters that killed them." He thrust his sword, the blow heavy with the weight of his temper. "Tides take you, Galbraith. Have you already forgotten Caolaig? The empty fishing boats. The bloated bodies washed ashore. The blood running through the cobbles. Have you forgotten my *father?*"

A hot surge of anger flooded Darce's cheeks. "Don't. Don't ever accuse me of—"

"It wasn't enough for you to let them kill him, was it? You had to swear your soul to one of them too, you oath-breaking piece of—"

Darce moved without thinking. One moment, Lachlan was in front of him, eyes heated with accusation. The next, he'd driven a boot into the middle of Lachlan's chest and brought his claymore down with a ferocious blow, clattering Lachlan's arm and knocking his cutlass from his grip.

Lachlan staggered, crutch slipping from under his arm as he lost balance. For a fleeting second, Darce thought about reaching for his arm, sparing him the fall. Then the chance was gone, and Lachlan landed on his back with a dull thud, pale cheeks flushed red.

"You're right." Darce tossed his own sword to the ground. "You *are* sloppy."

As soon as he said it, he regretted it. Lachlan wanted a reaction, and like a bloody fool, Darce had given him one. The words were exactly the kind of poison Lachlan craved—another measure of bitterness he could cling to and make his own.

The ensuing silence was thick with resentment, broken only by Lachlan's heavy breaths and the patter of rain. Around them, the towering garrison walls loomed grey and foreboding. This was not Blackwood Estate. Arburgh was not home. And as much as Darce tried to convince himself otherwise, this was not the Lachlan he'd once known. Perhaps he had to stop grieving the lad he'd lost, and accept the man he'd become.

"I'd have done the same for you," Darce said quietly. "I can't offer you my soul, but I swore to your father I'd give my life to protect you. That hasn't changed, no matter what you might think."

Lachlan snorted. "Where was your protection when Eimhir took my leg?"

Darce flinched. Sometimes when he woke, he heard the screams from that night in the winds howling outside the barracks. When he visited the officers' tavern, he was hit with the smell of the cheap liquor Muir had poured down Lachlan's throat. And every time he looked at Lachlan, he saw the dark pool of blood around where his leg should have been.

Before he could answer, Lachlan sighed. "I didn't mean that." His eyes were bleak and distant, fixed on the pinned-off folds where his breeches covered his stump. "You weren't the one who made the decision. I don't blame you for what happened."

The words should have brought Darce some kind of comfort, but they couldn't chase away the guilt. He carried it with him every day, a festering reminder of how he'd failed—not just Lachlan, but Isla, too. Lady Catriona and Laird Cormick had trusted him to keep their children safe, and he hadn't been up to the task.

He offered his hand and Lachlan took it, hauling himself back onto one leg with a grimace. His dishevelled hair fell across his face as he leaned over on his crutch to catch his breath. The fight had left him, replaced with an exhaustion Darce knew ran far deeper than the aches of a sparring session.

"You expect too much of yourself." Darce paused. "It's making you even more of an insufferable wee prick than usual."

Lachlan snapped his head towards him, eyes flashing. Then he let out a hoarse laugh, and the tension between them loosened, if only a fraction. "I suppose I deserve that. You were never shy about putting us in our place, nobility or not."

"You were never just another noble to me, little laird."

Lachlan shifted awkwardly, then leaned on his crutch to retrieve his fallen training sword from the ground. Rainwater dripped from his hair as he straightened again. "Thank you for the lesson, Galbraith. I might not act like it sometimes, but I'm glad you're here."

"As am I."

A rueful smile pulled at the corner of Lachlan's mouth, but if he'd heard the trace of a lie, he chose not to say anything. Instead, his gaze flicked to Darce's left hand, taking in the fresh bandage. "I see you and that seabird of yours still aren't getting along."

Darce turned to the ramparts above, half expecting to see the gannet circling there. The bird had been a tides-damned pain in his arse for months, ever since it followed him back to Arburgh. The fresh cut on his hand was only the latest in a series of wounds the wretch had inflicted on him with its razor-sharp beak. Featherblade, he'd taken to calling it, though why he'd seen fit to give it a bloody name was beyond him. The bird was nothing but a nuisance, and a violent one at that.

"Might be easier if I knew what it wanted," he said gruffly. "Seems to me it would have been happier staying on that island."

"Do you think it's drawn to your sentinel magic?" Lachlan looked pensive. "I thought it was only the Sea Kith who could summon birds, but maybe it's some gift of the auld blood we don't know about."

"Perhaps." If he'd been able to speak to Kerr, he might have learned more about the connection between him and the gannet, whether it was the same kind of bond Kerr shared with Shearwing. But the *Jade Dawn* hadn't been spotted in Silvish waters for months, and if Nishi had any sense, she'd be keeping well clear of Arburgh. Isla wasn't the only fugitive the Admiralty was hunting.

His thoughts scattered at the sound of hurried footsteps clacking across the cobbles, followed by an ashen-faced Blair Cunningham striding towards them.

Darce tensed. The lad had spoken in his defence at his trial, sparing him the noose and the gallows. Lachlan's influence, no doubt—the two young men had spent a considerable amount of time together over these last few months. But he was still the Grand Admiral's nephew.

"What is it?" Lachlan's jaw tightened. "Did something happen?"

Darce braced himself for the answer, dreading it as he always did. He waited for the lieutenant's eyes to darken, for his mouth to form the shape of Isla's name. Instead, Blair shook his head, his tousled curls bouncing under his Admiralty bonnet.

"The courtyard," he said, voice bleak. "Better you see for yourselves."

Darce led the way, followed by the scrape of Lachlan's crutch against the stone as he hobbled to keep up. Overhead, the clouds were black and angry, the rain more relentless than ever. It battered off the cobbles and soaked Darce's shirt until it clung to his skin. But if there was a chill in his blood, it wasn't from the foul turn in the weather.

A crowd had already gathered by the time they entered the courtyard. Darce saw the horror on their faces, the shock turning their cheeks white. These people were Admiralty officers, no strangers to violence and loss, whether it be on the waves or the streets of the capital. But Darce already knew this was no ordinary violence. This was no ordinary loss.

He pushed past a woman shaking in a sapphire cloak. Rainwater streamed over the cobbles, trickling through the grooves between the stones. But the water under Darce's boots wasn't clear; it deepened to a dark, violent red.

He stopped with a sharp breath. In the middle of the courtyard stood a solitary medical cart. Its tarpaulin covering had been peeled back and hung over the wheels, stained with blood.

Inside lay the naked bodies of four Admiralty officers, the flesh flayed from their backs.

Darce bit his tongue. He'd seen this too many times. Blackwood Estate, Caolaig, Arburgh. No matter where he was, this violence followed.

The closest body belonged to a young lad, neck twisted at an unnatural angle, eyes blank and glassy. The freckled skin of his back was stripped away in thin ribbons, leaving little behind but exposed muscle and the white nubs of his spine. Blood pooled under his body, dripping down the spokes of the cart's wheels.

"They were stationed at a wee fishing village five miles down the coast," Blair said. "A quiet posting—or it should have been. The raid happened this morning, before dawn. Only two officers and a handful of villagers survived."

Darce didn't say anything. He couldn't. The flayed bodies spoke loudly enough.

"Don't forget what they are, Galbraith." A pallor fell across Lachlan's face as he stared at the bodies in the cart. "This is what the skinchangers do, what they've *always* done. Her being one doesn't change that."

Something sank in the pit of Darce's stomach. Isla couldn't have known about this. She'd walked the blood-soaked shore with him at Caolaig. She'd helped him recover the bodies from the shallows. Selkie or not, she was the same woman he knew. The same woman he...

A raucous cry tore through the air, ringing above the downpour. Darce caught the familiar flash of a white belly as Featherblade swept overhead, circling the courtyard like a crow searching for carrion. Darce's heart plummeted, fearing the gannet might make for the cart and pick at the bodies with its beak, but instead it landed on the ramparts, its pale yellow neck arched as it observed the commotion.

Nobody else took notice of the bird. Lachlan's eyes were fixed on the cart, his knuckles white around the handle of his crutch.

"They didn't deserve this," he said, voice low. "It was a damn fishing village, just like Caolaig. We can't keep letting this happen."

"That's why I was sent to find you. Or rather, find the sergeant here." Blair turned to Darce. "I have a missive for you, Galbraith. I know you've ignored most of the others I've passed on, but believe me when I say it would be unwise to disregard this one."

He plucked a thin envelope from the pocket of his long-tailed coat and pushed it into Darce's hand, the force behind the gesture offering no room for argument.

Darce stared down at the rain-splattered envelope. He didn't open it. He knew what it was already—it was clear from the seal pressed into the sapphire Admiralty wax.

A wolf's head. The same wolf that snarled from the bow of the *Vanguard of the Firth*.

He scrunched the parchment between his fingers, ignoring the way it burned against his hand despite the chill in the air. He lifted his eyes to find Featherblade on the ramparts. The bird met his gaze with a sharp, blue-eyed glare, then let loose a rattling cackle from its throat, as if it knew as well as he did what was coming next.

Blair was right. There was no avoiding it anymore. He'd been summoned by the Grand Admiral himself.

CHAPTER FOUR

ISLA

The sweet, smoky scent of mackerel roasting over the fire's blackened embers drew a growl from Isla's stomach. She twisted the stick in her fingers as more of the skin crisped, ignoring the pained look Angus was making little attempt to hide.

It was different for him, she told herself. He knew nothing else but what it was like to hunt in the open waters, snatching a careless whiting or cod wriggling and whole. Over the last few months, Isla had learned to tolerate the raw taste in selkie form, but a part of her missed this—*needed* this. So when Eimhir had suggested they take a few hours' rest on a craggy islet, Isla had been eager for the chance to satiate the longing in her now-human belly.

She brought the stick to her lips and bit delicately, the skin crunching between her teeth. The flaky flesh was hot enough to burn her tongue as her mouth filled with the mackerel's rich, oily flavour.

It was apparently too much for Angus, who wrinkled his nose and trudged away towards the shoreline. The tide was high, and he stood with his bare feet in the water as he stared out at the dawn light bleeding over the horizon.

"It's a very human thing, to eat for enjoyment rather than out of necessity." Eimhir eyed the mackerel with a lopsided smile. "May I?"

Isla passed her the stick and watched as Eimhir took a bite out of the fish, chewing slowly. As she swallowed, her tongue darted out to catch a trickle of oil falling from her lips.

"Odd," she said. "But not entirely unpleasant."

"It could do with some salt," Isla conceded. "Or thyme, and perhaps lemons from Vesnia. But that might send Angus over the edge entirely."

Eimhir gave a throaty chuckle. "Aye, he is certainly Duncan's brother in that regard. Both set on keeping the auld ways. Or at least, that used to be the case. Never thought I'd see Duncan agree to a dive like this. I don't like it."

"You want to stop the gun-anam as much as I do."

"Not at the cost of your life, caraid." Eimhir's mouth drew tight. "I've already lost too much. My peltless baby brother to the sea, my mother and sister to mist sickness, Finlay to—" She took a steadying breath. "Fin to his own hatred. You're all the family I have left. My cousin. I can't lose you too."

Her words hung in the air. Isla saw the weight of them in the stiffness of Eimhir's spine, the creasing of her brow. She knew what fear looked like, what grief looked like. There was far more she shared with Eimhir than her selkie mother's blood.

"I have to do this," she said. "I'm the only one who can."

Eimhir cast her eyes over the pelt around Isla's shoulders, a troubled shadow falling across her features. "Aye, I suppose you are. But knowing that doesn't make it any easier to accept."

"Duncan seemed to accept it in the end."

A harsh laugh tore from Eimhir's throat. "Duncan has nothing to lose. If you get yourself killed, your pelt can be passed on to someone else, as long as your blood is spilled in the process. Why do you think he sent *him* with us?" She jerked her head towards Angus. "He's here to make sure your pelt is returned to Eileanan Selch if anything happens to you."

"I heard that," Angus called mildly.

"Do you deny it?" Eimhir shot back.

"Of course not." Angus's bare shins glistened with seawater as he traipsed over the shingle and sat on the other side of the embers. "If Mara's pelt—" He winced. "If *Isla's* pelt is lost, so is our chance of stopping the gun-anam. Only a dreamwalker can navigate our ancestors' memories. Only a dreamwalker can find a way to cross the haar into the soulless realm. Duncan knows what's at stake." He glanced at Eimhir. "There was a time you did too."

Eimhir snorted. "Don't talk to me about what's at stake. Was I not the one who went into exile and swore not to return until I'd found my aunt's pelt? The only difference between me and Duncan is I believe Isla can do this. He's just waiting for her to fail."

Isla swallowed the last piece of mackerel, the taste stale on her tongue. "Why give me the chance at all, then? Why risk losing my pelt to the depths when he could spill my blood across it himself and give it to someone he believes is worthy?"

Eimhir flinched, and Angus's eyes widened. "You *dare* suggest—"

"She doesn't know." Eimhir laid a hand on his arm, then turned to Isla. "It's true that the only way we can pass on our pelts is by spilling our blood across them. But the idea of any selkie killing another for their pelt... It's something unspeakable, unthinkable. Even when I lost my own and salt consumed my skin, I would have sooner surrendered myself to the sea than taken another's pelt by force."

Angus steadied himself, but an angry flush coloured his pale cheeks. "Only the most desperate, the most twisted, could even consider it. The scar it would leave on the soul..." He pressed his mouth into a thin line. "It would haunt any of us to madness. It's simply not done."

"We are a dying people," Eimhir added. "The sea gave us our souls, and each time one of our pelts is stolen, we return to it. Our numbers will forever dwindle until we are reunited once more with that which birthed us. No selkie would ever willingly hasten that fate. If we started killing each other for our pelts, we'd be no better than—"

"Humans," Isla finished, the word heavy in her throat. "I understand."

Silence fell between them. The only sounds came from the hushed lapping of the waves and the far-off cries from the fulmars and puffins stirring from their perches in the cliffs above.

Aineol, they chattered in their soft, mocking voices. *Stranger.*

Isla pulled her pelt closer, its dappled markings rippling in the morning light. She closed her eyes and breathed in the scent of the damp fur mingled with salt water and her own skin. It was hers; it belonged to her in a way nothing else ever had.

I have to do this, she'd told Eimhir. *I'm the only one who can.*

She pushed herself to her feet and scattered the remaining embers from the fire. The faint winter sun rose above the horizon, glittering across the breaking waves. It was time to go. Time to return to the sea.

Eimhir followed her gaze. "What is it you expect to find down there?"

Isla stepped into the water, its icy shock biting pleasantly against her skin. Her pelt responded with a gentle stirring, ready to return her to her selkie form. Somewhere, buried in the memories of her soulskin, the call of the depths beckoned her.

"Answers," she said, then sank into her pelt and dived.

Soon after they'd left the rocky islet behind, the seabed fell away, yielding to gloom. They swam close to the surface, breaching the waves. Isla savoured each gulp of salty air, filling her lungs greedily each time she burst through the swell. It wouldn't be long before she'd have to expel that precious breath. She already sensed the sand and stone of the sea floor retreating further with each mile they swam, as if the depths were sucking her down.

The call was stronger than she'd ever felt it, resounding in her bones. It was impossible to tell where it came from, only that it struck something in her soul she couldn't ignore.

We're close, she said, vocalising the words with a series of clicks. *Whatever it is, it's somewhere below us.*

Angus circled back. The vibrant warmth of his russet-brown pelt was lost to the muted grey of her selkie vision, but she recognised his sharp movements, the alertness with which he darted his head.

Wait here, he said. *I'll scout ahead, then come back for you.*

Before Isla could argue, he shot off into the waters below, leaving only a dark outline that quickly disappeared.

Eimhir stared after him. *Duncan was right. There's no better guide for navigating the depths. He'll tell us if he finds anything worth a closer look.*

You really don't want to go down there, do you?

Eimhir turned her unblinking eyes towards her. It wasn't difficult for Isla to imagine the expression that might have crossed her face in human form. *No*, she said. *And you shouldn't either.*

The warning note sent a prickle of unease through Isla. It wasn't like Eimhir to be afraid. When her pelt was stolen and salt scarred her skin, she'd faced her fate with a grim acceptance. But something about the depths unsettled her in a way Isla had never seen before.

The stirring of the water broke her from her thoughts, and she whirled around to find Angus returning from below, his hind flippers strong and steady as he pushed towards the surface. After refilling his lungs, he dropped back down, circling slowly.

The seabed is some quarter of a mile below us, he said. *As far as dives go, it's well within range. But whatever it is you're searching for, I don't think the seabed is where you'll find it.*

Eimhir let out a low, impatient whistle. *What are you talking about?*

There's a trench. How deep it descends, I don't know. But it's big. Angus flicked his black eyes to Isla. *If something is calling you, it must be down there. But I warn you—*

I know. Trepidation coiled in her chest. *But I have to try. For Eileanan Selch. For our people.*

Angus bobbed his head. *Then we dive.*

Isla floated to the surface, resisting the all-too-human temptation to fill her lungs. Instead, she exhaled, releasing the air keeping her afloat. Already her heart was slowing, her blood pushing through her muscles.

She spun around and thrust with her hind flippers. The water slipped over the slick curves of her body, offering no resistance as she propelled herself forward. Her whiskers twitched as she swam, picking up signals from the ripples and currents. The selkie part of her knew the sea. Here, she was home.

Before long, the sunlight fracturing the surface dissolved. Isla was grateful for the sharpness of her eyes, able to pick out the individual scales on a shoal of passing lanternfish. The distant seabed emerged slowly, sand and gravel scattered with sparse fronds of red algae. And there, splitting it down the middle like a wound, was the trench.

It was as wide as a river, falling away in sheer, rocky cliffs on either side. Isla couldn't see how far the gap sank. Whatever lay at the bottom—if there *was* a bottom—was shrouded in darkness. Yet there was no mistaking the thrumming in her bones, the urging of the currents. Whatever was calling her, it was down there.

This is it, she said. *That's where we have to go.*

Eimhir gave a disgruntled click, but said nothing.

Angus drifted closer to the mouth of the trench, flippers working slowly as he circled. *Stay close, and don't dive deeper than I do. You'll never make it back to the surface unless you stick to my range.*

He dipped his long body towards the fissure, and Isla followed. Already the weight of the water bore down on her bones, squeezing her organs with the pressure. The walls of the trench towered over her on either side, marred with deep cracks and crumbling rock. She startled at a ripple of movement, only relaxing when she spotted a slender tail retreating into a narrow hole as she passed, a stream of bubbles lingering in its wake.

Just an eel, she told herself. *Nothing more.*

Still, the creature's lithe, ribbon-like body stirred an unrest in her that was difficult to ignore. Sea serpents were rare in Silvish waters, but the old legends whispered at the back of her mind. Some said the Cirein-cròin had been slain off the coast of Silveckan centuries ago, its rotting teeth forming the jagged rocks rising around the port of Kinraith. Others warned the ancient beast only slumbered, waiting for its hunger to rouse it and send it on the hunt again.

She pushed away the thought before it turned to fear. The legend was just that—a legend. The only Cirein-cròin she'd ever encountered was her drunken old sot of an uncle, and he'd long abandoned the moniker the Admiralty had once bestowed upon him.

Grief twinged in her chest. Tides, but it hurt to think of him. It was Muir's compass that had led her to her pelt. Muir's compassion that had saved her from the Grand Admiral's clutches more than twenty-five years ago. She didn't know if he was alive, or if the Admiralty had got to him. He was just one more person she'd failed. One more person she'd lost.

Down there. The urgency in Eimhir's voice broke Isla from her thoughts. *Do you see that?*

Isla kicked her hind flippers, skirting around an outcropping to draw level with Eimhir. Further down, something pale and glistening caught her eye, wedged between two narrow shelves of rock. It was keeling at an unnatural angle, but there was no mistaking the curve of its hull, the spine of its masts.

A ship, lost to the depths.

One of the Admiralty's, most likely, Angus said, his flippers tense as he flitted back and forth. *Better here than hunting our people.*

Isla cast her eyes over the ship. Its pallid hull was torn asunder by the rocks it had impaled itself upon. No sails hung from its broken mast, not even tattered rags. *I'm going in for a closer look.*

Isla, wait, Eimhir said, strained. *I don't like this. Something isn't right.*

Somewhere, buried in the recesses of her mind, the part of Isla that was still human wanted to listen. It wanted to return to the surface. But the call from below was unrelenting. She couldn't ignore it. All she could do was follow where it led.

The ship loomed in front of her, held in place by the jaws of the narrowing trench. There was something strange about the colour of it; even with her greyscale vision, she knew it was too pale. The wood held an unnatural sheen despite the darkness, as if...

She froze. No, it wasn't wood at all.

The ship was made from bones. *Selkie* bones.

Dread washed over her, seeping through the barrier of her pelt into her flesh and muscles until she could barely move. The precious air stored in her blood froze, as if the water had turned to ice.

She searched for Eimhir and Angus, but she'd lost sight of them. The murky water thickened, clouding her visibility. She could barely see the pale gleam of the crippled ship through the mist.

The mist... No, the *haar*.

The sea fog appeared different underwater, but there was no mistaking it. It crept towards her, its icy touch squeezing like a vice around her organs. It was the memory of violence made real, a rupture into the soulless realm.

Tides, they were here. The gun-anam were here.

Fear seized her, turning her flippers to stone. She couldn't move. She could only watch as the gun-anam emerged from the haar, gliding through the water. It was impossible to tell where they began and the sea ended. They were wraiths of salt and spray, the twisted reflection of the sea itself. The only form to their presence was their seal-skull masks and cuirasses of bone, the same bone that had been fashioned into the crippled ship in front of her. But where the ship's hull had a pale, ghostly glow, the gun-anam's armour was blackened and dead, stripped of what it once was by the haar's consuming breath.

One of the wraiths reached for her, swirling the water into icy tendrils. Isla shook herself from her stupor and darted out of the way, releasing a burst of urgent clicks and whistles. There was no sign of Eimhir and

Angus. Perhaps they were lost in the haar. Perhaps they'd made for the surface at the first sign of the creeping mist.

Another wraith drifted towards her, and she thrashed her flippers, charging at its ribcage armour. The blow left her dazed, and she shot headlong into the fog, unable to find her bearings until a familiar, pallid sheen bloomed in front of her.

The ship. She'd found it again.

She slowed, examining the hull. The bones worked together seamlessly, smoother than any timber made from oak or elm. Though they'd splintered against the rock, they looked strong, from the underbelly of the keel to the tip of the forlorn, crooked mast.

They called her here. They *wanted* her to find them. They sang to her, echoing in her own bones. Even with the gun-anam circling, she couldn't ignore them. The ship beckoned her in, like a compulsion in her soul.

She floated closer and pressed her snout against the smooth surface.

All at once, the haar vanished. So too did the gun-anam. The pressure of the sea bearing down on her body lifted, and her lungs filled with the sweet relief of air again. The ship was still in front of her, but it had changed. The cracks and broken shards of bone were nowhere to be seen; instead, the masts stood tall and proud, the hull gleaming white and intact.

A shout carried through the air above her, and she craned her neck to catch sight of whoever was on deck. The woman barking orders was lanky and olive-skinned, with long brown tresses spilling across her shoulders and a fiery look in her eyes. But it wasn't her appearance that damn near stopped Isla's heart—it was the speckled, sand-coloured pelt around her shoulders.

This wasn't an Admiralty ship. It belonged to the selkies.

Before she could make sense of it, the world fell dark. Tightness seized her chest, squeezing the air from her lungs and sending her hurtling back to the crushing depths. The leeching chill of the haar returned, so thick she could barely move.

She flicked her flippers and spun around, pushing back from the bone ship's hull. For a moment, she saw nothing but swirling mist. Then, the shadow of a familiar presence emerged.

It was one of the gun-anam.

Isla's heart turned to ice. She knew this creature. It had stalked her ever since Blackwood Estate, where it had crept out of the mists atop its kelpie mount. She recognised the shape of its seal-skull mask, the fathomless stare of its empty eye sockets. It carried with it the stench of decay, like the sea itself was rotting around it.

Run, she told herself.

If she didn't move, its touch would freeze the blood in her veins. The haar clinging to its watery shadow would fill her lungs. She'd lose herself down here, with everything she'd fought for.

Isla, get out of there!

Eimhir appeared from nowhere, shrugging off the mist as she tore through the water. She charged at the gun-anam, teeth bared in a furious snarl. Angus was right on her hind, his long shape like a bullet unleashed. The two of them circled the wraith, jaws snapping as they forced it back.

Get to the surface, Angus said, his call strained. *We'll be right behind you.*

Isla forced her flippers into motion, shaking off the crippling touch of the haar. The gun-anam circled Eimhir and Angus, gliding through the water. She remembered the fear rooting her to the deck of the *Jade Dawn* as the wraith advanced on her all those months ago. Its dagger falling towards Darce, the heat lancing her belly as it caught her instead, the agony and anguish as Darce gave up part of his soul to save her.

She couldn't run. Not if it meant someone else would suffer because of her.

A shudder rippled through her as she whirled to face the gun-anam. Her head grew heavy, her flippers cramping as her air ran low. Maybe she was already too late. But if she was to lose herself here in the depths, at least she could help Eimhir and Angus get away.

You say you want to protect your home, aineol. Duncan's words in the enclave echoed through her head. *Prove it, and there may yet be a place for you here.*

Wasn't this what he meant?

Caraid, please. Eimhir's voice cut through the pounding in her skull. *This won't stop them. We need you for that. Our people need you.*

Darkness crept in at the edges of Isla's vision. She was out of time.

The surface, she managed.

She kicked with the last scrap of strength she could muster and propelled herself up through the shroud of mist. She barely noticed the distant sunlight streaming through the waves above. When at last she broke through, gulping air into her lungs, she felt no relief, only exhaustion.

Across the horizon, all was clear. No mist clung to the tips of the waves. But there was still no sign of Eimhir or Angus.

Each passing minute stretched longer than the last, laden with the unbearable weight of her fear. A bleak fatigue crept in, so heavy Isla couldn't shake it. The memories from the bone ship had taken their toll. She was in no shape to make the swim back to Eileanan Selch without help.

Then, finally, a shadow rippled below.

Angus burst through the waves, scattering spray into the air. A moment later, Eimhir followed. They bobbed in the swell, unable to speak as they refilled their lungs.

What happened down there? Eimhir asked eventually. *What did you see?*

Isla couldn't answer. The vision was already fading, but there was no mistaking how real it had been. Somehow, in touching those bones, she'd *been* there. She'd seen the ship and its selkie captain with her own eyes. She'd breathed the same air as them. The memories in her pelt had brought her there to show her something.

She just didn't understand what it meant yet.

Help me back to Caim, she said, each word a painful effort. *I need to tell the chieftains I know how to dreamwalk.*

CHAPTER FIVE

DARCE

Darce had never set foot in the Admiralty's headquarters before. Ever since returning to the garrison, he'd avoided the administrative buildings as best he could, sticking to the barracks and the courtyard and the few other places he was permitted to go without an escort. He had no desire to cross paths with Grand Admiral Alasdair Cunningham, even less so now he knew who he really was.

The ruthless bastard who ruled Silveckan's seas. The greatest selkie hunter in living memory. And—by blood, if nothing else—Isla's father.

The Grand Admiral's private office was as austere as the man himself. The pinewood floor shone immaculately under the dim light of the braziers. Oak panelling stretched to the ceiling in perfectly uniform lines, breaking only for the huge windows overlooking Arburgh's cliffs. The only aspect of the room betraying a trace of softness, a measure of emotion, was the oil painting hanging in a gilded frame over the desk.

Darce stilled. It was too familiar; a reminder of a raw wound. The tangle of sable hair, the dappled grey fur wrapped around her bare shoulders, the waves leaping in the distance. Part of him wished he could reach out and pull the woman in the painting around to face him, if only to see for himself.

"She looks just like her, doesn't she?"

He hadn't heard the Grand Admiral enter the room. He moved quietly and with purpose, joining Darce beside the portrait.

Darce didn't answer. He couldn't. Too much anger burned on the tip of his tongue. Instead, he gritted his teeth and forced himself into the seat the Grand Admiral gestured to with a dismissive flick of his fingers. There was nothing he could do but obey. That was the choice he'd made when he'd come here.

The Grand Admiral sat opposite him, interlacing his hands. There was nothing of Isla in his gaze. Her eyes were sea green and as fierce as the waves themselves, her emotions too wild to be contained. All he saw when he looked at Alasdair Cunningham was a keen, measured calm. Everything from his flinty stare to the thin line of his lips was cold and calculating.

"Sergeant Galbraith," he said. "I find myself in need of a sentinel."

The words were softly spoken, but they hung over Darce's head like the executioner's axe. He'd known this was coming. He'd dreaded it ever since he'd stepped foot back on Arburgh's docks. The only thing that surprised him was that Cunningham had taken this long to produce the shackles.

"I'll tell you the same thing I told your captains when they asked," he said stiffly. "I already made my oath."

"I don't need an oath from you, lad. I know better than most that it's no guarantee of loyalty." A shadow darkened Cunningham's expression. "No, what I need is for you to help me find my daughter."

Revulsion twisted Darce's stomach. He couldn't mistake the way Cunningham's voice curled over the words *my daughter*. The Grand Admiral wasn't the kind of man to relinquish hold on what was his. He would hunt Isla until there was nowhere in Silvish waters left for her to run.

"She's where she belongs," Darce said. "She's where she wants to be, where she *needs* to be. She won't let anyone take that from her." He met Cunningham's blue-grey eyes unflinchingly. "But you already know that, don't you?"

Cunningham's hand twitched towards his chest, so fleeting, so imperceptible, that Darce might not have noticed if he hadn't been waiting for it. Somewhere, hidden beneath the rich brocade of Admiralty finery, was the mark from the bullet Isla had put in him. The scar might have healed, but if Cunningham's face was anything to go by, the wound was a reminder still painful when pressed.

His expression smoothed again. "The Blackwood boy tells me you care for her. It's more than the oath for you, isn't it?"

When Darce didn't answer, a small smile spread on Cunningham's lips. "I thought as much. I assure you, she is in no danger from me. On that matter, I give you my word. All I want is to bring her back where she belongs." His eyes flicked up to the painting again. "I failed Mara. I won't fail our daughter."

"You would keep her a prisoner."

"I would keep her *safe*." An unforgiving edge crept into Cunningham's tone. "I have spent my life on Silveckan's seas. I know what horrors lurk in those waves. There is nothing I wouldn't do to protect Isla from them, just as I protect this city. Surely we have that in common, Sergeant?"

Darce turned his head to the rain-splattered windows. Aye, they did have that in common. That was what was so disturbing about this sorry mess he'd made for himself. It wasn't difficult to look at the Grand Admiral and see some kind of reflection of the man Darce himself could become. That kind of grief, that kind of fear, was easily twisted. It could consume a person, if they let it.

I am not afraid of sailing into a storm. But you keep trying to be my anchor, when all I ever needed was a wild wind to carry me through.

That was why he'd let her go. Why he *had* to.

"I can't help you," he said.

He half expected a shadow to fall across Cunningham's face, to see the cold rage in his eyes. But nothing changed in his expression. The lines on his brow were as severe as ever, but they held no more anger than before. Instead, he leaned back in his chair, tilting his head as if Darce was a puzzle to be examined.

"My nephew has been leading our western patrols with a confidence and ability far beyond his years," he said. "And it has not escaped me that where he goes, your young charge follows. His unfortunate...*impairment*...appears not to have hindered him in that regard. For now, at least."

Darce bristled. "What are you getting at?"

"I have a new commission in mind for Blair. With me, on the *Vanguard of the Firth*. Should I extend a similar offer to Lachlan Blackwood, I have no doubt he'll accept it." Cunningham leaned forward. "The deck can be a dangerous place, and the waters of the Strait are treacherous and unforgiving. It would seem to me he could use someone looking out for him."

The threat went unspoken, but was no quieter for it. Darce tightened his hands under the desk, willing his surging anger to settle. He drew a short breath, forcing calm into his voice when he spoke again. "If you do *anything* to that lad, if you let him come to harm, Isla will never forgive you. No matter what happened between them, he's still her brother. Her family. Are you willing to risk that?"

For a moment, the mask fell. All the rigid composure on the Grand Admiral's face was gone, replaced by a doubt that was too familiar, too human. In that heartbeat, Alasdair Cunningham was just a man, just a father. Then it was over, steel returning to his features as a wolfish smile stretched his thin lips. "Are *you*?"

Darce faltered. Tides, he was a fool. Cunningham had steered him into a position he couldn't retreat from, and Darce had handed him the bloody rudder. He couldn't stay here in the clutches of the capital while Lachlan sailed into selkie waters, and the Grand Admiral knew it. There was no way out of this but into the storm.

If Cunningham noticed his despair, he was in no mind to gloat over it.

Instead, he nodded, as if the two of them had come to some agreement. "I have a regiment of a dozen sentinels who serve on the *Vanguard* with their captains. You will join their company when we next sail. As far as anyone else is concerned, the Blackwood boy is the one you made the blood oath to. I shouldn't need to impress on you the importance of keeping the truth to yourself."

This time, the warning had an edge so sharp Darce felt it against his throat. "I understand."

"I thought you might." Cunningham rose from his desk, shoulders squaring as he offered an outstretched hand. "In that case, Sergeant Galbraith, I would like to extend a formal request for you to serve the Admiralty aboard the *Vanguard of the Firth*. Will you accept?"

Darce fought the laugh threatening to spill. Might as well ask a man at the gallows if he had any last words. The Grand Admiral didn't care about the answer. There was no other choice but to meet the finality of his grasp.

"Aye," he said. "I accept."

In the days that followed, the bars of Darce's cage expanded to the rest of the city. No longer was he confined under the watchful eyes of the barracks. No longer were his footsteps dogged by a jewel-toned cloak and a waiting musket. It wasn't a matter of trust—they simply knew he had nowhere to run. Lachlan had accepted his commission on the *Vanguard of the Firth*. They were both bound to that ship, for better or worse.

The snarling wind tugged at his hair as the ferry took him across the river to the city's southside district. If he looked back, he could see the Admiralty shipyards across the choppy grey-green waves, the *Vanguard* towering over the rest of the fleet. In a few short days, it would peel from the docks and head for the Strait of Silveckan in search of selkie waters.

In search of Isla.

Darce pulled the fur-lined collar of his cloak closer around his neck, as if that could stave off the shiver racing through him. It wasn't just that they were hunting her, or that he was helping them. No, it was that part of him *wanted* to find her, selfish as it was. He wanted to hold her close enough to smell the salt on her skin and feel the thrum of her heart against his, even if it meant standing in the cold shadow of Admiralty sails.

He stepped off the ferry and headed towards the Merchant Quarter. The midwinter markets were in full flow, and the narrow streets bustled with bodies as people picked their way from one crammed stall to the next. They flitted between spiced wine and roasted hazelnuts, stopped to watch grouse and venison smoking over a firepit. Some merchants boasted delicacies from beyond Silvish waters, tempting him with candied pears from Vesnia and colourful preserves from the Karzish Peninsula. After three months confined to the garrison, the colour and commotion threatened to overwhelm him. But more than anything else, it was a distraction, and that was precisely what Darce needed.

He parted with some coin and brought a tankard to his lips, savouring the warm honeyed rum as it trickled down his throat. Raised voices and lively chatter filled his head with a pleasant hum, drowning out everything else. His worries about the *Vanguard* and the Grand Admiral would return soon enough. For now, all he needed to focus on was weaving through the crowd, keeping his balance on the uneven cobbles underfoot.

His reverie was rudely broken as someone's shoulder jostled his. A ruddy-faced old sailor staggered back, eyes glazed as he looked Darce up and down.

"S-sorry, friend," he said, the words barely recognisable through the hiccup escaping his mouth. "Didn't see you."

"No harm done." Darce waved him away, already turning back to the heaving crowd.

Then he stopped and felt for the coin pouch on his belt.

"Shite!"

He wheeled around, eyes darting across the mass of bodies pushing in every direction. If he didn't spot the sailor quickly, it would be impossible to find him in the rabble. He had seconds, nothing more.

A dishevelled tuft of hair caught his attention, followed by a ruddy cheek as the sailor turned to check if he was being followed. When he saw Darce, he pushed through the crowd more vigorously.

Darce rushed after him, ignoring the aggrieved shouts as he elbowed through. Ahead, the sailor stumbled out of the main market square and darted towards one of the canal paths, his footsteps nimbler than Darce expected. It was all he could do to keep pace along the cobbled walkway, where one ill-placed step would send him sprawling into the filthy canal water.

The sailor glanced back again, letting out a grunt when he saw Darce was on his heels. He abandoned his route along the canal path, instead ducking into one of the narrow wynds snaking between the ramshackle tenement buildings.

Darce rounded the corner after him and was met with a fist in his gut.

He doubled over, fighting for breath as he fumbled for the rapier on his belt. Before he could get a grip, another blow cracked across the back of his head, and he fell to his hands and knees with a groan. A swift kick to the ribs followed, and as he collapsed onto the cobbles, he noticed two pairs of shit-stained boots in front of him.

There were more of them. They'd been waiting.

Darce cursed himself. Bad enough he'd been so sloppy as to let a cutpurse get the better of him. Worse that he'd taken the bait and followed him right into his trap. For the first time since returning to Arburgh, he regretted not having the sapphire brocade of his Admiralty cloak around his shoulders. Any southside thief would think better of targeting that kind of mark. But he'd been too eager to leave it behind in the barracks, too ashamed of what it meant.

One more mistake on top of all the rest he'd made this evening.

He braced himself for the next blow, but it didn't come. Instead, one of the cutpurses jerked his arms behind his back, securing his wrists with rope. The next thing he knew, a sack was shoved over his head, and everything went dark.

"Who are you?" he demanded, his voice muffled to his own ears.

Neither of the men answered. Instead, they dragged him from the ground, grip tight on his arms. He feared they meant to throw him in the canal, but when they shoved him forward, he was met with a damp wooden surface.

The stench of canal water filled his nostrils. He lay still, sensing a rocking motion. He must be on some kind of punt. Whoever the men were—and by now, Darce was certain they were no simple cutpurses—they had somewhere they wanted to take him.

A heavy boot pressed down on his back, forcing him flat against the bottom of the punt. They were on the move—he felt it in the wood groaning beneath him. Grimy water seeped through the sack into his mouth, and he spluttered to rid himself of the foul taste.

He stilled as a memory flashed into his head—a Sea Kith half-drowned on the deck of the *Jade Dawn*, Kerr drawing water from his lungs with his magic. He'd almost forgotten—wrists bound or not, he was a sentinel. He had a gift he could call upon, even in this sorry state.

He closed his eyes and thought of the filthy water pooling in the bottom of the punt. It was part of the canal, and the canal led to the firth, to the sea. Maybe he could reach the spirits dwelling in the open waters. Maybe they'd help him as they had before.

Can you hear me? he asked.

Only silence answered. There was no whisper from the waves, no ripple in his veins from the currents. All he could smell was the fetid damp from the sack, not the crisp bite of salt and seafoam. Perhaps the canal was too far from the sea, or else the spirits were in no mood to indulge him this time.

He sank against the floor, listening to the steady rhythm of the pole hitting the water with a splash. It was impossible to tell which direction they were drifting in, or how much time had passed. There was nothing else to do but wait.

When the punt finally came to a stop, Darce spoke to the men again. "Where are we? What do you want with me, if not my coin?"

The only response was a shove in the back as they dragged him from the punt. He found himself thrust down a winding spiral of stone steps, so narrow his captors had to walk behind him. He might have been tempted to run, were he not certain he'd only succeed in breaking his neck.

After a while, the air grew musty, making the inside of the sack reek. The ground at the bottom of the steps was rocky and slick, and he almost slipped on something slimy.

Seaweed, he thought. Tides, where were they taking him?

One of the cutpurses pushed him, and he stumbled into a chair. A sharp pain shot through his bound wrists as he fell against them, the rope chafing his skin.

Then something rustled behind him, and the sack was ripped off over his head.

Darce blinked. He was in a dark room, the only light coming from a lantern suspended from the rocky ceiling. Wooden panelling ran around one of the walls, giving way to the natural curve of the cavern roof above him. The opposite wall was a slab of wet limestone, boasting a crudely drawn mural. In the flickering glow of the lantern, Darce could make out the beady eyes and gaping jaws of a lithe, wriggling creature.

He let out a breath. *The Eel*.

For the first time, a trickle of fear crept in. The Eel. Southside's most infamous smuggler, wanted by the Admiralty and merchant nobility alike. His name was cursed every time a warehouse burned, every time an officer went missing and turned up a week later with broken fingers and a slit throat.

If he knew who Darce was, if he'd captured him because he was part of the Admiralty... Tides, he was already dead.

The dull thump of footsteps echoed behind him, but Darce kept his eyes fixed on the floor. It would do him no good to turn around. He already knew what was coming. Or rather, *who.*

A pair of serpenthide boots stalked into view, the scales glistening as they caught the dim light. Darce lifted his gaze enough to take in the frayed edges of a twin-tailed sailor's coat, the glimpse of a cutlass and fishknives beneath its folds.

"Sergeant Galbraith. You're a hard man to get hold of."

Darce froze at the voice, then forced himself to look up.

The man in front of him wore a surly expression, the lines on his dark brown skin deeper than he remembered. His long white hair fell across his shoulders in sailor's braids, and though his eyes were tired, they held none of their usual bloodshot glaze.

It was Muir. The Eel was Isla's tides-damned *uncle.*

"You'll have to forgive the manner of my invitation, but I can hardly stroll into the garrison these days." Muir gave a tight smile, but there was no humour in the glint of his eyes as his hand drifted to one of the fishknives on his belt.

"Now," he said, pressing the cold tip of the blade to Darce's throat, "tell me exactly where my niece is."

CHAPTER SIX

ISLA

Cold sweat streamed down Isla's skin as she awoke with a gasp. Each ragged breath resounded in her ears as she pushed herself onto her elbows and waited for the dream to fade.

"You're safe, caraid." Eimhir's voice came through the darkness, soothing despite the gravelly edges. "We made it home."

Isla sat upright, running a hand over the furs draped across the bed as she willed the frantic thrum of her heart to steady. The dream was gone. She was back in Caim. She heard the lapping of the loch beneath the crannog, the creak of the wooden bridges between the settlements. A small hearth burned on the far side of the room, smoke disappearing up the stone chimney as the flames cast shadows across the thatched roof. Yet despite the warmth, she couldn't help but shiver.

"What happened?" she asked, wiping loose strands of hair from her clammy forehead. "I don't remember getting back."

Eimhir rose from her own bed. "Aye, that doesn't surprise me. You barely had the strength to swim. You kept drifting off, slipping in and out of consciousness. Angus and I managed to keep you afloat, but when we got to shore, there was no waking you. This is the first time you've opened your eyes in days."

"Days?" That would explain the ache in her stomach. "I don't understand."

"Neither do we." The creases in Eimhir's brow deepened. "It seems this was no normal kind of sleep. You were dreamwalking, weren't you?"

Isla stilled. A thick fog clouded her head, but the mention of dreamwalking pierced it, offering a sliver of clarity amongst the confusion. Aye, she *had* been dreaming. But they didn't feel like dreams—they were something more. Flashes of memory, as real as the heat of the hearth on her cheeks or the comforting touch of Eimhir's hand on hers.

"I need to speak to the chieftains," she said, throwing the furs from her legs as she swung out of bed. "They need to know what—" She stumbled, her feet unsteady on the heather-woven carpet.

"The chieftains can wait," Eimhir said firmly, taking her arm and guiding her back to bed. "You need to gather your strength first. Stay there while I fetch you some food."

Isla wanted to protest, but a wave of dizziness made her head heavy. She sank onto the bed, fighting the urge to close her eyes. If she succumbed to sleep again, it would only bring more dreams, more fragmented visions she didn't understand. White ships made of selkie bones. Strange waters with black waves. A dark red sky holding no stars. And through it all, a tangled thread made from the mists of memory, so fragile she feared it might snap if she tried to unpick it.

A thread connecting her to Mara. Her selkie mother.

Before she could dwell more on it, Eimhir returned, carrying a wooden tray heaped with fresh fish. Isla's aching stomach grumbled, and she reached greedily for the marbled flesh of the tuna. She tore apart the pink meat between her fingers, gulping it down in chunks. The scallops she popped in her mouth whole, savouring their sweet, buttery taste as the roe burst between her teeth.

"I brought you this." Eimhir handed her a tankard, the liquid inside steaming. "A brew of rosemary and bramble. It should help keep your senses alert, stave off the exhaustion for a wee while."

Isla took the tankard and sipped, the warmth of the mixture spreading through her. Already her energy was returning, the fog lifting around her head.

She opened her mouth, then closed it again as she observed Eimhir's hunched frame perched on the end of the bed. Blue circles hung under her eyes. While Isla had been dreaming, it looked like Eimhir hadn't slept in days.

Isla nudged the tray. "You should have some too. Seems like you need it."

Eimhir snorted out a coarse laugh. "That's a kind way of saying I look like shite." She glanced at the food. "I've not had much of an appetite recently. Worry has a way of making you forget about your stomach."

"But—"

"Things will be better now you're awake again. For a moment, I..." A shadow fell across Eimhir's face, but she shook it away. "I'm glad you're all right, caraid. We've asked a lot of you, and I fear we'll have to ask for more before this is through."

"I can handle it." As the words left Isla's lips, she felt the weight of them like lead on her tongue. The dappled grey pelt around her shoulders shifted across her skin, as if it too knew what was at stake. "I won't let you down."

Eimhir softened. "I know," she said, squeezing her hand. "You never do."

It felt like no time had passed since she'd last stood in this room, the eyes of the six chieftains fixed firmly on her. This time, Isla stood taller, taking strength from what she'd seen in the trench. As she recounted what had happened, Eimhir and Angus remained by her side, supplying their own appraisals when called upon by the chieftains. But for the most part, she was the centre of their focus.

When she mentioned the ship, a dark look fell across Duncan's face. "Eimhir and Angus told us about it while you were recovering. We thought it bad enough that humans stole our pelts for trade and coin. Now they're using our bones to build their ships."

"No human built that ship." Isla glanced at Eimhir. "I didn't have the chance to tell you before. When I touched the hull, touched those bones, I saw something. A selkie captain on deck, her pelt around her shoulders. The ship belonged to *our* people, I'm certain of it. We built it. We sailed it. And somehow, we lost it."

A murmur of unrest rippled through the room, and Duncan narrowed his eyes. "I find that difficult to believe. We have no need for ships to traverse the sea, and given the number of selkie lives it must have taken to construct such a thing... You have much to learn if you think us capable of doing that to our own people, aineol."

"I was there," Isla said, heat rising in her voice. "It wasn't a dream; it was a memory. If I'd had more time, I might have been able to understand better what it was trying to show me. But the gun-anam..."

Her tongue turned to ice, and she let the rest of her words hang in a frosty silence. The mere mention of the soulless smothered the warmth from the firepit. The flesh on her arms prickled. Even here, in the heart of the Selkie Isles, the fear of the haar ran deep.

"The gun-anam," Duncan repeated. "And here we come to the most disturbing part of all. The soulless have never before attacked our people. Followed us, aye. Fed on the violence of a raid, aye. But until now, they've only ever set themselves upon humans. Never a selkie."

He didn't need to say anything more. The unspoken accusation rang around the room, thrown back at her with every furrowed brow, every drawn mouth. They thought this was *her* fault. She was half-human; *that* was why the gun-anam attacked. Maybe there was some truth to it. But all Isla felt was the barb of Duncan's words burrowing under her skin, the shame spreading through her. She wasn't one of them. She'd never be one of them, no matter what Duncan promised. She was still an outsider, still an aineol.

"I don't know what the gun-anam were doing in that trench," she said tersely. "The ship called to me—maybe it called to them. It's made of the bones of our people, after all. And the bones..." She paused, unravelling her thoughts. "They didn't carry the black rot of the haar like the armour the gun-anam wear. They were...alive."

One of the elder chieftains leaned forward. Her weathered, bony hands tightened around her pelt as she spoke. "You believe this ship is connected to the gun-anam? Could it be immune from the mist sickness, somehow?"

"I've spent the last few days lost in the dreams of my ancestors. I don't yet know how to navigate the dreams, but..." Isla looked at the chieftains. "I've seen flashes of memories from places I've never been. Sheltered coves, rocky bays—places a vessel might moor. I think there are more of these ships. Or, at least, there *were* more of them. If that's true, I need to find them."

Duncan's umber gaze was unmoving. "What makes you so sure you could?"

"Ever since I can remember, something inside me has pulled me out to sea, like a call I can't help but answer," Isla said. "I thought it would stop after I claimed my pelt, but it's stronger than ever. Something out there *wants* me to find it. Something is connecting me to these ships, and to Mara."

The lines across Duncan's skin deepened, but there was no ire in his expression, only a flicker of regret. "I've seen this before. If I'd stopped it then, if I'd stopped Mara then..." He pressed his lips together.

Beside her, Eimhir stiffened. "What are you talking about?"

"Before she was captured by the Grand Admiral, Mara had been spending a lot of time in the open waters. She said she was following the currents her ancestors left in their wake, and she'd hear nothing of taking a scout or an escort with her, no matter how many times I pressed the issue. I wasn't a chieftain then, and even if I was, I doubt she'd have listened." Duncan's mouth twitched. "She had a certain will about her."

"That's no surprise," Eimhir murmured under her breath. "Seems you inherited more than her pelt, caraid."

A swell of bittersweet emotion rose in Isla's chest, and she fought to keep the tremble from her voice as she turned to Duncan. "If she was searching for these ships, that's all the more reason for me to follow. She was a dreamwalker. Her memories led her to these places like they're leading me."

"Mara's memories led to her being captured," Duncan said. "And now the man who kept her imprisoned for years, the bastard who stripped her of her soulskin, is hunting you. If the Grand Admiral gets his hands on that pelt, I doubt he'll let it go a second time. Without it, we have no dreamwalker. Without it, we'll never find a way to put an end to the gun-anam and the mist sickness they carry."

"So we do nothing?" Angus spoke up, shooting Duncan a questioning look. "You wanted her to learn how to dreamwalk. She's proven herself capable. You can't ignore what she's seen because you don't like it."

If Duncan was surprised at his brother's outburst, he did little to show it. When he replied, he was as measured as ever. "We are ignoring nothing. But there is more at stake here than one life." He met Isla's gaze. "Mara was my friend. I let her go out there alone, and she never came back. But it was not just a friend I lost that day—it was the last remnant of our people's most precious gift. I won't make the same mistake twice." He glanced at the other chieftains. "We will confer on this. Until we have reached a decision on the matter, you are to stay ashore. We can't risk drawing the gun-anam to these isles."

His voice rang with finality, and Isla swallowed the temptation to argue. Instead, she nodded stiffly and followed Eimhir and Angus out of the enclave, filling her lungs with the crisp lochside air.

Angus stormed ahead, bare feet splashing in the water pooling across the bridge's wooden slats. His shoulders were tense under the russet folds of his pelt, and Isla caught a muttered flurry of selkie clicks carried with the breeze.

"I didn't expect him to speak against Duncan," she said.

"Duncan may be his brother, but Angus is his own person," Eimhir said. "You should talk to him, see what's on his mind. He isn't one of the chieftains, but his opinions are well respected. If we end up going after these ships, we could do worse than getting him onside."

Isla raised an eyebrow. "After what happened in the trench, I thought you'd try to talk me out of it."

"I might, if I thought I could." Eimhir nodded towards Angus's retreating figure. "Go after him. I'll catch up with you later."

Isla wrapped her hands in her pelt as she crossed the bridge. The loch itself was too deep to freeze, but crystalline spirals of frost clung to the rope handles and coated the wooden posts. Her breath clouded in front of her as she walked, reminding her too much of the mists and shadows of the gun-anam.

She found Angus on the loch's bank, his expression as grey as the water in front of him. He looked up as she arrived, blue eyes questioning, but said nothing as she sat next to him on one of the rocks littering the shore.

"I wanted to thank you for what you said in the enclave," she said. "I have to admit, I was surprised. Not many of the islanders seem willing to trust the word of an aineol."

Angus shrugged. "I was there. I saw the ship the same as you did. I saw the gun-anam. And as for trust..." The freckles on his forehead shifted as he knit his brows into a frown. "Eimhir garnered a great deal of respect from the clans when she went into exile to track down Mara's pelt. Not everyone agrees with her decision to allow you to take it, but nobody can deny she kept her word. She's earned our trust. And she trusts you, even after..."

Isla stilled. "After what?"

A flush coloured Angus's cheeks. "We all know Finlay went with her. He never came back. Rumour says you were the one who killed him."

"I..." Isla faltered. Thinking of that night was like returning to a nightmare she couldn't escape. Blood-soaked cobbles and ribbons of flesh flayed from bone. Lachlan lying in the rain, his leg a mangled, poisoned mess. Finlay's fingers around her throat, and hers around the hilt of a dagger, thrust into his exposed neck. "He tried to kill me first."

"If Eimhir blamed you, you wouldn't be here." Angus let out a heavy breath. "I don't know you, Isla Blackwood. Half of you is selkie, and the other half shares blood with the man intent on hunting us to extinction. But I know better than most that blood doesn't count for everything." He closed his eyes. "Did Eimhir ever tell you what happened to her brother?"

Isla nodded. "Humans stole the pelt meant for him when he was born. Without it, he weakened and withered with salt. She said her mother had to return him to the sea. It was the only way to ease his suffering."

"Aye," Angus said. "It was the same for me. I had no pelt to inherit either. The only reason I'm alive is because unlike Eimhir's mother, mine had no other bairns to live for. There was only me. Instead of giving me back to the sea, she spilled her blood across her own pelt and wrapped it around me. She gave her life, her soul, to keep me from suffering that fate. Duncan's father found me on the shore and took me in. We share no blood, but the clans are forged by stronger bonds than that. Some of us forget too easily."

Silence hung in the air between them, thick with grief. Angus's words burrowed close to the bone, pressing at a painful ache. She thought of Lachlan's tawny eyes, the wry twist of his mouth. It wasn't blood that made him her brother. It was the unspoken promises they'd made to protect each other, to stick by each other, to mend the rifts that opened between them. She'd never imagined some were too wide to close.

"I meant what I said the last time I spoke to the chieftains," she said. "This is my home. I'll do whatever I can to protect it, from the Admiralty and the gun-anam."

Angus shuddered. "I'd never seen one of those wraiths before the trench. I'm a scout, not a raider. My calling takes me to uncharted waters, and the haar only lingers in places where humans and selkies clash. It terrifies me to think that might have been my fate all those years ago. To think it still could be, if I ever lost my pelt."

"I often dream about the first time I saw them," Isla said. "I didn't know what they were, only that they struck a horror in me I'd never felt before. The darkness behind those empty bones, the fish-rot of their breath, the *cold*... I've never been so cold."

Angus gave her a sidelong look. "How many times have you encountered them?"

Too many, Isla thought, swallowing. But out loud, she said, "This was the first time since claiming my pelt. It felt...different, somehow. Like it left a shadow on my soul no light can chase away." She paused, an unwelcome thought clenching in her stomach. "How many times does it take for the mist sickness to set in?"

"If we knew, we might be better able to protect our people," Angus said. "That shadow you spoke of... It will spread each time the haar touches you until nothing is left but rot and despair. It will sicken your soul, and you'll eventually lose yourself to bloodlust and vengeance. That's why we have to stop them. No matter what the chieftains decide."

Isla stared at him. "You'd go against their decision?"

"If it came to it. If that's what it takes to protect our home." He stood, offering his hand. "Duncan may call you aineol, but the way I see it, you have as much to lose as any of us. If you need someone to help you find those ships, I'm with you."

Isla slipped her hand into his and pulled herself to her feet. The winter wind swept across the loch, but its chill didn't bite as deep as before. For the first time since arriving on Eileanan Selch, her course was clear.

The lost ships held the answer. All she had to do was find them.

CHAPTER SEVEN

DARCE

"**I** need a drink."

Darce snorted. In truth, he was surprised it had taken Muir this long. All through the questioning there was no fog of ale on his breath, no slurring in his speech. He seemed like a different man from the bullish drunkard he'd met the night of the selkie attack on the docks all those months ago. Sharper, more suspicious. Ready for violence, if the way he was palming the fishknife gave any indication.

The rope around Darce's wrists was cut, and Muir shoved a grubby tin tankard into his palm. "Here. You look like you need one too, from what you've told me."

Darce took a swig, choking on the acidic taste of whatever swill was in the jug. "And here I thought you were a changed man. Which is the truth? The drunken sot, or the ever-present menace in the Admiralty's waters?"

Muir grunted. "Can't it be both? There's an advantage to be had when you're the disgraced officer stuck at the bottom of a bottle. Most people don't want to look past the glazed eyes and bad breath to see what might be underneath. A lesson you might consider learning yourself, Sergeant." He rummaged in his coat pocket and tossed Darce a familiar-looking coin pouch.

Darce caught it in one hand. "Feels lighter than it was."

"Call it a tax on your stupidity. You can't afford mistakes like that, not if you want to survive the *Vanguard*."

The room was empty save for the two of them. Darce surveyed his surroundings as he rubbed the raw skin on his wrists. His eyes fell on the gaping jaws of the creature painted on the faded mural. "I know who you are. Do you expect me to believe you'll let me walk away from this? Back to the *Vanguard*, no less?"

"You're no good to anyone stuck down here. And now you've told me Isla is alive, I don't think she'd like it much if I killed you." Muir shrugged. "At least if I send you back, I might get some use out of you. Especially seeing as you were foolish enough to accept a place on that tides-damned ship."

"I didn't have a choice. Lachlan is all but a hostage."

"Of course he is. The Grand Admiral needs a way to control you. He needs a way to control all his captains and their sentinels, now he doesn't have one of his own." Muir slurped from his tankard, eyes gleaming. "He wants to find Isla, and he intends to use you to do it."

"I won't help him."

"Not even if he holds a blade to Lachlan's neck?" Muir flipped his fishknife between his fingers. "Not if he strings him up and threatens to keelhaul him until his back is ripped to ribbons? I've seen it before. Leaves less of a man behind than the skinchangers do with their flaying. Would you find it so easy to hold your tongue with the sound of his screams filling your ears?"

Darce shifted uncomfortably. "That's your nephew you're talking about."

"Aye, and Isla is my niece." Muir met his eyes with a sombre gaze. "There's a reason a sentinel can only make a single blood oath. If you had to choose, you would break."

"Like you did?"

Muir stiffened, the fishknife dangerously poised in his hand, and

Darce feared he'd pushed too far. A barbed silence fell between them, broken only by the distant echo of the sea through the tunnels.

Eventually, Muir leaned back in his chair, pocketing the knife. "Aye, like I did." He rubbed a hand over his weathered skin, as if that could somehow wipe away the weary lines of age and exhaustion. "There was a time I'd have given my life for Alasdair Cunningham. As it turned out, he got my soul instead."

"You were a sentinel," Darce said slowly. "*His* sentinel."

"A long time ago. Before the Admiralty became what it is today. Before Mara." A lump shifted in Muir's throat. "I sometimes wonder…if she'd known what would happen after, would she have pulled him from the water that day? There's a certain bond that comes with saving a life. It might not hold the power of a blood oath, but that doesn't mean it's any easier to break. At the time, I was grateful she'd done what I could not. She saved him, and in the end, that's what killed her."

Darce pursed his lips. "She should have let him drown."

"Perhaps. But back then, he was not the man you know as the Grand Admiral. Back then, maybe his life was worth saving." Muir gave a heavy sigh. "Alasdair changed before my eyes. He loved Mara, but it was a fearful, all-consuming love. He knew in his heart she belonged to the sea, and he couldn't stand the thought of losing her to it."

A chill ran down Darce's back. "That's why he stole her pelt."

Muir nodded. "He kept it from her, returning it just often enough to keep her alive. I was the only one who knew the truth of what she was. I was his sentinel. He trusted me like no other. I stood guard while she swam, keeping watch. Sometimes I tell myself I didn't know how she was suffering, I *couldn't* have known… But that's the lie of a washed-up seadog trying to survive the guilt of his past mistakes." He took a long, bitter gulp from his tankard. "I saw what it was doing to her every time I looked in her eyes. Sea green, like Cat's." He swallowed. "Like Isla's."

"Is that why you let her escape in the end?" Darce asked. "She reminded you of Lady Catriona?"

"She never tried to escape. Maybe she knew it was hopeless, or maybe there was part of her that couldn't let go of the man she'd saved. Or at least, the memory of him." Muir frowned. "Despite everything, I believe she loved him. But there was something she loved more."

"Isla." Her name came to Darce's lips in a painful breath.

"Mara didn't need to say anything. She just pressed my hand against the swell of her belly. She knew she wouldn't be able to hide it from him much longer. If he found out, her child would be as much a prisoner as she was." Muir grimaced. "In that moment, I was no longer a sentinel, no longer an admiral. Just a man who'd failed this selkie who reminded him so much of his wee sister."

"You got her out," Darce said. "You got them both out."

"Not soon enough." A dark look fell across Muir's face. "I commandeered a wee smuggling sloop and sailed out of Arburgh, praying the tides would be kind. But the waves have a will of their own, and they did not see fit to grant us safe passage. Not even my sentinel magic could tame them. The storm took us out to sea. We struggled for weeks in the open waters. Every day, Mara grew sicker. Her skin dried out and became scarred with salt. Her hair turned brittle, like kelp left too long on the shore. The green in her eyes turned misty and pale. I knew then what Alasdair had done when he'd taken her pelt. What I'd helped him do."

He tightened his fingers around the empty tankard in his hand. "She gave birth on the filthy deck of that sloop. All she had to cut the cord was a tiny sgian dubh she'd smuggled away in the folds of her pelt. When it was done, she cradled Isla in her withering arms. Then she passed me the babe and the blade, telling me to keep both of them safe. She said the sgian dubh had been quenched in their blood, that its bearer would always protect her." He chuckled. "I thought it nothing but a selkie superstition at the time, but I passed it on to Cormick all the same. Imagine my surprise all those years later when it turned up again in Lachlan's hands."

Darce's stomach lurched. "He saved her life with that blade. He still has it."

Muir didn't seem to hear him. His gaze was bleak and distant as he spoke, his voice heavy with regret. "It didn't take long after that. Mara hauled herself to the side of the boat and looked down at the waves. I think... I think it was the first time I ever saw her smile. Then she was gone, and I was left with a howling wean as pale as bone in my arms. I didn't know what to do until she opened her eyes. After that, I knew exactly where I needed to go."

"To your sister," Darce said. "To Blackwood Estate."

"Aye," Muir replied. "It was the safest place for her. She looked just like Cat, and it was a simple enough matter for her and Cormick to devise a story of a hidden pregnancy. The few who knew the truth were too loyal to ever have breathed a word of it. There was no trace of the babe's selkie heritage. Her skin stayed soft and free from salt. She had no pelt, needed no pelt. As far as the world knew, Isla was a Blackwood."

"You sacrificed everything to save her," Darce said. "You betrayed the man you gave your soul to. Yet you still came back to the capital."

"Staying would have brought the Admiralty's eyes north. I couldn't risk leading Alasdair to her. So I returned to Arburgh and pretended none of it had happened. I went back to my post. I stood by his side as he slaughtered selkies under the pretence of commerce—a thin excuse to hide his craving for vengeance. And when I could no longer bear the weight of my part in it, I told him at last the truth about how Mara escaped. I was ready to face the consequences." Muir raised his empty tankard. "You know the rest."

"You were disgraced. Cast out of the Admiralty, stripped of your rank." Darce shook his head. "I don't understand. Considering the Grand Admiral's reputation, I'm surprised he didn't kill you."

"I was his sentinel, remember? Perhaps he was afraid of what my death would mean for him. The blood oath is a powerful bond, after all. You should understand better than most." Muir gestured to his chest. "The pain never stops. It's an ache I've carried with me for more than twenty years. My only escape from it was the solace I found in the gutters of the city's southside; first, at the bottom of a bottle, then by helping the creatures Alasdair was hunting. Neither was enough to wash away what came before. Nothing will ever be enough for that."

He fell silent again. Every crease on his skin seemed etched in stone, deep with the weight of guilt and regret. For the first time, Darce could see both sides of the man in his weary features: the rebel and the wretch.

"Why did you bring me here?" he asked.

Muir lifted his head. "To help me fix what I broke," he said. "To overthrow the fucking Admiralty."

His words echoed around the room, ringing off the walls. Darce might have given a disbelieving laugh if his throat hadn't got so tight. This wasn't the slurred spouting of a washed-up drunk, as much as he wished it were. Every syllable had the edge of the blade behind it.

It was a declaration of war.

"You can't be serious," he said, voice hoarse. "The Admiralty is stronger than it has ever been. Cunningham is untouchable. How do you expect—"

"The Admiralty used to be more than one man's vendetta," Muir cut in. "There were tensions with the skinchangers, but nothing like the violence that has swept these waters ever since Mara's death. Alasdair won't cease his hunt until he's skinned every last one of them, save Isla. But if he could be stopped..."

"By whom?" Darce said. "Me? You?"

Muir glared at him. "By anyone who can get close enough not to miss."

"Isla tried that already. She shot him right through the chest. I don't know how he survived."

"You don't?" Muir gave a maddening smile. "Why do you think he keeps so many sentinels on the *Vanguard?* Consider all that auld blood, all it can do."

"They aren't *his* sentinels," Darce said. "If they've made their oaths already—"

Muir's smirk fell away. "The blood oath is a bond forged on both sides, an equal exchange between captain and sentinel. This is something different—a perversion of all that bond should be. If a sentinel willingly spills their blood for someone other than their captain, it can heal a mortal wound. But such a boon must be paid for, one way or another. It demands a life."

A cold realisation twisted in Darce's gut. "You're saying there are sentinels serving on that ship willing to sacrifice *their own captains* to save the Grand Admiral?"

"It should be unthinkable," Muir said. "A betrayal of the soul. That should tell you enough about how he has corrupted them."

"I don't understand," Darce said. "Sentinels were once Silveckan's guardians, protectors of our shores. What could he possibly offer—"

"Apart from obscene riches and the promise of power?" Muir barked out a laugh. "Believe me, Sergeant, that's enough for most people."

"Not all."

Muir's smile returned, tighter than before. "No, not all. And that might be the one chance we have."

Something in the edge of his voice caught Darce's attention. "Why do you want me on the *Vanguard?*"

"I need someone to take away his protection," Muir said. "Get close to the other sentinels. Make them doubt. Make them think twice about what he's asking of them. Then, when the time is right..." He left the rest in the air, hanging like a blade ready to fall.

Heat rose under Darce's collar. "This goes beyond treason, Muir. And I'm not as eager as you to risk Lachlan's life. Have you given any thought to what would happen to him if I failed?"

Muir fixed him with an unyielding look. "Then don't fail."

"Tides take you, you sanctimonious bastard."

"They will someday. I've already made my peace with that. But not before they take him. Not if I have anything to say about it." Muir shook his head. "I can't blame you for your reticence. Not when my own helped bring us to where we are. All I ask is that you let me show you what is at stake before you make up your mind."

"I know what's at stake."

The bleak smile dancing across Muir's lips was enough to send a shiver down his spine. "No, Sergeant. But you will."

Gallowgate.

Before Darce reached the square, the horror of it screamed in his blood. His sentinel magic hadn't fully awakened the last time he'd been here, and it was only now he realised how grateful he should have felt for it. Violence hung in the air like a rotting stench. Echoes of screams rattled through his head. Every fibre of his body was keenly attuned to the suffering in this place, to the scars left behind long after the blood dried and the bones crumbled.

The gallows in the middle of the square stood eerily empty, the worn rope of the noose waiting patiently for the next time it would jerk and snap. But behind the creaking wooden platform hung a row of gibbets, dripping fresh blood onto the cobbles below.

Darce's mouth ran dry. Behind the nearest cage's iron bars was the naked body of a selkie. A young lad, barely older than Lachlan. His skin was a sickly grey, and a layer of salt crept across his eyelids and around his blue lips. Blood oozed from a nasty gouge across his stomach, trickling down the bars before falling with a faint *tip* to the stone below.

A crow swooped from one of the surrounding buildings and landed on the side of the gibbet, talons wrapping around the bars. It cocked its head, then thrust forward with its beak, burrowing into the seeping wound.

The lad's eyelids fluttered, and a moan escaped his cracked lips.

Tides, he was *alive.*

Darce's hand flew to his rapier, but Muir halted him. "Unless you mean to use that blade to put him out of his misery, I suggest you keep it where it is," he said from under his hood. "There's nothing you can do for him that won't see you strung up yourself. I need you alive."

Darce tugged his arm free. "I already told you, I'm not—"

"You said you knew what was at stake. *This* is what's at stake." Muir gestured to the gibbets. "I know you can feel the ripples of what happened in this place. The auld blood *remembers*, Sergeant. Every violent end, every moment of suffering. It won't stop, not as long as he's alive."

"And what have you done about it?" Darce countered. "Skulking in the shadows, stealing from merchant vessels, smuggling the odd selkie or two out of the capital. Do you really think that's enough?"

"No," Muir said. "Not nearly enough. That's why I need you." He plucked the fishknife from his jacket pocket and drew the blade across his palm until drops of blood welled against his dark brown skin. "Do you know how I've evaded the Admiralty for so long? I haven't used my sentinel powers in years, ever since I turned my back on the man I made my oath to. The spirits of the sea don't answer my call anymore. They don't come to the kind of places I chose to survive in." He closed his fist, covering his bloodied palm. "They call me the Eel. A bottom feeder, hiding in the shadows of the canals. But there was a time I shared a name with a sea creature of legend. I was the Cirein-cròin. Would that they'd call me that again—that I'd deserve to be called that again. But that time is over."

He fell silent as a rattling caw tore through the air. A huge shape plummeted towards the middle of the square, and Darce's heart lurched as he caught a familiar flash of yellow across the bird's neck.

Featherblade.

The gannet fell on the scavenging crow with a screech, flaring its wings and jabbing at the smaller bird with its pointed beak. The crow abandoned the gibbet and flapped back to the sky, Featherblade swift on its wings as it chased it away.

Muir let out a laboured breath. "You asked me if I'd given thought to what would happen to Lachlan if you fail. Of course I have. The lad is my nephew, even if he's acting like a gutless wee shite. But what would have happened to Mara if I'd failed all those years ago? What would have happened to Isla?" He clenched his jaw. "I saved her, but I could have saved both of them. I could have done so much more. It's too late for me to make up for that, but you still have a chance."

Darce watched Featherblade circling the square. The gannet's great white wings spread wide as it came to land on the wooden beam of the gallows, webbed claws latching above the noose. It shrieked, then fixed him with its fierce glare, like it was waiting for him to do something.

"What do you want from me?" Darce murmured, not entirely sure which one of them he was speaking to.

Muir answered. "Get close to the Grand Admiral. Make him believe you want the same thing as he does—to find Isla. And when you get the chance, do what I couldn't. What Isla couldn't." He turned to him, his dark gaze every bit as intense as the seabird's. "Free this fucking island from the bloodlust of Alasdair Cunningham."

CHAPTER EIGHT

ISLA

The promise of open water filled Isla with a new sense of resolve. Caim's rocky shore was already far behind; out here, there was no land to disturb the steady line of the horizon, no safe harbour from the storms. It was as if the world itself had been swallowed, leaving only the sea.

A sharp sensation pulled behind her ribs, anchoring her to a place far deeper than the slick hide of her sealskin, deeper even than blood and bone. Back when she'd sailed with the Tidesguard, she'd navigated using the skies and her sextant, charting a course with the ink and parchment of her maps. Around Eileanan Selch, she let the currents guide her, their familiarity as easy to follow as a well-worn track.

This was different. The only thing she could rely on was the tug inside her, like a lodestone drawing the needle of a compass. If she followed it, she would find where she needed to go.

This way, she signalled with a low whistle, adjusting her flippers as the pull in her chest shifted course again.

Eimhir and Angus swam nearby, their presence quiet and certain as they shot through the water after her.

I still can't believe the other chieftains overruled Duncan, Eimhir said with amusement. *I won't forget the look on his face in a hurry.*

Angus barked a laugh, bubbles streaming from his snout. *It doesn't happen often, and for good reason. But they were right in their decision. We couldn't wait and do nothing.*

I don't understand why he was so reluctant in the first place, Isla said. *He seemed happy enough to let us investigate the trench before.*

That was different, Angus said. *The waters around Eileanan Selch are our territory. Until the gun-anam, there was little there to threaten us. But out here, we share the sea with the Admiralty. Its patrols are becoming more and more difficult to avoid, especially when their sentinels can sense us. If they latch on to our presence…*

He didn't need to say anything more. Isla already knew what would happen if they were caught. For Eimhir and Angus, it might be over quickly—throats slit, pelts ripped from their limp bodies. But for her… The Grand Admiral didn't just want her pelt. He wanted his daughter.

I won't go back, she said, half to herself. *I won't let him do to me what he did to Mara.*

Angus slowed. *I didn't know Mara, but I know Duncan sees her in you. More than he wants to admit. When you told him you could dreamwalk, when you spoke of the same places she'd been trying to find… It might not seem like it, but he fears the same thing you do.*

He fears losing the dreamwalker pelt, Eimhir said. *Don't pretend he cares about what happens to Isla.*

He cares about what happens to our people, Angus countered. *All our people.*

Even an aineol? The question escaped Isla's throat in a burst of clicks before she could stop herself. It hung between them, unanswered, slowly drifting away with the current.

We should keep moving, she said, once the silence was too much to bear. *Let's do what we came here to do.*

She propelled herself forward with a swift kick of her hind flippers. The further they swam from Eileanan Selch, the stronger the pull in her chest became. Following it was the only thing that mattered. If it led them to another lost ship, if it led them to a way of stopping the haar and the gun-anam...

Angus paused, his whiskers flicking against the current. *This isn't right. We were heading deeper into the Strait of Silveckan before. We've changed course.*

This is the way my pelt is pulling me, Isla said.

Towards Arburgh?

Isla slowed, an unsettling fear sinking deep beneath her sealskin. *What are you talking about?*

This isn't the way you were taking us before. We've drifted into another current, one that will take us right to the capital. Angus's tone was mild, but there was no mistaking the thin note of accusation.

I thought... Isla fought to clear her head. *I'm sure this is where it wanted me to go.*

Eimhir drifted to her side. *I believe you, caraid. But don't forget, your pelt is not the only soul you carry with you.*

Her words struck at Isla's heart, reaching a place she'd tried to keep buried. The ache resurfaced, bringing with it all her memories of that night on the *Jade Dawn*. The rain lashing down on the deck, soaking her shirt to her skin. Darce's hands holding her close. The sting of a salty kiss, the flash of a blade, the blood pooling from her stomach. She'd given her life to save his, and he'd brought her back with the gift of his soul.

If tides be kind, we'll find our way back to each other, he'd said.

Eimhir was right. She was running to *him*.

I... I didn't realise, she said. *I didn't think about which part of me it was calling to. Believe me, it was never my intention to lead us anywhere near Arburgh. I have more to lose than any of us by returning there.*

She couldn't read any kind of expression in Angus's selkie features, but something in his posture loosened. *I don't pretend to understand what's calling you. As a scout, I can only rely on the currents, not the pull of my soul. Perhaps if you tried to dreamwalk again, the memories in your pelt might guide us back on course?*

Aye, Isla said shakily. *I can try.* She closed her eyes and let her body drift to the surface. By the time her nostrils broke through the waves, the trance of float-sleep had already taken hold. The human part of her mind faded into a dreamless torpor, watched over by the animal instincts of her selkie form.

She waited for the dream to bloom, for her pelt to show her the places her ancestors once walked. But this time, there was no shifting of the darkness, no memories to carry her mind to. Instead, all she felt was a presence on the horizon, something familiar and strange at the same time. Something that called not to her soul, but the blood pulsing through her sleeping body.

A growl from Angus startled her awake, and she dived back below the waves to find him and Eimhir tense and alert.

What happened? she asked. *What's out there?*

Not anything we want to cross paths with, Eimhir said. *Do you remember me telling you how Finlay and I tracked you through the Wilds after the attack on your home?*

You said you followed the trail of the auld blood, Isla said. *At the time, we thought it was Darce. But it was me all along, wasn't it? It was my blood you sensed.*

Aye, Eimhir said. *The auld blood calls to selkie and sentinel alike. It allows us to sense each other's presence when it is spilled. We can't connect it to a specific person, but it draws us to their proximity. That's what you're feeling. There's a wounded sentinel close by.*

Or a selkie, Isla ventured.

Not a selkie, Angus said. *Selkies don't travel on ships.*

Isla stilled. She felt it now, the restless rippling of the sea, disturbing the currents. Something big was heading their way, too distant to be seen. But the water knew.

We need to put distance between ourselves and that ship, Eimhir said tightly. *If we can sense its sentinel, all it will take is one wound for them to sense us.*

She shot off through the water, and Isla followed, willing her tired muscles to carry her. Already the vastness of the sea seemed smaller with the ship bearing down on them. No matter how hard she pushed, how fast she swam, she felt the cedar and iron of their pursuer eating up their wake, closing the distance between them.

A flash of movement from the surface caught her eye, a dark silhouette skimming the waves above. Even from here, she could make out the long span of black wings, the white flash of its belly.

A razorbill.

Isla thrust forward and burst through the waves. As she leapt, the seabird let out a low caw, banking to avoid the spray. Its beady eyes seemed amused as it hovered above her before flapping its huge wings and heading back in the direction of the ship.

The shape in the distance was closer now; Isla saw three proud masts stretching towards the sky, sails billowing in the wind. The narrow prow pointed straight at them, cutting through the water with ease.

It would catch them soon. But if the razorbill was any indication, perhaps that wasn't the death sentence she'd first thought it was.

There was one way to find out.

The first thing she felt as she began to shed her pelt was the cold. Layers of fur and blubber melted from her skin, exposing her to the sea. The water seeped through to the bone, seizing her lungs in a vice-like grip.

Are you out of your mind? What are you— The rest of Angus's words shifted into a series of barks and clicks her now-human ears were unable to decipher.

Isla couldn't answer through the mouthful of salt water she'd gulped down. She flailed her weak human arms and legs, fighting to keep her head above the waves as the currents threatened to drag her under.

She focused on the horizon. All the muted tones of her selkie vision disappeared, replaced with colour once more. The blue sea roiling around her. The yellow outline of the sun shrouded by clouds. The emerald sails of the ship heading towards them.

An exhausted laugh spilled from her chattering teeth as her chest flooded with relief.

It wasn't the Admiralty. It was the *Jade Dawn*.

Being back on the deck of a ship brought Isla a comfort she hadn't realised she'd missed. She felt the beating heart of the *Jade Dawn* through the green-stained timber beneath her bare feet. Its canvas sails buffeted in the wind as it skimmed across the waves, cutting through the swell as easily as any sea creature.

Captain Nishi sauntered down from the quarterdeck, a half-smile tugging at the corner of her mouth. Her copper eyes gleamed as she extended an arm, her rolled-back sleeve exposing the swirling patterns of her Sea Kith tattoos across her brown skin. "It appears the tides have decided to bring us together once more, Blackwood."

Isla clasped her hand. "It's good to see you again, Captain. I never got the chance to thank you for what you did for us. If you hadn't taken us to that island, we'd never have found Eimhir's pelt."

"She saved one of my crew. I owed her a life." Nishi nodded to Eimhir. "You're looking better than the last time I saw you, selkie. I'm glad you were able to reclaim what was taken from you."

"As am I," Eimhir said. "The Grand Admiral does not part easily with his trophies."

"Yet here you are with two of them." Nishi glanced at Isla's pelt, quirking an eyebrow. "The last time you were on my ship, I told you the sea was in your blood. Seems I was right, though not in the way I expected."

Isla pulled the damp fur around her, shivering as the salt water trickled down her skin. "Believe me, I didn't expect it either. When I went to that island, I found more of myself than I'd ever bargained for."

The words left a stale taste on her tongue as they evaporated into the wind. Her ears rang with the parts she'd left unsaid, the truth echoing too loudly. She sensed Eimhir stiffen beside her, Angus's eyes on the back of her neck.

Aineol, the wind whispered.

"You said the Grand Admiral does not part easily with his trophies," Nishi said, breaking into her thoughts. "Well, let me give you this warning: nor will he hesitate in taking them back. He doesn't like being robbed, that much is certain. You're not the only ones to have faced his wrath out here on the waves."

"You had a run-in with one of the Admiralty's patrols?"

"Aye, you could call it that." The gold of Nishi's lip ring caught the light as she grimaced. "I've done my best to keep the *Jade Dawn* out of Silvish waters ever since we took you to that island. Reckoned the Admiralty would be none too happy about us helping you escape Arburgh. But their ships have been scouring the Strait of Silveckan, leaving naught in their wake but burnt wrecks and bloody waters. We got too close and paid the price."

Dread curled in Isla's stomach as she thought of the sentinel they'd sensed from the water. "Kerr. Is he—"

"Come now, do you think we'd be sailing this smoothly if the Admiralty had managed to kill me?"

Isla spun to see a familiar flaxen-haired figure crossing the deck, a grin on his face and a sling holding his bandaged forearm across his chest. This close, she heard the call of his sentinel blood singing in her ears. It came from everywhere and nowhere, whistling in the wind and roaring with the crash of the waves.

The giant razorbill from earlier circled above, letting out a gravelly cry from the hollows of its black beak before it swooped down and landed on the gunwale. It fixed Isla with a sharp look, then whistled a low trill.

"I see you've been reacquainted with Shearwing," Kerr said, amused. "I couldn't understand where it was leading us at first, but if a guidebird changes course, it would be a foolish thing for the Sea Kith not to follow. The tides must have wanted us to meet again."

"I'm glad it was you who picked up our trail rather than the Admiralty." Isla gestured to his injured arm. "Speaking of which, what happened?"

"Cap'n refused a less-than-courteous boarding request from the commander of a brigantine that spent a good two days chasing us down the edge of the Strait," Kerr said. "I was on the forecastle calling up a storm to carry us away when one of their officers shot me clean through the arm. Made a bit of a mess on the deck, but at least I managed to get our sails full before I collapsed."

"You shouldn't have been on the deck at all," Nishi muttered. "If they'd boarded us, a sentinel would have been their first target. Or did you want to be forced into servitude?"

"I wanted to get us away," Kerr said mildly. "If it meant taking a musket shot to my arm to succeed, I'd say that's a fair price to pay. More than fair, seeing as your plan involved taking on their entire crew with nothing but your pistol and rapier. Or is there a new addition to the *Jade Dawn's* articles that decrees you're the only one allowed to risk their neck on this ship?"

"I am your *captain*," Nishi said, running a weary hand across her face.

"And I am your sentinel," Kerr replied. "I don't need to remind you of what that means, or how it came to be."

Isla flinched. Kerr's words wrenched at the aching bruise behind her ribs, reminding her of the part she was missing. Darce's absence was like a scar she couldn't see, one she couldn't help running her fingers over, wincing every time the wound reopened.

She found Nishi staring at her, expression gentle. "Where is your sergeant?"

Isla bit her tongue. It was a question that would be easy to answer. She only had to follow the constant pulling in her chest, and she'd find him again. Instead of pushing away the ache until it was too much to bear, she only had to give in. All it would take was leaving behind everything she'd fought so hard to find.

Her fractured soul had already dragged her adrift. She needed to get back on course.

"You say the tides must have wanted us to meet again," she said. "I hope that's true. We could use your help."

Nishi frowned. "I like you, Isla Blackwood. I might go as far as calling you a friend. But helping you is the reason we're being hunted by the Admiralty in the first place. I won't put my crew in any more danger."

"You won't need to. It's information we need, nothing more." Isla glanced at Eimhir and Angus. "We're searching for something. Something that might help stop the haar, and the wraiths that come from it. Do you remember—"

"Aye," Nishi said. "I remember. Blood and seafoam soaking the deck. The air turning so thick with salt I could hardly breathe. And the cold…" She shuddered. "Sometimes I still feel its touch."

"It doesn't leave you," Eimhir said. "Even on the warmest days, you'll shiver in its shadow."

The wind dropped, and the green sails above fluttered gently, making no sound. Even the crashing of the waves quietened, leaving an unnatural stillness across the deck.

Nishi fixed them with a solemn stare. "I lost too many of my crew on that crossing. If you plan to dispel the mists and stop those horrors, I'll gladly tell you anything that might help. What is it you're searching for?"

Before she could answer, Angus let out a deep growl. Eimhir muttered something back, her throat quivering with each guttural noise.

Isla held her hands tight by her side. "You both know I can't make sense of the selkie tongue in human form. If you have something to say, it would help if I could understand it."

Only silence answered her. Then Angus spoke. "I said it's a mistake to involve humans in this. What we seek is no business of theirs."

"If it wasn't for them, I would be one with the salt and spray, and the

Grand Admiral would still have Isla's pelt," Eimhir said testily. "Human or not, they've earned our trust."

Nishi tilted her head, eyes glinting as she took the measure of Angus. "I've never found myself with any reason to quarrel with your people. I don't see why that should change, unless you want it to." She rested her hand lightly on the hilt of her rapier, but the smile in her voice tempered the warning.

A flush spread beneath Angus's freckles. "I don't go looking for fights. I leave that to the Admiralty."

"The Sea Kith are not the Admiralty," Isla said. "The open water is their home as much as it is ours. They can help us." She turned to Nishi. "You've sailed the entire Strait. Have you ever come across an unusual kind of wreck? A white ship, not painted like the *Jade Dawn*, but made of bone?"

Shearwing opened its beak and gave a low, rattling croon. It shuffled its webbed feet along the timber, then leapt off, spreading the impressive might of its wings to take back to the skies.

Nishi and Kerr exchanged a look.

"What is it?" Isla asked.

"We've seen a ship like the one you speak of," Nishi said. "An old wreck dashed on some rocks, its shattered hull gleaming white in the sun. Whether or not it was made of bone, I couldn't tell you. We gave it a wide berth."

A chill prickled Isla's spine. "The mists?"

Kerr shook his head. "No mists. But something wasn't right about the place. We kept our distance when I felt the unrest in the currents below. Shearwing refused to fly anywhere near it. Whatever happened there, it was enough to trouble the sea spirits. Enough for them to warn us away."

"It could be the place." Isla met Eimhir's gaze. "This might be our best chance of finding another ship."

"That might not be all you find," Nishi warned. "The ship we saw was wrecked on a small island northwest of the Drift. To reach it, you'll be cutting through one of the Admiralty's main trade routes. There are more patrols in these waters than ever before, and if they spot you…"

Her words hung in the air, but Isla brushed them off. "We don't have a choice. The mist sickness is getting worse. If we don't stop it, there won't be anyone left to stand against the Admiralty when its fleet arrives on selkie shores. The Grand Admiral will win." A bitter lump rose in her throat. "We can't let that happen. *I* can't let it happen."

Eimhir placed her hand on her shoulder, grip strong and steady. "It won't come to that. Not if I have anything to say about it. We'll get you where you need to go. And if any Admiralty patrol tries to stop us, we'll give them a taste of what to expect if they dare try to breach Eileanan Selch."

Angus's shoulders tensed, but he relented with a tight nod.

"Our course is set, then. We'll head north and make for the Drift." Isla released a breath and turned to Nishi. "Thank you, Captain, for everything. We didn't realise how lucky we were running into you all those months ago in Kinraith."

Nishi's lips stretched into a smirk. "Luck had little to do with it, Blackwood. The tides have a will of their own, fickle though it may be. I only hope they carry you safely, so we might have the chance to meet again."

Isla moved to the gunwale, running her hands along the green-stained wood. In front of her, the horizon was clear. Yet it was easy to imagine a gathering storm, dark with the shadow of Admiralty ships.

"Aye," she said quietly. "I hope for that too."

CHAPTER NINE

DARCE

After spending so much time confined within the walls of the garrison, Darce had forgotten the stench of the docks. The brackish smell was like a slap to the face, waking him from the haze that had settled over him. Each breath was thick with brine and the must of wet timber as he walked the length of the jetty, eyes trained on the monstrous ship moored at the end.

There it was.

The *Vanguard of the Firth* loomed over the docks. Even with its black sails stowed, the galleon seemed to leach all light from the morning sky, turning its surroundings as bleak as it was. The hull groaned and creaked as it rocked with the waves, grating on Darce's ears. Everything about the ship told him to stay away. He didn't belong here. He wasn't *welcome* here.

"It's something, isn't it?" Blair appeared beside him, curls bouncing as he nodded towards the ship. "I wager you've never set foot on a man-o'-war like this before."

"You'd win that bet."

He lifted an eyebrow at Darce's expression. "No need to look so uneasy, Sergeant. The *Vanguard* is the pride of the Admiralty fleet. There's nothing in Silvish waters that can stand against it."

That's precisely what makes me uneasy, Darce thought. It was only now, standing under the ship's cold, dark gaze, that he realised what he'd agreed to. When the *Vanguard* unfurled its sails and met the open water, it would be hunting Isla.

Here he stood in boots of serpenthide, the bite of their soles promising him grip on the slickest of decks. He wore soft buckskin breeches that kept the wind's chill from his skin. Around his torso was an exquisite leather brigandine trimmed in teal and gold, boasting the snarling wolven features of the *Vanguard's* figurehead.

Obscene riches and the promise of power, Muir had said.

It felt like a bargain struck, a deal he couldn't renege on. Whatever his reasons were, however desperate he'd been, he'd accepted this. He'd *chosen* to be here.

And he didn't know if Isla would ever forgive him for it.

Beside him, Blair gave an irritated sigh. "What is *he* doing here? A baron's business is with the merchant docks, not the Admiralty ship-yards."

Darce glanced over to see a familiar figure strutting down one of the *Vanguard's* gangways. His red hair was perfectly coiffed, and he wore a smile every bit as sharp as the ornamental dagger gleaming from his belt—both for show, but no less dangerous for it.

Nathair Quinn.

When he caught sight of Darce, his smile widened like a trap ready to snap shut. "Sergeant Galbraith, I see they finally let you out to play. I must say, Admiralty colours suit you better than irons. I'm sure Lachlan is pleased you saw sense in the end."

Anger rose in Darce's chest, but he fought to keep his voice even. "Come to talk him out of his commission, have you? Or will you just move your attentions to the next noble you can use to help further your schemes?"

"You sound just like her." Quinn chuckled. "Our dear Isla never did manage to grasp the subtleties of the capital. We do what we must to get to where we need to go." His eyes flicked across the emblem on Darce's uniform. "It appears you learned that lesson better than her."

An unwelcome flush rose up Darce's neck. "This is only—" He caught himself, remembering Blair's presence. "Whatever I'm doing, it's because I have her best interests at heart."

"Do you suppose Isla will see it that way?" The smile never left Quinn's lips, but his eyes hardened with a knowing glint. "When she sees you on the *Vanguard's* deck, at the side of the man she tried to kill, do you think she'll believe you have her best interests at heart? Or will she see it for the betrayal it is?"

Darce couldn't answer. His chest turned cold, hollowed by the dread creeping through him. Quinn's words were an echo of his own fears, brought to the surface when all he wanted was to keep them buried.

A satisfied expression stretched across Quinn's face. "Delightful to see you again, Sergeant, and may the tides carry you swiftly to your quarry. I hope for your sake she's in more of a forgiving mood than she was when I crossed her." He lowered himself into a graceful bow, then strode back towards the docks, cloak swaying in his wake.

Blair stared after him, jaw twitching. "Prick."

Of all the things to find common ground over, Darce thought. Aloud, he said, "You don't hold the baron in high esteem, then?"

"I don't hold him in any kind of esteem." Blair snorted. "He bought his title with something my uncle wanted. Aye, he may dress in fancy furs and talk like a noble, but coin and a sharp tongue won't be enough to get him to the places he's trying to go."

"I wouldn't be so quick to underestimate him," Darce said. "Nathair Quinn didn't get where he is by being satisfied with his lot. He'll always want more, and he'll do whatever it takes to get it."

"And Lachlan?" Blair cleared his throat. "I mean to say, how does he fit into his schemes?"

Darce raised an eyebrow. "Concerned about him, are you?"

"That's not—" He broke off, cheeks reddening. "I don't understand why Lachlan trusts him, that's all."

Because Quinn was there for him when nobody else was. The truth rose bitterly in Darce's throat, impossible to swallow. Isla had been too focused on saving Eimhir, and he'd been too focused on protecting Isla. They'd let Lachlan slip from their sights into the shadow he resented. All it had taken to lose him was Quinn's lure of a path back into the light.

"Quinn knows how to make himself valuable," Darce said. "Lachlan is no fool, but it's easy to make allowances for someone whose knives end up in the backs of your enemies."

Blair pursed his lips. "I only hope he's given some consideration to the possibility that one of those knives might end up in his." He glanced towards the gangway. "At any rate, we should head aboard. We're to set sail at the turn of high tide, and the Grand Admiral won't want any delay."

Darce followed him up the gangway. The main deck bustled with crew, the jewel-toned colours of their Admiralty cloaks stark against the black timber. They grappled with knotted lines, hauling the seaweed-laden ropes over the gunwale and securing them in place. More of them sat high on the rigging, fingers working to loosen the gaskets. Soon, the *Vanguard's* huge sails would unfold, catching the wind that would carry them out of the firth.

By then, it would be too late to turn back.

He stole a glance at the gangway, but the wooden walkway had already been hauled up. The ship rocked more insistently, loosed from the strangling lines tethering it to the docks. It wanted its freedom. It wanted the sea.

Inch by inch, they peeled away, swinging towards the open water. Darce made his way to the front of the ship, blinking as the wind whipped spray into his eyes. Far below, the waves leapt in the bleak winter light, scattering into foam as the *Vanguard* crashed through them.

As he peered over the edge, he caught sight of the ship's wolven figurehead carved into the prow. From here, he could only see the back of its great, shaggy head, but he'd seen its snarling jaws too many times not to recognise it for what it was. The talisman of the *Vanguard*, the sigil of the Grand Admiral himself.

Wolf cub. The thought flashed through his mind, painful and unbidden. How many times had that old nickname passed carelessly through his lips? How many times had Isla bristled upon hearing it? Every time he'd uttered it, he'd spoken a truth neither of them had realised, an omen of what was to come.

"She's out there, isn't she?"

Darce flinched at the sound of the voice. It carried over the wind with ease, demanding to be heard.

The Grand Admiral stood behind him, casting his gaze over the swell. The furrowed lines on his forehead seemed more severe out here, like they'd been cut into stone. Darce half believed the force of his glare could command the waves as much as any sentinel, such was its intensity.

"I don't know where she is," he answered.

"No, Sergeant, I'm afraid you'll have to do better than that." Cunningham moved alongside him, his dark grey hair catching the wind under the brim of his tricorne hat. "I didn't bring you aboard for you to test my patience with lies. We both know what failure will cost you."

On the main deck, Lachlan stood in conversation with one of the *Vanguard's* captains. His fingers tensed around the handle of his crutch as he braced himself, adjusting his weight to the ship's swaying.

The deck can be a dangerous place, Cunningham had said. *And the waters of the Strait are treacherous and unforgiving.*

Darce swallowed. "I mean it. I don't know where she is."

"But you can find her." Cunningham fixed him with a steel-eyed stare. "You have the gifts of the auld blood. For the sake of your young charge, I suggest you use them."

For the briefest of moments, Darce thought of drawing his blade. He could stop this right now. He could run his sword through Cunningham and accept the fate that would surely follow. His own life was a price he was willing to pay to keep Lachlan safe. To keep them *both* safe.

But if what Muir said was true, if the other sentinels on the *Vanguard* were willing to sacrifice the lives of their own captains to save the Grand Admiral from a mortal wound... No, it wasn't the time. All he could do was wait, and pray the tides would find a way to frustrate their hunt until he was in a position to strike Cunningham down for good.

He closed his eyes, reaching for the part of him connected to Isla. If it was frayed, he only had himself to blame. He'd forced her hand. He'd sent her running to the water when she begged to stay by his side.

His breathing slowed, then sharpened as the pain returned. Whatever it was holding them together, it was still in place, buried so deep he wouldn't know how to dig it out even if he wanted to. It was more than the call of the auld blood they shared. He'd given her part of his soul. He'd pressed his hand against the gushing wound in her stomach and offered the tides all he had to save her.

And they'd answered.

The sea knew where she was. He sensed the wake she'd left behind like a current leading him towards her. All he had to do was follow it, and he'd find her.

When he opened his eyes, Alasdair Cunningham was watching him with an immutable expression. He didn't need to ask a second time. Darce was all too aware of the noose around his neck, ready to snap tight if he stepped out of line.

He forced the unwilling words from his throat. "West. We need to sail west."

Cunningham turned on his heel and made for the *Vanguard's* helm. The sapphire tones of his twin-tailed coat rippled as he walked, the soft material doing nothing to disguise the stiffness of his spine, the square set of his shoulders. This was a man who was utterly relentless. A man with the will to defy the tides themselves, and enough power to do it.

Somebody on deck barked a command, and then came the clap of sails. They unfurled from the spindle-like masts, blocking out the sky as they caught the wind. As the pale grey light disappeared behind billowing black canvas, Darce fought the shiver spreading over his skin as he was left in shadow.

The wide mouth of the firth lay ahead, beckoning them to open waters. As the *Vanguard* sailed to meet it, Darce prayed he hadn't set them on a course he couldn't take back.

CHAPTER TEN

ISLA

Everything *ached*.

Isla pressed her thumbs into the bare skin of her thighs, trying to work some feeling back into her muscles. They'd been swimming for days, and float-sleep did little to help the exhaustion. She'd never felt more grateful than when Angus spotted a rocky skerry in the distance, and Eimhir suggested they stop and rest. The terrain was nothing but rough slabs of limestone strewn with seaweed, but it was a respite all the same.

"I forget you're not used to such distances," Eimhir said. "We've been by each other's sides so constantly these past few months that it's difficult for me to remember a time that wasn't the case. It feels like you've always been one of us."

"At least someone thinks so." Isla glanced at the choppy waves. Angus was still out there, his russet-brown head bobbing above the water as he circled the skerry. When his black eyes locked with hers, she looked away.

Eimhir followed her gaze. "You're upset with him."

"I thought he was beginning to trust me. He was ready to defy Duncan's orders to help me hunt down the ships. But every time I think I'm getting somewhere…" Isla pressed her hands against the rock. "I'm afraid I'll never be enough for them, no matter what I do."

Eimhir placed her hand over hers. There was a time her fingers would have bitten like ice against Isla's skin, but now, all she felt was the beat of their shared blood.

"You are already enough, caraid," Eimhir said, squeezing gently. "Whatever other doubts you may have, never doubt that."

"The chieftains hate humans. Angus hates humans."

Eimhir sat silently, her features hard as she stared out at the bleak horizon. "Tell me of the night your home was attacked."

Isla flinched. "Why do you—"

"Please. You've never spoken about it before."

The dull ache of grief swelled painfully in Isla's chest. She didn't want to dredge up the memories she'd so desperately tried to bury. The anguish of that night was too closely entwined with the sting of guilt, the blistering of resentment, holding her to account for all the things she'd done, all the things she'd failed to do.

"When Darce burst into my room, his face was covered in blood," she said. "My father's blood, though I didn't know it at the time. He died on his bedroom floor, his leg cleaved open by a selkie axe. I didn't... I didn't get a chance to say goodbye." She took a shuddering breath. "We escaped through the servants' stairwell into the kitchens. There was a cook, her name was Rowan. Her body was on the floor, dress ripped open. And her back..."

Eimhir stilled. "The flaying."

"Aye." Bile rose in Isla's throat, thick and pungent. "Her skin was torn to ribbons, peeled back like a pair of wings. I could see the white of her spine." She shook her head violently. "And Caolaig... The cobbles streamed with blood by the time we reached it the next morning. The shore was wet and red and scattered with bodies. Skin like wax, lips blue. Some of them... Some of them were *bairns*, Eimhir. How could they... How could anyone—"

"How indeed," Eimhir said softly, and a chill raced down Isla's back.

"I hated them," she murmured. "I *still* hate them."

"Yet here we are. Something must have changed."

A sudden sense of understanding raked at Isla's heart, its claws sharp and bittersweet. "Aye, it did. I met you. Long before I knew you were my cousin, before I found the part of me that was lost, you were my friend. I found something deeper than the wounds that ran between us."

"We both did," Eimhir said. "And I will forever be grateful for it. But few selkies are as fortunate as I. Angus has never met a human he's had reason to trust. He's only ever known the violence of the Admiralty. He's seen friends dragged from the water and gutted on deck like a fresh catch. Bodies dumped into the sea, stripped of their pelts. Can you blame him for hating humans, like you once hated us?"

"No," Isla said heavily. "I only wish things were different."

She pulled her pelt tighter, sinking into the fur's damp warmth as the wind showered her bare arms with spray. The dappled tones rippled in the dreich light, clinging to her like a second skin.

"I keep holding on to the thought that if we can stop the mist sickness and banish the gun-anam beyond the haar, there might be a chance for both parts of me to exist in this world," she said. "Then I remember the way Duncan's voice changes when he speaks to me. The look on Lachlan's face when he realised what I was. I can't change that I am human as much as I am selkie. I don't *want* to change that."

Eimhir roped an arm around her shoulders. "You won't have to, caraid. It's the world that will have to change. That's why we're doing this. Stopping the gun-anam is the first step on the path to us being able to live freely, live in peace. We'll walk it together, no matter what it takes." She pushed herself up from the rock, offering her hand. "Come, the Drift is not too much further. If we find this lost ship, we might also find the answers we seek."

Isla rose, wincing as her foot scraped against the rough limestone. Eimhir was right. They weren't far. Her weary muscles could carry her this final stretch.

Before she could dive into the waves, Angus reappeared, leaping from the water and shedding his pelt in a single fluid motion. The red-brown fur melted from his skin, gathering around his pale arms and legs. He ran a hand through his wet hair, breathing heavily.

"We'd best move," he said. "There's a ship heading this way, and I doubt we'll be so fortunate as to come across your Sea Kith friends a second time. We're in the heart of the Admiralty's trade routes. It's likely one of the capital patrols."

On the horizon, the rain thickened across the waves. Isla could barely see a hundred metres in front of her. "How do you know?"

"The currents. Better to trust them than your eyes. Now, let's hurry, before they—" He broke off, paling. "Shite, Isla, your *foot!*"

She startled at the vehemence in his voice. Then she looked down and understood.

A stream of blood trickled across the rock, mingling with the puddle of seawater beneath her feet. She lifted her leg, exposing the serrated edge of a limpet shell stained red. That was the scrape she'd felt when Eimhir hauled her to her feet. The rough tip of the shell had sliced her skin.

She hastily dipped her hand into the water and wiped the blood away, wincing at the sting of salt. "It's just a scratch. Nothing to worry—"

"A scratch is all they need," Angus said sharply. "If that is an Admiralty ship, if they have a sentinel on board…"

"Back to the water," Eimhir said. "Now."

Isla nodded, the folds of her pelt already spreading across her skin. The wet fur soaked into her arms, across her legs, until it became one with her flesh. Her organs squeezed and shifted, her bones twisting and crunching as she returned her to her soulshape.

The last thing she saw before her vision turned grey was the traitorous red droplet quivering on the shell of the limpet.

She leapt into the water, breathing out through her new-formed nose. Her limbs had sewn themselves together, fingers and toes yielding to strong, leathery flippers. The swollen heart in the cavity of her chest thumped hard and fast, sending precious air through her blood. Her muscles would need it. She'd need everything her selkie body could give her.

Angus was already swimming. *Don't slow. Don't stop.*

His words thrummed through the water in a tone that chilled Isla's blood. He knew what was chasing them. He was afraid of it.

I'm with you, she said. *Let's go.*

He shot off through the water, and Isla pushed her protesting muscles to dart after him. The rain thundered down against the waves above, pockmarking the surface and filling her ears with a muffled echo. Ahead, there was only darkness, so dense she could barely make out the seabed. All she could do was continue into the gloom, and hope it would lead them to safety.

As she swam, she pushed away the cold grip of fear and retreated into her seal mind. But the animal in her was afraid too. It knew what it meant to be hunted. Just because these waters were home, it didn't mean they were safe.

She pushed her flippers, willing her aching body to respond. The effort of each stroke strained her muscles as she fought through the angry currents. It was as though the sea itself had turned against her.

The agitated growl from Angus confirmed her fears. *They've got a sentinel*, he said. *Be on guard. They're trying to slow us down.*

She felt it now, the magic disturbing the water. It swirled to her hind flippers, winding around them in a stream of violent ripples. As she kicked, the sea dragged her back. It was like the currents had come alive. They grasped for her with claws of salt and foam, churning the water.

She'd never understood why selkies reviled sentinels so much, why they *feared* them so much. The glimpses of magic she'd seen from Kerr were selfless: drawing seawater from the lungs of a half-drowned deckhand, drying the soaked powder in her pistol when she'd fallen into the river. This was different. She sensed the sentinel's distant hand manipulating the currents, yoking the sea spirits to their will. The sea had become hostile when it should have been their sanctuary.

Eimhir thrashed wildly, snapping her jaws as if she could bite through the invisible tethers. Her long back arched as she wrestled and writhed like a stricken fish caught in a net. Eventually she broke free and circled back, her black eyes glittering furiously.

No, she snarled. *I won't let them trap me in the waters that are our home, waters they have no place in. I'd rather give them the fight they're after.*

They'll kill you. Angus was calm, but Isla saw him straining against the current. *Don't forget, I know these patrols. I know what they're capable of. We have a chance of getting away. Their sentinel won't be able to keep this up forever.*

They won't need to, Eimhir shot back. *It's only a matter of time before they go to full sail to hunt us down, if they haven't already. Their muskets and harpoons will find us easy targets if we exhaust ourselves. Better go on the attack while we still stand a chance.*

The ferocity in her voice was enough to make Isla slow. The thought of meeting the pursuing Admiralty ship head on filled her with dread. But worse was the thought of it running them down until they were too tired to swim, too tired to put up a fight. They'd strip her pelt from her back, robbing her of all she'd fought for, all she'd given up to find that missing part of herself.

She couldn't let them take it. Not like that.

She splayed her flippers and circled back towards Eimhir. *I'm with you, cousin.*

Through the gloom, she could already see the subtle turbulence in the distance, the currents and eddies shifting around the ship's bow. It wouldn't be long until it was upon them. At least now, it would be their choice.

This is a mistake, Angus said.

Aye, Eimhir replied grimly. *Theirs.*

CHAPTER ELEVEN

DARCE

Despite being surrounded by the sea's ever-stretching expanse, Darce's cage was smaller than ever. On the *Vanguard*, there was no getting away from his fellow officers. No escaping the Grand Admiral's vigilant eyes presiding over the quarterdeck. Every day, the ship's wooden jaws closed tighter around him, until he wondered whether they would ever let him go.

Integrating himself with the other sentinels hadn't been as easy as he'd hoped. His attempts to find common ground were met with reticence and suspicion, like he was crossing an unspoken line. There was some kind of current lurking below the façade of duty, the lure of fame and riches. Darce felt it tugging at him, but the truth remained slippery and elusive.

It didn't help that out here, the call singing to his blood was stronger than ever. The sentinels used their magic to harness the waves, compelling the sea spirits to carry them swiftly across the swell. The spirits' presence was like a thrum in his veins, a whisper in his ears. He couldn't ignore it. Not on this ship, with everything it had witnessed. The timber may have been washed clean, but he sensed the selkie blood spilled here.

Echoes of their writhing agony, their stark fear, lingered in the grain. They screamed to him, demanding justice. Demanding vengeance.

If only Darce could give it to them.

A shrill cry tore across the wind, shaking him from his thoughts. He glanced up to find the familiar shape of a gannet circling overhead, its white belly bright against the darkening sky. It tucked its wings and swooped down, landing in a clatter of webbed claws.

Darce met its baleful glare, folding his arms so the wretch couldn't get to his fingers. "I see you decided to join me after all. I hope you'll prove more of a help than the night Muir's lackeys hauled me off the streets. The one time I might have appreciated your vicious beak, and you were nowhere to be found."

Featherblade squawked and jabbed furiously at his face, but Darce had been on the receiving end of enough nips to duck neatly out of the way.

"Save it for the Grand Admiral," he said. "The tides know I'll need all the bloody help I can get."

The bird stared back, its pale blue eyes boring through him with an intensity that made Darce feel like he was being judged. The yellow patch on the crown of its head shone in the faint winter sun as it ruffled its feathers and turned away, deciding it'd had enough of him.

"It's still following you, then?" Lachlan joined him, resting his crutch against the wooden railing. In the few short days they'd been aboard, he'd become adept at managing his balance on the rolling deck, even through rougher waters. Some of the crew still gawked, but fewer of them muttered their doubts about his place on the ship.

Darce couldn't help but smile. Lachlan always did take a spiteful kind of satisfaction in proving people wrong.

"Looks like it," he said, glancing at Featherblade. "I thought it might have stayed behind in Arburgh, but clearly it had other ideas. I don't understand why it's so attached to me."

"The taste of your fingers, undoubtedly."

Featherblade threw back its head and let out a piercing cackle. Then it shuffled its wings and took off, soaring towards the clouds.

Darce watched it go. "Tides, sometimes I wonder how I ended up here."

Lachlan snorted. "I think we both know the answer to that."

He didn't say Isla's name. He didn't need to. Even unspoken, it rang through the air between them, impossible to ignore.

"Have you thought about what will happen if we find her?" Darce asked, voice low. "Do you hate her so much that you'd see her as the Grand Admiral's prisoner?"

Lachlan shifted his gaze to the water. "As I understand it, they're family. Whatever happens is for them to work out."

"You can't seriously believe that." Darce fought to swallow his anger. "Do you have any idea how much she'll suffer if he takes her pelt? The salt will eat through her skin. Her organs will shrink and waste. Every moment will be agony, and he'll return her pelt only enough to keep her alive when she'd rather die. Would you stand by and let that happen?"

Lachlan blanched. "Don't make this about me, Galbraith. This is *her* fault. Everything that has happened is because of her."

"What are you talking about?"

"She brought them with her." He curled his hands into fists. "You know as well as I do the raids were never as bad before she came back. It's because she's one of them. *She's* drawing them out. Not just the skinchangers, but those wraiths, the ones that came from the mist. It all traces back to her."

Darce opened his mouth to argue, but something in Lachlan's words stilled him. He thought of all the times the haar had crept in, bringing with it the shadows of the gun-anam.

Blackwood Estate. Arburgh's docks during the selkie attack on the capital. The *Jade Dawn* on the treacherous crossing through Beira's Passage.

Isla had been at the centre of each one.

An unsettling chill crept through his veins. What if Lachlan was right?

What if the gun-anam were following Isla, stalking her across Silveckan? If she didn't know, if she hadn't made the same connection...

"I thought you didn't believe in the gun-anam," he said, trying to push the fear from his mind.

"I didn't believe Eimhir's story," Lachlan said. "She was only using us for her own ends. But I saw that wraith emerge from the mists at Blackwood Estate. I felt its blade pierce my flesh." His hand drifted to his shoulder. "You did a good job stitching the wound, but it lingers even now. It's always cold, stinging like salt."

"Isla would never have wanted to put you in danger."

"Whether she wanted to or not, she did," Lachlan said bluntly. "What happened to our home, what happened to our father... Tides *take* her, it would never have come to pass if she—" He broke off, eyes glittering. "This is pointless, Galbraith. There's no changing my mind."

"She is still your sister," Darce said. "No matter what else she may be, she is your family. Perhaps all that is left of it."

For a moment, he thought he might have forced a crack in the wall Lachlan had barricaded himself behind. A pained look flashed across his face, revealing a glimpse of the lad who'd lost all he cared about in a single night.

Then it was gone, and the youngest Blackwood drew more out of his reach than ever.

"She's made it clear who she considers family," Lachlan said tightly. "Isla chose her path. I will not apologise for choosing mine."

He tucked his crutch under his arm and swung away, leaving Darce with nothing but the weight of regret as he watched him go.

"Very well," he said softly. "Then neither will I."

Each night, Darce drifted to sleep with the sea whispering in his ears. It was a sound not even the walls of his cabin could keep out; it came to him not through the waves crashing against the hull, but in the pulsing of his sentinel blood. It yawned and sighed in his dreams all through the night, only fading with the grey light of morning.

This time, when he woke, there was no light. Somebody grabbed his arm from below his bunk, jolting him to his senses. His hand slid towards the stiletto dagger concealed beneath his pillow, but he stopped upon recognising the wide-eyed young cabin boy.

"They sent me to wake you, Sergeant Galbraith," he said in hushed tones. "The Grand Admiral needs every sentinel on deck."

Isla, he thought, heart hammering as he climbed down from the bunk. Had they found her already?

He threw his tunic over his head and pulled on his boots, fingers fumbling at the straps. No, if Cunningham had Isla in his grasp, the last thing he'd want is an audience. This was something else. Something grave enough to warrant calling every sentinel on the ship to action.

He slid his rapier into his belt, then ducked through the doorway and hurried up the steep wooden steps to the main deck.

The night was still, eerily so. Darce hardly dared to breathe for fear of disturbing the silence. The wind dropped, leaving the *Vanguard's* huge sails hanging limply from the masts. Someone had dimmed the lanterns, and the glow of the moon was half-obscured by clouds, offering no reprieve against the darkness.

Eventually, he reached the aft of the ship, taking his place next to another sentinel. The waves below ebbed gently, as black as the night sky. The *Vanguard* barely seemed to be moving at all; no foam churned in their wake, no spray leapt against the hull. Everything had just...stopped.

He glanced at the sentinel next to him, a woman around his age called Rhona. Her brown hair was tied in a knot, and her brow furrowed in concentration as she murmured to the water. She moved her arms in slow, steady gestures, casting protective wards across the waves. Her muscular forearms were half-hidden behind tattoos—not the skin-toned, subtle patterns of the Sea Kith, but bold lines in green ink winding from her wrists to her elbows.

She shot him an inquisitive look. "Fancy helping, or did ye just come here to watch?"

"I don't know what's happening," Darce said. "One of the cabin lads came to fetch me from below."

"Hard luck. You'll probably wish ye'd slept through this." She nodded to the waves. "We've caught the attention of a sea serpent."

Darce leaned over the gunwale, training his eyes on the water. He couldn't see anything through the darkness. In truth, he wasn't sure he wanted to. He'd never encountered a sea serpent before, but he was familiar with the old sailors' tales. He knew how they could summon broodlings to swarm a deck. How they could wrap their supple bodies around a ship and break it in two.

"There," Rhona said, pointing to the middle of the hull. "You see it?"

The moon broke through the veil of clouds, scattering its light against the waves. At first, all Darce saw was a glimmer reflecting off the water. Then, he realised the reflection was coming from something *under* the surface.

"I see it," he said, mouth dry.

It was moving so slowly he'd mistaken it for the rolling waves. Only now did he recognise the rippling outline of the long, lithe shape next to the ship. Moonlight danced off its scaly hide as it glided through the water, the length of it stretching further than the *Vanguard* itself.

Rhona muttered something under her breath, her inked forearms flexing as she cast another ward.

"You're calming it?" Darce asked.

She grunted. "Trying to. Care to give us a hand?"

The water rippled as the serpent slipped under the keel. Darce imagined it rearing from the waves on the other side, jaws spread open, the hot stench of its sea-rot breath spilling across the deck. The rapier tucked into his belt seemed pitifully inadequate. They couldn't fight a monster like that. Couldn't run from it, not even on the *Vanguard*.

He focused on the cresting waves. The sea was in his blood. It coursed through his veins, ice cold and sharp with salt. Its distant call echoed in his ears, rising and falling with a hushed whisper.

Auld blood, it said in a deep, fathomless sigh. *Sentinel*.

Darce closed his eyes and reached out. In his mind, salt water filled his throat. The weight of the waves surrounded him, holding him in a watery embrace.

A familiar presence brushed his thoughts. Featherblade. He sensed the gannet's alertness as it nestled in one of the portholes. It had been sleeping, but something had disturbed it. It too felt the ripples through the water below, the huge coil of scales and sinew circling the ship.

Darce withdrew from the seabird's mind, reaching instead for the other consciousness, the one lurking below the surface. His temples turned cold as he grasped for it, his blood like ice as it pulsed through his head.

Aineol, the serpent whispered.

The unfamiliar word slid through his ears, awash with seafoam and spray. The creature *knew* he was there. It sensed their connection and spoke to him in a slippery tongue he couldn't understand.

He cracked open an eye. Rhona's face was impassive as she concentrated on the water. "You didn't hear that?" he asked.

"Hear what?"

"I thought... It's nothing." Darce fell silent, shivering at the serpent's lingering whisper as its strange mind brushed against his own. The creature circled the *Vanguard*, curious and wary. Not afraid. No monster like this could be afraid of something built from mere timber and canvas.

We are no threat, he thought. *We're just passing through.*

The serpent gave a low, gurgling hiss in the confines of his mind, sending pain through his temples. *Lies.*

Darce turned cold. The magic singing in his veins roiled and seethed, like the sea itself had raised its voice in protest. He thought of the long-dried blood soaked into the *Vanguard's* deck, the soulskins ripped from gutted selkie bodies. The memory of suffering lingered in the ship's timber like rot. He sensed the ghosts here. It was little wonder the serpent could, too.

We shouldn't be here, he said, as much to himself as to the serpent. *We're not meant to be here.*

He felt the creature's long, sinuous body slide beneath the ship, so close its scales scraped off the barnacles encrusting the keel. Part of him wanted to hold his breath, as if that might cause the serpent to lose the interest it had taken in them. A wrench of that coiled tail around the *Vanguard's* throat, and it would be over with a crack as the timber splintered and water flooded the remains of the deck.

"I think it's leaving," Rhona said, rasping.

Darce stilled. The oily, writhing presence of the serpent's mind faded, untangling from his own. Warmth rushed back to his blood, flushing his cheeks and neck.

Rhona was right. The serpent was gliding away, disappearing into the depths.

Above them, the *Vanguard's* huge black sails fluttered. The wind returned, carrying with it a ripple of relief as the ship pushed through the waves once more.

Rhona's eyes glittered in the darkness. "Well, ye got there in the end, I suppose."

"It's my first commission. I've not exactly done this before."

"Aye, I can tell." She snickered. "Who's your captain?"

Darce hesitated as he forced out the lie. "Lachlan Blackwood."

Surprise flickered over her face, but she smoothed her expression. "The Grand Admiral doesn't take on new captains without good reason. I look forward to seeing the young laird prove his worth."

There was a soft curl to her voice that left Darce unsure whether she was mocking him. "What about you?" he asked. "Who did you make your blood oath to?"

"Mhairi Mackenzie," Rhona said. "You might not have seen her around much. She's a quiet one, prefers her own company. I don't think she'd have come here if it wasn't for me. But when the Grand Admiral offers ye a place on the *Vanguard*…"

"It's not easy to say no," Darce finished, bitterness rising on his tongue. "I know that feeling."

Rhona sent him a sidelong look, then turned back to the waves. "At least we were able to calm the beast. The tides were on our side tonight."

"Do you ever question why?" The words left his mouth before he could stop them, hanging in the air between them like treason. "I only mean… Well, the *Vanguard* is no friend to the sea, or the creatures in it. Sometimes it's difficult to understand why the tides answer our call."

"You *are* new to this, aren't ye?" Rhona snorted. "The *Vanguard* may not be a friend to the sea, but its sails have defied week-long squalls. Its hull has battered through waves that would sink any other vessel. Its deck kens the taste of blood from monsters that would see us dead. There is power in that. More power than either you or I command."

Her words rang against the bite of the wind. Darce couldn't be sure if they were a rebuke or something deeper, something carrying the same undercurrent he often heard in his own voice.

"And without its sentinels?" he ventured. "Where does its power come from then?"

Rhona stared at him, her expression inscrutable. "You're asking some dangerous questions."

"Dangerous for who?"

Something gleamed in her dark eyes, and Darce thought he might have imagined the ghost of a smile at the corner of her lips. It was as if an unspoken understanding passed between them, too tenuous to give voice to. Then it was gone, and Rhona turned away. "You should head below and get some rest while ye can. Feels like there's a storm brewing out there."

The sky was clear now, the stars like pinpricks in the deep cloak of night. Moonlight shimmered off the tips of the waves, casting a fractured glow over the water. Yet as he trudged back to his cabin, Darce couldn't help but sense Rhona was right. Whether the other sentinels knew it or not, they were heading straight into a storm. One of the Grand Admiral's making.

And if Darce had his way, he'd make damn sure Cunningham didn't emerge out the other side.

CHAPTER TWELVE

ISLA

By the time Isla realised they'd swum straight to their deaths, it was already too late.

The ship's keel rumbled towards them, shuttering out the light streaming through the surface. This close, she could make out the slithering fronds of seaweed clinging to the timber, the barnacles clustered like patchwork. More and more of the sea was swallowed by the looming shadow, until there was nowhere left to run.

That was the point, she told herself. But her earlier determination paled upon seeing what was coming for them. No courage warmed her. All she felt was the knot of fear, the knowledge that a decision, once made, was not so easy to unmake.

Another harpoon shot through the waves, leaving an angry stream of bubbles churning in its wake. Isla darted away in time to see it fly past and disappear into the murk below. The spears were meticulously crafted, their ashwood shafts boasting barbed arrowheads made from antler and iron, filed to murderous tips. If one caught her, its teeth would bite clean through her pelt, sinking into her blubber and tissue. There would be no dislodging it as the hunter on the other end of the gun hauled in the rope, dragging her punctured and bloodied body onto the deck.

Keep moving, Eimhir barked. She sported an ugly gash across her flank where one of the spears had nicked her. *Don't let them line up another shot.*

Isla followed her into the shadow of the ship's hull as another harpoon plunged through the waves. They were outmatched. The ship—a single-masted sloop—wasn't particularly large, but it tore through the waves with formidable speed and had unloaded the full force of its arms on them. The muffled crack of black powder echoed each time another harpoon was unleashed. It wouldn't be long until one found its mark.

We can't keep this up much longer, Isla said. *We need to get out of reach of those tides-damned harpoons.*

We had our chance to run, Angus replied tightly. *We've no choice but to see this through. Stay close, and when you see me leap, make sure you follow. This ship is no galleon or brigantine—we should be able to reach the deck from the water, with a wee bit of help from the tides.*

You mean to meet them on deck? Isla asked.

It's no use fighting on their terms, Eimhir said. *We'll make them fight on ours.*

Before Isla could ask what she meant, she was off, racing after Angus with swift, powerful strokes. Isla followed in their wake, gliding through the water as quickly as the currents allowed. The ship's sentinel must have tired like Angus expected, but their command hadn't slipped away entirely. She still felt the sea spirits trying to bind her with chains of salt and foam.

Ahead, Angus angled his lean body towards the surface. His hind flippers flexed as he thrust forward with a burst of speed and shot through the waves, leaving a stream of frothing bubbles in his wake.

Stay close, he'd warned her.

Isla leapt.

The moment she burst through the surface, she concentrated on shedding her sealskin. As she flew through the air, she was already changing shape. Her bones shifted. Her lungs shrank. Her fur receded, falling in wet grey folds around human shoulders, human legs.

She landed barefoot on the deck, feet slipping against the rain-soaked timber. Out of habit, her hand flew to her waist, grasping for the pistol she'd once kept tucked in her belt. But her fingers only met the fur of her pelt. The pistol was gone. Another thing she'd given up to claim the life stolen from her.

Before she had time to adjust, an Admiralty officer advanced on her, cutlass drawn. His face twisted with loathing as he lunged, slashing at her with his blade. All Isla could do was scramble back until her spine hit the gunwale.

Rain streamed down the blade of his cutlass as he raised it again, a sneer curling across his lips. The next time he struck, it would be blood dripping from the steel. *Her* blood.

A whirl of speckled, fawn-coloured fur tore between them, and Eimhir barrelled through, smashing her elbow into the officer's chin. The blow rocked him, sending him stumbling back.

He fumbled with his sword, but Eimhir was too quick. Blood oozed from the wound in her leg where she'd taken the harpoon blow in selkie form, but it didn't slow her as she fell upon him and wrapped her wiry arms around his waist.

"Let's see how useful that blade is in the water," she growled.

Her arms tightened, muscles in her forearms twitching as she squeezed the air from his lungs. Then she dragged him to the edge, keeping her fingers locked as she threw them both into the waves.

Isla rushed to the edge, watching as the officer's cloak billowed and sank beneath the waves.

It's no use fighting on their terms, Eimhir had said. *We'll make them fight on ours.*

Now, she understood.

The staccato click of a musket cocking jolted her attention back to the deck, and she spun to see another officer taking aim at Angus. She rushed towards them, her selkie strength lending more power to her legs than a human possessed.

But it wasn't enough.

A crack tore through her ears, and the air fizzled. Angus staggered, blood spreading across the russet-brown fur around his shoulders.

There was no time to check on him. Her momentum sent her flying into the officer, and she hauled her to the deck, knocking the musket loose. The officer scrambled for the dagger on her belt, but Isla grabbed her wrist and squeezed until something snapped.

An agonised shriek tore from the officer's mouth, but she didn't stop her struggle. Her other hand shot up to rake at Isla's eyes, her face contorting.

"Selkie bitch," she spat.

Isla rolled and grabbed a handful of the officer's cloak to drag her to her feet. The gunwale was only metres away.

A flash of stark realisation widened the officer's eyes. "No. Please, you don't—"

The rest of her words were lost to a winded grunt as Isla slammed her into the wooden railing. Below, the waves dashed hungrily off the side of the hull, sending spray flying into the wind.

They were calling her home. Who was she to ignore them?

She pulled the Admiralty officer close and toppled over the gunwale. The icy water hit her before she had time to sink back into her soulskin, and her human lungs seized with shock. Then her pelt rippled, spreading its protective barrier over her skin, returning her to her selkie form.

The officer thrashed in the swirling currents, fighting to loosen her sodden cloak. She tore it off, then reached up, fingertips stretching for the waves above her.

She wouldn't reach them. Isla would make sure of it.

She darted forward and sank her teeth into the officer's boot. The serpenthide scales were tough and sharp, slicing the inside of Isla's mouth as she jerked her head to pull the officer towards the depths. The metallic taste of her own blood spread across her tongue, but she refused to loosen her hold.

You hunted me, she thought, dragging her down. *Likes a tides-forsaken animal. You would have sunk one of those spears through my heart and ripped my pelt from my body. I didn't start this. You did.*

The officer didn't hear her. She didn't understand. She'd die never knowing what it was she would have stolen. Already her eyes were bulging, the muscles in her neck straining from the effort not to open her lungs. She was desperate for breath, desperate for the air she'd taken for granted.

Then she opened her mouth, and the sea rushed in.

It only took seconds for the struggle to end. The officer's flailing arms spasmed one last time, then fell still. Her glazed, lifeless eyes stared blankly at the surface as she slowly sank.

There was nothing left for Isla to do. The depths would claim her for their own.

She turned back to the ship and thrust herself from the waves onto the deck once more. As she straightened her human legs, she saw Eimhir grappling with another of the sloop's crew. Her face was pale, her hair ragged, but she sported no wounds other than the seeping gash running down her thigh.

Angus, on the other hand...

Isla darted her head to where he'd fallen, but the only trace was a red stain soaking the wood.

Fear seized her heart. Angus was right. This was a mistake. The sloop was a small ship, but the crew had still been too many to take on between the three of them. They should have kept running. They should have—

"Are you hurt?"

It was Angus. He appeared beside her, cheeks pallid as he clutched his bloodied shoulder.

Isla stared at him. "No, I'm all right. But you... I saw you get hit. I thought—"

"Eimhir dug the shot out. Didn't want to risk returning to my soul-shape with a lump of lead buried in my flank. I'm bleeding, but I'll survive." He turned his attention to the deck. "We need to end this. You know how quickly spilled blood brings about the haar. We don't want to be here when the gun-anam come."

Isla looked around. The carnage had quietened. The lingering stench of burnt powder drifted away with the wind. Blood splattered across the deck, not all of it Angus's. The only crew member she could see was a haggard man propped against the mast, his breathing slow and laboured.

"Their sentinel," Angus said. "A powerful one. He drew the water from my soaking pelt and forced it into my lungs. I may have broken his ribs fighting him off."

"He's the only one left?"

"We got lucky." Angus gave a grim smile. "It's a wee ship, by Admiralty standards, and they weren't expecting us to attack. Believe me, it doesn't usually end like this."

A wave crested over the other side of the gunwale, and Eimhir leapt from it, pelt melting from her skin as she landed. Her leg was still bleeding, but she paid no attention to it as she strode over to them.

When she saw the ship's sentinel leaning against the mast, she stopped. "He's the last of them?"

Angus nodded. "I didn't know if you wanted to—" He hesitated, eyes darting to Isla. "Our raiders always leave a message. To remind the Admiralty of the consequences of stealing our pelts."

"No," Isla said flatly. "I won't have any part in that kind of *message*."

"He would have ripped your pelt from you, if he'd had the chance. It would be your right."

"I don't want it," she snapped. "I've seen too many flayed bodies to ever want it. Let's leave him and get away from this ship. We've already wasted enough time."

"Caraid..." Eimhir's voice was soft, but there was a flintiness to her eyes that made Isla shiver. "We can't leave him. We're all bleeding, and this is one of the Admiralty's main trade routes. If another ship picks him up, he'll have a clear trail to follow."

Dread wound tight in Isla's gut. This was what it came back to. Blood spilled led to more blood. The hunting, the raids, the flaying—it was all part of the same vicious cycle, forever ending the same way.

She turned to the old sentinel. His eyes were half closed as he leaned against the mast, his lips wet with blood.

"You're the one he's searching for," he said as she approached, spluttering on the words. "That pelt... As delicate a grey as the morning cloud. Patches that ripple like ink of midnight blue. A sealskin with an aspect beyond measure. He wanted it intact. Wanted you alive."

An unsettling chill crept over her, burrowing bone-deep. She could almost see the Grand Admiral's reflection in the sentinel's bleary eyes. His shadow loomed over her shoulder. His voice whispered in the wind at her ear. No matter how far she ran, he would follow. He would find her.

"We can't let him report back," Eimhir said. "The Grand Admiral will bring the entire fleet down upon you. We need time to find what we're looking for at the Drift. We won't have it if we let him go."

Isla swallowed. "I know."

Eimhir walked away, returning with a small dagger in her hand. As she took up her stance behind him, blade poised at his neck, the sentinel locked eyes with Isla. There was no malice in his expression, just resignation.

"We weren't selkie hunters," he said. "You'll find no pelts in our hold, only a shipment of healing ointments and tonics bound for Breçhon. Our muskets were meant for pirates, our harpoons for sea serpents."

"Yet you still chased us," Isla said. "You still hunted us."

"Aye, we did." He bowed his head, shoulders slumping. "If only you understood. If only anyone understood." His eyes darted up, frantic and shining. "Please, you have to listen—"

Eimhir drew the blade across his throat. "No," she said. "We don't."

Blood pooled from the thin red line, splattering on the wet timber. The sentinel's body crumpled, hitting the deck with a muffled thump.

Isla stared at his prone, unmoving frame, her chest constricting.

And there lies the truth too terrible to admit, Eimhir had told her once. *The men are the monsters, and the monsters men. This violence belongs to all of us. It will continue as long as we let it.*

And tides, Isla had let it.

She tore her gaze from the sentinel's body and moved to the gunwale, digging her fingertips into the wood until her knuckles turned white. Below, the waves crashed against the hull, swallowing all trace of the bodies they'd taken to the depths. But the remnants of what had happened here would linger. She knew that all too well.

Eimhir joined her, watching the horizon with discerning eyes. "It might not feel like it, but it's out there. The answer to saving our people. Once we find it, we'll be able to end this."

Isla only wished she could be so certain.

CHAPTER THIRTEEN

DARCE

A sharp sensation caught in Darce's gut, piercing him like the barbs of a fishhook.

At first, he thought he'd imagined it. But as he glanced over the *Vanguard's* deck, he saw he was not the only one affected. One by one, the other sentinels reacted, their spines straightening as the magic caught them too.

Spilled blood. Auld blood.

The earlier rain swept away, and the air was crisp and clear as dusk closed in. Darce trained his eyes on the horizon, heart pounding as he searched the waves for some kind of violence. He knew what the singing in his veins meant.

High above, Featherblade shrieked, the flash of its belly stark against the purple sky as it banked starboard. A moment later, there came a cry from the crow's nest.

"Sails!"

Darce hurried to the other side of the deck. Across the waves, he could make out the distant billowing of canvas around a single mast—a cutter, or perhaps a sloop. From this far away, the ship seemed impossibly small, haplessly drifting.

The hum of magic in his veins was quiet and insistent. Something had happened here.

A hushed murmur spread as the Grand Admiral stepped down from the helm. Deckhands and officers parted, cloaks of teal and sapphire rippling as they drew back. Cunningham strode through in his long-tailed Admiralty coat and raised a spyglass under the brim of his tricorne hat.

"It's the *Silent Wind*," he said. "No sign of any officers on deck. No sign of any skinchangers, either. Whatever happened here, we arrived too late to stop it." He let the spyglass fall to his side. "Tell the helm to bring us alongside. We'll do a sweep for survivors, unlikely as it is we'll find any. I want every captain and sentinel on alert."

The crew began to disperse, but as Darce moved to join them, Cunningham called out in a brusque voice, "Not you, Sergeant."

Darce paused. "Something you need from me?"

"The same as always." Cunningham's eyes hadn't left the ship. "Was she here? Should we expect to find some trace of her on board the *Silent Wind?*"

"I don't know."

Cunningham turned his gaze on him. "I didn't think I needed to remind you of the importance of your cooperation."

"You don't." Darce gritted his teeth. "Something happened on that ship, but whether the blood spilled was from selkie or sentinel, I can't be certain. Either way, if Isla was here, she wouldn't be so foolish as to tarry. We would do well to take heed of that and leave."

Cunningham laughed bluntly. "I admire your persistence, Sergeant, though I wonder if the Blackwood boy would feel the same if he realised the precariousness with which you were handling his life. But if you expect some idle threats to be enough to deter me from searching for my daughter, you are gravely mistaken. If any trace of her remains on that ship, we will find it. *You* will find it." He paused. "Take the lad with you. He is playing the role of your captain, after all. I'm sure his presence will be all the impetus you need to work swiftly."

"I am not threatening you. I'm trying to *warn* you," Darce said tersely. "If the *Silent Wind* suffered violence, if the waters around it tasted blood, we'll face a fate worse than its crew if we linger."

A thin smile stretched the corners of Cunningham's lips. "Then you better make haste."

He walked away, leaving Darce with nothing but the cold grip of dread. Already, the *Vanguard* was shifting course, prow pointing towards the empty ship in the distance.

He couldn't stop what they were sailing into. All he could do was be ready to face it.

By the time they pulled alongside the *Silent Wind*, only the last vestiges of daylight remained, the sky streaked with lilac and lavender lingering on the western horizon. It was a clear night, at least for now.

Lachlan joined him as the deckhands set the wooden gangway in place between the two ships. "What do you suppose we'll find over there?"

Darce turned to the fulmars circling above the stricken ship. They hovered on pointed wings, piercing the air with their rattling calls. Every so often, one of them would swoop down and disappear below the gunwale, flitting back to the air with a bloodied beak.

He'd been right to warn the Grand Admiral. Whatever had happened on the *Silent Wind,* its violent echoes rippled, stoking the call of his sentinel magic.

"Nothing good," he replied shortly. "Keep your eyes sharp and tell me if the weather changes."

"The *weather?* What do you mean by—"

The rest of his words scattered into the wind as Darce walked ahead, taking his place at the edge of the gangway. The wooden slats swayed in front of him as the two ships heaved with the waves. Below, the water churned, restless and black under the shroud of night. One slip, and it would gladly swallow him whole.

The wood bowed under the weight of his feet, drawing a groan from the timber. Every cautious step filled him with more foreboding than the last.

When he reached the other side of the gangway, he paused. The scavenging fulmars circled the mast, their stuttering calls resounding in his ears. His blood sang stronger than ever, thrumming in his veins until it felt like they might burst. Auld blood was near, and he wouldn't have to look far to find it.

The stench of death hit him. A stale, coppery tang hung in the air, mixed with the reek of piss and loosed bowels. As Darce slunk across the deck, he saw where it was coming from. A man lay against the timber, face down in a pool of his own blood. His cloak fell limply across his shoulders, ragged and stained.

Darce knelt beside the man's body and rolled him over. His grizzled face was translucent, his eyes glazed.

A single wound scored his throat, a gash that had opened him to the bone.

Lachlan stood behind him, a pallor falling across his features. "Part of me hoped... I don't know what I hoped. Just not this."

"It was a quick death," Darce said. "A merciful death."

"So we should feel grateful the bastards didn't flay him alive? That they didn't cleave his skin from his bone and leave his back in ribbons for the sky to see?" Lachlan shook his head. "Tides, Galbraith. Sometimes I wonder whose side you're really on."

Darce fixed him with an even stare. "I know exactly where my loyalties lie. There was a time you did, too."

He ignored Lachlan's sharp intake of breath, turning away before the lad had time to draw him into another argument. The more time he spent on this ship, the more oppressive the air felt. Something was closing in. The sooner they returned to the *Vanguard*, the better.

He closed his eyes, willing his thoughts to settle as he reached out with his magic. The *Silent Wind's* sea spirits were cowed, hiding in the shadows of the hull. Their sentinel had called on them, but now his lifeblood dribbled through the cracks in the deck, and they'd lost the tether to the ship they'd once called home.

Was she here? he asked.

In the silence of his head, his words echoed in the Grand Admiral's voice. Each soft-spoken syllable tasted like the dark shadow of his own heart, his own desires. It would be easy to want her as much as Cunningham did, to use his magic to tear the seas apart until he found her. Maybe when she was back at his side, he wouldn't care what it cost him.

Isla, the tides whispered.

They breathed her name like the sigh of a wave. It filled his ears with the crash of spray, muffling everything else. He pictured her barefoot on the deck, dappled grey pelt clinging to her skin, sable hair dripping wet around her shoulders. Then she was gone, leaping into the waves, leaving only salt water behind.

He had to pick up her trail. If he knew where she was headed, he could lead the *Vanguard* astray, buy himself more time to turn Rhona and the other sentinels to his side.

Or you could follow her, a voice whispered. *You could have her back in your arms.*

"Galbraith."

Darce furrowed his brow, pushing away the sound of Lachlan's voice. Isla had been here. He felt her in the memories of the sea-soaked sails, the heartbeat of the timber. The aching in his chest pulled taut once more, tugging him towards—

"Galbraith!" Lachlan's voice was an urgent hiss.

Darce opened his eyes. "For the sake of your own life, little laird, I suggest you let me work. If I don't give the Grand Admiral what he wants—"

"The weather," Lachlan said. "You told me to watch for a change in the weather."

His face was a ghostly shade of white, and his hand trembled as he pointed at something over Darce's shoulder.

An icy chill burrowed through Darce's skin as he slowly turned to see what Lachlan was staring at.

The horizon had disappeared. No moonlight reflected off the waves, no stars peeked out from behind drifting clouds. Instead, a dense, misty veil rolled across the sea, clinging to the tips of the waves as it crept towards them.

It was the haar—the sea fog heralding the arrival of the soulless.

The gun-anam were coming.

"It's like Blackwood Estate," Lachlan murmured. "I remember my dream turning cold. And when I woke..."

The wraith's shadow. Isla's scream. A blade driving into Lachlan's shoulder.

Darce grabbed the lapel of his coat. "Get back to the *Vanguard*. Tell them to make ready to sail."

"And leave you alone?" Lachlan's face clouded. "I don't think so."

"*Must* you be so stubborn? If you don't warn them, we'll all be killed. I'll be right behind you, as soon as I've picked up Isla's trail."

Lachlan wavered, his expression torn. Then he snapped his mouth shut and nodded tightly, turning back to the gangway. The haar was already thickening around the edge of the ship, shrouding the *Vanguard* behind a curtain of drizzle. By the time Lachlan crossed over, the only trace of him Darce could sense was the dull, muffled thump of his crutch knocking against the wood.

Then that too faded, and he was alone.

He drew his rapier from the scabbard on his belt. The blade held no sheen in the density of the mist. The steel was dull, coated with quivering droplets from the damp air closing in.

A shiver crept down his spine. The last time he'd brought a blade to bear against the gun-anam, one of the wraiths had caught it in its spectral hand, shattering it. He'd been left with no weapon to defend himself against the wraith's ghostly dagger falling towards his heart.

The dagger Isla took for him instead.

Something in his blood surged at the memory. This wouldn't be like last time. He'd given his soul to save Isla's life, and that oath had awoken his sentinel magic. He could wield more than a sword; he could harness the power of the sea itself.

But only if the tides saw fit to answer him.

The *Silent Wind* rocked gently, its hull releasing a low groan. Everything else fell still. The haar smothered the deck until it felt like the ship had been cut adrift from the *Vanguard* entirely.

That was when he sensed the first of the gun-anam.

He'd forgotten what cold truly meant. For weeks, he'd stood in the face of the open sea, winter wind gnawing at his skin, squeezing his lungs with an icy grip. Yet none of it carried the unnatural chill he felt now. A deep frost spread through him, burrowing its roots into his bones. His fingers turned numb around the hilt of his sword. His breath froze into shards that shattered when they fell.

A low rumble reverberated through the air. The storm had arrived, as he'd known it would.

From the mist's rippling depths, a shadow crept towards him. It was a shapeless thing, too faintly formed to behold. Then it swirled, and the dark tendrils solidified and became armour of bone: a cuirass made of skeletal black ribs, a seal-skull helm with gaping jaws and empty sockets for eyes. It carried the stench of ocean rot, of death and decay.

Rain fell on the deck, pattering against the wood. The gun-anam drifted forward, leaving a trail of silvery droplets in its wake. With each gliding step, the haar drew closer, draining the warmth from Darce's face.

He rolled his rapier in one hand and lunged.

His blade struck something, resounding with a harsh, watery clang. The impact sent a shock through his arm and he jolted back, eyes fixed on the gun-anam. The wraith held a shimmering sword, its ghostly edge made from the same shadow as the gun-anam itself. Darce had seen a blade like that before. He knew how easily it cleaved through flesh, how it clashed against steel with the roar of the sea.

The wraith stopped, looking at him through the sockets of its seal-skull mask. Then its empty stare crept to the fallen sentinel, the dried puddles of blood, the remains of the fight that had taken place here.

She's drawing them out, Lachlan had said. *Not just the skinchangers, but those wraiths. It all traces back to her.*

Darce's mouth turned dry. "She's not here."

The gun-anam stilled. A strange sound rippled from behind its seal-skull mask, like it was speaking with the voice of the depths. Darce's ears filled with water, and he shook his head violently, trying to dispel it.

"She's not here," he said again, spitting the words out. "She's already long gone. You won't find her on this ship."

The gun-anam circled him, filling his head with whispers from the sea. The mist was so thick it was suffocating. Darce drew it into his lungs, each breath cold and brackish.

Help me, he thought, reaching for the spirits. *Please.*

There was no answer. His blood froze in his veins. Reaching for his magic was like trying to grasp the tides themselves, leaving him unable to do anything as they slipped through his fingers.

The gun-anam reached for him. Darce's lungs tightened, and he dropped his sword with a clatter to claw at his throat. He was going to drown. The sea rose in his chest, ready to swallow him. He'd be just another soul lost to these wretched waters, to this ill-fated ship they never should have—

A familiar screech tore through the air, and a flash of white wings burst through the mist.

Featherblade.

The gannet lunged with its huge webbed feet and raked its claws through the wraith. The tendril burst, scattering silvery droplets across the deck.

Darce stumbled, clutching his throat. The tides might not have answered him, but that brute of a bird had. He'd never been so glad to see its blue-rimmed glare and vicious beak.

The thunder roared, and the gun-anam wailed with it, its cry like a wave dashing against the rocks. Featherblade banked on its pointed wings and flew straight at the wraith's seal-skull mask, taking aim at its empty eye socket. The mists swirled, and then the shapeless shadow was gone, leaving nothing behind but a silvery puddle on the deck.

A muffled shout echoed close by, and Darce lifted his fallen sword. The ship was not a battleground he'd have chosen. His feet were unsteady on the slippery wood, and he could barely see more than a few inches in front of him.

A shadow came charging through the fog, and Darce readied his blade, only to pause at the familiar *thunk* of a crutch.

Lachlan emerged from the gloom, eyeing the raised sword with a smirk. "Hardly the time for a lesson, Sergeant. I thought you'd have more pressing concerns."

"Hardly the time for your glib tongue either, yet you seem to manage." Darce grunted, relief flooding his chest. "I thought I told you to return to the *Vanguard*."

"I did. The Grand Admiral sent me back with reinforcements." Lachlan's smile tightened. "It seems you're too valuable to risk losing."

"That's not the honour you think it is, little laird. You don't understand what that bastard—" He broke off. "Get behind me!"

Another gun-anam rippled from the mist, leaving a trail of vapour in its wake. Darce barely had time to lift his sword before it was upon him. Its icy breath clouded in front of him, thick with the stench of brine.

He brought his rapier around in a fierce, swirling arc, cutting through the wraith's wisping form. More silver droplets scattered the deck, but the haar swept across them, drawing them into its shroud.

These creatures couldn't be killed. They had to run, even if it meant risking Cunningham's wrath. And if it also meant leaving behind the chance to find Isla, perhaps that was for the best.

Beside him, Lachlan thrust his own sword, fending off another wraith. His lips were cracked and blue, his cheeks deathly pale as frost spread across his skin. The haar grew thicker around them, turning the moisture in the air to ice, freezing the puddles on the deck until they were silver and brittle.

"Need to get back...to the *Vanguard*," Darce managed, each word straining. "Can't...fight them."

Lachlan shuddered. "Which way?"

Darce could see nothing but the haze surrounding them. No sails, no mast, no sky. They were stranded, lost to the haar's depths.

"Put your hand on my shoulder," he said. "I'll find the gangway."

Lachlan stiffened. "I need one hand for my crutch. If I'm to cling to you like a bairn with the other, I won't be able to use my sword to defend myself."

"I can defe—" Darce stopped himself before he added salt to a wound still raw. Instead, he moved behind Lachlan, grabbing a fistful of his fur-lined cloak. "Then you lead the way. It makes no matter to me, so long as we both get out of this together."

He couldn't see Lachlan's face, but his shoulders loosened as he moved, his crutch scraping with each cautious step. Each soft thump of the rosewood against the deck echoed in Darce's ears, reminding him how much had changed, and how much hadn't.

I swore to your father I'd protect you, Darce thought. *If that means protecting your pride when you need it most, I'll do that too.*

Ahead, the mist was thinning. Muffled cries and the clash of steel filled his ears once more as Lachlan stopped dead in front of him.

"Tides," he whispered, voice catching. "Look at them."

More than a dozen gun-anam drifted across the deck, dripping seawater from their dead bones. Around them lay the scattered, lifeless bodies of several Admiralty officers, their cloaks like shrouds over their corpses. Some of them bore jagged wounds, frostbite forming around the weeping gashes. Others lay glassy-eyed and open-mouthed, seafoam frothing between their lips.

Darce's warning hadn't been enough. Nothing was enough to prepare for the paralysing horror of seeing a gun-anam for the first time. These poor bastards must have frozen, unable to move from the terror of looking into the shapeless face of a creature with no soul.

Something behind him roared, and he hauled Lachlan behind the gunwale as a huge wave crashed over the side of the ship. The water swept across the deck in fury, scattering the mist and driving the gun-anam back.

Lachlan staggered upright, his soaked hair dripping across his brow. "What was that?"

Darce glanced to the forecastle, recognising the swirling green ink on the forearms of the woman standing there.

Rhona. The Grand Admiral had risked one of his sentinels to bring him back.

Her face contorted as she let her arms drop, and the wave dispersed through the cracks in the deck. "Now, Mhairi!"

Darce hadn't noticed the second figure in the mast's shadow. A girl no older than Lachlan advanced, drawing two stiletto daggers from her belt. She was a slight wee thing, wheat-haired and rose-cheeked, but her eyes glittered like iron as she stalked towards the nearest gun-anam. Her wrists flicked too quickly to make sense of, but the splatter of silver droplets flying across the deck told Darce she'd hit her mark.

She spun, then stopped dead. A snaking coil of mist crept around her left arm. Her fingers turned blue against the handle of her dagger, her skin hardening with glistening frost.

Darce flinched. He'd seen what the ghostly vapour could do. His old blade had shattered in its grip, reduced to shards of steel. The girl's soft flesh and delicate bones would offer no resistance.

"Mhairi!"

Rhona stormed down from the forecastle, eyes dark and furious as she closed in. She threw up an arm mid-stride, clasping her fingers around an invisible tether.

The *Silent Wind's* sails snapped taut, releasing all the seawater soaking their canvas. The droplets hovered in the air, shimmering like rain waiting to fall. Then Rhona twisted her fingers and cast a ward.

Mhairi just had time to draw a breath before the torrent of water crashed down on her. The wave knocked her to the deck, sending her sliding across the wood, but the mist winding around her arm vanished, dispersed by the force of the water.

She staggered to her feet, clutching her wrist. Rhona rushed to her side and peeled back the sleeve of her coat. Mottled blue blotches marred Mhairi's skin, and the fair hairs on her forearm stood rigid with frost.

Rhona turned to him, drawn and pale. "Anyone else alive?"

"Not that I've seen." Darce trailed his eyes over the deck, the timber half-hidden under a bloodied carpet of Admiralty cloaks. "We can't stay here any longer. These wraiths are drawn to places of violence, places that know the taste of blood spilled between human and selkie. We need to get back to the *Vanguard* before more come."

"The Grand Admiral's orders—"

"Fuck his orders." Darce nodded to the gangway, its wooden slats disappearing into the mist. "Take your captain and go. We'll be right behind you."

Another rumble of thunder sent a tremor through him. The storm was on top of them. Rain hammered down, streaming across the deck in miniature rivers every time the ship rolled. The *Silent Wind* wouldn't last much longer without its crew, not when the tides were this hungry for its wooden bones.

Rhona reached the gangway first and pulled Mhairi in front of her, guiding her along the slippery surface. Before they were halfway across, the mist swallowed them. Darce only hoped they'd made it to the other side.

He turned to Lachlan. "You next. Do you need—"

"I can manage," Lachlan said curtly. He lifted his crutch onto the platform and pushed himself up, the wind whipping his soaking hair across his face as he inched into the chasm between the ships.

As Darce edged onto the gangway behind him, the swell surged, and the *Silent Wind* gave a low, wounded groan. He resisted the urge to put a steadying hand on Lachlan's shoulder. They were almost across. He could see the looming shadow of the *Vanguard* emerging from the mist.

A monstrous wave crashed against the hull, and the ship reeled.

For a moment, he thought they'd made it. The *Vanguard's* deck was right in front of him. Blair lurched to catch a stumbling Lachlan, hauling him on board before turning back with horror in his eyes.

The gangway buckled and slipped, and Darce fell.

CHAPTER FOURTEEN

ISLA

The Drift loomed in front of them, its huge sea stacks rising like pillars from the waves.

Finally, they were here.

Isla held her snout above the heaving swell and breathed in the salty air until her lungs could hold no more. They'd swum without stopping since the Admiralty attack, and her aching limbs had little left to give. All she wanted to do was find a scrap of land to rest on until her muscles felt normal again.

Nishi said the island was northwest of the sea stacks, Eimhir said. *But Kerr was right. It's like the currents are fleeing from that direction. Like something out there doesn't want us to find it.*

Isla reached for the fragment of her soul calling her. The currents brushed against her, skimming over her pelt, dancing between her flippers. They were streaming away from something, like Eimhir said.

I don't think it's us the currents are trying to keep at bay, Isla said. *The tides are protecting something.*

One of the ships? Angus asked.

I hope so.

They swam through the Drift's towering sea stacks, passing under scores of seabirds circling the jagged rocks. Puffins and petrels, skuas and guillemots, all of them distant shapes against the low canopy of clouds. Their cacophony of cries carried with the wind, piercing through the crashing waves. It felt peaceful, despite the noise. A rare place untouched by human or selkie. For a fleeting second, Isla wished she could linger, safe in a world that would ask nothing of her.

Then she remembered the mists, and the thought dissipated.

Before long, the Drift was behind them, and Isla caught sight of a shape on the horizon. She could barely make out the hint of land above the shoreline, but it was there, just where Nishi and Kerr said it would be.

Let's take a closer look, she said. *The wreck should be on the other side of that ridge.*

Be careful, Angus said. *Those Sea Kith warned us something wasn't right about this place. Now we're here, I can feel it too.*

As she drew nearer, Isla understood what he meant. The island was a desolate scrap of sandstone and scrub abandoned in the sea. No gulls flitted overhead, no trees rose from the heathland; the only things growing around the rocky shore were wild clumps of bracken and heather. It was like a shadow hung over the whole place—invisible, but no less cold for it.

She cast off her pelt and clambered ashore, picking around the rockpools and swathes of seaweed guarding the higher ground. The terrain was uneven, disturbed by sprawling roots and brittle fronds of dead bracken.

"There won't be much ground to cover, at least," Eimhir said. "If the ship is here, it can't be far."

"It's here," Isla said. "Ever since we passed the Drift, I've felt the call again. This is where we need to be."

It was strange to think how many years she'd sailed these waters on the deck of a ship, using all the tools at her disposal to guide her. Her charts and her sextant, a compass and the stars. It had all seemed so precise, so reliable. Now, all she had was the calling of her soul, the elusive thread connecting her pelt to all those who had worn it before. It felt *right*, somehow. It felt like belonging.

"I see something," Angus said, eyes narrowing. "It might be a mast, but it's pitched at an odd angle."

Isla followed his gaze. The overgrown thicket of heather and bracken fell away on the northern shore, and through one of the gaps, she caught a glimpse of something pale against the grey sky. It was crooked, like Angus said, but she imagined how it might rise towards the clouds, boasting billowing sails from its yards.

It was one of the lost selkie ships. It had to be.

Her feet moved of their own accord, legs lengthening their stride as she pushed through the rest of the overgrowth to reach the shore. She barely registered her heart pounding against her ribs, her ragged breath echoing in her ears. The ship was calling her, and she had to reach it.

"Isla, wait!"

She stuttered to a halt. The edge of the ridge fell away in front of her, yielding to the sea. Several rocks thrust from the waves, their scarred surfaces thick with seaweed and lichen. They looked like crumbling teeth rising from the swell—ancient, but no less sharp for it. And there, gutted between their jaws, lay the scattered carcass of a ship.

Isla stiffened. Part of her had hoped to find it intact. Wrecked, perhaps, but still holding the semblance of a ship. But the remains in front of her had been chewed up and spat out. Pieces of hull speared by the rocks. The bowsprit, broken in half. And the mast Angus had spotted earlier, listing on its side, stripped of the sails it should have carried.

Eimhir cast her eyes over it. "What do you think happened?"

"I'm hoping it will tell us," Isla said.

She slipped down, sliding her hands across the slabs as she waded into the water. The waves lapped at her waist, icy against her human flesh. This close, the rocks seemed more menacing than ever, holding pieces of the ship aloft like trophies. They'd torn it apart. Not out of any malice, but because the ship had drifted somewhere it was not meant to be.

A section of the mast towered in front of her, impaled on the rocks. The bone had splintered, but it held its ghostly white glisten. It wasn't like the black rot of the gun-anam. It was still alive.

Isla took a breath, then placed her palm on it.

The winter wind chased around her neck, snarling at her hair as she waited. Her skin was dry, her limbs heavy with exhaustion. Yet somehow, she knew all the pain would be worth it, if only she could find what she was looking for.

Her fingers trembled, the mast's surface slick against her skin. Still, nothing happened. The ship had no answers. Its brittle bone was reticent, offering only silence.

She let her hand fall. "I… I don't understand. The vision came so easily last time."

Angus frowned. "You didn't see anything?"

"Nothing at all." She gave a frustrated sigh. "It doesn't make any sense. This is the same kind of ship we found in the trench. It *must* be one of ours."

"Perhaps you were mistaken back in the trench." Angus pursed his lips. "The gun-anam took us all by surprise last time. You could have been confused about—"

"I was not confused," Isla said sharply. "I know what I saw."

"Peace, caraid." Eimhir placed a hand on her shoulder. "We've been swimming for days. We're exhausted, all of us." She shot Angus a pointed look. "It's a wonder any of us have the strength to stand, let alone call on the memories of our ancestors. I say we rest for what's left of the day, then try again at sundown."

Angus hesitated, then nodded. "You're right. The journey was a long one, and none of us want it to have been for nothing. We can't give up, not when we might be close to finding answers."

"There was a sheltered cove back along the shoreline," Eimhir said.

"We can gather some bracken for beds and sleep there, as long as someone is keeping watch in the water. I'll take the first patrol."

Isla glanced at the wound on her leg. The blood had dried around the gash, but it looked painful. "You need rest as much as any of us."

"And I'll get it." Eimhir gave a faint smile. "Don't worry about me. I can take care of myself."

She slipped into the water, her fawn-coloured pelt sliding over her shoulders. Isla watched her go, heart heavy. Ever since she'd claimed her pelt and the life it had given her, Eimhir had been by her side. Being separated, even if only for a short time, brought with it an entirely new ache.

Caraid. Cousin. Family. Eimhir had become so many things to her, none of which she could bear losing.

Angus cleared his throat. "We should make for the cove. It's not far."

Isla followed him around the shore until they came across a tiny inlet of white sand nestled against the ridge. A shallow cave was hollowed into the rock, and although it was damp and musty, it sheltered them from the bite of the wind.

By the time they'd started a fire and lined the floor with a bed of bracken, Isla was ready to sink into the welcoming arms of sleep. But when she closed her eyes, she couldn't help the unease keeping her from drifting off.

She sat up and ran a weary hand across her face. Angus was hunched in front of the fire, the russet colours of his pelt more vibrant than ever in the light of the flames. His freckled forehead creased, and when he sighed, it carried more than the weight of his own breath.

"You're meant to be sleeping," he said.

"I could say the same about you."

He gave a short laugh. "I'm not the one carrying our people's hopes in the pelt on my back. That burden is yours alone, I fear. No matter how much Eimhir tries to protect you from it."

Something in his tone made Isla tense. "What do you mean?"

"She'd do anything for you. Sometimes I think she'd accept the end of our people if it meant keeping you safe. There are times I wonder if she regrets not taking the pelt for herself, if only so she could take the weight of it from you. But that is a choice neither of you can take back."

"I don't *want* anyone to take it back." Isla buried her hands in her pelt, the damp fur like home between her fingers. "I found the part of myself I was missing. The place I belong. If there's a burden attached to that, I'll gladly bear it."

"And what if you can't bear it?" he asked. "What if this legacy you've been laden with is too much?"

This time, it was Isla's turn to laugh. It was a bitter sound, scratching her throat. "Sometimes I think you *want* me to fail. You and Duncan both. You can't stand the thought of an outsider, an aineol, holding the power to save our people."

"That's not what I—" Angus breathed sharply, running a hand through his hair. "I don't want you to fail. But that doesn't stop me considering what this might cost us. Some of us more than others."

Isla stilled. "You're talking about Eimhir."

"I'm worried about her. The way she acted when we were fleeing from that Admiralty ship..." Angus drew his mouth into a reproachful line. "It was reckless. She knows better than to go looking for a fight."

"She also knows what it's like to have her pelt stolen. You can't blame her for wanting to fight rather than be hunted down. And it worked, didn't it? We won."

"This time. Next time, we might not get so lucky. And where would that leave us?" He shook his head. "Your pelt, your dreamwalking gift, is the only hope our people have of escaping our fate. I have as much reason as any of our kind to want the Admiralty to bleed, but it is a distraction we cannot afford. I thought Eimhir understood that."

"As I recall, *Eimhir* wasn't the one who suggested flaying their sentinel."

A shadow fell across Angus's face. "I only meant to offer you the same vengeance any selkie has the right to claim. You are one of us now, after all. Perhaps it was ill-judged of me, but I was trying to show you that."

Something curled in Isla's stomach. Angus's words felt like a peace offering, but it was difficult to take any kind of comfort from them, not when they were wrapped in memories of blood-soaked cobbles and flayed flesh. If that kind of violence was her right to claim in the name of vengeance, she wanted no part of it. No matter who it was for.

"When does it end?" she asked quietly. "Even if we find the soulships, even if we rid the haar of its corruption... How do we ever escape this?"

Angus didn't answer, and silence fell between them as he turned back to the fire. Isla lay down on the bracken, ready to close her eyes, when he spoke again.

"It's no easy thing, being the first to lower one's blade. Especially if you don't trust your enemy to follow suit." He fed a twig into the flames. "The history between human and selkie is written in blood, and blood has a long memory. Sometimes, I fear there's no escaping it."

Despite the warmth of the fire, a shiver crept across Isla's skin. She nestled into the lining of her pelt, trying to push away the chill. But as she waited for sleep to take her, all she heard was the hollow echo of Angus's words ringing in her ears like a warning.

By the time Isla woke, the fire had dwindled to embers and the sky was cast in streaks of orange as the sun slipped below the horizon. Her muscles still felt weary, but at least the ache in them had subsided.

She peeled away a frond of bracken clinging to her cheek as she sat up and stretched, noticing Eimhir at the entrance to the cavern. "You're back."

"Angus took over a couple of hours ago. We didn't want to wake you." Eimhir turned around with a smile. "You looked like you needed the rest."

"You're one to talk." Isla surveyed her pale cheeks, the shadows sinking under her eyes. "Have you slept at all?"

"It's been difficult," Eimhir said. "I might not have your gift, but that doesn't mean my nights are free from dreams. The things I see when I fall asleep... Well, I'd rather take my chances with exhaustion."

Isla joined her at the cave's entrance, placing her hand around Eimhir's cold fingers. "What do you dream about?"

A storm gathered in Eimhir's grey gaze. "The *Vanguard of the Firth*. The Grand Admiral. You. I know the dreams are born of fear, not prophecy, but part of me wonders..." She swallowed. "I'm afraid of what might come to pass. Afraid that one day, they might not be dreams anymore."

"You won't let that happen," Isla said. "Every time I have ever needed you, you've been there. I trust you with my life, with my soul. I am whole because of you." She squeezed her hand. "You already take on so much. At least leave the dreams to me."

Eimhir gave a strained laugh. "I'll try, caraid. I can promise you that much."

Night fell across the sky as they ventured along the shore to the ship's scattered wreck. The mast lay across the rocks, its white sheen cast in a pale glow. As Isla waded out to it, a shiver that had nothing to do with the icy water raced down her spine. She couldn't fail again. It *had* to work this time.

She stopped in front of the mast, the waves lapping at her stomach. The only thing defying the darkness was the gleaming bone.

"Please," she whispered, reaching out a hand. "Show me what happened to you."

Her fingers met the surface with no response. Once again, the bones remained silent to her touch, unable or unwilling to give her the answers she needed.

She let her hand drop to her side, fighting frustrated tears. The ship called to her. Its shattered bones summoned her here. Yet now she was in front of it, all she felt was the sting of rejection.

Aineol, the sea sighed.

The water rippled, and a familiar russet-brown head reared up from beneath the waves. Angus stared at her, his seal eyes black and expressionless, and Isla realised what she had to do.

She sank into the water as her pelt spread over her skin. The sky disappeared, replaced by the shimmering underside of the waves. Down here, the darkness was not so absolute. The colour in her vision might have turned grey, but the muted spectrum showed her things her human eyes had failed to notice. The shifting sand below. The outline of the rocks. The splintered base of the mast.

This was how she was meant to see the world.

She touched her snout against the bone, and everything changed. In a heartbeat, her surroundings melted away, yielding to memories that didn't belong to her. Her feet found a smooth surface, cold and slick with seawater. The currents dissipated, replaced by salty air and a stiff breeze. The mast, once broken, stood proud and tall as it stretched towards the clouds.

She was on the ship. More than that, she *belonged* here. The deck beneath her bare feet welcomed her with each step. It knew her gait. It recognised the blood pulsing through her soles as she walked. It called to the pelt around her shoulders, the pelt carrying the souls of her ancestors in these forgotten memories.

"They're closing in." A grim voice cut through the air, and a haggard old selkie trudged down the forecastle stairs, his weathered forehead creased.

"Whalers?" Another selkie crossed the deck to meet him, walking through Isla like she was a ghost.

"Aye, looks like it. We might not be their usual quarry, but that won't stop them." He pursed his lips. "Better find Murdoch. Tell him it's time, if he's still willing."

"He will be."

The memory shifted like a change in the wind, carrying Isla with it as it blew. Time held no meaning here. Everything had happened long ago. Yet her pelt remembered. It hung around her shoulders, soaking her skin as it opened her eyes to what it had witnessed.

The selkie they'd called Murdoch stood in the middle of the main deck. He wore no pelt; his naked skin was dull and pallid in the sunlight, crawling with streaks of salt. The scarring ran deep across his flesh, encrusting his knuckles and elbows with bloodied crystals. Dark shadows under his eyes gave him a hollowed-out look, but there was no despair in his expression. Instead, he pulled his flaking lips into a smile and bowed his head.

"Finally," he said, his voice rasping and brittle. "This suffering is at an end."

The old selkie fixed him with a solemn stare. "It will not be forgotten. Neither will your sacrifice."

Murdoch knelt against the deck, pressing his withered hands against the white bone. "My soul has been stolen, and I have become gun-anam. I am already dead. All that remains of me are my blood and bones." He lifted his head, taking in the gathered crowd. "I gift these to you, my people, so you may carry them home."

The old selkie moved behind him, drawing a small dagger from the folds of his pelt. There was something familiar about the blade, the intricate carvings on the handle.

A sgian dubh. *Lachlan's* sgian dubh.

It belonged to your mother, Muir had told her. *It was meant to protect you.*

And tides, it had. Twice, Lachlan had saved her life with the blade. The third time, he'd held it against her neck in grief and anger. Then he'd released it and let her go.

But it had never belonged to him, or to Lady Catriona. It was Mara's blade, handed down by her ancestors. A *selkie* blade.

The old selkie held the sgian dubh against Murdoch's throat, his hand strong and steady. Murdoch stretched his torn lips into a faint smile, then closed his eyes.

The blade flashed, and blood spilled.

Isla tried to step back, but the memory arrested her in place. All she could do was watch as the glistening deck splattered with scarlet. Murdoch slumped, the ghost of his smile tracing the corners of his lips as blood poured from his throat.

Something trembled. The ship swallowed Murdoch's blood, drawing it into the bone in thirsty gulps. It was as though it were alive. As though Murdoch had *given* it life. She heard the sea spirits as they raised their voices—not in pain, but in song.

"We thank you for your sacrifice, Murdoch," the old selkie said. "Your bones will hold us when we sail. Your blood will take us from the reach of our enemy. Though your soul is lost, we will carry your body with us."

He lifted his head skywards, and Isla followed his gaze. It was only now she realised the ship's towering masts held no sails. They stood tall and lonely against a wind they could not catch.

Then, a haze of silver droplets rose from the sea. Glittering threads of water intertwined, forming shimmering ropes along the yards of the mast. They stretched out like a veil of rain, filling in the spaces that should have held sails. When the wind gusted, they billowed into a vapour that Isla might have mistaken for a thin sheet of canvas had she not seen it so many times before.

The haar. The selkie ships sailed using the haar.

"Take us through," the old selkie said.

The mist thickened, shrouding the ship in its damp, salty haze. Isla braced herself, but no deathless chill breathed across her skin. This haar wasn't the same as the one she knew, the one that brought with it the shadows of the gun-anam. It hadn't been corrupted by their frigid touch, their brackish stench. Instead, it clung to the masts in wisping cloud-sails, carrying them across the waves.

Then, as suddenly as they'd descended, the mists cleared, and Isla's heart stopped.

The sun disappeared, but it was not night. No moon hung in the sky, no stars glittered from the dark canopy above. There was only a wash of opaque colour, a red so deep and rich it was almost black. Beside the ship, the waves stilled. The sea was like glass, untouched by the slightest ripple.

This was the soulless realm. The realm of the gun-anam.

It was like looking through a dream. The ship sailed through the same waters as before, but passing through the haar had changed something. There was a veil between worlds, and they were on the other side.

Isla leaned over the gunwale. The pursuing whaler ship drew near, its prow jutting out fiercely as it cut through the swell. This close, she could see the bundled nets on deck, the racks of deadly spears. But the crew didn't rush towards them, readying themselves for an attack. Instead, they leaned out over the waves like she did, as if they were searching for something.

Closer the ship came, and still the nets lay untouched. Still the spears lay unhandled. The whaler vessel slipped past, leaving them in the eddies of its wake, as oblivious to their presence as if they were ghosts.

The haar had carried them to safety, to a place the whalers could not find them.

To a place the *Admiralty* could not find them.

Isla jerked back, and the memory melted away. In front of her, the mast lay splintered once more, a shattered remnant of what it had been. But if it could be mended, if one of these lost selkie ships could be made whole again...

Eimhir swam towards her. *Are you all right? What did you see?*

The answer was too impossible to hope for, but Isla felt it rise in her all the same.

A way to end it, she said.

CHAPTER FIFTEEN

DARCE

I n Darce's dream, he was drowning.

He fought against the swell, arms clawing towards the surface, but the sea's unforgiving grip only dragged him deeper. The cold squeezed his ribs until he was sure they would crack. All he wanted to do was gasp in precious air, but the salt stinging his lips was a painful reminder it was too far out of reach.

Yet, when he gave in and opened his throat to the sea, no water rushed into his burning lungs. Instead, he tasted stale, musty air like a sweet relief. His mouth was dry, his windpipe raw, but he was breathing. He was alive.

He opened his eyes and blinked away the blurriness in his vision. The cabin was dim, but he could make out a hunched figure slumped in the chair in the corner, crutch tucked under one elbow while he slept.

"Lachlan?" The word left his throat in an unintelligible rasp.

Lachlan's eyes snapped open. He pushed himself up from the chair, hand grasping the handle of his crutch as he crossed to the bunk. "I didn't think you'd wake so soon. That auld blood in your veins must be stronger than we thought."

"What...happened?" Each syllable strained Darce's windpipe, and fresh pain flashed across his chest as he tried to sit up. "I remember the gun-anam, the gangway slipping..."

"You fell," Lachlan said. "You were swallowed by the waves before I had time to move. I didn't know what to do. But Blair did."

"Blair?"

"He didn't waste a second. Secured a length of rope around his waist and leapt in after you." Lachlan swallowed. "It felt like hours before he resurfaced with you. All I could do was stare at those waves, watching them churn, thinking you both were lost beneath them. Knowing I could do nothing about it."

The bitterness lacing his voice hung in the air between them, and Darce took a heavy breath. "There's no use dwelling on what might have been, little laird. I'm alive, and I'm grateful for it. I suppose there's some value in being the Grand Admiral's pawn after all."

"You think that's why Blair went in after you? You misjudge him, Galbraith. He's...he's not his uncle."

Darce averted his eyes from the flush spreading across Lachlan's face. "I hope that's true. For your sake."

They sat in weighted silence, an unspoken understanding resting between them. For a moment, Darce could pretend they were back at Blackwood Estate, when the tensions between them came from nothing more than trivial indiscretions and youthful rebellion. A time before this grief, this loss, that burrowed through them both.

"On the matter of the Grand Admiral..." Lachlan grimaced. "I'm sorry, but I was told to bring you to the main deck as soon as you woke. He seems unusually...*impatient*."

Darce stiffened. "We're not heading back to Arburgh? Even after the losses we suffered against those gun-anam?"

"Not yet. Not when he believes we're so close." Lachlan fixed him with a measured look. "You called yourself his pawn. I didn't understand before, but I do now. He's using you to find her, isn't he? Using the blood oath you made."

"Aye."

Lachlan chuckled. "I wasn't so foolish as to think I received this commission on merit, but I thought it was Blair who'd pulled some strings. I should have realised it was you they wanted all along. No wonder he was willing to risk his sentinels to make sure you survived."

"You think I wanted that? You think I want any of this?" Darce swung his legs over the side of the bunk, grunting as his feet touched the cold wooden floor. "I can't lead him to her. If he takes her pelt, she'll become one of those wraiths we fought last night. Surely you could not wish that fate on her, not after what you've seen."

"The only fate awaiting her is a life of status and power in the capital," Lachlan said shortly. "He wouldn't be going to such lengths to find her if he meant her harm."

"You don't need to mean harm to cause it." Darce nodded towards the stump of his leg. "I thought you'd understand that."

Lachlan's fingers shifted around the handle of his crutch. "Careful, Galbraith. That almost sounded like you were coming to my side."

"There were never any sides. You were the only one who couldn't see that." Darce slipped on his boots, his legs stiff as he pushed to his feet. His cloak hung on a nail in the corner, heavy with seawater. He wrapped it around his shoulders, then turned to Lachlan. "Be careful. I'm not the only pawn here. The Grand Admiral only sees you as something he can use to control me."

"A poor choice of hostage, what with you seeming perfectly content to risk my life to lead him away from her."

"You think I would allow him to harm you?" Darce clenched his jaw. "You are the closest thing I have to a brother, Lachlan. I don't need to make a blood oath to know I would give my life to protect you."

"You wouldn't need to protect me at all if you gave the Grand Admiral what he wants. But you won't do that, will you?" Lachlan flashed a tight smile. "There were always sides, Galbraith. And you're still on hers, even now."

His words rang around Darce's ears as he climbed the stairs to the *Vanguard's* deck. Their echo rattled deep, an accusation he couldn't shake.

If you had to choose, you would break, Muir had told him.

Maybe this was what it felt like.

The crisp air stung his raw throat when he stepped outside. All he could taste was the sea, the same sea that had tried to swallow him only a few short hours ago. But the storm had passed, and the waves were calmer, rising and falling in gentle crests. The mists had scattered too, leaving behind a dreich horizon offering no end.

Alasdair Cunningham stood on the quarterdeck, silhouette stark against the pale wintry light. The brim of his hat cast his face in shadow, and his eyes were as flinty as ever.

"I'm glad to see your recovery was a swift one," he said as Darce approached. "We have work to do, and last night's events cost us precious time."

"I warned you," Darce said. "Where humans and selkies meet in violence, those wraiths will follow. If you persist in this hunt, more of your people will die. Is that what you want?"

"You know what I want, Sergeant." Cunningham fixed him with a look of steel. "I will bleed the Admiralty dry if that's what it takes to find my daughter. If you don't wish the Blackwood lad to bleed with them, I suggest you help make up for the hours we lost. She was on that ship, wasn't she?"

On the lower deck, Lachlan emerged from a stairwell, crutch tucked under his elbow as he fought to keep his balance on the slippery wood.

"Aye," Darce said. "She was there."

"And where is she now?"

A raw edge scratched Cunningham's curt, clipped words. All Darce could see was the hollowed-out grief of a desperate man. A *dangerous* man. A man who would never stop.

The call sang again, anchoring him to Isla. How easy it would be to follow her, to search for her until she was his again. How easy it would be to become the same kind of monster as the man across from him.

North, the sea whispered.

All he had to do was speak the word, and he'd see her again.

He locked eyes with Lachlan across the deck. It was difficult not to flinch at the understanding in his expression, the wry pinch at the corner of his mouth.

There were always sides, Galbraith. And you're still on hers, even now.

Resentment had always run deep in the younger Blackwood, but there was a time Darce had known how to navigate those currents. Now, he feared his choice might drown them both.

Darce swallowed his guilt, and readied his tongue for the lie. "South. We follow them south."

For once, the tides were on his side. Over the next few days, winter turned its wrath on them, besieging the *Vanguard* with raging winds and flurries of snow. Not even Alasdair Cunningham had the temerity to defy a Silvish westerly, and they had no choice but to reef the huge black sails and wait out the storm, guiding the ship downwind as the swell heaved beneath them.

Darce shifted his grip on the gunwale, trying to coax some life into his numb fingers. Though he and the *Vanguard's* other sentinels fought to subdue the worst of the waves, the snow still fell thick and fast. It drenched his cloak, seeping into his skin.

"Fancy a dram?" Rhona appeared beside him, a pewter flask in hand. "Looks like ye could use one."

"I'm on duty."

"Nae use being on duty if you freeze to death." Rhona took a swig, then held the flask out again. "Go on. I can keep a secret."

The metal rim was so cold it stung, but the sharp relief of whisky gliding down his throat brought a warmth that spread through Darce's insides. He savoured the burn of each smoky mouthful, licking his lips to catch every last drop.

"Thank you," he said, handing her the flask. "That ought to keep the chill away for a wee while, at least."

"Until those wraiths come back, ye mean?" Rhona fixed him with a measured look. "You ken more about them than you're letting on."

"I wish I didn't." He shivered. The gusts of snow couldn't compare to the cold that clung to the gun-anam. "It's not the first time I've encountered them."

"Aye, I thought as much," Rhona said. "Everyone the Grand Admiral sent over... We froze. I couldn't move. I've never looked at something and felt so...*wrong*." She pulled the fur-lined collar of her cloak close around her neck. "I saw Dugald clutching his throat, seafoam spilling from his mouth. Erin falling to a blade drawn from the mist. Two sentinels I've known for years, two friends, leaving this world without raising a blade in spite. Mhairi and I might have joined them, if it wasn't for your captain."

"What do you mean?"

"Lachlan Blackwood. He put his cutlass between me and one of those wraiths. Held it off long enough for me to come to my senses and start fighting." She arched an eyebrow. "Ye seem surprised. The lad wields a sword well for a man with one leg. Of course, when I told him that, he looked at me like he was trying to find the insult."

A wry smile tugged at Darce's lips. "That sounds about right."

"He said he had a good teacher."

Her words struck him like a blow to his sternum. "Not good enough," he managed. "For all the right I've tried to do by him, I've failed him more times than I can count."

Rhona stared at the waves, fingers white as she gripped the gunwale. The wind gusted, sending snow swirling through the air.

"I ken that feeling well," she said. "Sometimes I wonder if we're fated to spend our lives trying to make up for the sacrifice they made for us." She turned back to him, eyes glittering in the dim light. "Is that how the Blackwood lad lost his leg? When you made the blood oath?"

Darce blanched. "Aye," he said, the lie burning his tongue. "And there's not a day goes by that I don't regret it, that I don't wish there had been another way. If I could have spared him that—" He swallowed the rest of his words before they betrayed him. "What about you? How did you come to make the oath to Mhairi?"

"I was an enforcer for one of the southside smuggling rings," Rhona said. "Mhairi was a street urchin I got used to seeing on my rounds. I kept an eye out for her, kept her out of trouble when I could. Still not sure why. There was something *there*, a connection I couldn't explain." A rueful smile pulled at the corner of her mouth. "The job paid well enough, or it would have, if I'd been able to resist gambling all my coin on a hand or two of Bloody Gambit. A few years ago, my debts caught up with me, and I ended up cornered down the arse-end of some alley with a pistol levelled at my head. I heard the shot, but there was no pain. Just Mhairi, lying across my knees with blood soaking her filthy clothes."

"She saved your life."

"And then I saved hers. You ken how it works as well as I do." A pensive look fell across Rhona's face. "I'd never seen a sentinel before. I didn't know I had the auld blood in me. But somehow, I knew what I had to do. She'd given her life for mine; it seemed only right to offer mine for hers. I didn't realise what it would do to me, to us both. That day changed everything."

Darce glanced at her. The first time they'd spoken, he thought he'd imagined it. But there it was again, that tension in her voice, the dark undercurrent beneath the shape of her words. "Do you still gamble?" he asked carefully.

"Don't we all?" She huffed. "I've got my reasons for being here, but I doubt they're the same as yours. You do a shite job of hiding your rancour towards the Admiralty."

"Or perhaps I'm not as practised at it as you."

Rhona's hand twitched, fingers flexing towards the dagger in her belt. Then she relented, a guarded smile cracking her composure. "Best watch your step, Sergeant. These waters you're testing are dangerous, and there might not be someone to pull you out next time ye find yourself floundering in them."

"I'll keep that in mind."

A dry chuckle escaped her throat as she screwed the pewter lid back onto the whisky flask and returned it to her pocket. "Aye, I'm sure you will."

Her footsteps faded across the deck as she headed back in the direction of the cabins, but their conversation lingered in Darce's ears long after she'd gone.

I need you to take away his protection, Muir had told him. *Make them think twice about what he's asking of them.*

He thought of the shadow behind Rhona's eyes, the hidden edge buried in her words.

The time to make a move against Cunningham was fast approaching. The *Vanguard* had already lost two of its sentinels. Perhaps now, Darce had found another to stand by his side.

Over the next week, the snowstorms scattered, giving way to clearer skies. The air was so crisp it burned Darce's lungs, but it was a small price to pay for a bright horizon and favourable wind. Every wave the *Vanguard* cut through carried them further away from the distant ache in his chest. Further away from Isla.

A satisfied smile flitted across his lips. The decision he'd made loosened some of the pressure in his chest, lifting his spirits. Isla was safe, at least for now. He'd bought himself time to test the waters with the other sentinels. But he had to move quickly. It wouldn't be long before the Grand Admiral realised they were chasing a lie. And when he did, Darce would have no choice but to strike.

At the side of the deck, Lachlan stood in conversation with Blair. His golden hair had grown long enough to tie back, and his jaw was shadowed with the beginnings of a beard. He was unrecognisable from the soft noble lad he'd been at Blackwood Estate. The sea suited him like it suited Isla. But that didn't make the waves any less dangerous. The Grand Admiral's threats were all the reminder Darce needed of that.

"Ahoy!" A cry carried down from the crow's nest, jolting him from his thoughts. "Ship on the horizon, north-northwest!"

He joined Lachlan and Blair, peering across the choppy waves. The ship was little more than a speck in the distance. Without a spyglass, there was no determining what banner it flew under.

"No Admiralty patrols scheduled for these parts," Blair said. "Most likely a merchant runner from Silveckan blown off course. Still, it doesn't hurt to make sure, especially after what happened to the *Silent Wind.*"

"Indeed." Alasdair Cunningham's voice cut through the air as he strode towards the quarterdeck steps. "Call the captains to their posts. Regardless of who or what is on that ship, the *Vanguard* will be ready to meet it."

Blair nodded, but before Darce had time to move, another cry rose from the crow's nest.

"Sails! Green sails!"

Darce stilled. He'd seen hundreds of ships in his lifetime, but there was only one whose sails caught the light like emeralds, whose hull was stained the colour of seaweed.

"The *Jade Dawn*," Lachlan said, the same understanding flashing across his face. "It must be."

Cunningham flicked his head towards them. "The Sea Kith vessel? The one my patrols have been hunting?"

"Aye, the ship that brought us to Arburgh," Lachlan said. "The ship that helped my—that helped Isla escape."

"Then it appears the storm did us a favour." Cunningham straightened his spine, barking orders over the wind. "Bring the *Vanguard* about and take us to full sail. I want every sentinel working the waves until we catch that ship."

"Grand Admiral—" Darce started forward, but the look from Cunningham stopped him in his tracks.

"No, Sergeant," he said, voice silky. "My patience is wearing thin. If you can't take me to her, I'll find someone who can."

"They don't know anything. Aye, they helped us flee, but they weren't involved in anything more than that. They won't know where she is."

Cunningham smiled. "For their sake, you'd best hope you are mistaken."

For a fleeting moment, the restraint Darce had so carefully guarded threatened to snap. *Let us be done with this*, something in him urged, and the twitch in his fingers agreed. With a single stroke, he could slice his rapier across the Grand Admiral's throat. It didn't matter if the other sentinels came running, not if he managed to throw his body overboard by the time they got there. Let them try to revive his corpse from the sea's depths.

His hand flew to his belt, but before he could draw his sword, a tight grip seized his shoulder.

Lachlan stood at his side, eyes imploring as he dug his fingers in. He didn't say anything, just gave an indiscernible shake of his head. Behind him, two sentinels swept across the deck, their sapphire cloaks streaming behind them as they took their positions at the gunwale only metres away.

Fuck.

Darce bit the inside of his mouth, hand trembling. He was so close. This would all be over if he could only...

Don't fail, Muir had told him.

He stepped back, releasing a shaking breath. This wasn't the time. Not if he wanted to succeed. Not if he wanted to get Lachlan out of here alive.

"To your posts, all of you," Cunningham said. "And ready the cannons. If these pirates won't answer to the Admiralty, they'll answer to the tides."

Darce stood by as the crew rushed around him, hastening to their duties. Already he felt the sea singing in his blood as the other sentinels called on their magic to harness the currents to the ship's favour.

He leaned over the gunwale, reaching out to the waves. Their crash echoed in his ears, promising to carry them quicker.

Don't listen to them, he thought, grasping for some hold over the swell. *Take us away from here. Set us adrift. Anything but this.*

The sea roared, paying no mind to his desperate bargaining. Darce wrestled for some kind of control, but the will of the waves slipped through his fingers. It was no use. There were too many sentinels urging them towards their quarry, filling the full might of *Vanguard's* angry black sails with the wind. The *Jade Dawn* was a swift, agile ship, but Kerr alone was no match for the ten sentinels the Grand Admiral had at his disposal.

A raucous shriek tore through the air, and Darce snapped out of his daze to see Featherblade perched nearby, regarding him with a fervent kind of expectation.

Guilt churned in his stomach. The *Jade Dawn* and its crew didn't deserve the horror coming for them. He already owed them more than he could repay. But without the tides on his side, there was only one thing left he could do to help them.

He moved closer to the gannet, keeping his fingers out of its reach. "You have to go to them. Make them understand this isn't a fight they can win. If Nishi wants to save her crew, she must yield."

Featherblade squawked furiously and lunged for his hand, beak flashing with malice.

Darce whirled away, cursing as a fresh gash opened across his knuckles.

"You tides-forsaken wretch, I'm trying to *help* them! Sea Kith or no, they don't stand a chance against the *Vanguard's* cannons when we get broadside. If they don't lower their colours, they'll all be killed."

Featherblade spread its wings to their full length and pushed off the gunwale with a screech. The wind lifted it above the waves, carrying it higher and higher until it disappeared.

"What are ye doing?"

Darce wheeled around to find Rhona staring at him, her inked forearms crossed stiffly in front of her chest. Her brown eyes narrowed as she looked at him, then to the clouds above.

"I saw ye talking to that bird," she said.

"You saw nothing," he said, moving to push past her. "I should get to—"

She grabbed his arm, fingers like iron. "Ye think me a fool, Sergeant? You've been working to your own agenda ever since ye stepped on this ship. I don't know what kind of grudge you've got against the Grand Admiral, and truth be told, I don't care. I only care that you don't take the rest of us down with you when it all goes to shite."

He wrenched his arm away. "All I'm trying to do is stop more blood being spilled in this senseless pursuit."

"At the cost of your own? Of the Blackwood lad's?" She leaned in, lowering her voice. "You're meant to be his sentinel. His fate is tied to yours. Have ye considered what would happen to him if you get caught?"

"Caught doing what? Shooing a seabird away from the ship?"

"That's all you were doing, aye?"

"For the moment, *aye.*"

The words slipped from his mouth in anger, too quick to take back. Rhona's eyes widened, but all she did was shake her head as she moved out of his way. "Tides protect ye, Sergeant. If you keep heading down this path you're on, nobody else will."

This time, she didn't stop him as he pushed past to take his place at the starboard bow. He placed his hands on the wood and fought to gather himself. The splinters pricked at his palms, as if the *Vanguard* itself knew his treachery.

Rhona was right. He was getting reckless. The longer he remained on this ship, the tighter the noose chafed around his neck.

He shook the thought from his head and tried to focus. The sentinels' magic was at work, reining the swell to their side. Waves leapt alongside the hull, eagerly pushing them on. The wind billowed in the sails, filling his ears with the roar of flapping canvas. He should have been helping, but the thought of doing anything to turn the sea spirits against the *Jade Dawn* was a betrayal he couldn't stomach.

"We're gaining on them!" one of the deckhands shouted. "Their stern will soon be in range of our forward cannons."

Darce leaned over the railing, craning his neck. The *Jade Dawn* loomed in the distance, its flowing green sails drab and muted through the drizzle between them. They were still running. Maybe Featherblade hadn't been able to deliver the message. Maybe Nishi hadn't listened.

"Ready a warning shot." The Grand Admiral's command carried from the quarterdeck, terse and unyielding. "On my signal."

The *Jade Dawn* seemed impossibly far away, but Darce knew how quickly the distance could be cut with a favourable wind. As soon as the *Vanguard* got within a mile, its formidable cannons would be ready. A well-placed shot would rip a hole through the stern, tearing the hold to pieces in a blast of lead and timber. If Nishi wasn't ready, if any of them were caught in the way...

"Fire."

The roar of the cannon tore through Darce's ears. A cloud of smoke belched from the *Vanguard's* bow, but when it cleared, the *Jade Dawn's* green flag was still raised high in defiance.

"Reload!" came the shout from one of the gunners. "Ready our next shot."

On the quarterdeck, the Grand Admiral stood steely eyed and stone faced. There was no mercy in the hard lines etched on his skin, no quarter to be given. If the *Jade Dawn* kept running, he'd blow them to pieces.

"Strike the flag," Darce begged under his breath, turning back to the waves. "Don't throw your lives away."

Ahead, the *Jade Dawn* was limping, wounded from the solitary shot. It would be easy for the *Vanguard* to unleash the full might of its cannons. A volley of lead against the broadside would decimate the hull. Darce's stomach twisted at the thought of the carnage: shards of shrapnel flying, bodies crushed and ruptured, tattered sails askew. Nothing would be left but scraps of driftwood and the dead.

The Sea Kith didn't stand a chance, not against this ship.

A cry carried from below as the gunners reloaded the forward cannon and waited on the command from the quarterdeck. Cunningham's mouth drew thin as he surveyed the waves, offering no forgiveness.

"Hold!" someone called from the crow's nest. "They're striking their flag."

For a moment, it seemed like nothing had changed. Then the emerald flag atop the *Jade Dawn's* main mast fluttered feebly as it slowly lowered to the deck.

Darce whipped his head back to the Grand Admiral. Cunningham wanted answers. He wanted Isla. If he destroyed the Sea Kith and their ship, he might never get them.

It should have been a relief when he raised his hand to stay the next shot. But the slow, wolfish smile across Cunningham's lips terrified Darce more than the thought of a hundred cannons.

"Prepare to board. And bring me their captain."

Darce grunted as someone elbowed past, jostling him out of the way. The deck swarmed with bodies, jewel-toned cloaks whirling in every direction as the *Vanguard's* crew set to work. They'd done this before. They knew exactly what the Grand Admiral wanted.

He turned his gaze skywards to see Featherblade circling against the clouds. The gannet didn't land, but it released a mournful cry that rattled in Darce's bones.

Tides, I hope I've done the right thing.

All he could do was wait. The *Vanguard* leapt through the waves, hungrier than ever now its quarry was within reach. The *Jade Dawn* diminished in its shadow, flag lowered and once-proud sails stowed. This close, it was clearer than ever the Sea Kith hadn't stood a chance. Not against the flagship of the Admiralty's fleet. Not against Cunningham's wrath.

As the gangways were readied, Darce held his position, fighting the urge to run to the *Jade Dawn*. Interfering would only make things worse. He needed to bide his time and find a way to help Nishi and Kerr.

The captured crew soon began to trickle across to the *Vanguard*, wrists bound and weapons surrendered. A gauntlet of muskets welcomed them onto the deck, the threat of black powder hanging in the air. Some of the deckhands were wounded, the more fortunate sporting only bloody gashes rather than crushed limbs. Even the single warning shot had shown no mercy.

Darce kept his eyes on the gangway, heart lurching when he caught a glimpse of a solemn-faced Kerr, and behind him, Nishi.

She held her chin high as she strode onto the *Vanguard's* deck, gaze locked firmly with the Grand Admiral's. Her brown skin was swollen around her right eye, and blood oozed from her lips as she curled them. "Took you fucking long enough."

Cunningham ignored her, instead turning to Blair. "Take the pirates to the brig. Then send a captain and complement of officers to their ship. We'll take it back to Arburgh with us."

"Arburgh?" Nishi wrestled with the manacles around her wrists. "It's no surprise your first thought is to run to dry land, you salt-shy coward. I knew you were afraid to face us out here."

"And fetch a rag for this one's mouth," Cunningham said, each word dripping with disdain. "Best she saves her voice for the capital, for I intend to hear her sing when we get there."

"Let's go." Blair grabbed Nishi's arm. "Don't make this worse for yourself than you have already."

Something glinted in Nishi's eyes, and her lips stretched into a blood-stained grin.

"Wouldn't dream of it," she said, and leapt.

She was on him before anyone had the chance to react. One minute, Blair was in front of her, grip tight around her arm. Then came a bone-splitting crack, and the young lieutenant reeled back, blood streaming from a gash on the bridge of his nose.

Nishi grinned wider. She raised her shackled wrists and stormed forward, but before she could land a second blow, Blair gathered himself and sent a fist into her stomach. Nishi barely had time to gasp for breath before he advanced again, sending her to the floor with a swinging arm.

The deck erupted. Furious shouts rang out from the Admiralty and Sea Kith alike as Nishi scrambled to her feet. Fresh blood poured from her mouth, but the insolence in her eyes hadn't faded as she stalked around Blair in a half-circle.

"Try me again, lad," she hissed. "Better yet, let me out of these chains so I can show you what a so-called *pirate* can do against a piss-poor excuse for a sailor."

A shrill caw rattled the air, and Darce glanced up to see Featherblade joined in the sky by the huge, black-winged frame of Shearwing. Both birds circled frantically, their shrieks adding to the din.

Blair whipped his hand to the scabbard on his belt, and Darce froze as the low sun caught the edge of drawn steel. This was madness. If Blair struck Nishi down, the killing wouldn't end there. The Sea Kith would fight to avenge their captain. They'd be slaughtered, every one of them.

He had to do something.

The staccato clatter of cocked muskets rattled across the deck as he stepped in front of Nishi. "Listen to me," he said, low and urgent. "Nothing good can come from this, do you hear me? *Nothing*. For the sake of your crew, for the sake of us all, you have to stand down."

Nishi stopped dead, meeting his gaze for the first time. The swelling around her eye was dark and angry, and her forehead was slick with crimson. She didn't say a word. She didn't have to. He saw all he needed to in the heat of her glare.

"Stand down," he said. "*Please.*"

The ring in her lower lip twitched as she drew her mouth into a sneer, and he thought she might fly at him too.

"Captain." Kerr's voice rang across the deck, clear and calming. "We agreed."

Nishi stilled, shoulders softening at his words. "Aye," she said hoarsely. "That we did."

Long, heavy seconds passed, until finally she stepped back with a cold look of disgust. She held her manacled wrists towards Blair, offering her submission with fire burning in her eyes.

Blair glanced between Nishi and the Grand Admiral. When no command was given, he sheathed his sword and took her by the arm, leading her to the hold. This time, Nishi didn't resist. She followed Blair, pausing only to look over her shoulder.

Darce met her eyes with a steady gaze. *Trust me*, he thought.

Her only response was to spit a red glob of blood at his feet.

CHAPTER SIXTEEN

ISLA

I n the short weeks she'd been away, Caim had changed.

It wasn't just the tightening of winter's grasp around the heart of the Selkie Isles, though that was part of it. Snow covered the once-green slopes in a white shroud, and the sky remained grim and surly, impatiently waiting for night to hasten in. The thatched roofs of the crannog buildings glistened with frost, and shards of ice dangled precariously from the overhanging reeds.

But it wasn't the bone-aching cold that struck Isla deepest. It was the feeling, for the first time, that she was *meant* to be here. Every time she clambered down to the underwater cavern connecting Caim to the surrounding sea, the ancestors that had once felt like strangers walked by her side. Each time her bare feet splashed through the icy water, she imagined herself retreading the long-forgotten steps of those who came before her. It had taken dreamwalking to make them real, to make her realise she carried them with her.

"Eimhir said you'd be down here."

Isla turned her head at the padding of heavy footsteps. Seconds later, an imposing figure appeared over the ledge, his black pelt blending in with the cavern's gloom.

She took a sharp breath. It was Duncan.

He regarded her evenly. "For someone who claims they want to be one of us, you seem to leave every chance you get."

"I wasn't *leaving*. I was only trying to make myself useful while you and the other chieftains deliberate over what to do about my vision." She pursed her lips. "Have you decided—"

"Useful in what way?"

She swallowed her irritation and replied, "Dreamwalking. I discovered I can't do it in the loch. I need to be out in the open water, surrounded by the sea."

"You think there is more to learn? More than you've told us already?"

If there was an accusatory note in his voice, she chose to ignore it. "This pelt holds the memories of every selkie who inhabited it. I've barely brushed the surface." She smoothed her hands over the folds, marvelling at how the dappled fur shone in the darkness, the grey rippling with traces of heather-purple and cloud-blue. "Mara gave up her soul to save me. I can't imagine the strength that must have taken, the pain she must have suffered. I won't let it be in vain."

Duncan's umber eyes betrayed nothing. He gestured to the pool of water lapping at the bottom of the steps. "Let's go. Show me what you've learned."

Isla stilled. Something about Duncan's countenance made her uneasy. He was too calm, too guarded for her to glean any sense of what he wanted. What would he do if she followed him? Worse, what would he do if she refused?

When she didn't move, Duncan approached the pool. His ink-black pelt slid across his broad shoulders, melding with his skin until it covered it completely. Without waiting to see if she would follow, he dived into the water and disappeared through the submerged tunnel.

She had no choice. She had to go after him.

The icy water hit with a sharp relief, skimming over the sweeping curves of her selkie body as she thrust with her flippers. Through the darkness, subtle ripples brushed her whiskers, guiding her through the snaking tunnel towards the sea.

A glimmer of sunlight refracted off the waves above as she emerged from the cavern into the open water. She caught sight of Duncan, his selkie form powerful and swift as he swept around a shoal of pollock and snatched a fish in his jaws.

There will come a day when Caim's waters are no longer safe for us to hunt in, he said, circling back to her. *I fear that time will be upon us sooner than any of the chieftains are willing to admit. The larger the Admiralty grows, the greedier its captains become, the more danger we face. Eileanan Selch is the last place in Silvish waters untouched by their ships, and even that is under threat.*

That's all the more reason to search for the lost ships, Isla said. *They were built from the bones of our people, selkies who'd lost their souls and gave their blood—their lives—to summon the haar. And in turn, the haar protected them. It shrouded their ships, kept them safe from human eyes. If we could do the same—*

And what chance did those ships have against an ever-growing fleet of men-o'-war and heavy frigates? Duncan countered. *They were hunted to extinction, haar or no. Even if we found one intact, why should I believe our fate would be any different from those who once sailed on it?*

His eyes gleamed like he was throwing down a challenge. But in the vibrations of his voice, she felt the currents of desperation.

He was afraid.

She expelled the last of the air from her lungs, allowing herself to sink further beneath the surface. Through the layers of fur and blubber, the cold bite of the sea seeped into her bones. All the human instincts in her mind screamed at her to swim, to fight through the waves. But she quietened that part of herself and let her seal mind take over.

The sea shifted, and she found herself in a dream.

Far above, on a ridge overlooking Caim's fearsome peaks, a selkie woman with smattered freckles and fire-red hair shrank back. "Don't come any closer. You won't be able to stop me, and I don't want to take you with me."

When Isla spoke, it was in the burr of a man's voice. "You don't have to do this. We can find another way."

"There is no other way." The red-haired woman spread her arms. Spirals of salt cut across her skin, leaving it cracked. Her lips were raw and peeling, her eyes bloodshot. "The anam-long are gone. If I cannot give my blood to our ships, there is nothing left for me but this suffering. Nowhere left to go but the sea."

"Your pelt—"

"Is *lost*. And without it, without a soulship to carry my bones, so am I." She smiled, blood welling through the gaps in her teeth. "Remember me, caraid. Let me live on in the dreams of those who come after you."

Isla reached out an arm, but it was too late. Her fingers—the man's fingers—found only thin air as the red-haired woman pushed herself back over the edge. She hung there, glassy-eyed and smiling. Then she was gone, leaving nothing behind but a faint, irrevocable splash.

A violent shudder tore through the dream, blurring Isla's vision. She thrashed her flippers, but found only weak human limbs.

What had she done?

Panic set in as she flailed her arms and legs. The sea closed around her, squeezing her in its icy grasp. She tried to gulp down a breath, but water rushed into her fragile lungs, filling her chest as she choked and spluttered.

Somewhere in the distance, she heard a name that might have been hers. It was so far away, so out of reach. All she saw through the salty sting of her eyes was the darkness of the depths, swallowing her until only the void remained.

"You pushed her too hard! I warned you, and you took her out there anyway."

Raised voices pounded against Isla's skull. She tried to open her eyes, but her lids felt bruised and heavy.

"I needed to see for myself." Duncan spoke evenly. "I witnessed Mara dreamwalk on enough occasions to know what it looks like. I had to be certain she was telling the truth, not a lie born out of desperation to belong here."

Something hot and watery rose at the back of Isla's throat, and she rolled over, spluttering seawater and bile. The sodden folds of her pelt spilled over her shaking arms and legs as she pushed herself to her knees, blinking away the haze in her vision.

"Isla." Eimhir rushed to her side. "Sit still, will you? You're shivering."

"What happened?" She pulled her pelt around her shoulders, burying herself in the warmth of its fur. "I don't remember."

"You nearly bloody drowned, that's what happened." Eimhir glared at Duncan. "Are you satisfied? Did she pass your test?"

Isla lifted her chin to meet Duncan's dark, unyielding gaze. His arms were folded across his pelt, dripping with seawater. A thick silence hung around them, fraught with the echo of Eimhir's unanswered question. Isla didn't want to be the first to break it. It felt too much like giving in.

Eventually, Duncan turned to Eimhir. "Head back to the crannogs. I'd like to talk to our dreamwalker."

"But I—"

"It wasn't a request, Eimhir."

Eimhir's grey eyes clouded over like a storm ready to break. For a moment, Isla thought she might refuse. She *wanted* her to refuse. But it seemed even Eimhir knew this was not a fight she could win. Not against her chieftain.

She made for the steep steps leading out of the cave, pausing only to cast a warning look back at Duncan. "You once thought I was the last hope for our people. But it's not me. It's her. You would do well to remember that."

After her footsteps faded, Duncan fixed Isla a measured gaze. "It appears I have misjudged you. Or your capabilities, at least. You have Mara's gift."

Something of the tension in Isla's shoulders loosened, but it wasn't enough to drop her guard. "You believe me?"

"I watched you lose yourself in that dream. You looked just like Mara, before..." He grimaced. "What did you see?"

"They were talking about the ships. The anam-long, they called them."

"Soulships." Duncan's gaze turned sombre. "A fitting name. A name to remind us of what was lost so they might be built."

Anam-long. Soulship. The word struck a place deep inside her. There it was again, this weight her ancestors carried, the calling that had come to her. She couldn't ignore it. She'd never been able to ignore it, ever since she was a bairn splashing in the shallows, always wanting *more.*

"Our deaths had purpose, once," she said. "When we lost our pelts, we sacrificed what was left of our bodies to build those ships. We lived on through them. And now that they're gone, there is nowhere to go for a selkie suffering the loss of their soul, only the sea. That's how the gun-anam came to be. That's what we have to make right, if we want to survive."

"We've forgotten so much," Duncan said. "The anam-long, the sgian dubh and blood sacrifice... Fragments of a bygone culture, whispers from legends of old. Thanks to these dreams of yours, we're beginning to see the shape of what was lost."

"I can do more," Isla insisted. "All I want to do is help our people. Why can't you see that?"

Duncan shook his head. "Seeing it was never the problem. I just know the wake you follow."

"You're talking about Mara." Her name was a struggle to speak. The selkie woman whose pelt she wore. The mother she'd never met. The current forever pulling her to sea, no matter who she had to leave behind.

Lady Catriona. Lord Cormick. Lachlan.

Darce.

A violent ache rose in her chest, and she pushed it down again. "What was she like?"

"Stubborn. Reckless. You remind me of her." Duncan closed his eyes. "You remind me of her far too much."

The steady depths of his voice trembled, giving way to something Isla recognised well. She knew how sharply the splinters of grief scratched the throat. She knew the hollow echo of loss. But there was something else lurking under the surface, dark and bitter.

She'd seen how pain could twist a man into a monster. The Grand Admiral wore those scars as well.

Duncan opened his eyes, his expression once again like stone. "I needed to be sure. Now I know the truth in what you've seen, I'll tell the rest of the chieftains we must go after the lost soulships. Angus will lead the scouts across the breadth and depth of Silvish waters until they find an anam-long that remains seaworthy."

"*They?*" Isla echoed. "I'm not to go with them?"

"No."

The word was so blunt, so unyielding, she couldn't help but rock back. "Have you forgotten I was the one who found the first two wrecks? Their bones call to me. Finding the others will be an easier task with my dreamwalking."

"Your dreamwalking is precisely why you cannot go," Duncan said. "Eimhir is right. Nobody else can do what you do. Your gift is the only hope we have of reaching the soulless realm. We can't risk losing you."

"Losing me?" Isla countered. "Or losing my pelt?"

"They are one and the same."

"Much to your disappointment, I imagine."

Duncan snapped his head towards her. All at once, the distance between them seemed too close. All she felt was the ripening of the tension in the air, the frantic thrum of her heart.

Eimhir's voice floated in her ears. *The idea of any selkie killing another for their pelt... It's something unspeakable, unthinkable.*

"I was drowning," she said slowly. "You could have left me to die, but you brought me back. Were you not tempted to..."

Duncan stared at her, a vein pulsing in his temple. She wanted to shirk away, but she didn't dare move.

After what felt like an age, the rattle of his breathing subsided, leaving the air cold with silence once more. Isla waited, digging her fingers into her palms.

Finally, he spoke. "Angus will send word once he's located a soulship in good enough condition to make the crossing into the soulless realm. Until then, you'll remain here on Caim."

"You said if I proved myself, I would have a place here," Isla said. "I did not think you meant a prison."

"You believe you have proven yourself?" Duncan gave a strained laugh. "How could you possibly do that, aineol, when you know as well as I do what we face? Finding the lost soulships won't stop the war that's coming. When the Admiralty falls upon us, how will you find it in yourself to stand against your own blood?"

Isla turned cold. Lachlan's face swam before her, eyes accusing. She remembered the bite of his blade against her throat, the tremble in his hand as he released her. He hadn't been able to kill her back then. What if that had changed?

"It won't come to that," she whispered, half to herself. "Lachlan is—"

"I wasn't talking about your brother."

It took her a moment to understand what he meant. Then it hit, as winding and unexpected as a blow. "*Him?* The Grand Admiral? Call me aineol all you like. Tell me I'm a stranger, that I'll never belong here. But don't you *dare* accuse me of having any loyalty to that bastard. I would never choose him. How could you possibly think—"

"Because Mara did."

He spoke the words as softly as a confession. Isla stared at him, unable to believe what she'd heard. Not *wanting* to believe it. Every empty second stretched longer than the next, filled with the echo of what he'd said.

"She saved his life, and in return, he killed her for her pelt," Duncan continued. "That's what I thought. That's what we all thought. But years later, I learned the truth. I saw it with my own eyes." He lowered his head, lips twisting. "Knowing she'd stayed with him willingly was like losing her all over again."

"That's not true," Isla said, mouth dry. "She *couldn't* leave. He stole her pelt."

"But he didn't keep it from her, did he?" A muscle twitched in Duncan's jaw. "He allowed her to return to her soul shape, return to the sea."

"Only under guard," Isla said, heat rising in her voice. "Hidden on an uncharted island, somewhere the Admiralty would never discover what she was. I know that place. I've been there. It's where..." She trailed off, memories flooding her mind. The turquoise water, the rustle of beachgrass amongst white sand, the granite tomb holding a faded grey pelt. The same pelt she now wore around her shoulders. "You *knew* about it? Why didn't you help her?"

"There was always someone watching. I couldn't get close. Not until his faithful sentinel got careless one day and let me slip into the bay unnoticed." Duncan grimaced. "I thought I could get her away from him, bring her home. But when I found her, she refused to leave."

"That doesn't make any sense. Why would she..." Isla trailed off, regret burning her tongue as the half-finished question died in the air. The memory of Alasdair Cunningham's voice echoed in her ears, offering an answer too painful to accept.

I loved her, and she loved me.

All she wanted to do was push his words away, to unhear the raw, aching truth. But it sat there in the bruised hollow of her chest, unable to be ignored.

"She chose to stay," she said, surprised at the bitterness on her tongue. "She had the chance to escape with her pelt, with her soul, and instead she stayed with him."

"I never told anyone what happened that day," Duncan said. "Mara was my soulkith, my closest friend. I didn't want to tarnish her memory with her betrayal. By the time the scouts found her body in the Strait, almost a year to the day after I left her, I'd already made peace with the fact she was gone. I knew how her choice would end, even if she didn't."

"You didn't know," Isla said. "She *did* leave, in the end. She left for me."

As she spoke, the words tasted empty. It didn't seem enough. Nothing would ever be enough, now that the truth pared like a knife.

I loved her, and she loved me.

"She chose him," she whispered. "Before she left, she stayed."

When she gathered the courage to meet Duncan's eyes, she could almost see Mara's reflection in his gaze.

You remind me of her far too much, he'd said.

The realisation hit her squarely in the chest. *This* was why he'd never be able to accept her, why he'd never see her as anything more than an outsider. Her presence carried with it the far-reaching ripples of Mara's choice. The choice he feared she too would make.

"This is my home," she said, voice straining. "This is where I belong."

A rueful smile caught the edge of Duncan's mouth, and when he spoke, all Isla heard was the resounding knell of his disappointment.

"Time will tell, aineol," he said. "Time will tell."

CHAPTER SEVENTEEN

DARCE

Being back on dry land should have lifted a weight from Darce's chest. Instead, he felt more trapped than ever.

He'd stalked the barracks' hallways every day since returning to Arburgh, unable to occupy himself long enough to chase away the fear of what might be happening to Nishi and Kerr. Whatever torture the Grand Admiral was inflicting in his search for answers, Darce was the one who'd brought it on them. He'd told them to surrender, fearing for their lives if they'd tried to run.

Now, he couldn't help but wonder if they'd have preferred death after all.

This morning, the rain was ceaseless, pelting off the cobbles so ferociously it sounded like thunder. Darce could barely see the other side of the training yard through the downpour. His linen tunic and buckskin breeches were drenched, but he readied his sword for another drill.

The straw-stuffed pell in front of him had already taken a beating, but he set himself on it again, slashing the sack until it split. His fingers were numb, but still he hacked at the training bust, even as straw spilled from its innards into the puddles below.

He contemplated the mess, blinking away the water streaming into his eyes. It was easy, in the end. A heavy swing, the blade's edge bared at the right angle, and it was over. It was what he should have done on the *Vanguard*. He hadn't taken his chance then, and now it was too late.

"Was it something he said?" Rhona crossed the courtyard, face shielded by the hood of her woollen cloak. She slipped out one of her wiry, inked forearms to cast aside the puddles as she walked. The streaming rainwater dissipated before her boots, snaking through the grooves between the cobbles.

"Didn't give ye much trouble, I see," she remarked. "I have to say, I've never met another sentinel who takes his swordsmanship as seriously as you." She raised an eyebrow at his soaking clothes. "Or did ye forget you had magic?"

He grunted. "The tides don't always answer. At least a blade will be there when I need it."

"A blade won't solve all your problems either."

Before Darce could respond, another figure emerged from the drizzle. As his eyes fell to the sling around her arm, he remembered the tendrils of mist crushing her wrist on the deck of the *Silent Wind*.

"Mhairi," Rhona said, tight with disapproval. "You're meant to be on bedrest."

"Needed some fresh air." Mhairi lifted her face to the sky, grinning as the rain bounced off her skin. "Silvish winter, eh? Only thing more miserable is—"

"A Silvish summer," Darce finished, familiar with the old joke. "It's good to see you up and about, Captain Mackenzie. How is your injury?"

"Sore." Mhairi shrugged. "Broke my wrist in a couple of places, but I'll be on the mend soon enough."

Darce doubted that. He knew the touch of the gun-anam, the shadow it left on a person. Even now, he often woke with salt on his tongue, starving for breath, the walls of his throat icing over.

"There's nae need to rush," Rhona said. "We've been taken off the

Vanguard's roster, in any case."

Darce glanced at her. "You sound relieved."

Rhona folded her arms, rainwater trickling along the ink of her tattoos. Her dark-eyed gaze bored into him, carrying the same guarded warning he'd seen so often during their time on the *Vanguard*. But there was more to it than caution; it simmered with traces of what festered underneath.

Fear. Resentment. Anger. Feelings he knew only too well.

Mhairi cleared her throat, eyes darting between them. "In any case, I didn't come out here for a wee wander in the rain. I was asked to pass on a message to Sergeant Galbraith."

Darce stiffened. "What is it?"

"The Grand Admiral wants you to go to the garrison prison and verify the information he was able to...*extract* from the Sea Kith."

The hesitation in the tail of her sentence was enough to churn his stomach. "Are they hurt?"

"I'm just the messenger." A flicker of disquiet passed across Mhairi's pale features, but before she could speak again, Rhona stepped in.

"Ye have your orders, Sergeant. I suggest ye see them through. We both know what will happen if you don't."

Her words rang in his ears long after they left him to pack away his sword. Something wasn't right. There were too many secrets hiding under the surface, too many tacit warnings. If he was to have any hope of swaying the other sentinels to his side, he had to find out what it was, this truth they were afraid to speak.

He turned to the portcullis leading towards the garrison prison. Whatever Rhona was hiding, it would have to wait. For now, he had some old friends to visit.

The prison was buried under the garrison itself, carved into the cliffside. As Darce descended the steep steps, a fetid smell hit him: piss and shite mingled with the unmistakable tang of stale blood. The cells were bleaker than he'd imagined, their stone walls dripping with moisture, the narrow tunnels draughty with the sea air creeping in through the cracks.

He followed the guard to the end of the tunnel. The brazier on the wall did little to chase away the darkness here. The rocky floor was slimy underfoot, the air thin and musty. It felt less like a prison and more of a hole to die in.

The guard gestured to the cell at the end, and Darce edged forward, half-afraid of what he might find. The formidable iron grate across the mouth of the cell was rusting, with metal flakes peeling from the bars. Beyond them, he could faintly make out the outline of two figures inside.

"Nishi?" he said tentatively. "It's me, Sergeant Galbraith."

One of the shapes stirred, and a low groan echoed off the walls. Then came a sharp noise, and the other figure slowly approached the bars.

The light from the brazier danced across Nishi's face. Her cheeks were gaunt and thin, but the mottled bruising had faded and she didn't seem to bear any fresh wounds.

She leaned against the bars, copper eyes burning. "Fuck you."

"Nishi, I..." Darce drew back. "He would have killed you. He'd have sent the *Jade Dawn* to the fathoms, and all of you with it. I was trying to buy you some time."

"I don't want to hear it." She cast a contemptuous glare over the sapphire-trimmed cloak around his shoulders. "Look at you, wearing their colours, doing their dirty work. It's little wonder Isla refused to speak of you when I last saw her."

Her words caught him squarely. "You've seen her? Where? Please,

Nishi. I'd never give her up to the Admiralty."

"They already know. I told them."

"You…" Darce's mouth ran dry. "Why would you do that?"

Nishi pressed her lips together, the fury in her gaze as relentless as ever. Then, the other figure in the shadows stirred again and slowly crawled to the bars.

It was Kerr.

Darce blanched, the warmth draining from his face. Kerr's hair was matted with filth, his left cheek swollen around a nasty gouge weeping with yellow pus. He wrapped his hands around the rusting bars, revealing bloody stumps at the ends of his fingers, their tips ragged and misshapen.

When he tried to speak, only a garbled moan left his lips, and Darce saw the empty place his tongue had been.

"Tides," he whispered. "What did they do to you?"

"*This* is what you bought us," Nishi said coldly. "They didn't lay a hand on me. They didn't need to. For all his ignorance, the Grand Admiral understands the bond between sentinel and captain better than you." She narrowed her eyes. "You made an oath when you spilled your auld blood for Isla. An oath you broke."

"I didn't, I would never—" He shook his head, gut churning. "I didn't mean for this to happen. I was trying to protect you, like I'm trying to protect Isla."

"Protect us?" Nishi snarled. "*Look* at him, Galbraith! They call us pirates, brand us as savages, yet this is what they do in the service of those cloaks they wear. The same cloak *you're* wearing."

"It's not what it looks like. I'm working—" He glanced around, ensuring there were no guards in earshot before lowering his voice to speak again. "I'm working *against* the Admiralty. I'm trying to take Cunningham down before he gets to Isla. You have to believe me." He turned to Kerr. "I am sorry for what they did to you. Your suffering is on my hands, born from my mistake, and I'll never be able to make that right.

But you're a sentinel. You know what it means to make the blood oath. I could never betray Isla, not after what we've been through."

Kerr looked up, eyes glazed. There was none of Nishi's anger in his gaze, just a quiet acceptance.

"You *believe* him?" Nishi demanded. "After what he's done?"

Kerr gave a silent, solemn nod.

Nishi swore and moved back from the bars. The swirling patterns of her Sea Kith tattoos looked like scars in the dim light as she stared blankly ahead. The Admiralty jailers might not have tortured her like they had Kerr, but she carried the weight of it all the same.

"Isla was heading north, to the Drift," she said, voice heavy. "I told the Grand Admiral the moment he threatened Kerr. I am fond of Isla, but she is not Sea Kith. I don't owe her that which I owe my crew. But it wasn't enough. He knew as well as I did that by the time he readied a ship, she'd be long gone. So he asked me for something else, something I couldn't give him."

"What did he want?"

"The location of a place even we Sea Kith do not know. A place I've never once thought to seek out. The Selkie Isles." Nishi smiled bitterly. "Of course, my ignorance didn't please him. He tortured Kerr over and over, as if the sound of his screams would uncover some kind of knowledge I couldn't possibly have. Eventually, I told him the only thing I could think of that might spare Kerr. I told him he needed a guidebird to find such a place. He needed Shearwing."

Darce stilled. "Is that true? Could Shearwing find the Selkie Isles?"

"Perhaps. The tides have a will of their own, and those birds understand it better than we do. In any case, it convinced the Grand Admiral to keep Kerr alive." She shook her head. "Why did he send you here, Sergeant? Did you come to do his bidding, or your own?"

"Cunningham wanted me to confirm your story." Darce glanced at Kerr. "Maybe he wanted to show me what will happen if I go against him. It doesn't matter. I'm not giving him what he's after."

He stepped back from the bars, heart thumping with the rush of a decision made. He'd hesitated too long. Isla was being hunted like an animal. Lachlan slipped further away each day. Now, Kerr bore the wounds of his reluctance to act.

There could be no more hesitation. No turning back, whatever the cost.

"Hold out as long as you can," he said. "I'll get you out of here."

Nishi gave him a wary look. "And how do you mean to do that?"

"With help," Darce said, "from someone who knows a thing or two about smuggling Admiralty prisoners out of the capital."

The last time he'd visited Arburgh's undercity, all he'd been able to see was the inside of a musty sack as Muir's lackeys dragged him blindly through the vaults. He didn't know the path they'd taken. Finding his way back to the Eel's lair would be impossible using his senses alone.

Fortunately, Darce had other gifts to draw on.

He stopped at the bottom of the winding steps. Somewhere, far in the distance, the sea called to him. It whispered from immeasurable depths, its voice trembling with the rolling crash of waves, the scattering spray on the wind.

In his mind, he pictured the smuggler's cavern where he'd met Muir. The moisture clinging to the limestone walls. The brackish smell of sea-weed near the entrance. The echo of waves carrying through the tunnels. The sea left a mark—it left a trail to follow.

He gathered himself and started forward. The vaults were the dark underbelly of a city that was already dour enough. The crumbling re-mains of once-cobbled streets branched off into narrow wynds and dead ends, places a lost traveller would never find their way back from. There was no sun, no sky, no rain to wash away the filth, just a perpetual dusk clinging to each corner. The only light came from hanging oil lamps, and their glow only made the shadows darker.

The sea brushed his ears again, each wave a far-off, heaving sigh. Darce followed the sound through the murky passageways, unable to do anything but trust where it led him. Derelict tenements lined the alleys, occasionally interrupted by the odd boarded-up whorehouse or dimly lit gambling den. A pang of sympathy pulled at his chest as he caught a pallid, underfed street urchin peering at him from behind an overturned merchant's barrow. The vaults were no place for anyone to live, let alone a lad barely more than a bairn.

Eventually, he found himself in rockier tunnels where the ground was damp and the air sharp with salt. The distance between the glow of each oil lamp grew wider and wider until the light disappeared entirely. But it was not until he heard the crunch of broken glass beneath his boots that he realised it was no accident.

These tunnels had once been lit. Which meant somebody no longer wanted to be found.

He kept moving, trailing his hands along the walls on either side. The darkness was absolute—there could have been a man an inch in front of him and he wouldn't have known. All he could do was edge forward, each step testing the slick, uneven ground.

"Who goes there?" a voice called out from further down the tunnel, bouncing off the walls.

Darce cleared his throat. "My name is Sergeant Galbraith. I have business with Mu—with the Eel. He'll know why I'm here."

There was no reply. Darce crept closer, listening for whoever was ahead. The hushed whisper of the sea was stronger. He'd been here before—the sea spirits singing to his blood were proof of that.

A muted orange glow cast off the tunnel wall ahead, and Darce quickened his pace. He'd done it. He'd found his way back to Muir's lair, and with it, a chance to turn the tides on the Grand Admiral's plans.

He rounded the corner to see Muir in low, urgent conversation with a scrawny young man in serpenthide boots and a leather cuirass. When Muir caught sight of Darce, a scowl fell over his features.

"And here I hoped you were hearing things," he said to the lad, shoving him in the shoulder. "Go, get back to your post. And next time, don't ask questions first. Just raise the alarm."

The young man nodded, scurrying to the tunnels with red-tinged cheeks.

"Bloody tenderfoot," Muir muttered. "Lost too many old hands recently. It's bad for business."

He produced a tin flask from his waistcoat pocket, slurping down a mouthful of whatever foul-smelling liquor was inside. "And *you*..." He wiped an errant dribble from his chin, taking the opportunity to shoot Darce another glare. "What were you thinking, coming here? Are you trying to get us both killed?"

"I need your help getting some friends out of an Admiralty prison."

Muir gave a tight-lipped smile. "Is that all, aye?"

"Don't act coy. I know the Eel has managed it before."

"Is Alasdair still alive?" When Darce didn't answer, Muir snorted. "I thought as much. More than a month you've been away, with nothing to show for it. Meanwhile, the nets here are tightening. The Admiralty is closing in, and I'm running low on bodies."

"There must be something you can do. Those Sea Kith helped Isla. We owe them."

"I'm in no position to pull off a jailbreak. And even if I were, I'd be foolish to try it when Alasdair is on such high alert." Muir ran a hand through his braids. "We're running out of time, Sergeant. If you don't end this soon, we're both done for."

"You think I don't know that?" Darce said. "Not a single day passed on the *Vanguard* when I didn't consider striking him down. I couldn't risk it. Not with the other sentinels so close by. Not if it meant Lachlan paying the price if I failed."

"And what price do you suppose he'll pay if you do nothing?" Muir countered. "That lad will never be free. Alasdair will line his pockets with gold while he holds a blade to his throat. He'll use him to yoke you to the *Vanguard*, and as the years pass, you'll begin to justify all the things you're forced to do in his name." He shook his head. "I should never have let you walk onto that ship. You don't have the stomach to see this through."

Heat rose in Darce's chest. "*I* don't have the stomach? How many years did you stand by and do nothing when you could have acted? How many times did you stay your hand? All the things Cunningham has done, all the blood he's spilled—it's on your hands as much as his. But I suppose it's always been easier for you to look into the bottom of a bottle rather than a mirror, lest you remind yourself what you really are."

A dangerous glint danced in Muir's eye. "Watch yourself, Sergeant. If you think I won't—" He broke off, hand tightening around the flask. "Did you hear that?"

Darce listened, but he heard only the whistle of wind through the tunnels, the far-off lapping of the waves.

Then came the crack of black powder and lead.

Muir froze, a pallor falling across his dark skin. "You bloody fool. You've led them right to us."

Before Darce could speak, the thump of frantic footsteps echoed off the walls, and Muir's sentry stumbled into the cavern, a sheen of sweat across his ashen forehead.

"They're here," he managed. "They're coming to—"

His words died the moment he did. Darce didn't hear the second shot. All he saw was the stain blooming across the sentry's chest, the whites of his eyes rolling back as he sagged to the ground, blood pooling under him.

"Go," Darce said, turning to Muir. "You know these tunnels better than they do. I'll slow them down, give you a chance of getting out of here."

Muir curled his lip. "To what end?"

"The same as it's always been. To overthrow the fucking Admiralty." He grabbed a fistful of Muir's collar. "You told me of a time you were more than an eel of the canals. A time they called you the Cirein-cròin. It's time to stop hiding. Time to remind them why you were given that name." He released him with a shove. "Go. For Isla's sake. For all our sakes."

Muir hesitated, the deep lines of his brow furrowing. Then he gave a grim nod before disappearing into the shadows at the rear of the cavern.

Darce turned to the mouth of the tunnel. His hands yearned for the weight of his old claymore, but all he had was the blade the Admiralty had given him. He drew the rapier from his belt, readying himself for whoever emerged.

The only sound was his muffled heartbeat. Then came the slow, rhythmic clip of boots on stone, growing closer and closer until a tall, immaculately dressed figure rounded the corner.

Darce tightened his hand around the hilt of his sword. "You."

Nathair Quinn flashed a smile, the edges as sharp as a blade. "Really, Sergeant, what else did you expect?"

He looked too out of place to be real, standing in the cavern entrance with polished dress boots and a long-tailed velvet coat. His red hair was swept back, and he walked with the assurance of a man who knew no harm could come to him.

"I came close once before," he said, stepping over the lifeless sentry. "One of my men followed Isla down here after I fed rumours to her selkie friends about the Eel offering shelter to their kind. But he's a slippery bastard. Always on the move, always washing away his markers and shattering the lamps. I lost him that day."

"Looks like you lost him again."

"Indeed." His eyes flicked to the painted mural on the wall, taking in the wriggling body, the gaping jaws. "Though it seems I have more than enough evidence he was here, and you were with him. Even when I lose, I rarely come away with nothing." He whistled, and a young lad came scarpering from the tunnel to Quinn's side.

It was the urchin boy Darce had spotted in the vaults.

"Fetch the lieutenant," Quinn said. "There's something here he'd like to see." He sent Darce an amused glance. "You should pay better attention to your surroundings, Sergeant. These tunnels might belong to the Eel, but they've never been short of rats."

A moment later, Blair emerged from the darkness. He cast his gaze over Darce, expression stony. "I didn't want to believe it, but it seems you're making treason into a habit, Galbraith." He unclipped a set of irons from his belt and tossed them across the floor. "I'd be grateful if you didn't make this any harder than it needs to be. For Lachlan's sake, if not your own."

As he spoke, more footsteps rumbled through the tunnel, and a dozen more Admiralty officers spilled into the cavern. One by one, they lifted their muskets, barrels levelled squarely at Darce's chest.

It was over. He couldn't fight them. Running would only result in a shot burying itself between his shoulder blades. There was only one thing he could do.

He dropped his rapier, the blade clattering at his feet. Then he knelt and picked up the irons, fastening their metal jaws around his wrists as he met Blair's gaze. "Fuck the Admiralty and your charges of treason. I'm doing this for Lachlan, no one else."

Quinn glanced at Blair, his smile widening. "A most desirable outcome, we can both agree. As long as your uncle makes good on our arrangement."

"The arrangement was that you'd deliver us the Eel," Blair said curtly.

"And I would have, were it not for one of your own men getting twitchy on the trigger and allowing him time to scuttle off." Quinn shrugged. "In any case, I have delivered you something far more valuable. I have delivered you a traitor."

A look of distaste flashed across Blair's face. "You'll get what you were promised. A berth in the Admiralty shipyards for your merchant sloops, and all the dock security that entails. I expect you'll need it, with the Eel still out there."

He turned back to Darce. He had the same steely eyes as the Grand Admiral, the same proud jaw, but there was something boyish about Blair's features that once softened the similarity.

Now, they looked more alike than ever.

"I went in after you when you fell from the *Vanguard*," Blair said. "Not for the Admiralty, or my uncle, but for Lachlan. He loves you like a brother. Do you know what it will do to him to watch you hang?"

"I would have spared him this, if I could. I would have spared him all of it."

"But you didn't." Blair shook his head. "I hope it was worth it, Galbraith."

As he was led from the cavern, shackles biting his wrists, Darce peered back at the shadows. There was no trace of Muir, only the faint echo of the words Darce had tried to reach him with. A reminder of a better man he feared was lost for good.

I hope it was worth it, Blair had said.

The words needled Darce's skin. He'd failed Nishi and Kerr. He'd used up all his chances, run out of luck. Now, the noose waited for them all.

Hope, however desperate it was, was the only thing he had left.

CHAPTER EIGHTEEN

ISLA

Waiting for the scouts to come back to Caim was like waiting for a tide that refused to return to shore. The passing weeks stretched longer than seemed possible. Each day, Isla traversed the wooden bridges between the crannogs to visit the chieftains' enclave, desperate for some kind of news. And each day, she was sent away with only disappointment to accompany her.

"You know as well as I do how vast these waters are," Eimhir said, trying to reassure her. "Angus and the scouts need time."

"They need *me*," Isla replied stoutly, and Eimhir fell quiet again.

It wasn't just the resentment about being left behind, though that was part of it. Her soulskin ached for the sea—not the safe, windswept waters around Eileanan Selch, but the unending reaches of what was beyond.

"We don't even understand how the soulships work," Eimhir said. "It's one thing getting to the soulless realm, but what are we to do once we're there?"

They sat by the lochside, droplets of moisture clinging to their hair from the light drizzle. Isla took a bite of the half-eaten perch they were sharing, swallowing chunks of the flaky white flesh as if she were in her selkie form.

"I've been thinking about the haar," she said, wiping her mouth. "We know it carries the mist sickness infecting our people. But there was a time it was free from that corruption; a time it protected us. If we could somehow return it to what it used to be..."

"You won't be able to," Eimhir said. "Not as long as the gun-anam exist."

"What do you mean?"

Eimhir's gaze fell across the surface of the loch. "I remember how it felt when my pelt was stolen back in Arburgh. The salt gnawing at my skin, the shadow creeping in where my soul once was. If you hadn't found my pelt when you did, I would have surrendered to that anguish, that death of hope. The sea would have devoured my bones, and I would have rotted in the darkest reaches of the depths until I became one of them—one of the gun-anam. I had but a *taste* of that torment. Think how many of our people have succumbed to that fate. All that suffering, all that violent loss... It doesn't disappear. It has to *go* somewhere."

"The haar." Isla's voice was barely more than a whisper. "Our pain is what changed it. *That's* what is causing the mist sickness, driving selkies to mindless bloodlust."

"Aye," Eimhir said. "And that's why this will never end."

Isla reached for her hand, squeezing her fingers around Eimhir's cold skin. "That's not true. If we find a soulship—"

"Nothing will change." Eimhir's eyes darkened. "It won't stop the Admiralty hunting us. It won't stop them tearing our pelts from our backs to line their own pockets. It might slow the death of our people, but it won't stop it."

Isla stilled. Eimhir's hand was like ice, her pulse faint. "What are you talking about?"

"Our people's existence depends on us passing the most precious parts of ourselves to those who come after us. Our pelts, our blood, our bones—even our memories. Without the soulships, the gun-anam were stripped not only of their pelts, but of their purpose." Eimhir stared at her. "There is nothing left for them but vengeance and violence. That's what's infecting the haar. We can't save them from that kind of pain."

"You don't mean that," Isla said. "The first time we met, you told me you wanted to end their suffering. You said that without pain, perhaps there was a chance for us all to heal. I believed you then. I need you to believe me now. I'll ensure no more of our people suffer the fate of the gun-anam. Once we have a soulship, we'll cross into the soulless realm and find a way to reverse the haar's corruption. We'll end the mist sickness once and for all."

Eimhir met Isla's gaze, features softening. "I'm sorry, caraid. I fear I'm finding myself on the brink of despair too often in these times. Sometimes I wonder what I would do without you to pull me back."

"I'll *always* be there to pull you back."

Eimhir gave a weak smile. "You believe this will work, don't you?"

"It has to." Isla sighed. "I feel like the answer was always there, just out of reach. Do you recall the *Mistbreaker*, back in Kinraith? That bastard of a captain spilled selkie blood across the deck, claiming it would protect the ship. Strange to think he was so close to the truth, yet so ignorant of it."

"We selkies have long known there is power in blood, but that power is granted through sacrifice," Eimhir said. "The *Mistbreaker* was cursed the first time its deck tasted unwilling blood. Such things cannot be taken by force."

Her words were intended as a comfort, but Isla couldn't help the prickle across her skin. She pictured Duncan in the cave, the way he'd changed when she pressed him about her pelt.

"Do you think..." She swallowed, unsure whether she wanted to give voice to the fear. "Would Duncan ever—"

"Wait." Eimhir leapt to her feet. "The crannogs. Something is happening."

Isla followed her gaze. The interlinking bridges between the crannogs were bustling with bodies, busier than she'd ever seen them. From the shore, she could hear the disquiet, the air carrying the hum of voices over the water.

They hurried along the lochside and joined the crowd pushing over the bridges. Most of the selkies were gathered around the chieftains' enclave, and as they moved closer, Isla leaned in to hear snippets of hushed conversation.

"Didn't expect them so soon—"

"—still not said anything, either."

"Will they send someone to—"

Eimhir grabbed one of them by the arm. "What's going on? Is it the scouts? Have they returned?"

The selkie's eyes widened. "Not the scouts. *Sails.*"

Isla's heart stopped. Sails, here in Eileanan Selch. The one place that remained untouched by the Admiralty. The one place that should have been safe.

If they were here, it was over. It didn't matter that the rocks surrounding Caim were ferocious enough to tear even the *Vanguard of the Firth* to splinters. The Grand Admiral knew better than anyone how much a selkie needed the sea. All he had to do was set up a blockade around the island and wait for them.

Wait for her.

She shuddered, remembering the crack of the pistol in her hand, the red stain blooming across his shirt. She could have ended this. She *should* have ended it.

"I didn't kill him," she whispered. "But he's been haunting me ever since that day."

Eimhir slipped her hand into hers. "I won't let him take you."

Isla nodded, but the comfort of Eimhir's steadfast grip couldn't stop the lurch of her heart, the coldness seeping through her. The Grand Admiral had come for her, as she knew he would. She was the last living part of Mara. He would never let her go, not as long as he lived.

She turned towards the overcast sky. Clouds closed in around the summits of the surrounding crags, threatening rain. The storm petrels were stirring from their cliffside burrows, taking to the skies with low, chattering calls.

"They know when a squall is coming," Eimhir said. "We'd do well to take heed."

The petrels were specks against the thickening shroud, their trills muffled by the rising wind. As they flitted between the crags, their cries grew sharper.

Then, all at once, they scattered, disappearing into the clouds.

"What are they..." Isla stared at the sky. Something had spooked them—a black shape with huge wings and a flash of white in its belly. A shape she knew too well to mistake for anything but a giant razorbill.

Shearwing.

A dismal wail rattled from its throat as it circled high above the loch. The bird seemed agitated, flapping its great wings haphazardly as it passed overhead. If it had seen her, it gave no sign. It just swept around in another aimless circle before flying off over the crags once more.

Isla turned back to the selkie Eimhir had spoken to, her heart thudding. "The sails... Did you hear what colour they were?"

"Colour?" The selkie looked at her, bemused. "What should that matter?"

"Were they green? Did anyone see—"

"Stop talking," Eimhir hissed, pulling her to the side. Her expression was agitated as she stormed ahead, and Isla hastened to keep pace with the frantic length of her strides.

"What's wrong?" she asked, gathering her breath. "It's the Sea Kith that have found us, not the Admiralty. We don't have anything to fear from Nishi and her crew."

"We might have nothing to fear, but the Sea Kith do." Eimhir wheeled to face her. "How do you think Eileanan Selch has remained safe from the Admiralty for so long? If a ship enters these waters, it's already doomed to the depths. If the rocks don't get it, our raiders will."

"But the Sea Kith would never—"

"I know that, caraid. But Duncan and the other chieftains..." Eimhir shook her head. "They don't trust humans, and they have good reason. They'll never let them leave here alive."

Isla stiffened. "Then we have to get to them first."

The wry twist on Eimhir's lips might have been amusement or exasperation. "I had a feeling you'd say that. And I might have tried to talk you out of it, were it not for the fact that their presence here troubles me." She paused, brows knitting together. "Nishi wouldn't risk coming here without good reason. I would rather learn what that reason is than see them killed."

Some of the tightness released in Isla's chest. "Then you're with me?"

Eimhir smiled. "Always."

They slipped away to the sea cave, following the underwater passage through the cliffs to the open waters. Isla ignored the muffled patter of rain hitting the waves above and instead focused on the wooden hull in the distance. Her selkie vision showed her none of the green stain on the timber, but she knew the shape of it all the same. It was the *Jade Dawn*.

There was already a rope waiting for them by the time they reached the ship. It hung suspended in the water, its fraying tail strangled with seaweed as it drifted with the currents. Nishi was expecting them, it seemed.

Isla swam to the surface and shed her pelt, shivering as the shock of water seeped over her human skin. Her fingers were numb as she grabbed the rope, and she dug them in as the rope jerked upwards.

She spluttered out a mouthful of seawater. "They're not waiting around, are they?"

Eimhir looked up at her as she swung on the rope below. "Something is wrong. It's like thunder in the air, waiting to break."

Before Isla could reply, the rope slithered over the gunwale and she landed on the deck in a clatter of limbs. A pair of salt-worn boots slowly stepped into her vision, followed by an outstretched hand covered in familiar ochre ink.

She allowed herself to be hauled to her feet, then froze.

Eimhir was right. Something *was* wrong.

The Nishi staring at her was not the sea-hardened captain she remembered. Something had been stripped from her, leaving her cheeks gaunt and her gaze bleak. The brightness that once danced in her copper eyes had become haunted, and there was a tremor in her jaw that Isla had never seen before.

"We found you," Nishi said, voice heavy. "The tides haven't forsaken us completely."

A loud caw rattled through the air, and Shearwing swooped down. This close, Isla could see the dullness in its feathers, the despondency in the way it hung its neck. It looked at her with its beady eyes, then released a stuttering cry.

"Kerr?" she whispered, bracing herself for the answer.

Nishi shook her head. "The Admiralty has him. Or what's left of him, at any rate."

"He's alive?"

"Barely. It might be kinder if he weren't."

Her voice broke, so raw and exposed that Isla felt its sharpness in the air. That pain, that grief... She knew how deep that kind of anguish cleaved. Kerr was Nishi's sentinel. He'd given her his blood, his soul. For them to be separated like this... She knew how that felt.

"How did you get away?" she asked.

"We didn't. The Grand Admiral let us go. He even had his finest shipwrights repair the *Jade Dawn* before handing it back to me." Nishi barked out a harsh laugh. "I'd have sooner seen my ship sunk in the firth than leave that wretched city without Kerr, but I had no choice. He made that excruciatingly clear. That's why I'm here, Blackwood. I'd never have ventured into your selkie waters if it wasn't my sentinel's life at stake. The Grand Admiral wanted me to find you, to deliver a message."

Something in her tone turned Isla's blood cold. "What message?"

Nishi reached into the pocket of her long-tailed sailor's coat and pulled out a small mahogany box. It was a delicate thing, with carvings across the rich red-brown wood and shining silver clasps across the seam. Under different circumstances, Isla might have expected it to contain some exquisite gift, but when she took the box from Nishi, all she felt was rising dread.

"I'm sorry," Nishi said quietly.

Isla swallowed, her fingers trembling around the clasps. Then she slowly prised them open and lifted the wooden lid.

The first thing that hit her was the tang of stale blood. The rotting stench filled her nostrils, and she pressed her mouth shut to hold back the wave of nausea. Dark red stains bled across the silk lining the lid, and she let out a choking gasp as her eyes fell on the tattered lump of flesh nestled in the middle of the box.

It was an ear. He'd sent her a bloody *ear*.

"Who?" Her voice sounded unrecognisable to her own ears. It pulled tight, fraying at the edges, ripping her throat as she forced the words out. "Who did he..."

"It's your sergeant," Nishi said. "The Grand Admiral has him too. He said..." She grimaced. "He said you can return to Arburgh of your own free will, or he can keep sending you pieces of your sentinel until there's nothing left of him to carve."

Isla stared at the box, throat tightening around the painful lump lodged there. The ear was encrusted with dried blood, the tissue ragged where it had been crudely hacked off. It was difficult to accept that this grisly piece of flesh belonged to Darce. To have part of him within reach in such a cruel manner...

She snapped the lid shut, squeezing her fingers around the box until her knuckles turned white. "I'm going to Arburgh."

"Isla, wait." Eimhir placed a hand on her shoulder, brow creased with worry. "You need to think about this before you rush off so rashly. If you go to the capital, you'll never leave it again. He'll never *let* you leave. Remember what he did to Mara."

I loved her, and she loved me.

Isla pushed the thought away, chest hot with anger. "I won't leave him there."

"You would join him instead?" Eimhir shot her a pained look. "Please, caraid. If we lose you, we lose a future free of the Admiralty, free of the mist sickness and the gun-anam. Our people need you."

"Then take my pelt. I'll give it to you freely. I'll spill my blood across it, and you'll be able to claim it as your own."

Eimhir reeled back. "Don't. Don't *ever* say such a thing. How could I take your pelt, your soul, knowing what its loss would do to you? I remember the pain of the salt spreading across my skin, the ache of the sea abandoning my body. It would destroy all I am to see you suffer like that."

"Then you understand why I must go." Isla squeezed her hand gently. Eimhir's fingers were cold, all sinew and bone. "If I lose him, part of me will die too."

Speaking the words aloud brought a sharpness to her chest. She'd been unable to admit it to herself, this splitting of her soul, this agony she'd pushed down to a place she was afraid to look at. Now it rushed to the surface like a wound reopened, and there was no salve that would ease it. Not until she was made whole again.

Eimhir's eyes clouded. All Isla could see was the anguish in her furrowed brow, the conflict warring across her face.

Eventually, Eimhir nodded. "I understand. As long as you understand there is no place you can go where I will not follow."

"No," Nishi cut in. "You can't go to Arburgh. Neither of us can.

The Grand Admiral made it clear what will happen if Isla doesn't come alone."

Eimhir opened her mouth to protest, but Isla pulled her close, wrapping her arms around her. The damp fur of her pelt was indistinguishable from her own, the salty scent as familiar as her own skin. Eimhir was family. She was *home*.

She drew back and pressed a kiss against Eimhir's forehead. "I have no intention of becoming a prisoner. Arburgh will not hold me. The Grand Admiral will not hold me. I'll get Darce and Kerr out of there, and then I'll come back. We'll finish what we started, together."

Eimhir's eyes were pale and bleak, but she cracked her lips into a smile. "Fine words. If they came from anyone else, I might have a hard time believing them. But the tides themselves cannot sway you when you set your mind to something. Once your course is set, there it stays. I could not ask you to change it, even when it grieves me. I am proud to call you my cousin."

She drew back, turning to Nishi. "You should go. Eileanan Selch does not forgive humans who trespass in its waters. Our raiders will do whatever it takes to defend our home, and I won't be able to protect you if you're here when they arrive."

"I understand, selkie," Nishi said. "I hope one of these days, we'll meet in a place free from the shadow of the enmity between our people. We Sea Kith share more in common with you than that which divides us. We would sooner be your allies than your enemies."

Eimhir met Isla's gaze. "If that day is ever to come, we need you to come back. *I* need you to come back."

"I will. I promise."

She watched with a heavy heart as Eimhir leapt onto the gunwale. Her sea-soaked hair fell down her back, melding with the fawn-coloured fur of her pelt as she transformed and dived into the waves.

Isla dug her nails into the green-stained wood, staring at Caim through the veil of rain. Ever since she'd fled Silveckan, she'd called this place home. She'd even started to believe it. But standing at the prow of the *Jade Dawn*, she saw it for the first time through her human eyes. The grim, foreboding peaks. The roar of the spray as it crashed off the rocks protruding from beneath the waves.

If she lost her pelt, the island would not welcome her back as a human. And it would never welcome Darce.

"I can take you as far as the firth," Nishi said, breaking into her thoughts. "I dare not venture up the river itself, not when Kerr's life hangs in the balance. But we'll be waiting out there, Shearwing and I both. If you—*when* you get them out, we'll be there." She glanced up at the huge emerald sails. "This ship isn't the same without its sentinel, but the wind is on our side, and the crew is ready. That will be enough to get you where you need to go."

Isla nodded tightly. "Thank you, Captain."

Nishi headed for the helm, the click of her boots fading across the deck. Before long, the *Jade Dawn* would be on the move, and Eileanan Selch would disappear into the distance like a dream chased away by the harsh light of morning.

"I will come back," Isla murmured.

On the other side of the ship, the horizon waited in the distance, a grey line between sky and sea. Somewhere out there, Arburgh was waiting. The Grand Admiral was waiting.

Darce was waiting.

A memory stirred in her mind—a promise made on a distant shore. *If tides be kind, we'll find our way back to each other.*

The old adage echoed in her ears, stirring something bitter in the hollow of her chest. She'd long forgotten a time the tides had ever been kind. They were forever determined to separate her from those she loved. Lachlan. Darce. Eimhir.

Not anymore, she thought. No longer would she allow the will of the waves to steer her fate. She would sail into what was coming, and meet it head on.

She had no need for the tides to be kind, not if she became the fucking storm.

191

CHAPTER NINETEEN

DARCE

Darce awoke to something warm trickling down the side of his head, oozing from the place where his ear had been.

He pushed himself upright, dabbing gingerly with his shackled wrists. A sharp pain shot through his temple as he pressed too hard, and he snatched his hand away, fingers wet and bloody. The wound must have burst in his sleep again, ripped open on the cold floor of his cell.

Forgive me, Galbraith.

He closed his eyes, as if that could keep out the echo of Lachlan's anguished whisper. The words rattled around his head like they were trapped, unable to escape through the ear they'd been spoken through.

The ear Lachlan had taken from him.

The memory flooded his mind, refusing to release him from his torment. Lachlan's hand had trembled from the moment he reached into his boot and retrieved the shining blade of his sgian dubh. As he approached, his knuckles whitened, and the dagger wavered as he fought to hold it steady.

"Be brave, little laird," Darce murmured, so only he could hear.

Lachlan faltered. He glanced at the Grand Admiral, eyes pleading.

Every tendon in his neck strained as he waited for a reprieve that would never come.

Cunningham's face was like stone, his voice like steel. "You can take his ear, or the noose will have his neck."

The blade glinted as Lachlan moved closer, its edge sharp and wanting. Darce tried not to look at it; instead, he fixed his gaze on Lachlan. Sweat pearled across his forehead. His cheeks were ghostly pale.

"Forgive me, Galbraith," he whispered.

The blade bit against Darce's skin, sinking into the flesh between his earlobe and his neck. At first, all he felt was a rush of warmth and something wet dripping on his collarbone. Then the pain seared hot, and he bit his tongue to stop himself screaming. Lachlan's hand was reluctant, his grip quaking. Every fraction the blade moved brought with it a fresh burst of pain—skin stretching, steel forcing through sinew and cartilage.

A low, guttural moan ripped through Darce's chest, and then the pressure released. He sank back, the edges of his vision blurry.

Cunningham held open a wooden box, his expression hard and unblinking as Lachlan approached with red-stained hands. He waited expectantly for Lachlan to present the lump of bloody flesh he held in his palm, then pressed the lid shut with an irrevocable crack.

"The Admiralty commends you for your loyalty, Laird Blackwood," he said crisply. "I am all too familiar with what it is like to have one's own sentinel turn traitor. Take comfort in the knowledge that Sergeant Galbraith's misdeeds do not reflect on you. You have proven that today."

Even as the memory faded, the side of Darce's head remained ablaze, the air stinging the exposed mess Lachlan had left behind.

Forgive me, Galbraith.

Tides, he was trying. But all he had for company were the damp walls and his own dark thoughts. He didn't know how long it had been since they'd dragged him from the garrison and left him to rot here. Days? Weeks? All he could think about through the throbbing in his head was the flash of the blade and the look on Lachlan's face, haunting him like a ghost.

He must have fallen asleep again, for the next thing he remembered was the groan of the cell door jolting him from his dreams. He heaved himself up against the wall, his back aching from the cold floor. Outside the cell, there was only darkness, until the faint glow from an oil lamp cast away some of the shadows, followed by the familiar scrape of a crutch.

It was Lachlan.

He set the lamp down and bent awkwardly on one leg to slide a key into Darce's shackles. The irons fell with a clang, and Lachlan straightened, hand tight around his crutch as he looked away.

"I was ordered to bring you to the garrison," he said stiffly. "The Grand Admiral wants you made presentable for when she arrives."

"When who arrives?"

The pained look told Darce all he needed to know. Dread knotted in his stomach as the pieces fell into place. The blade, the box... It hadn't been to make him suffer. It was to lure Isla back to Silveckan, to a cage she'd never break free from.

Lachlan's eyes were firmly fixed on the wall as he angled himself away from him. "We should go."

"Lachlan..." Darce pushed himself to his feet, stretching his aching legs. By the time he'd hobbled to the cell door, Lachlan was already moving.

"Wait." Darce set after him, wincing as he struggled to keep up. "Tides take you—will you stop and look at me?"

Lachlan whirled around. "It's *you* the tides should take, Galbraith. How could you put me in that position? Do you think I wanted that? Do you think I took any pleasure in what he made me do?" His voice cracked, and he turned away again, cheeks flushing. "Don't ask me to look at you. Not when it means looking at what I did."

"It was the knife or the noose, little laird. You did what you had to."

"Just like Isla did when she let Eimhir take my leg?" A bitter smile curled at the edge of his mouth. "If I forgive myself for what I did to you, I'd have to forgive her, too. I can't do that."

"It's not about your leg. It never was." Darce grabbed his shoulder and pulled him around. "Isla took something much more important than that, didn't she? She took away being your sister."

Lachlan paled. "I don't know what you're—"

"The thing you can't forgive is her being who she truly is, who she's *always* been. Saltblooded. Unfettered. As wild as the wind and the waves." Darce tightened his grasp on his shoulder. "She is a selkie. As much as she loved you—loves you still—part of her belongs to the sea. You could never have kept her from it. Neither of us could. Your mother and father tried, and all it did was push her away. The Grand Admiral wants to do the same, even if it kills her."

Lachlan shoved him off, catching himself on his crutch as the motion tipped him off balance. His face was ashen, his fists clenched, but buried under the quiet fury in his eyes was a glimpse of the wounded lad who'd lost everyone he'd ever loved. A lad who lashed out when he was hurting, because those around him would bear it for him.

Before Darce could say anything more, Lachlan leaned down, reaching into his boot to retrieve the sgian dubh. Though the blade was wiped clean, Darce squirmed at the memory of blood clinging to it, the threads of flesh it cut away. Lachlan's hand had shaken around it, like it was shaking now.

"My father gave me this on my twelfth name-day," Lachlan said. "He said the sgian dubh was a special blade, that it had come to me so I could protect my sister. But it was just another thing that belonged to her, another thing I was never meant to have."

"Cormick didn't lie to you. It *is* a special blade. A selkie blade, touched by selkie magic. It cut Isla's cord. It quenched itself on her blood."

Lachlan narrowed his eyes. "How would you know such a thing?"

"Muir told me."

"Muir? But he's..." Lachlan frowned. "They recovered a body from the canals months ago. The jacket had his old sailor's pin attached. It was suspected he fell in drunk and never managed to climb out again."

Darce bit his tongue. He had to be more careful. Despite Nathair Quinn's best efforts, the Admiralty hadn't discovered the Eel's true identity, and if Muir was to survive, it needed to stay that way. Better for Lachlan to believe his uncle was dead than to be the cause of it.

"Isla spoke with him before she fled Arburgh," he said carefully. "He told her everything. Muir was the one who gave your father the blade. And Cormick passed it to you for a reason. He trusted you with your sister's life."

Doubt flickered across Lachlan's features. For a moment, he was within reach. If Darce could only grasp for him before the swell of hurt and grief carried him away again...

Lachlan shook his head, grip steadying around the sgian dubh's handle. "I never could live up to his expectations. Why should this be any different?" He held out the blade. "I don't want to carry another memory of the shadow I lived under all those years. If it was meant for someone who would protect her, you should have been the one my father gave it to."

Darce cast his eyes over the dagger. Its silver handle was engraved with a swirling pattern, and the small blade was flat and pointed, seeming too delicate to inflict any kind of harm. But he'd seen it save Isla's life. He'd felt it carve through his own skin. It knew how to draw blood. It knew to do what was asked of it.

He brushed his fingers over the handle, lifting it from Lachlan's hand. "If I'm caught with this, if they realise it's yours..."

A rueful smile tugged at the corner of Lachlan's mouth. "Don't worry, Galbraith. It's not mine. It never was."

He set off into the corridor once more, leaving Darce with nothing but the echo of his words and the smallest sliver of hope, balanced on the edge of a blade.

The garrison's main hall had always boasted a haunting kind of grandeur, but today it was made all the more eerie for how empty it was.

The last time Darce had set foot here, the pinewood floor was barely visible under the feet of dancing nobles. Now, it stretched uninterrupted from wall to wall, so untouched he could see the wood grain in each polished plank. The long table perched atop the dais was draped in silken finery and laden with enough food for a feast, but it presided over an empty room.

He ran a hand over his chin, shaven clean by one of the garrison's attendants earlier that evening. The ragged ends of his hair were smoothed and slicked back into a tidy knot at the nape of his neck, and he'd been dressed in a new linen shirt and a long-tailed coat of exquisite brocade. Sitting at Cunningham's right hand, he looked every part the loyal Admiralty cur.

And it would be the first thing Isla saw.

He leaned back in his chair, sinking against the velvet padding. The sgian dubh shifted where he'd tucked it into his sleeve, and he prayed the blade would not slip and clatter on the polished floor.

If Cunningham noticed his fidgeting, he paid no attention to it. His steely eyes were fixed on the heavy oak doors at the other side of the room. With each passing minute, the creases in his brow deepened. It was the first time Darce had seen a trace of unease in his hard-edged features.

There were too few of them around the table for the size of it. Blair sat on the other side of his uncle, his boyish curls teased and tamed, while Lachlan was further down, next to the empty chair awaiting the guest of honour. He kept glancing at it, jaw tight, as if he expected Isla to materialise before his eyes.

The only other presence in the room was the small retinue of Admiralty guards standing by the doors, far enough away so as not to intrude, but close enough to call on if they were needed.

Darce laced his fingers around the stem of the goblet and brought it to his lips. After living off the stale scraps he'd been fed in the cell, he couldn't help but savour the rich taste of the ruby-coloured wine, but he stopped himself from gulping down more than was wise. If he was to survive this night, he needed to keep his head clear and his wits sharp.

The grand oak doors at the hall's entrance stood silent and unmoving. Darce turned to Cunningham, unable to stifle the twinge of satisfaction on his lips. "What do you suppose will happen when they open?" he asked. "Do you really think Isla will walk happily into the life you want to impose on her? Or do you plan to keep her a prisoner like you did her mother?"

A vein pulsed in Cunningham's temple. "I suggest you hold your tongue, Sergeant, or I'll have it taken as quickly as I did your ear."

"You don't know her. If you did, you'd never—"

"Enough." Cunningham silenced him with a cold gaze. "Do not make the mistake of thinking you can test me without consequence. I can make you suffer in ways far more permanent than pain. I thought you understood that."

Darce stilled, the edge of Cunningham's words pressed against his throat like a blade. He was right. Lachlan might have been seated at the Grand Admiral's table, honoured as one of his captains, but that didn't mean he was safe. The threat hung over him, waiting to fall if Darce stepped out of line.

The low rumble of the doors opening broke him from his thoughts as a young officer in dress regalia strode into the room. "Grand Admiral. Your guest... She's arrived."

Darce stared, hardly able to breathe. Part of him desperately hoped for the officer to be mistaken, for Isla to be anywhere else in the world but here. But his body betrayed the truth in the sharpness between his ribcage, the seizing of his heart. He wanted to see her. He *needed* to see her.

Cunningham's hands flexed at his sides. "Send her in."

The officer moved to the side, motioning to the doors. Then, from the dimly lit hallway on the other side, Isla walked into the room.

A painful wrench pulled at Darce's chest. It had been close to half a year since he last saw her, but she looked the same as the day she'd left him on the shore. Her dark hair was twisted in a tangled braid, loose strands falling across her cheeks. The wet grey fur around her shoulders clung to her like a second skin, its dappled colours rippling under the light from the chandeliers.

She walked towards them barefoot, trailing salt water across the polished wooden floor. Darce willed her to spare him a fleeting glance, but she kept her gaze fixed ahead. It wasn't until she reached the table that she stole a look at his missing ear. Something hardened in her expression, and when she turned to the Grand Admiral, her sea green eyes held all the wrath of the waves in a winter storm.

Cunningham glared at the young officer by the doors. "I told you to see to it that she had everything she needed to be comfortable. You were to set up her quarters, arrange for clothes, provisions—"

"He did," Isla said. "I told him I had no need for any of it. I didn't come here for your hospitality."

She turned to Darce, and he saw the fierceness of the woman he knew. The woman his soul belonged to.

"I came here for my sentinel."

CHAPTER TWENTY

ISLA

Isla sat in the empty chair waiting for her, sinking into the velvet cushion. The table was resplendent, dressed in a sapphire brocade cloth and brimming with dishes she hadn't tasted in years. Dried figs stuffed with creamy cheese and dripping with sweet honey. Olive paste on hunks of crusty bread. Lemon-garnished octopus, thin strips of ham with juicy melon, tender cuts of venison falling off the bone.

A grotesque display of the rewards of the Admiralty's trade routes, with no regard for the blood spilled to create them in the first place.

She stared at her plate, unable to bring herself to touch the food piled there. The rich smells made her mouth water, but she pinched her lips and folded her hands in her lap. No matter how hungry she was, she wouldn't eat his food. Not now that she understood the cost of it, the selkies killed for refusing to give up their territory.

Lachlan sat beside her, eyes fixed determinedly on the table. His jaw twitched as he pushed around his food, refusing to look at her.

I was never really your family, was I? he'd said the last time she saw him.

The memory wrenched at her heart. All those years of bickering and playfighting in every corner of the estate, sneaking forbidden treats from the kitchens, huddling under the sheets when a storm raged outside. What was blood compared to that? What had they been, if not family?

She pushed aside her thoughts. The Grand Admiral was no fool. He knew what he was doing by bringing Lachlan here, having him sit by her side. He wanted her weak, wanted her vulnerable. If she didn't guard herself against it, he'd win.

Maybe he already has, a voice in her head told her. *He wanted you to come here, and here you are.*

She curled her hands into fists under the table. There had been no other choice. Not after what he did to Darce.

The remains of his ear had been cleaned and stitched, but that didn't stop the rage when she looked at it. The ragged flesh, the bloody scar... It was a reminder of the lengths Alasdair Cunningham would go to.

The Grand Admiral caught her staring and pulled his mouth into a disapproving line. "A regrettable necessity. I offered the sergeant a place on my ship, and he repaid me by turning traitor."

Isla bristled. "You had him mutilated to send me a message."

"By rights, he should have met the noose. He should consider himself fortunate he was more useful to me alive. I needed your attention, and young Laird Blackwood needed to prove his loyalty to the Admiralty."

She snapped her head towards Lachlan, stomach lurching. "*You* did this?"

He didn't answer. All the colour drained from his face, and his hands shook around the polished handles of the cutlery he was holding.

She turned back to the Grand Admiral. "And what would you do with my attention, now that you have it? Is there a point to all this violence, all this cruelty?"

For the first time, his expression faltered. The composure he wore like a mask faded, replaced by something softer, something she was afraid to look at. "If I have been cruel, it was only to spare you worse cruelty at the hands of the skinchangers. I needed the chance to speak to you without their influence, to make you understand there is a place for you here. *This is where you belong.*"

"Like Mara belonged here?"

He tilted his head. "You look like her, you know. You have her eyes. There were times I thought I might be content to drown in the way she looked at me, with all the beauty of the sea, and all its dangers."

"Yet you kept her from it." Something in her voice broke. "She loved you. She could have left, but she *chose* you. She would have given you everything, but there was a part of her you had to take for yourself."

"I made a mistake. I never should have kept her pelt from her."

A harsh laugh escaped her throat. "I don't believe you."

"I don't expect you to. I know the lengths to which your skinchanger friends will go to justify their bloodlust, their hunger for violence. It's no surprise their lies have taken root. But I have never lied, not about Mara. Not about you." He fixed her with a sombre gaze. "I didn't understand then, but I do now. I know what it's like to have the most precious part of you stolen."

Isla's stomach twisted. It would be easier if she could push his words away, dismiss them as the lies of a man willing to do anything to reclaim what he'd lost. But there was no cunning edge to his voice, no deception lurking under the surface. Just a confession of a mistake made, raw and laid bare.

I know what it's like to have the most precious part of you stolen.

His daughter. Her.

The thought made her want to dig her nails under her skin and rip out the parts of her that belonged to him. But there was no way to disentangle herself, no escaping what she was.

Aineol, she thought bitterly.

He stared at her. "Ask me about her. I'll tell you whatever you want. I'll tell you the truth."

An angry retort rose in her throat, but she swallowed it down. Biting back would only draw blood, and she'd learned where that led. She couldn't change what he'd done to Mara, to Darce. But she could use what he knew to give the selkies, *her people*, a chance at a future free from his violence.

"You..." Isla took a breath. "You said she saved your life."

"Aye, she did." His eyes crinkled at the corners. "I was thrown from my ship, and she carried me to shore. She breathed life back into my lungs. I knew from that moment I could never lose her."

"You could have stayed with her after she rescued you. You didn't have to go back to the Admiralty."

"Where would we have gone?" He laughed softly. "She dragged me onto a barren skerry off the Southern Reaches. There was no shoreline in sight. If a passing Admiralty ship hadn't happened upon us, I'd have died in her arms on that tides-forsaken scrap of rock."

Isla's heart thumped against her ribs. This was what she needed to know. Mara had been searching for the soulships in the Southern Reaches when she went missing. If she traced her steps, if she found the place she'd been scouring when she rescued the Grand Admiral...

Cunningham was still looking at her. "If she had only told me about you, things might have been different. I thought the skinchangers took her from me, and I never forgave them for that. By the time I realised the truth, it was too late." He shook his head. "Twenty-five years of spilled blood stands between us and whatever chance of peace there might have been. Mara is to blame for that as much as I am."

"She knew what you were. She gave her life, her soul, to shield me from it."

"And what good did it do?" He smiled. "At the end of it all, you're here, right where you should be. And I cannot regret the cost of what it took, no matter how high it was."

His words rang with years of grief and pain. There was no cruelty in what he said, no malice. That made it all the worse.

"My presence here was paid for in blood," Isla said coldly. "And not just selkie blood, either. The Sea Kith had nothing to do with this, yet you hunted them like animals."

"They're pirates."

"They are my friends." She folded her arms. "Enough of this. Before I hear any more from you, I want to see Kerr."

The entire room seemed to hold its breath. The only sound came from the rain hammering against the tall stained-glass window behind Cunningham's chair.

His hand tightened around the stem of his wine goblet. Then his shoulders loosened, and he motioned to one of the guards by the doors. "Fetch the prisoner. I shall not rob my daughter of the chance to say goodbye before his execution."

The table fell into silence once more. The lingering echo of *daughter* wound itself through Isla's head, laying claim to her, its tendrils taking root. She couldn't unravel it, no matter how much she wanted to. His blood ran through her as much as Mara's did.

That was why he would never let her go.

The thought sank deep, and she tried to push away the ripples of dread as the oak doors opened again and Kerr was dragged into the hall.

Her heart lurched. He was filthy, dressed in the ragged remains of his linen shirt and stained breeches. His flaxen hair was matted, falling across a face more gaunt than she remembered. A nasty scar ran across one cheek, the edges red and weeping with infection.

She pushed out of her chair and strode towards him. When she knelt in front of him, a slow smile stretched his cracked lips.

"The *Jade Dawn* is waiting in the firth," she said in a low whisper. "Nishi is here. She came for you."

I know, he mouthed. The inside of his mouth was black, a bloody stump in the place his tongue had been.

A cold rage spread through her as she rose. She buried her fingers in her pelt, but it wasn't enough to stop her arms from shaking.

"We are leaving," she said, voice rasping. "Kerr, Darce and I. If you've learned anything from what you did to Mara, you'll let us go." She flicked her eyes to Lachlan. "I would have you at my side, but I won't make your choice for you, not again. Whatever happens here is for you to decide, wee brother."

He stared at her, expression inscrutable.

"You're not going anywhere." Cunningham pushed his chair back, the scrape of it sharp across the wooden dais. All traces of his mild countenance faded, replaced by a familiar cruelty. The edge of his jaw, the steel in his glare... It spoke of a man who would not compromise. *Could* not compromise. "You are my child, my daughter. You belong here."

"I *belong* here?" The words left Isla's throat in a snarl, ripping free with a burst of satisfaction. He was not the only one who could drop the mask. He was not the only one with teeth to bare. She gestured to her bare feet, the dried salt streaking her arms, the dirt and sand beneath her fingernails. "Look at me, at the animal I am. Do you believe I *belong* here? Do you think these walls could ever be enough to keep me from the sea?"

He regarded her impassively. "Don't be a fool. You have no weapons."

"The wind needs no weapons. The sea needs no weapons." She pulled her pelt close, the dappled fur shifting as she walked back to her chair. "You invited me to your table making the mistake of thinking I am your daughter. I am not. I am everything you hate, and everything you fear." A slow smile unfurled across her lips. "I am the storm."

She wrapped her fingers around the edge of the chair and heaved its wooden frame into her arms. There was no time for anyone to react as she lunged from the dais and hurled the chair straight at the towering, ornate window directly behind the Grand Admiral's head.

The glass shattered, and the storm rushed in.

Cunningham stood as rain swept around him, the raging wind billowing his fine satin cloak. He didn't flinch. He didn't survey the damage she'd wrought. He just stared at her, hard as stone, fingers wrapped around the ebony handle of the pistol tucked in his belt.

But when he moved to raise it, he wasn't looking at her.

Darce, she realised, her blood turning cold.

She locked eyes with him, dread clutching her chest. But there was no alarm in his expression, no panic in his movements. He met her gaze, then shifted his arm to reveal a glint of silver up his sleeve.

It happened in a heartbeat. The tiny dagger slid into his waiting palm. His fingers tightened around the hilt.

Then he drove the blade into the Grand Admiral's neck.

CHAPTER TWENTY-ONE

DARCE

Darce wrenched the sgian dubh from the crook of Cunningham's collarbone, a river of red gushing from the wound he'd left.

He stood dazed, hardly daring to believe he'd managed to sink the blade into his flesh. Then Cunningham staggered and fell across the table, eyes wide as he clutched desperately at his neck. Blood spilled across the brocade, soaking into the fabric.

He'd done it. He'd fucking done it.

It only took a second for chaos to erupt. An outraged cry rose from the guards as they reached for their muskets. Darce barely had time to duck out of the way before a volley of shots tore across the room, peppering the walls.

Gunfire echoed around his missing ear, muffled and distant. He waited under the table for the barrage to end, eyes watering from the burnt stench of black powder in his nostrils.

A hand tightened on his shoulder, and he whirled around, raising the sgian dubh against his attacker.

Lachlan stared back at him, stricken. "Galbraith, what did you do?"

Darce lowered the blade. "What I had to. What I should have done on the *Vanguard*, the moment he threatened your sister. The moment he threatened you."

"They'll kill you for this."

Before Darce could reply, a shriek pierced the air, and Shearwing hurtled through the broken window. Lachlan backed away, dragging his crutch with him as the razorbill swept overhead. Its huge black wings flared as it circled the hall, beady eyes searching for Kerr.

One of the guards aimed with her musket, and Darce stiffened. "Watch out!"

The barrel exploded in a burst of smoke, but Shearwing was already banking sharply. It released a furious cry and raked its curved claws through the guard's chest, knocking her to the floor.

The gun fell, splattered with blood. It was only metres away. If he could reach it...

He slid around the corner of the table, stretching his fingers towards the barrel. Then came the familiar click of a hammer cocking as another Admiralty officer stood over him, pistol levelled squarely at his forehead.

Darce froze, waiting for the flint to spark, for the chamber to rattle. But something was happening. The rain gusting through the window gathered in a shimmering spiral, writhing through the air like a serpent. It encircled the pistol, seeping into the barrel...

Soaking the black powder inside.

The officer squeezed the trigger, but the gun only spluttered and choked. This was his chance.

Darce leapt to his feet and charged, tangling with the officer's flying fists as he fought to wrestle the pistol away. The man was broad and stocky, throwing his weight behind every blow. A punch collided with Darce's ribs, then another, knocking the breath from his lungs. He grunted through the pain and barged forward, throwing the officer against the wall.

This time, the pistol came loose.

He wrenched it away, then brought the handle around to crack against the officer's face. The blow sent the larger man sprawling to the floor, the bridge of his nose burst and bloody.

Kerr limped to his side, arms outstretched. A wry smile spread across his cracked lips as he let the ward drop and the rest of the water pattered to the floor.

He'd saved him.

Auld blood, Kerr mouthed. *Use it.*

Darce glanced at the gaping window. The call of the sea rose, stronger than ever. He could almost taste the salt on his lips, the chill in his veins.

At the other end of the table, Isla huddled against one of the oak chairs, shielding herself from an onslaught of gunfire. The lead shots bit through the sturdy frame, sending scraps of velvet and wood flying.

A memory flooded his mind. His hand wet and stinging from the gash he'd scored across his palm. The ice of her skin as he'd pressed against it and whispered a promise.

I was always yours.

Something welled inside him like the crest of a wave. He raised his arms, calling the rain to him. The droplets might have been stripped of their salt, but it didn't matter. They had come from the sea, and the sea had seen fit to answer him.

He twisted his wrists and sent a funnel of water at the guards. It slammed into them, rushing into their noses, forcing open their mouths. Their muskets fell in a clatter as they clawed at their faces, drowning in front of him.

Darce dropped his hands, ignoring the guards' frantic gasps for breath as he hurried to Isla's side. She was bleeding from a cut on her cheek, the end of a splinter lodged in her skin.

She tugged it out with a wince. When she finally met his eyes, she faltered, like she was seeing him for the first time. "Darce... I—"

Another gust of wind and rain roared through the window, sending shards of glass falling. A flurry of feathers shot past, and a moment later, Featherblade landed.

The gannet hopped towards him with a shrill cackle, then prodded at his missing ear with its beak.

"You bloody—" Darce hissed, clamping a hand to his head. "And here I was thinking I was glad to see you for once."

Featherblade hung its head, blue-rimmed eyes contrite.

"Don't give me that. You're only sorry you weren't the one to take it. Or is it just my fingers you have a taste for?" Darce reached out his hand. The wind howled, bringing with it the salt from the sea, a reminder of what he was. His blood sang with the call of the distant waves, and he felt their ripple in return.

Featherblade regarded him, then laid the crook of its curved neck across his palm and let out a low croon.

"I need your help," Darce said, scratching its head. "I know you won't like it, but I need you to fly to the sea caves and find the Eel, wherever he's hiding. Lead him to the docks, to one of his boats."

The bird squawked indignantly.

"We'll never get out of here without him. You have to make him understand. Snap *his* fingers off, if that's what it takes."

Featherblade glared at him like it was sizing him up for another jab. Then it gave a reluctant caw and spread its great white wings, departing through the window into the night.

"The Eel?" Isla asked, staring after it. "A guidebird? I don't understand."

He wiped a trickle of blood from her cheek, thumb brushing against her skin. All he wanted to do was let his touch linger, to hold her close enough to make up for all these months she'd been beyond his reach. "I'll tell you everything as soon as we're out of the Admiralty's grasp. But right now, we need to get out of here, before..." He trailed off, stomach turning cold. "Tides...no."

"Before what?" Her brow furrowed at his expression. "Before *what*, Darce?"

He'd been so focused on the guards he hadn't noticed the oak doors open. He hadn't noticed the two figures enter the room and stride towards the high table.

One of the *Vanguard's* captains. And a sentinel.

He staggered to his feet, hauling Isla with him. Cunningham lay across the table, eyes blank as Blair pressed his hands against his neck, trying to staunch the bleeding. Lachlan stood beside him, face ashen. The tablecloth was drenched in red. Blair's forearms were dripping up to his elbows. It should have been over. For any normal man, it would have been over.

Cunningham's head lolled towards the sentinel, blood bubbling from his lips as he formed words that wouldn't come.

It didn't matter. It was enough.

The sentinel was older than Darce, with flecks of grey peppering his long hair and dark brown beard. His eyes hardened as he reached for the scabbard on his belt.

Nobody noticed. Nobody moved. Not until the sentinel drew his sword and whirled around to plunge it into the unsuspecting heart of his own captain.

Next to him, Isla screamed. The sentinel pulled his bloody sword from his captain's breast, then turned to the Grand Admiral, muttering something Darce couldn't hear.

Another oath. This one twisted, perverted by the one he'd broken.

"We have to go." Darce grabbed Isla's hand, her fingers cold in his grasp.

"That's how he survived," she whispered. "They kill their captains to keep him alive."

"Isla, *please.*" He ushered her towards the window, knocking loose shards of glass free from the frame. "We have to get out of here while we still can."

She tore her eyes away, cheeks pale as she clambered over the ledge into the night. Kerr followed closely, his breathing ragged.

Darce turned back to the table. Blair's eyes were wide with horror as the Grand Admiral writhed and thrashed in front of him. Lachlan stood by his side, arm tight around his shoulders.

Their gazes met for only a moment, but it was all Darce needed to know Lachlan wasn't coming. Not if it meant leaving Blair.

You misjudge him, Galbraith. He's…he's not his uncle.

Darce swallowed. If Lachlan was wrong, he'd end up paying the price for Darce's treason. If he left him here…

"Darce!"

Isla's call swirled with the wind through the shattered remnants of the window. He couldn't wait any longer.

He climbed over the ledge, landing in front of Isla and Kerr. "Let's go."

Rain thundered against the cobbles as they ran, its relentless echo ringing through Darce's missing ear from every direction, making his head spin. All he could think about was the flash of the sentinel's sword and the life dimming in his captain's eyes. The poor bastard hadn't known. His own sentinel had driven his blade through his heart, and he'd had no idea it was coming. No reason to expect it.

It should be unthinkable, Muir had told him. *A betrayal of the soul. That should tell you enough about how much he has corrupted them.*

Streams of rainwater cascaded down the steep streets, rushing through the gutters. Darce's magic surged like the roar of the waves, granting him aid he didn't know how to ask for. Raindrops sprang free from his eyelashes, clearing his vision. Puddles evaporated before his boots reached them. It was like the tides themselves had rallied to his side, throwing their will behind him.

A piercing cry tore through the sky overhead. Shearwing was barely visible against the black clouds apart from the flash of its white belly, but soon Featherblade appeared over the rooftops, yammering triumphantly.

Both birds swooped down, flapping their huge wings as they led the way.

"Follow them," Darce said. "They'll take us where we need to go."

The Admiralty Bridge loomed in the distance, its grand stone arches rising over the river's mile-long breadth. On the other side lay the merchant docks. If they reached Muir, they might have a chance.

As they drew close, the rain hammered harder, bouncing off the vaulted wooden roof covering the bridge. The sound drowned out their frantic footsteps, muffled their laboured breaths. All Darce could hear in the tinny hollow of his ear was the roar of the storm.

Until the capital bell tolled.

Boom.

The deep, resounding clang brought him staggering to a halt. He knew that noise; he'd heard it months ago during the selkie attack on the capital. The brassy tones drilled deep into his bone in a sombre warning, a call to arms.

Isla faltered. "He's locking the city down. They'll close the bridge."

"Then we need to hurry."

He raced forward, leaping up the steps to the bridge. The roof provided a welcome respite from the wind and rain, and he took a moment to shake out his clothes. His skin shivered under the soaked fabric. Even the auld blood coursing through his veins couldn't protect him from the chill.

Ahead, two figures marched along the bridge, jewel-toned cloaks swirling behind them. Their tricorne hats sat low across their faces, but Darce noticed a sling around the arm of the shorter figure, and rolled-up sleeves revealing inked forearms on the other.

"Let me handle this," he muttered.

Rhona looked up from under the brim of her hat, eyes widening. Beside her, Mhairi reached one-handed for the stiletto dagger tucked into her belt.

"Don't," Darce said quickly. "The last thing I want is any more blood spilled tonight. Please."

Rhona stared at him, expression cool. "I heard ye'd been left to rot in the garrison prison. Either I'm misinformed, or you've managed to get yourself into deeper shite than I imagined." She flicked her eyes over Kerr and Isla, breath catching when her gaze landed on the rippling folds of Isla's pelt. "Sergeant, what have ye done?"

He moved in front of Isla, shielding her from view. "Listen to me—"

"She's the one we've been hunting, isn't she? She's the reason you joined the *Vanguard* in the first place, the reason you've been rankling under every one of the Grand Admiral's commands."

"Aye, she is," Darce admitted. "I'm not Lachlan's sentinel. I'm hers."

If Rhona was surprised, she gave no sign of it. Instead, a wry smile stretched across her lips as she surveyed Isla. "I'll wager you're more than that." She turned to him, humour fading. "What about the Blackwood lad?"

He opened his mouth, then faltered as grief and guilt constricted his throat.

This time, it wasn't just Isla who'd left Lachlan behind. He had, too.

A glimmer of understanding dawned in Rhona's eyes. "Shite. You...you should go. Quickly, before the patrols come."

"You want to let him leave?" Mhairi shot her a disbelieving look, fingers lingering on the hilt of her dagger. "Rho, he's a traitor. If anyone finds out—"

"We're outnumbered," Rhona said bluntly. She jerked her head at Shearwing and Featherblade, perched on the wall. "You've already got a broken wrist. Do ye really want to take on these nasty bastards, not to mention the two sentinels and a tides-damned selkie?"

Mhairi hesitated, dropping her hand. "Aye, I reckon you're right. But if we're letting them go, it's best we leave too." She backed away, watching them warily as she retreated towards the bridge exit.

"Thank you." Darce turned to the others. "Go on ahead. I'll be right behind you."

For a moment, he thought Isla might refuse. He recognised the stubbornness in her jaw, the flash of defiance in her eyes. But she nodded tightly and set off after Kerr, her ice-cold fingers brushing his with an aching touch as she passed.

He approached Rhona, lowering his voice. "There's something I need to know. You're a sentinel. You serve him. Do you—"

"Don't." She spat the word at him. "You were never one of us. You don't have the right to ask that kind of question."

"Does Mhairi know?"

Rhona stared at him. "I suggest ye get out of here before it's too late for both of us. And let me give ye fair warning, Sergeant—this is the only favour you'll have out of me. The next time we cross paths, I'll do what's asked of me. I can't afford anything less."

"There doesn't have to be a next time. The Sea Kith are waiting in the firth. You could leave the capital, and Mhairi too."

Something twitched in her face, a pained expression that might have been hope or anguish or both of them dashed together like spray on the rocks. "Is he dead?" she asked, barely whispering.

He shook his head.

"Then I can't leave." Rhona fell back, a rueful smile straining at her lips. "Tides be kind to ye, Galbraith, wherever you're going. At least I can take a wee bit of comfort now that I ken one of us has broken our shackles."

She dipped her hat and turned away, following Mhairi from the bridge into the street below. He watched them go, heart heavy.

He might have broken his shackles, but after what he'd seen tonight, he wasn't sure he'd ever be free.

CHAPTER TWENTY-TWO

ISLA

The familiar stench of gull shite and damp timber hit Isla's nostrils as they approached the merchant docks. Empty lobster creels lay scattered across the sprawling wooden jetties, rats gnawing at the scraps tangled in the nets. Coils of rope waited for the bustle of dawn, their knotted lengths draped in slithering fronds of seaweed. Over the years, she'd sailed from dozens of harbours like this one.

Never had she been so desperate to leave.

Above, the two guidebirds soared through the rain, taking turns to raise their mewling voices over the roar of the wind. Shearwing was the larger of the two, its huge black wings casting a comforting shadow as she ran. The other one, the gannet... It stayed closer, watching her as fiercely as Darce.

A painful twinge pulled at her heart, full of grief for the time she'd lost, the things she'd missed. She'd locked the pain of leaving him in a place she thought would no longer hurt her, only for the wound to burst open as raw as it ever was.

One of the birds cawed, and soon both were circling the mast of a small cutter moored at the end of the jetty. The boat sat rigged and ready for them, bobbing on the waves. As they approached, a cloaked figure climbed out, face shrouded behind a fur-lined hood.

Isla halted, but Darce's hand found her shoulder. "Don't worry. It's the Eel. He's on our side."

"You made a deal with the capital's most ill-reputed smuggler? How could you trust him to follow through?"

Darce grimaced. "Probably best you see for yourself."

The cloaked figure stopped. A weathered hand reached for the hood and drew it back, revealing white sailor's braids and an unblinking stare.

Isla drew a breath. "Muir?"

His eyes narrowed. "Of all the ways the tides have punished me over the years, their cruellest trick must surely be bestowing upon me a niece whose reserves of good sense hold all the depth of a rockpool. How could you be so bloody foolish as to come back after—"

She threw herself into his chest, cutting off the rest of his tirade. He smelled of leather and stale liquor, and as his arms tightened around her, she couldn't help the pang of realisation that this, too, was home.

"I thought you were dead, you crabbit old sot," she said, tears pricking the corners of her eyes. "I came to find you all those months ago, but all you left behind was a puddle of blood and that old compass."

"The blood wasn't mine. The compass, well..." He drew back, running his hands over the fur around her shoulders. "Looks like you know all about that by now."

He smiled, and something in her heart wrenched at the glimpse of a man she'd long forgotten. The lines in his dark brown skin seemed fainter, the glint in his eyes sharper, like from a time before the bottle took hold.

"You saved me." She choked the words out. "You helped Mara escape. You carried me away, out of his reach. All those years, I never understood why my mother and father wanted me to stay so close. I resented them for it. But they were trying to keep me safe."

"I made Mara a promise," Muir said. "Cat and Cormick would have done anything to help me keep it."

She wiped her eyes and tried to settle her breathing. "There are so many things I need to ask you, uncle. So many things I still don't know."

"Aye, I imagine so. The sergeant will be able to tell you some of it, but now isn't the time for answers." Muir gave a tight smile. "You need to get out of here."

Isla faltered. "You're not coming with us?"

"Not this time, lass. Not while I have a job to do." He turned to Darce. "You were right in what you said before. Seeing her only makes it clearer. I owe you my thanks." His mouth twitched. "And an ear, it seems."

Darce barked out a laugh. "You came through for us with the boat. Let's call it even."

She climbed into the cutter, hands trembling. It should have been easier to leave. Her people needed her. But as she gripped the edge of the boat, something inside her dragged like an anchor, unwilling to let go.

"Why stay?" she asked. "What's left for you here?"

Muir's eyes crinkled at the sides. "Dark be the water, and darker still the creatures that lurk within." He leaned over and pressed a kiss on the top of her head. "The Eel served his purpose, but there is no creature darker than the Cirein-cròin. It's time I reminded Alasdair of that."

The cutter peeled away from the jetty, rocking on the waves. As Darce and Kerr began to row, she remained at the stern, unable to take her eyes off the jetty. She'd thought her uncle a drunkard, then she'd thought him dead, and now she didn't know whether she'd ever get the chance to make up for the time she'd missed with the man he truly was.

With every stroke of the oars, Muir's outline grew more distant, lost through the veil of rain between them. When he slipped out of reach, Isla released a long breath, praying she hadn't laid eyes on him for the last time.

It didn't take long for the *Jade Dawn's* huge emerald sails to unfurl, setting the ship across the waves with all the swiftness the wind provided, and then a wee bit more. Darce and Kerr stood on opposite sides of the prow, casting wards to call the tides to their will. The swell rose eagerly at the beckoning of their magic.

"They'll give us a head start, at least," Nishi said. "But I've seen the *Vanguard* up close. I know the speeds that monster can reach with its army of sentinels on board. It's only a matter of time before they hunt us down."

"Can't we lose them? They don't know our heading."

Nishi's copper eyes flitted to the prow. "Kerr's wounds will be slow to heal. Your sergeant still bleeds, too. The moment one of the Grand Admiral's sentinels gets a whiff of their auld blood, they'll be able to find us."

"Then what can we do?"

"The only thing left." A fierce smile danced on Nishi's lips. "We find a storm, and pray to the tides only one of us sees the other side of it."

Isla followed her gaze. If Nishi was seeking a storm, she wouldn't have to sail far to find it. The clouds had only grown darker since leaving the firth, and the wind had picked up, sending spray flying across the deck every time the ship pitched over the waves. Tension closed in as the air became stale and oppressive.

There might have been a time she'd feared the horizon turning black. Now, she welcomed it.

Shearwing and the huge snow-white gannet flew alongside the ship, screeching as they chased each other over the waves. Every so often, one of them would plunge beneath, disappearing for a few seconds before bursting through the surface. Something about their playful squabbling lifted the shadow across Isla's heart, and she couldn't help but laugh.

Nishi quirked an eyebrow. "You wouldn't be so amused if they were really fighting. I've seen the mess such a scrap can leave. At least Featherblade is friendly. We were picking feathers from the deck for weeks the last time Shearwing got on the wrong side of another guidebird."

"Why would another guidebird attack Shearwing?"

"The Sea Kith are bound by the life we chose, a life on the sea, but not all of us sail the same way." Nishi shrugged. "There's a reason some call us pirates. Others call us guardians. No two Sea Kith ships are the same. Sometimes we quarrel like any family."

Isla turned back to the birds. Featherblade's wings cut a stark shape against the clouds as it soared high, cackling over the wind. "How is it that Darce was able to bond with one of them? He's not Sea Kith."

"Guidebirds seek out those who are lost," Nishi said. "Most sentinels in the capital know exactly who they are. Or, at least, who holds their chain. They've never needed help from the sea to find themselves."

Below, a huge wave crashed over the prow as the *Jade Dawn* lurched, soaking Darce with spray. The droplets streamed across his skin as he continued casting his wards, fingers flexing to the ebb and flow of the swell. She'd never realised how much it suited him out here—his hair slick with seawater, the wind whipping up the loose strands at the nape of his neck.

"I once told him he was trying too hard to be my anchor," she said. "It's strange to think of him ever being lost. He was always so...steady."

"It's no easy thing to be separated from part of your soul. You should know that better than most." Nishi shifted her hands on the wheel. "I thought your sergeant sold us out to the Admiralty. I blamed him for what happened to Kerr. But he was willing to live as a slave to keep you out of the Grand Admiral's reach."

Heat rushed to Isla's cheeks. "I told you before, he's not *my* sergeant."

Nishi snorted. "I didn't believe you back then, and I certainly don't now. If it wasn't for us needing his magic on deck, I'd wager the two of you would be—"

A low rumble of thunder echoed across the waves. The air had gone still. Shearwing and Featherblade fell quiet, their quarrel forgotten as they fled to their perches. Isla held her breath as the seconds ticked by, each longer than the next. Then a blinding light illuminated the storm clouds in the distance.

The gold ring in Nishi's lip glinted wickedly as she stretched her mouth into a grin. "About bloody time."

She spun the huge wooden wheel through her hands as she barked orders to the *Jade Dawn's* crew. Deckhands scrambled up the rigging and hauled in the sails, stowing them where the savage winds couldn't rip them to shreds. Metre by metre, the green canvas shrank and folded away, until it was only the swell carrying them.

Darce left his position at the ship's bow and climbed the stairs to the quarterdeck. "You're sure this is necessary?"

"We don't have much choice." Nishi nodded towards the starboard side of the ship. "Look."

It took Isla a moment to notice anything. The night was dreich, the clouds hanging so low they clung to the crests of the waves.

Then she saw it. A shape darker than the storm. Three masts rising tall, disappearing into the clouds. Black sails billowing furiously in the wind.

The *Vanguard of the Firth*.

"How?" she whispered. "How did he manage to catch us?"

"He'll leave nothing to chance, not when it comes to you," Darce said. "That ship was fully rigged and ready to go as soon as he gave the order. Part of him knew you would run."

"He should be dead."

"You saw what happened back there. We both know how powerful the sacrifice of auld blood can be." He moved closer, hand flexing as if he were about to reach for her. Then he stilled, leaving her with nothing but the ghost of a touch that never came. "He's coming. I don't know what kind of state he'll be in, but he's coming all the same."

Nishi scowled. "That ship is an abomination. No vessel so large should be able to sail so swiftly. I'll wager there are more than a hundred cannons on that thing, yet it slices through the waves as fast as a sloop."

"We don't have to worry about the cannons. Not this time," Darce said. "Cunningham has too much to lose."

Isla glanced at him. "You speak as if you know him."

"I do. Better than I'd like." A shadow fell across his face, and he looked away. "They'll board us. And when they do, he'll come straight for you."

"But first, they must board us," Nishi said. "And I don't intend to make that easy for them. The tides will show them no mercy if they follow us into the squall. The depths will feast on their timber tonight."

"Or ours," Darce pointed out.

"You doubt the *Jade Dawn* can survive a storm, after everything you've seen?" Nishi shot back. "You asked me to trust you, Sergeant. I'm asking you to do the same."

She hauled the wheel around again, and the *Jade Dawn* answered, leaning into the wind as she guided it towards the tempest creeping closer across the waves.

"Everyone to their posts," she called over the wind. "Let them try to catch us, if they dare."

Isla moved alongside one of the Sea Kith deckhands and wound her fingers around the rigging, bracing for what was to come. The water turned dark, frothing angrily as it battered the hull with all its weight. Spray washed over the deck as the *Jade Dawn* pitched harder, its prow crashing into the ever-deepening troughs between the waves. The only sound she heard over the wind's roar was the yelling between the crew as they worked to secure ropes around anything loose on deck.

Nishi stood above it all. Her woollen coat was drenched from the rain, her black hair gathering around her shoulders in slick coils. She grinned, greeting the storm like an old friend.

"Hold steady," she yelled. "The fathoms are hungry, but I don't intend to let them feed."

The waves were relentless, crashing over the deck. Isla could barely see more than a metre in front of her. They were in the thick of it, suffocated by the storm closing in.

A shout came from above, and Isla lifted her head towards the crow's nest. The *Jade Dawn's* spotter clung to the rigging as the wind raged. He gestured frantically with his spyglass and yelled again, and this time, she caught his words.

"Ship on our starboard approach!"

The *Vanguard* hadn't given up its chase. It had followed them into the squall.

"Admiralty bastards!" Nishi wrestled with the wheel, her feet slipping against the sea-soaked deck. "We can't let them get broadside. If they board us, it's over. I won't let the *Jade Dawn* fall into their salt-forsaken grasp again."

The masts creaked as the ship rolled steeply. Isla sucked in a breath before a monstrous wave crashed over the side, sweeping her feet from underneath her. She squeezed her eyes closed and dug her fingers around the rope she was clutching, praying her grip wouldn't fail. The sea held no danger for her, but if she fell, she might not make it back on board. She couldn't leave the *Jade Dawn* to the Admiralty. Not when it was her they were after.

When she opened her eyes again, the wave had cascaded across the deck. She spat out a mouthful of salt water and filled her lungs, noticing the deckhand next to her was gone, swept into the sea.

Guilt pulled tight in her stomach. Even if they managed to slip free, what would it cost?

A roar of thunder filled her ears, making her wince. Less than a second later, a blinding flash lit up the clouds.

The *Vanguard of the Firth* towered over them.

Nishi stared up at it with grim resignation. "Prepare for boarders."

Isla released her hold on the line and ran to one of the weapons racks.

It had already been picked to the bone, but a small axe stood propped up in the corner. It wouldn't cleave a skull in two, but she'd be able to cut through any grappling lines the Admiralty threw.

"There's still time to run."

She turned to find Darce in front of her. He was dressed in the Admiralty finery they'd forced him into, shimmering cuts of teal and sapphire trimmed in gold. She might have forgotten he was on their side, were it not for the fierce ache that squeezed every time she looked at him.

He moved closer, and the rain streaming over her face trickled away. The brush of magic sent a shiver scurrying down her spine. She'd forgotten what it was like to be this close to him, to feel the stirring of the part of himself he'd given her.

"You can run," he said again. "Return to your selkie form and get away while you can. We'll buy you the time you need."

She shook her head. "I won't leave you, not again."

A pained smile crept across his lips. "Tides take me for my selfishness, but part of me hoped you'd say that."

He closed the distance left between them. Rain lashed down, but not a drop touched her skin. He was shielding her, protecting her like he always did. Like he'd done ever since she could remember.

She closed her eyes as he reached for her, his fingers winding to the nape of her neck.

"I want you to stay," he said, low and rasping. "I will *always* want you to stay."

His hand tightened in her hair, then fell away. When she opened her eyes again, he'd stepped back, his jaw clenched as he turned to the gunwale.

"Darce, wait. What's—"

She stopped short as something whistled through the air. Then came the *thunk* of iron biting into timber, and the teeth of a grappling hook latched over the wooden edge.

Darce moved before she could, slashing his cutlass through the rope trailing from the end of the hook. He'd barely stepped away when another metal claw shot through the air, this one landing against the deck before finding its mark around the gunwale.

He eyed the axe in her hand. "I recall you telling me you preferred pistols."

A reluctant smile tugged at the corner of her lips. "A pistol wouldn't do me much good in this rain. I might get one shot away, if I'm lucky."

"At least they'll be without their muskets, too," Darce said. "With the way this storm is blowing, the *Vanguard's* sentinels will have bigger things to focus on than drying out black powder."

The deck swayed, tilting to the starboard side as more grappling hooks sank into the railings, pulling the *Jade Dawn* towards the looming shadow alongside it. Through the rain, Isla could make out the huge frame of the *Vanguard's* hull, the rows of gunports hiding cannons. If the Grand Admiral wanted, he could turn them into scraps of flotsam in a single barrage.

She locked eyes with Darce. "If they take me..."

"They won't." He readied his blade. "You'd best get ready to use that axe. They're coming."

The first boarder was an Admiralty officer with a scar across the bridge of her nose and a fishknife between her teeth. She threw the knife at Darce, who scrambled out of the way. Then she turned to Isla, mouth splitting into a broken-toothed smile as she registered the pelt around her shoulders.

"You're the one he wants," she said. "The tides must favour me, to place you right in my path."

She lunged, reaching for a handful of pelt. Isla jumped back and swung with her axe, catching the woman across the cheek.

The officer pressed a hand to her face, then reached into her belt and drew a sabre. "Careful, lass. I'm sure he'll forgive me for making you bleed a little, as long as he gets you back."

Isla answered with another swing of her axe. The older woman brought her blade to meet it, snarling as she parried the blow. A second later, a bright red line scored Isla's knuckles. She hissed as the sea spray stung the wound, lifting her axe just in time to fend off another strike.

The impact jolted through her arm, knocking her off balance. She stumbled to regain her footing on the slippery deck, and the officer's smile grew wider as she advanced again, blade levelled at Isla's throat.

Then, suddenly, she stopped. Her eyes widened, a trickle of blood spilling from her mouth.

That was when Isla noticed the steel protruding from the officer's chest.

Darce stepped out from behind her, pulling his cutlass free with a fluid motion. The woman fell, blood pooling under her body.

A cry rang out further down the ship, lost to the roar of the wind. More Admiralty cloaks clambered over the side, spilling onto the *Jade Dawn's* deck in a whirl of teal and sapphire. Blades flashed. Bodies fell. The water streaming underfoot turned red as it seeped through the cracks into the ship's belly. Even the rain wasn't enough to wash it away.

More blood. More death. All because of the man who called himself her father.

On the quarterdeck, Nishi grappled with a burly man holding a dagger to her neck. Nearby, Kerr ducked away from the jab of a spear as he twisted his fingers into wards. There was only so long they could hold out against the sheer numbers of the *Vanguard's* crew. The Sea Kith would be slaughtered, and she...she would be taken.

One of the ropes pulled taut under the weight of another boarder, and Isla readied her axe for whoever was next to climb over.

A wiry arm appeared, bare skin pale and streaked with water. Isla rushed forward with her axe raised as the sea-soaked figure tumbled onto the deck in a blur of blonde hair and fawn-coloured fur.

She stopped mid-swing, heart hammering. "Eimhir?"

Eimhir rose to her full height, grinning behind the huge axe clamped between her teeth. She removed the haft from her jaws to spit seawater onto the deck, lips quirking. "You were expecting to repel me with *that?*"

"I wasn't expecting you at all." Isla dropped her arm and pulled her into a hug rich with the familiar scent of salt and sodden fur. "What are you doing here?"

"I came for you, of course." Eimhir gestured down the deck. "We all did."

Isla followed her gaze. The Sea Kith and the Admiralty were locked in a violent tussle, blades flashing, blood splattering across the deck. But there were others in the fray—swift-moving shapes with bare arms and lean shoulders, armed with daggers and axes. They danced across the deck, trails of water dripping from pelts of every colour, from glistening white to the richest brown.

The selkies had come for her. *Her people* had come for her.

Something in her heart seized, and she turned to see Eimhir smiling. "You think we would leave you to face this on your own? Even Duncan is here."

Isla spotted him in the middle of it all, the black folds of his pelt rippling like the night's reflection in the waves. He moved with purpose and power, offering no quarter to the Admiralty officers surrounding him.

One darted forward, opening a gash across Duncan's golden-brown skin. Duncan didn't flinch. In a single movement, he shot his hand out and grabbed the officer by the throat, lifting him up until his feet were writhing above the deck. The officer clawed at his arms, but it was no use. Duncan snarled and hurled him into the roiling water below.

He met her gaze, expression hard. "I'd ask you to come with us to safety, but I fear I already know what your answer would be."

"You do."

He curled his lip. "They are humans. You would choose them over your own people?"

"They are my people too," Isla said fiercely. "I won't abandon them, not when their lives are threatened because of me."

"And what about your life? Have you forgotten what's at stake, what we stand to lose?"

"How could I forget? I carry it with me everywhere I go. I feel its weight around my shoulders in the memories Mara passed to me." She gestured to her pelt, fingers tightening around her axe. "You fear I'll follow in her wake, make the same choices she did. But I am not her. I will chart my own course. I will take us where we need to go, as soon as my friends are safe."

Duncan stared at her, water dripping from his coiled hair as his shoulders heaved with ragged breaths. It was impossible to read anything in his umber eyes, but they terrified her all the same.

His mouth pulled into a grim line. "You know what will happen if we fight here. What it will cost."

The weight of his words hung in the air between them. He didn't need to say anything more.

"Aye." She swallowed, her skin prickling with a ghostly chill. "I know it all too well."

CHAPTER TWENTY-THREE

DARCE

The *Vanguard's* black hull towered over the starboard deck, blocking out the horizon. All Darce could see was the dark timber, the hatches of the gunports, the rigging rising into the clouds. Both ships were locked together, tangled in a bloody embrace with grappling lines and gangways stretching from deck to deck. Every so often, some poor sod trying to traverse between them would slip and fall, swallowed by the churning waves.

He slipped away while Isla was locked in tense conversation with Eimhir and the other selkies. It would do neither of them any good if she followed him. All that mattered was keeping her out of the Grand Admiral's reach long enough for Darce to finish what he'd started.

The gangway shuddered, making his stomach lurch. He edged forward, willing the timber to hold steady. This time, he wouldn't be able to rely on Blair to save him if he fell. Not after what he'd done.

He reached the end and staggered onto the *Vanguard's* heaving deck. Several Sea Kith had made the perilous venture over as well, putting the Admiralty officers on the back foot by taking the fight to their ship. The same rotten smells hung in the air as on the *Jade Dawn*: the copper tang of spilled blood, the reek of loosed bowels and pissed breeches.

Nobody was winning this fight. Nobody would gain anything from it.

He spotted Lachlan locked in a frantic tussle with a Sea Kith gunner Darce had spoken to a few times on the *Jade Dawn*. He rushed over to separate them, holding up his hands in surrender as the gunner turned on him instead. "Easy, friend. This one isn't the enemy."

"You sure about that?" The Sea Kith sent Lachlan a dirty look and spat on the deck.

"Please. Let me take care of this."

The man gave a begrudging nod, retreating towards the same gangway Darce had come over.

"What are you doing, Galbraith?" Lachlan was breathing heavily, holding his sword in one hand and the handle of his crutch in the other. Purple shadows ringed his eyes, and there was a desperation on his face Darce hadn't seen before.

"Exactly what it looks like, little laird. Pulling your arse out of trouble, just as I've always done."

Lachlan scowled. "You think I'm in need of your assistance? You're the one who's going to get yourself killed. I can't believe you had the nerve to come back to this ship after—"

He broke off, flinching, and Darce felt the cool kiss of a blade under his chin. The edge bit against his skin, promising to draw blood if he moved an inch.

"Draw your sword, Sergeant." Blair's voice was cold at his ear. "As much as I crave your death, I won't dishonour myself by killing an unarmed man, even if he is a traitor."

Darce turned slowly, hand drifting to his cutlass. "I have no wish for this to turn ugly between us."

"It's a wee bit late for that, don't you think?" Blair choked out a laugh. "Now *draw your sword*. I won't ask you again."

"Blair, wait—" Lachlan's voice was lost to the clatter of steel as Darce raised his cutlass and Blair lunged to meet it. The young lieutenant was swift and strong, and Darce's arm rattled with the impact after fending off the blow. He sidestepped neatly out of the way and countered with a slow, deliberate riposte, giving Blair enough forewarning to parry it easily.

"I don't want to fight you," he said. "I've never considered you my enemy."

"Then you've done a piss-poor job of showing it." Blair's face contorted as he pushed forward again, narrowly missing Darce's ribs with a well-aimed thrust. His eyes burned bright with anger as he parried another of Darce's half-hearted attempts. "You tried to kill my uncle."

"But I didn't succeed, did I? You witnessed what happened as much as I did, yet you still refuse to see him for what he is." Darce ducked under a wild swing and slashed back, ripping open Blair's sleeve with the edge of his cutlass. "Do you have any idea what it would take for a sentinel to turn on their captain? He's corrupted them. He's perverted their oaths so he has a steady supply of bodies to keep himself alive."

Blair drew back, touching his hand to his torn sleeve. His fingertips came away bloody. "Every sentinel knows what might be asked of them one day. They choose to serve on the *Vanguard*. It is an honour."

"Do you really believe that? If your uncle told you to spill Lachlan's blood to save his life, would you do it?" Darce glanced at Lachlan. "Could you trust him not to follow that order, or would you find it an *honour* to die for the Grand Admiral too?"

Lachlan turned ashen. "Galbraith, stop."

"If you think I'd leave you in the hands of someone who would gladly carve you up and offer you to that bastard on a damned plate—"

His head snapped back, and he tasted blood. It took him a moment to realise Blair's sword had clattered to the deck, and the throbbing in his cheek had come from the lieutenant's bare knuckles.

Blair wrung out his fist, his breathing ragged. "I would *never*," he said, quavering with rage. "He is—you don't—"

"Enough." Lachlan stepped between them. "Whatever our grievances are, this isn't the time to act on them." He grabbed Darce, gaze unyielding. "You should get back to the *Jade Dawn* before it's too late. No matter what has happened, I don't want to see you die here."

Darce opened his mouth to retort, then froze. An unnatural hush fell across the ship. Admiralty officers stopped in their tracks to crane their necks towards the quarterdeck, where a pale, ghostly figure emerged from the shadows.

Tides, it was him. Cunningham had risen already.

The brim of his hat was pulled low, but Darce could still see his hard-edged features. His skin was pallid, stretched over his bones like he was a walking corpse. The veins underneath looked black against his pallor, snaking across his cheeks and under his eyes. As he surveyed the deck with pursed lips, the gaping wound on the side of his neck fluttered open like it was trying to breathe.

Darce's stomach twisted. He'd plunged the blade into Cunningham's flesh and watched as the blood poured over his hands, staining his skin with the reminder of what he'd done. It should have killed him. It would have killed any normal man. But no blood ran from the gash now. It had run dry, leaving only a ragged hole behind.

It wasn't right. It wasn't *natural*. The Grand Admiral's survival was a second chance bought with an unwilling sacrifice. How many more would die for him before this was over?

He turned back to Lachlan, who was staring up at the quarterdeck with a stricken expression. "Come with me. Let us be done with this."

Lachlan tore his eyes away, shaking his head. "I can't. There is nothing for me on that ship. Everything I have is here."

He didn't glance at Blair, but Darce knew him well enough to understand the twitch in the side of his jaw, the flush creeping up his neck.

"What I said earlier..." He lowered his voice. "Are you certain you can trust him? Do you believe he would protect you, if you needed him to?"

A wry smile pulled at the corner of Lachlan's mouth. "As much as I can trust anyone these days."

The sting of the old bitterness haunted every syllable, and it was all Darce could do not to bite back, to speak the excuses and justifications on the tip of his tongue. But in his heart, he knew it was no use. He'd made his choice. He couldn't deny Lachlan the same.

He headed towards the gangway, squeezing Lachlan's shoulder as he passed. "I hope he proves himself worthy of you."

Lachlan nodded. "Take care, Galbraith."

Darce clambered over the slippery wooden gangway as quickly as he dared. The *Jade Dawn's* deck was a bloody sight. The green timber was stained red, scattered with limp, blank-eyed bodies. But as he pushed through the fray, he noticed more and more Admiralty officers retreating to the *Vanguard*, weapons sheathed and cloaks ragged. Eimhir and the other selkies were turning the tide. They might get out of this yet.

No sooner had the thought crossed his mind than a chill crept over his skin. As it spread, it left a trail of frost along the hair on his forearms and turned the tips of his fingers blue. His lungs seized like the cold had stolen his breath.

A dense mist shrouded the far side of the ship. A mist he'd encountered too many times before.

The soulless. They had come to feast on the blood spilled here.

He looked up at the helm and found Nishi wearing the same horror he felt in his bones. "Captain, you know what's coming. We have to go."

"Aye." Nishi swallowed. "Tell our selkie friends to push off the gangways and sever every grappling line they see. If those Admiralty bastards have any sense, they won't waste time trying to stop us."

Darce went to work, hacking through the lines and dislodging every grappling hook he could find. Featherblade and Shearwing circled overhead, screaming raucously as they ushered the Sea Kith back onto the *Jade Dawn*.

His fingers were so numb he could barely close them around the hilt of his sword. The blade was encrusted with frozen shards, coating the steel in glittering patterns. His next breath filled his throat with splinters of ice. It was an abyssal cold, one that buried itself so deep it was impossible to dig out. The kind of cold that lingered for a lifetime.

They were too late.

A shadow stirred, and he braced himself for the wraith to emerge. Its rotten bones, its brackish breath, a touch that would freeze the blood in his veins.

But the wraith never came. Instead, Isla staggered out of the haar, dragging Eimhir alongside her. Her lips were blue, and her pelt dripped with the silvery vapour of a vanquished gun-anam.

When she saw Darce, her eyes filled with relief. "We can't stay here. Nishi has to—"

"I know. She'll get us underway as soon as the last tethers are cut."

"Good." She glanced at Eimhir. "She's in a bad way. Put herself between me and one of the wraiths. It was like the haar was drowning her. It kept pouring down her throat, turning her face blue."

"I'm fine." Eimhir's voice was brittle as she untangled herself from Isla's arm. "It's not the first time I've faced these monsters. I just need—" She buckled over, spluttering salt water over the deck. The bile was thick and rancid, and Darce noticed flecks of blood floating in its midst.

"Nishi!" Isla waved towards the helm, eyes wide and frantic. "We need to get clear of the haar."

Darce peered down the broadside of the ship. Most of the lines had been cut loose, and only one gangway remained. The *Vanguard's* crew seemed more occupied with the gun-anam than the *Jade Dawn*. One of the wraiths reached out a tendril, wrapping coils of spray around an officer's neck. The woman's cheeks turned red, then paled as she spluttered. Bubbles spilled from her lips and dribbled down her chin as she fell to the deck, eyes blank and glassy.

He'd almost torn himself away when he caught sight of a familiar, loping gait further down the *Vanguard's* deck. It was Lachlan, cheeks ruddy from exertion as he swung on his crutch at a desperate pace. His eyes were bright with fear, his mouth forming a name Darce couldn't hear over the raging wind.

Blair lurched back to avoid the ghostly blade of a gun-anam. His feet slipped on the slick timber, leaving him teetering on the edge of the deck.

Then he fell to the hungry black waves.

"No!"

Isla was at his side in a second, searching the water. "What is it? Who—" Her gaze found Lachlan across the narrow gap between the two ships. She must have seen the anguish as well as he did: the horror in the whites of his eyes, the stricken grief on his face.

He realised what was going to happen too late. Isla was already on the gunwale, barefoot and ready to leap, by the time it hit him.

She'd never been able to bear her brother's pain. Not if there was something she could do about it.

Before he could call her back, she was gone.

He rushed to the edge, scouring the waves for any sign of her. The swell churned furiously between the hulls of the two ships, ready to swallow anyone who plunged beneath the surface.

Eimhir joined him, knuckles white around the wooden railing as she sucked in ragged gasps of air. Isla was right. She wasn't in a good way.

She made to swing a leg over the railing, but Darce held her back. "You're in no condition to follow her over there. Don't be foolish."

Eimhir drew her lip back in a snarl. "You have no right to tell me—"

"Think about Isla." He squeezed her shoulder. "If you go after her, it will only mean she has two people to save. You need to trust her."

She shoved his arm away, but made no move to climb over. "There was a time you'd have followed her over there yourself, auld blood."

"Aye, and I'd have been wrong. It took me too long to learn that." He turned back to the water, heart leaping as a lithe shape burst through the surface. "See for yourself."

Isla fought through the waves towards the *Jade Dawn*, the collar of Blair's doublet hanging between her jaws as she dragged him with her.

The lieutenant's face was bone-white, his eyes glazed.

Someone threw a rope, and Isla slipped out of her selkie form to grab it. Darce couldn't help but marvel at how seamlessly the grey fur melted from her glistening wet skin, settling into damp folds around her shoulders. It was like bearing witness to a part of her he'd never seen before.

This was who she was, who she'd always been.

She pulled Blair into the crook of her arm and held him as the Sea Kith deckhands hauled the rope up. Below, the waves leapt against the hull, furious to be denied their prey. The *Jade Dawn* bucked and heaved until Darce thought the ship might keel over entirely.

He turned to Nishi, who was at the helm with a horror-struck expression. "Captain, all the lines are cut. We're free of the *Vanguard*. We need to go."

Nishi's brown skin took on an ashen hue. She stood transfixed, her eyes trapped on the monstrous hull opposite them. "We can't," she choked, her voice so brittle it sounded like it might shatter. "Kerr. He's on the ship."

"What? Why would he—" Darce spun, trying to pick out Kerr amongst the chaos on the *Vanguard's* deck. The haar fell across the ship, shrouding the deck in a haze. More gun-anam spilled out from its midst. It was a ship of ghosts and corpses, and none looked closer to death than the Grand Admiral himself, standing on the quarterdeck with a ghastly pallor and bloodshot eyes.

Standing with his pistol levelled directly at Kerr's head.

"What is he doing?" Darce hissed. "He had no reason to be over there. He—"

"He is the *Jade Dawn's* sentinel," Nishi said. "He'd do anything for his crew."

Darce followed her gaze. He saw it now—the rips in the *Vanguard's* enormous sails, the waves pouring in through a splintered hole in the hull. Remnants of sentinel magic clung to each wound, a dozen or more scars covered with Kerr's fingerprints.

Kerr faced the Grand Admiral, gaunt-cheeked and bent at the spine. There was a spark of defiance in his eyes as he stared down the barrel of the pistol, a fire that left no room for regret.

He'd crippled the *Vanguard*. He'd given them a chance to escape. But at what cost?

A piercing wail tore through the wind from the *Jade Dawn's* mast. Darce didn't need to look up to know it was Shearwing. The pain in the razorbill's cry made it clear enough.

"Stop!"

Isla stormed across the deck, dragging Blair behind her. She set him roughly against the towering pillar of the mast, a fishknife pressed against his throat. Darce saw the tip of it nick the skin, drawing tiny droplets of blood. A vein pulsed in Blair's neck. All it would take to open it was a swift flick of Isla's wrist.

Across on the *Vanguard*, Lachlan rushed to the edge of the railings, paling as he took in the scene in front of him. He shot a desperate glance towards the Grand Admiral.

Cunningham hadn't moved. He stood as still and silent as ever, the ebony barrel of his pistol pressed firmly against Kerr's forehead. No rain touched the gun; one of the sentinels must have been shielding it.

"Let Kerr go," Isla shouted, her voice catching. "Send him back to us and we'll return your nephew unharmed. Better we all live to fight another day, no?"

Cunningham stared at her like she was a ghost. Of all the times Darce had seen him most human, it had been when he was looking at Isla. Now, there was no trace of that man. Only a husk left in his place, resurrected by a sacrifice that should never have been made.

He pulled his mouth into a cruel smile. "No," he said, and squeezed the trigger.

Nishi screamed. Lachlan's face drained of colour. Kerr's head flew back, blood and bone splattering from his skull. Darce watched in horror as he fell, tumbling over the gunwale into the restless waves below.

He was gone.

Shearwing released an infernal shriek and spread its wings, hurtling from its perch with outstretched claws.

Cunningham was too quick. He drew his second pistol, a mother-of-pearl twin to the ebony gun he'd used to kill Kerr, and pointed the barrel at the sky.

The powder burned. The shot tore loose. Shearwing gave a stuttering cry, then fell.

Darce froze, his mouth dry, as the razorbill's limp body hit the waves and sank.

The *Jade Dawn's* deck fell into a heavy silence, disturbed only by the echo of the gunshot. Cunningham slid his pistols into his belt and looked across the widening chasm between the two ships with an inscrutable expression.

Isla's hand trembled around the handle of the dagger she held to Blair's neck. Her fingers were blue. The blade glistened with ice, freezing the droplets of blood welling at the tip. All around them, the haar grew colder, the air thickening with the stench of rot.

"Nishi." Darce tried again. "The lines are cut. We need to leave. If we stay here, the gun-anam will take us all."

He wasn't sure if she could hear him. Her eyes were slack with desolation, her mouth bloody where she'd bitten at her lip ring. She tightened her hands around the ship's wheel, staring at the *Vanguard* like she could sink it through pain and spite and grief alone.

"Aye," she said, her voice fraying at the edges. "He wouldn't want us to join him too soon. I can give him that much. I can give him—"

The rest of her words were lost to the sob in her throat.

Isla dropped the blade from Blair's neck. "There's been too much blood spilled in your uncle's name already. Count yourself fortunate I haven't the heart to add to it tonight."

The dagger clattered to the deck with a muffled thud as the wind roared. High above, the Sea Kith worked to unfurl a section of sail, letting the canvas catch the fierce gusts. The *Jade Dawn* reeled, drifting further from the *Vanguard's* looming shadow. It wasn't long before Darce lost sight of the other ship, the shroud of the haar swallowing it up.

"They'll find it hard to follow us through this," he said. "By the time we clear the mists, they'll be long behind us."

Isla wiped her cheek, the trail of her tears frozen on her skin. "He'll come for me. Kerr won't be the last to suffer because of me, because of what I am to him. This is only the beginning."

The foreboding in her words left him with a chill that buried deeper than the deathless cold of the haar.

Not if I can help it, he vowed, hoping it would be enough.

CHAPTER TWENTY-FOUR

ISLA

The groan of creaking timber was a comfort in the confines of the cabin. It reminded Isla of a different time, a simpler time, when the walls of a ship held the home she'd chosen for herself. She'd sailed for years, charting a course with the stars and her sextant, searching for her place on the waves. Never realising the answer had lain beneath them.

She'd once thought the sea would bring her freedom. But there was no freedom to be had as long as the Grand Admiral hunted her.

Eimhir moaned in her sleep, and Isla pressed her hand against her forehead. Her skin was cold and clammy. Though they were long clear of the haar, it was like part of it lingered in the cabin, stealing the colour from Eimhir's cheeks, the breath from her lungs.

Isla placed a gentle kiss on her head and left the cabin, closing the door behind her. One of the other selkies from Caim stood outside, observing the corridor with wary eyes. She gave Isla a solemn nod as she passed, then shifted in front of the door, folding her arms stiffly.

It was just another sign of the tension hanging over the *Jade Dawn*. The Sea Kith were not the Admiralty, but they were still human, and that was enough for distrust to fester. It clung to the walls and seeped between the gaps in the timber, until Isla worried that before long, the whole ship might be infected by it.

She climbed the wooden staircase to the foredeck. The late-morning sky was pale and bright, washed clean after the storm. No clouds worried the horizon. No trace of mist clung to the waves. For once, their course was clear.

She found Duncan at the prow of the ship, the heavy folds of his ink-black pelt cascading down his bare shoulders. His eyes remained fixed on the horizon as he asked gruffly, "How is she?"

"No worse. We can only wait for the chill to pass." When he made no reply, she added, "You worry for her, don't you?"

"I worry for all our people."

"Even an aineol?"

"You most of all." He pursed his lips, a shadow flashing across his usually impenetrable expression. "Your sentinel... You know there will never be a place for him on Eileanan Selch."

Isla stiffened. She wondered if Duncan could hear the quickening of her heartbeat, the ferocity with which it pounded against her ribs.

"Even if such a thing were not forbidden, there is no way for him to set foot on Caim," Duncan continued. "He can't exist in the place you call home. You will leave it for him, just like Mara did."

She gritted her teeth. "It's not the same."

"Isn't it? You were willing to risk the future of our people to save one man, one *human*. Mara did that, too. And in the end, that's what got her killed."

"Darce isn't—he would never—"

"You think I call you aineol because you are half-human, because I can't separate the fact that you are Mara's from the fact that you are also the Grand Admiral's." Duncan fixed her with a steady gaze, betraying no emotion. "You are wrong. I call you aineol because part of you will always belong to one of them. This sergeant... You carry his soul with the same weight you carry Mara's. You'll never be at home on Eileanan

Selch. Not because of me, but because of him."

Isla couldn't speak. There was no malice in Duncan's voice, no accusation behind his words. Just a truth she'd refused to consider, even when it ached and clawed and pulled inside her like a cord that couldn't snap.

Darce had offered his soul for her life. They were tethered by blood in an oath that couldn't be broken. An oath she didn't *want* to break. She couldn't separate herself from him, not any more than she could separate herself from her pelt. She would find her way back to him, no matter what it cost.

"You're right," she whispered. "If I stayed, if he wasn't there... Part of me would always be missing."

Duncan turned away, eyes hardening. "Then it is as I feared."

"No," Isla said forcefully. "Whether or not my future lies on Eileanan Selch, it is still my home. I have not forgotten the promise I made to protect it. We know Mara was searching for the lost soulships when she went missing. When I was in Arburgh, the Grand Admiral spoke of how she saved his life. He mentioned her carrying him to a barren skerry in the Southern Reaches."

Duncan regarded her cautiously. "You think we might find one of the soulships there."

"Most of the islands in the Southern Reaches are uninhabitable, untouched. If one of the ships ran aground there, or was left for some season..."

"It might be intact. For the most part, at least." Duncan tilted his head, considering. "The Southern Reaches are beyond where our scouts usually venture, but these soulships sailed in a different time, a time when the Admiralty's grasp did not extend as far as it does now. It's possible Mara found one there. If she did..."

"It could be the chance we've been waiting for," Isla finished. "I have to go there. I have to follow her, to make sure it wasn't all for nothing."

Duncan shot her a piercing look. She couldn't tell if she imagined the way his eyes slid to her shoulders, to the dappled fur hanging around them. He didn't want to let her pelt out of his sight again, she realised with a chill. If he tried to stop her…

"Go," he said abruptly. "Find where Mara went. I'll return to Caim and wait for Angus and the other scouts. Once we've gathered our forces, we'll meet you at the Southern Reaches and finish this."

She tried not to let her surprise show as he stalked past to gather the other selkies. Part of her expected him to change his mind and insist she return to Caim. It wasn't until he leapt from the *Jade Dawn*, plunging through the waves in a ripple of black fur, that she allowed herself to breathe normally again. He was gone, and with him, the uneasy shadow that followed his gaze.

A fierce swell rose in her chest, pushing out the fear and dread that had rooted deep these last few days. The horizon was bright and clear. A strong wind filled the *Jade Dawn's* emerald sails. There was no storm in the air, only something Isla dared to think might be hope.

She climbed to the helm, but she only found the Sea Kith second mate. The young woman gave her a pointed look, then gestured to the side of the quarterdeck.

Nishi sat with her forehead pressed against the wooden railing, legs dangling through the gaps. In one hand she held a bottle, its cork nowhere in sight. She didn't look up as Isla approached and sat beside her, just gave a rough hiccup and took another lengthy swig from the bottle.

"It's quiet," she said, slurring her voice. "Too fucking quiet. Do you know how much of a headache that tides-damned razorbill used to give me with its incessant squawking? I keep looking for it in the sky, thinking it will fly out of the clouds like this was all some cruel jape. But it's not, is it? Shearwing is gone. Kerr is…"

She choked, the rest of her words caught in her throat. Isla gently took the bottle and brought it to her lips, gulping down a mouthful of the rum. The sweet, spicy taste burned her throat, and she savoured the warmth of it on her tongue before handing the bottle back to Nishi.

"I should have left the moment we got clear of the firth," she said. "It's me he was after. It's me he wants. Nobody else should have paid the price for that."

"It wouldn't have changed anything," Nishi said. "The *Vanguard* would have run us down all the same, and we wouldn't have had your selkie friends to come to our aid. Your people defended my ship, saved my crew from slaughter. I won't forget what I...what *we* lost, but I'll remember that."

A weighted silence fell between them, thick with grief. It seeped through Isla's skin, pressing on her own wounds. Lady Catriona. Laird Cormick. The only mother and father she'd ever known. She'd buried her pain like she'd buried them, and the sorrow she'd stitched up welled back to the surface, ready to burst at the seams.

"What does it feel like?" The question left her lips before she could call it back. The time was still too raw to ask such things. She wasn't sure she could bear hearing the answer.

"To have part of your soul ripped from you?" Nishi let out a harsh laugh, waving the rum bottle in her hand. "It feels like I want to die. Like I want to drown myself in this bottle, then throw myself from the bowsprit and drown again in the fathoms." She set the bottle down on the deck. "I know Kerr waits for me down there, but he would never forgive me if I joined him so soon. So I must endure. I must go where the tides take me, until the tides take me."

"What happens to the blood oath?"

"In death, it is broken. Oftentimes, that is enough. The death of the sentinel means the death of the captain. But not always. Not if they have a reason to go on." She gave a grim smile. "And I have a reason."

The quiet rage in her words charged the air, sending a shiver across Isla's skin. "You can't mean to take on the Admiralty alone."

"Not alone," Nishi said. "And not yet. But Arburgh's reign over the waves has grown too tight, stretched too far, and we Sea Kith can no longer ignore what that means for us. If we don't stand against the

Admiralty, we'll only be caught in its grasp."

"We have that in common, I fear," Isla said. "My people won't survive a war either, not without drawing the gun-anam to every skirmish and spreading the mist sickness. If we're to have any hope, I first have to find a way to cross the haar so we can return it to what it was."

"And you believe the answer lies in the Southern Reaches? I heard you talking to the chieftain." Nishi sent her a pointed look. "That's a long way to swim, even for a selkie. But for the *Jade Dawn*…"

"I can't ask for any more than you have given already."

"You don't have to. The tides have brought us together too many times for it to be happenstance. What kind of Sea Kith would I be to ignore their will?" Nishi turned to the waves. "Something stirs on the horizon. It's not a storm, not this time. Its currents run deeper than that. What's coming is *change*, Blackwood. And I intend to be there to see it."

The *Jade Dawn's* sails fluttered fiercely, their emerald canvas bright against the sky. Perhaps Nishi was right. There *was* something different in the air, the promise of a shift in the wind.

But if change was waiting beyond the horizon, it would not reach them on its own. They would have to sail to meet it.

That night, she woke from a dream with blood blocking her nose and salt thick on her tongue. It took her several rasping breaths to recognise the low ceiling and panelled wooden walls of the cabin she shared with Eimhir. Trails of sweat trickled down her breastbone, and she winced as she wiped them away, half expecting her skin to crack and peel with the motion.

It was getting worse. Ever since leaving Arburgh, the dreams—the memories—came to her every night, even in human form. They dragged her to places she didn't want to see, left her with scars that weren't her own. A glimpse of familiar blue-grey eyes that held none of the coldness she now knew. Salt stains crawling up her arms as she lowered herself into crystalline water. The sweet relief of her pelt soothing her broken skin, and the ache of knowing it was only for a fleeting moment.

She pushed away the thin cotton sheets and climbed out of her bunk, listening to make sure the low rumbling coming from Eimhir's side remained undisturbed. The cabin was too confining. She needed to set her eyes on the unending line of the horizon, to fill her lungs with the crisp bite of sea air.

The deck was still, the only light coming from the oil lamps. She padded across to the bow, the timber damp against her bare feet. Nobody else was around apart from a solitary figure by the prow.

As she ventured closer, she realised it was Darce. He'd disposed of his jewel-toned Admiralty finery and instead wore a woollen tunic over creased, sea-stained leathers. His hair was loose, its tousled lengths covering his missing ear as it hung around his jaw.

"Bad dreams?" he asked, without turning.

She joined him at the bow. "Aye, you could say that. Though it would be easier to push them from my mind if they were only dreams. Knowing parts of them were real, parts of them happened..." She grimaced. "I feel the memories like they're my own, the suffering like it's my own. I came up here hoping to forget that, even if it's just for a wee while."

He nodded, taking a step back. "I'll give you peace. Best I head down below, before—"

"Wait." She reached for his hand, but it was already gone, leaving her grasping for his touch. Her cheeks flushed, shame burning in her chest.

"I thought I was imagining it," she said softly. "But ever since I came back, you've been pulling away from me like the tide from shore."

"No, that's not..." He shook his head, forehead creasing with weary lines. "You don't understand. I spent months fighting to keep you out of the Grand Admiral's reach, yet the moment I saw you again, I was undone. All it took was you coming back for me to realise there's nothing

I wouldn't do to keep you by my side. And I fear where that might lead me. I've *seen* where that might lead me."

"It's not the same. *You're* not the same."

"But I could be." He gave a weak smile. "I've looked into his eyes and seen my own reflection. The same fear, the same grief." He swallowed. "I haven't the strength to let you go a second time."

"You don't need to." She edged closer, breathing in the scent of him so she might commit to memory the musk of leather and wool, the sharpness of salt and steel. "I never wanted to leave. Part of me will never forgive you for firing that shot and forcing my hand. For suffering his wrath when it should have been me." She reached towards him, delicately pushing his hair back from his temple. His chest hitched against hers as her fingertips found the scar around his missing ear. "I'll never forgive myself, either."

He wrapped his fingers around hers, guiding her hand away. "I'd have given more than an ear to find my way back to you."

She tightened her grip as he pulled back again. "Don't."

They were separated by only a breath. She felt the pulse in his wrist, his heartbeat in the sliver of space between their ribs. For months, she'd endured the vastness of the sea dividing them. How could it be these final few inches were the widest to close?

"I'm afraid, Isla." Darce trailed a hand over the curve of her shoulder, fingers brushing lightly across her pelt. "Afraid to touch you. Afraid if I start, I might not be able to let you go." When he reached her bare skin, he paused, his touch agonisingly close, the whisper of it tracing the length of her neck.

She tilted her head. "I don't want you to let me go."

He took a sharp breath, his dark brown eyes fixed on hers. Then his hands were on her jaw, soft and firm and wanting all at once as he brought her mouth to his.

She met his lips with a faint cry, learning anew the taste of him, the way his mouth moved against hers. The cold nip of the night sky melted away as she folded into the hollow of his chest. Every shared breath, every brush of his tongue against hers, sent a new ripple of warmth through her. His hands wound around the nape of her neck as he held her. It was a grasp she never wanted to escape from, a home she never wanted to leave.

He drew back, eyes glittering in the dim light. "I feared I might never get to do that again. But I've thought about it every night since I last saw you."

His lips were wet and parted, begging her to close the distance between them again, to crash into him with all the hunger and yearning she'd kept locked away.

The moment she leaned in, an ear-piercing shriek rattled through the air.

She leapt back as Featherblade landed on the bowsprit in a tussle of wings. It curved its neck to preen its feathers, seemingly oblivious to what it had disturbed.

"Tides take that bloody nuisance of a bird." Darce glared at it, but there was no anger behind his words. The loss of Shearwing hung over them all. The *Jade Dawn* was a lonelier place without the razorbill's shadow flitting over the deck, its low, gravelly caws echoing from the mast.

Featherblade crooned, then jabbed its beak towards the portside horizon. Dawn's first light bled into the clouds, casting the purple shroud with flecks of orange.

"To the south, then," Darce said. "And whatever awaits us there."

His hand was warm as it wrapped around hers, and a fresh rush of blood raced to her cheeks as she followed his gaze to the sunrise. "Together, this time. No matter what happens."

"Together," he agreed, then paused, brow furrowing. "I doubt you've had time to consider this with everything that's happened, but there's still the matter of the lieutenant down in the brig. There are only a few ports left between us and the Southern Reaches. It's better we cut him loose sooner than later."

"Cut him loose?" Isla repeated. "You want to let him go? He's the Grand Admiral's nephew."

"He's also your cousin," Darce said. "I know it might be difficult, but you should speak to him. Lachlan seems convinced he's not the same kind of man as his uncle. You might find you have more in common than you realise."

She opened her mouth to protest, but something stopped her. She pictured Lachlan's face as he leaned over the gunwale—cheeks white, frantically searching the waves that had swallowed Blair whole. She'd gone into the water without a second thought, carrying the lieutenant's dead weight to the safety of the *Jade Dawn*. She'd watched the salt water spilling from his throat, his blue lips forming the shape of her brother's name.

Perhaps Darce was right. Perhaps they shared something more than the Grand Admiral's blood.

She took a steadying breath. It was time to see what Blair Cunningham had to say.

There wasn't much to distinguish the brig from the rest of the *Jade Dawn's* hold. The Sea Kith weren't in the habit of transporting prisoners, and the makeshift bars separating one small corner of the room from the rest didn't seem like they'd hold up to any real force. Still, they were enough to contain a single prisoner, and Blair didn't appear to be holding any ambitions of escaping.

He was sitting on the floor as she approached, his linen shirt torn open at the collar, the fabric ragged where she'd sunk in her selkie teeth to drag him through the waves. His light brown curls fell over his face as he rested his arms on his knees. If there was any fight in him, he was hiding it well.

"I have nothing to say to you," he said, without looking up. "If you're here to kill me, get on with it."

Isla paused. "What makes you think I want to kill you?"

"That's what your kind do, isn't it? I don't know what reason you had for plucking me from the waves, but it's not enough for me to forget what you are, what you're capable of."

She knelt in front of him, keeping her distance through the bars. "I'm not the monster here. I think you know that."

"Don't talk to me about monsters." He lifted his chin, meeting her gaze for the first time. His blue-grey eyes were like his uncle's, but there was a fire in them she'd never seen in the Grand Admiral's. "You know, I was never meant to join the Admiralty. My parents were merchant sailors. They spent most of their lives on the Adrenian Sea, carrying supplies to Breçhon, to Vesnia, to the Karzish Peninsula. Until one day, their ship was set upon by raiders. *Selkie* raiders." He shook his head. "They never recovered their bodies. Perhaps that was a kindness, after seeing what those beasts did to those they did find."

Bile rose at the back of Isla's throat. She'd seen the aftermath of too many raids to pretend she didn't know what he was talking about. Flesh torn to ribbons, muscle and sinew lying loose and ragged, chalk-white bone exposed to the elements. She knew how that kind of torture could leave a scar on those who witnessed it.

"I am sorry," she said. "I understand your grief better than you think. My own father was killed in a selkie raid on our home."

Blair looked flummoxed. "Your father is—"

"My father is—*was*—Laird Cormick Blackwood." She cut him off firmly. "No matter how much your uncle tries to lay claim to me, that will never change."

Blair's frown deepened. "Lachlan told me what happened that night. The things he saw, his friends maimed and killed... I don't understand how you can blame him for how he feels. He lost everything."

"Not everything," she said tightly. "Not until later."

A tense silence stretched between them. Of course Blair knew what had happened between her and Lachlan. He'd shared in her brother's grief, borne his resentment. It was only natural he'd believe the worst of her. Part of her believed it too.

"I don't blame Lachlan," she said. "I don't blame you, either. I pity you. You choose to hate me, hate *all* selkies, because it's easier that way. Otherwise, you might have to look at your own people, your own family, to see where the blame truly lies." She studied the lines between his brows, the circles ringing his eyes. "You know, don't you? You *must* know what he is. Tell me, is Lachlan in danger?"

Blair shot her a prickly look, but said nothing. After a long, tense minute, his shoulders slumped as he picked at the heel of his boot. "I don't know. I wish I could be sure."

"I think you *do* know. I had my blade to your throat, and your uncle still killed Kerr. He wanted to send a message, and he was willing to pay the cost of it with your life."

"He knew you wouldn't kill me."

Isla gave a blunt laugh. "Even *I* didn't know I wouldn't kill you."

"Then perhaps he understands you better than you think." Blair fixed her with a cool gaze. "You didn't save me out of kindness or mercy. You saved me for Lachlan's sake. My uncle saw that. He knows how much your brother means to you. That's the one thing giving me faith that Lachlan is safe. If my uncle kills him, he loses his last piece of leverage over you."

"My brother is not fucking *leverage*."

"No, he's not." Blair's mouth tightened. "On that much, we can agree."

This time, the edge around his words didn't feel like it was aimed at her. Instead, it sounded like a peace offering.

Or perhaps that was what she wanted to believe.

She pushed herself to her feet. Blair had chosen to serve on the *Vanguard*. He'd chased them into these waters. The consequences should have been his to bear as much as anyone's.

He's not his uncle, Darce had said.

No, he wasn't. And as much as Isla hated to admit it, perhaps that was worth keeping him alive for.

As she turned to the staircase, Blair's voice rang out behind her, thin and frustrated. "Is that it? No blade, no noose? What do you intend to do with me, if not kill me?"

The answer danced on the tip of her tongue, but she swallowed it down. Better to let him fester in his thoughts a wee while longer, in the hopes he might learn something from them.

Blair would get his freedom. And if she was making a mistake, its ripples would follow soon enough.

CHAPTER TWENTY-FIVE

DARCE

The south brought with it milder weather on the wind. There was still a bite to the air, especially in the grey mornings, but the *Jade Dawn* skimmed over the waves smoothly, and for once, the horizon was clear of haze and drizzle.

Nishi joined him at the prow, her lip ring glinting in the sunlight. She carried her grief in the slump of her shoulders, but there was a fresh rigour to the way she set her jaw, a determination that hadn't been chiselled away.

She peeled back the sleeve of her emerald jacket, revealing the intricate ochre patterns of her Sea Kith tattoos. They rippled against her brown skin like they were part of her flesh, and Darce noticed raised marks around a fresh set of swirls.

"For Kerr?" he asked.

"Aye. And Shearwing. Tides watch over them both." She rolled her sleeve down, eyes narrowing as she focused on the distant horizon. "We're not far. I only hope Blackwood finds what she's searching for."

"So do I," Darce said. "It's only a matter of time before the Admiralty regroups and Cunningham orders the *Vanguard* back to the hunt. The gun-anam won't stop them. There are times I fear nothing will."

Nishi sent him a sidelong look. "On that point, Sergeant...I wanted to ask you for a wee favour. I'd like to borrow that gannet of yours to send a message to the other Sea Kith. The more I feel the Admiralty breathing down my neck, the more I find myself wishing for allies. I'd like to put out a call and see if I get any answers."

"You think they'll listen?"

Nishi shrugged. "We've never been a unified folk, but what threatens the *Jade Dawn* threatens the rest of them—every sloop and schooner, every galley and galleon. We've steered clear of the Admiralty in the hopes Cunningham would leave us alone, but the truth is, he'll come for us eventually. He'll not be satisfied until the Admiralty controls every inch of water around Silveckan's shores and beyond. That leaves no place for the Sea Kith to exist."

"I'll do whatever I can to help. Whether or not Featherblade listens to me is another matter, however."

Nishi chuckled. "Obstinate creatures, so they are. Shearwing was the same, back in the beginning. Give it time. The bond between you will only strengthen. You saw how it was at the end, when Kerr..."

She trailed off, and in the hollow of her words Darce heard the echo of Shearwing's last cry, the splash as the razorbill's body hit the waves, following Kerr to the fathoms. A ball of anger tightened in his stomach, its threads fraying with all the grief and desperation he'd been picking at for months.

"We'll do it for them," he said. "For every soul the Admiralty has left in its wake."

Nishi nodded, pulling down the edge of her tricorne hat. She didn't need to say anything else as she turned back to the helm. Darce understood. When the sting of loss dulled, its weight remained. All anyone could do was learn how to carry it.

Her footsteps soon faded, leaving him with only his own thoughts for company. He gave a laboured sigh, allowing himself to savour the weak sunlight doing its best to warm his skin.

When he looked across the deck again, he caught sight of Eimhir further down the ship, her fawn-coloured pelt loose around her shoulders. She stared at the waves, eyes slack and unfocused. When he called out to her, she made no reply.

He joined her at the gunwale, reaching a hand to her shoulder. "Eimhir—"

She whirled to face him, expression darkening. Before he had time to say anything more, her hand closed around his wrist, fingers like ice as she squeezed. "What are you doing?"

"I didn't mean to startle you." He held his other hand out in appeasement. "I'm sorry. I only wanted to see how you were."

She released his wrist, but there was still a trace of hostility in the way she looked at him. "What concern is it to you?"

"What concern is it? Are we not friends?"

She stared at him, shoulders heaving. Then something in her softened. "Aye, I suppose we are." She slumped over the railing, running a hand through her windswept hair. "Forgive me, auld blood. These past few weeks have been draining, to say the least. I've hardly had time to catch my breath. And being around humans again... It's taking some getting used to."

"You're around *allies*," he reminded her. "We want the same thing."

"Do we?" She gave a crooked smile. "Did Blair Cunningham want the same thing? Is that why you let him go?"

"Isla let him go. She couldn't bear any more blood spilled on her account."

"And what if the cost of that is her own? What will you do then?" Eimhir shot him a pained look. "You and I want the same thing, Sergeant. I believe that. But I fear you've been around the Admiralty too long. You're looking for decency where none exists."

"Not all of them are like the Grand Admiral."

"What difference does it make, if they follow him anyway? What good is their regret if they stain their hands on his behalf?" Bitterness curled at the edge of her lips. "Maybe we are friends, but you're still human. You'll find a way to make excuses for them, a way to forgive them. Because you *are* them. Our blood is on your hands too."

"I—" Heat rushed up Darce's neck, and he balled his hands into fists. "Perhaps you're right. But there was a time not so long ago you believed Isla was human. You didn't know she had selkie blood. You didn't know she was your cousin. Yet you called her caraid anyway. You loved her anyway."

Something flitted across Eimhir's face, and the clouds darkening her features lifted. "Aye, I did. Sometimes I forget that." She turned to the waves, her brow troubled as she gathered the speckled folds of her pelt and pulled them close. "The wind is fierce this morning. I can feel it biting to my bones."

"We'll get through this, Eimhir. You have to trust that."

"If only it were so simple." She pushed back from the edge. "I'm heading below. You're safe to drop your wards."

Darce stiffened. "My wards? What do you—"

Eimhir gave a low chuckle. "You are a sentinel, and I am a selkie. Even if we are friends, those truths will never cease to exist. Neither will our nature."

Below, the once-calm waves churned restlessly, splashing seafoam against the *Jade Dawn's* hull. There was no wind whipping them up, no swell making them surge. Just a singing in Darce's blood, coming from a place so deep he hadn't known it was there.

Only then did he realise his hands were still balled at his sides.

He loosened his fingers, and the waves settled into a rolling calm. The water glittered in the sunlight, showing no trace of the unrest he'd suffused it with.

"I—I didn't—" He turned back to Eimhir, but she was already gone. The only trace of her was the red marks she'd left around his wrist, the imprints of her fingers leaving a lingering chill against his skin.

He wiped his hands against his coat, casting a wary glance over the waves. How easily they had leapt to his will, without him consciously calling on them. Had they sensed some kind of danger in Eimhir? Or was it as she'd said, that their very nature would always set them against each other?

Are we not friends? he'd asked her.

The weary sigh of the swell washing against the ship was his only answer.

Later that day, the crags of the Southern Reaches rose out of the waves to greet them. Tall peaks of slate towered over the turquoise waters like proud sentries. Each of the isles seemed more unwelcoming than the last, their jagged ridges and sheer slopes too inhospitable for any kind of settlements.

This was where the Grand Admiral had ended up all those years ago. This was where Mara had dragged him when she'd saved his life. There was no doubt in Darce's mind that if it hadn't been for her, Cunningham would have died alone out here. The isles were remote and isolated from Silveckan's south coast, with little in the way of passing trade. The only signs of life came from the seabird colonies nestled high in the cliffs.

It was the perfect place for something to remain lost.

He stood with Isla and Eimhir at the edge of the quarterdeck, searching the rising crags and skerries for any sign of the bone ship Isla had described. All they'd come across were rocky peaks and tiny spits of land bearing nothing but a thin layer of soil and bursts of heather and campion.

Above, Featherblade circled the *Jade Dawn's* emerald sails, occasionally leaving the vicinity of the masts to weave between the towering sea stacks or chase a flock of seabirds. The sky was a cacophony of caws and cries, thick with the calls of guillemots and shags, puffins and kittiwakes. Darce caught a glimpse of black wings, and his heart lurched in recognition before he realised the razorbill was too small to mistake it for Shearwing.

Featherblade swooped down, its long neck bobbing in excitement as it rattled out a series of low, urgent croaks.

Darce's heart quickened. He met Isla's eyes and saw in them the same anticipation, the same desperate hope. This could be it. It *had* to be it.

"Go," he said to Featherblade. "Show the way."

The gannet spread its huge wings and flapped to the sky, a triumphant cry bellowing from its throat. It soared ahead of the *Jade Dawn's* prow, leading them to one of the islands.

Darce peered towards the cluster of rocks. At first, all he could see was the same crumbling stone and overgrown foliage. Then a glistening flash of white caught his eye, and he craned his neck around the corner of a towering sea stack.

There it was: a mast, rising from behind an outcropping of slate, shining bright against the pale sky. It stood tall and proud, not wood but bone. *Selkie* bone.

"I was right." Isla moved beside him. "This is why Mara was in the Southern Reaches. She must have been searching for the lost soulships when she found the Grand Admiral instead."

A growl rumbled from Eimhir's throat. "If only she'd continued her search instead of saving his life, everything might have been different."

The *Jade Dawn* rounded the island slowly, Nishi taking care not to run aground on the submerged rocks hidden in the shallows. As they drew closer, the steep cliffside fell away, yielding to a narrow cove. And there, listing on the shore, hull unmarked and gleaming white, was one of the soulships.

Eimhir eyed it guardedly. "It looks...whole."

She was right. Isla had spoken of the other bone ships she'd come across—little more than wrecks, their splintered carcasses strewn across the rocks or lost to the depths. But this ship seemed intact. Its curved hull held a dull sheen in the fading light, and there were no holes Darce could see. It was like it had been left for them to find.

They rowed over in the tender, oars slapping against the waves as Nishi and Eimhir took them to shore. This close, the soulship blocked out the light from the dying sun, casting a long shadow across the pebble-covered shore. The tender landed with a crunch, and they stepped into the shade of the soulship's keel.

"It's…magnificent," Nishi said, breathless. "I've never seen anything like it."

Neither had Darce. It was smaller than the *Jade Dawn*, around the size of a small schooner. The timber panelling on the arc of the hull wasn't timber at all—it had no knots or graining and held nothing of the damp wooden smell he associated so strongly with the docks. No seaweed clung to its prow, no barnacles clustered along its belly. Instead, it was smooth and white, shimmering with an ethereal kind of light that reminded him of the lustre of a selkie pelt.

"I've never seen one so *alive* before," Isla said. "Only in my dreams." She trailed a hand across the bone. "I'd like to go up on deck."

Nishi nodded. "I'll return to the *Jade Dawn* for supplies. If the ship was careened here on purpose, it might need some repairs. But from what I can see, it looks seaworthy enough. It shouldn't take much to get it back on the waves."

By the time they made it on board, the sun had started to slip below the crags, casting the ship's empty deck with reflections of purple and orange from the sky. Every step Darce took felt out of place, like he was walking somewhere he had no right to be. He couldn't shake the knowledge that under the soles of his boots were the bones of Isla's people.

Our blood is on your hands too. Eimhir's words echoed in his head, sending a chill down his back.

Further down the deck, Isla stood alone, the wind tugging at her hair. As she changed, the dappled fur of her pelt thickened and spread over her skin. It chased away her pale human flesh, shining in ripples of grey and black. Her eyes bulged as she fell to the deck, catching herself on strong, sturdy flippers. She lay against the bone, pressing the long, curved form of her seal body flat as her breathing slowed and stilled.

"Dreamwalking." Eimhir moved beside him. "The memories of our ancestors live in her. That's what my people sent me to find. *She's* what they sent me to find."

"I'm glad you did. You showed her where she belongs." His words caught painfully in his throat. "Even if there are parts of her that will never be mine, places she must go where I cannot follow, I could never regret her making that choice. Not after seeing what she has become. Who she was meant to be."

After a while, Isla rose from the deck, her pelt retreating from her skin and settling across her shoulders once more. The fur spilled across her breastbone and hung loose around her bare legs as she walked towards them, eyes bright with tears.

"Is something wrong?" Eimhir asked. "Did something happen here?"

"This ship..." Isla whispered. "It was their last hope. They knew if they lost this one, they'd lose the only way they had to navigate the haar. They would have come back for it. They *should* have come back for it, but..."

"Humans," Eimhir said tightly.

"They were caught by Vesnian poachers on their way back to the Selkie Isles. They never got the chance to tell the clans what happened to the last soulship. Every one of them was slaughtered. All their pelts were lost, save one." Isla's knuckles turned white as she buried her fingers in the folds. "Their souls only exist in memory. My memory."

Darce flinched. "Isla, I—"

"It can't be undone," she said. "Nothing we do will bring back those we lost. But this ship can change what's coming. *We* can change it."

A slow smile spread over Eimhir's face, and the shadow darkening her eyes lifted as she reached for Isla's hand. "I never doubted that, caraid. The moment you spilled your blood onto that pelt, I knew you would be the one to save our people."

"Not just me." She squeezed Eimhir's fingers and sent Darce a steady look. "All of us. Together."

Darce nodded, reaching for the resolve in her words, clutching it close. It nestled between his ribs like a heartbeat, echoing with a promise.

The next two days passed in a breathless haze, punctuated by aching muscles and snatches of restless sleep. Every time Darce looked up, he saw the *Jade Dawn's* tender sailing back and forth between ship and shore, carrying the supplies they needed to repair the careened soulship and return it to the sea. The Sea Kith worked tirelessly under Nishi's watchful gaze, the crew holding the soulship in the same kind of reverence as their captain.

"The *Jade Dawn* has its sea spirits, aye," she said, striding across the deck to join him and Isla. "But this ship carried something more. I might not have the auld blood, but I can feel that much. When it speaks, you would do well to listen, Blackwood. Bones and timber alike hold long memories."

Isla smiled. "I'll keep that in mind."

Nishi flicked her eyes to the stark, empty mast stretching towards the clouds above. "*That* will be a problem, however. I thought the sails might have been taken down for repairs and stowed in the hold, but there's no trace of them anywhere. You won't get far on oars alone, especially if the Admiralty happens upon you."

"There are no sails," Isla said. "A soulship needs no sails. What it needs is someone whose blood sings to the waves, someone who can call on the spirits and beckon them to our side." She turned to him, her gaze green and bright. "What it needs is a sentinel."

"You need a selkie," Darce said. "I might have the auld blood, but I don't know how to cross the haar."

"He's right." Eimhir appeared from the lower deck, blonde hair slicked back and pelt dripping wet. "The soulless realm is no place for a human, even one with auld blood. He cannot take us there, and even if he could, you'd be a fool to bring him. He doesn't belong there, caraid. You know this."

"We have little choice in the matter," Isla said. "In my memories, it was the auld blood of the gun-anam that was used to summon the haar. Blood from a selkie who had lost their pelt, who was willing to sacrifice what was left of their body. We don't have that, but we do have Darce. His sentinel magic is bound to my blood. He can help us."

"You think Duncan will agree to that?"

Isla stilled. "He's here?"

"He arrived with Angus and the others just now." Eimhir nodded towards the shore. "We should speak with him before making any decisions."

Isla pursed her lips. "I'll go to him."

Darce reached out an arm as she passed, fingers brushing against her skin. "Do you want me to come with you?"

She shook her head. "These are my people. I have to do this alone."

There was a time he might have argued with her, but that old urge had faded. He knew the stubborn set of her jaw, the determination pulling her brows tight.

He imagined Duncan did as well.

He watched from the foredeck as she traipsed to the shore and waded to where the selkies were waiting for her. Two of them stood in waist-high water, arms folded across their bare chests, the tails of their pelts floating in the waves. One was tall and lean, with a crop of unruly red hair and smatterings of freckles across his face and shoulders. The other was at least a decade older and built more broadly, his golden-brown skin dense and muscular under his rippling black pelt.

From what Isla had told him, the older selkie could only be Duncan.

He carried a weight the others didn't, a presence heavy around his shoulders. He didn't look like the kind of man to yield easily.

"Ears burning?" Nishi joined him. "I don't think they're happy we're here."

"I don't blame them. They have good reasons not to trust humans."

A familiar shriek tore through the air before Nishi could reply. Seconds later, Featherblade landed on the gunwale, its blue eyes glinting with their usual self-satisfaction.

Nishi reached to stroke the underside of its curved neck, and Darce found himself grappling with a mixture of wonder and irritation that her fingers remained unscathed. "I suppose that answers your question about whether Featherblade would be happy flying with you while you search for the other Sea Kith."

She sent him a sideways glance. "You won't sail with us? I could use someone like you, Sergeant."

"I'm needed here."

"You mean to go with them?" Nishi frowned. "This deathly mist they intend to cross... Do you believe you'll survive it?"

"I don't know," Darce said. "I don't think any of them know. But I understand why they're desperate enough to risk it. For years, the Grand Admiral used people like me to hunt them down and steal their souls. If there's a chance I can help right some of those wrongs, I have to try."

Nishi pressed a hand to his shoulder. "Kerr was right about you. He saw something in you, even before you made the blood oath."

Sorrow and shame welled in his stomach. "Nishi, I never intended—"

"Stop." She cut him off with a shake of her head. "He knew what kind of man you were. I let my grief blind me to that back in Arburgh. I won't make the same mistake again. You'll always be kith to the *Jade Dawn*, Sergeant. If tides be kind, we'll meet again on the other side of this."

Featherblade spread its great white wings and released a long trill into the evening sky.

"If tides be kind," Darce echoed.

CHAPTER TWENTY-SIX

ISLA

Night had not long fallen when the *Jade Dawn* slipped away, leaving behind only the eddies of its wake as it faded into darkness.

Isla followed the shoreline around the corner of the cliffs, keeping the ship in her sights as long as she could. Watching it diminish into the distance weighed heavy on her heart, like it was taking part of her with it. There was something about its vibrant sails, its green-stained deck, that let her think of it as home, at least for a wee while. Perhaps that was what *home* truly meant—knowing a place deeply enough that leaving it left a mark.

Finally, the ship disappeared, leaving her with no company but the wash of the waves against the shore. She shifted her bare feet against the pebbles as the rising tide lapped at her ankles. Her body could withstand the sea's icy touch now that she'd claimed her pelt, but some kinds of cold buried deeper than the selkie in her could endure.

As she turned back to the main beach, something in the water caught her eye. A shadow moving beneath the surface.

Moving towards her.

She jerked back as a huge shape rose from the waves, sending spray into the air. A scream threatened to tear loose from her throat, but she managed to stifle it when she recognised what the shadow was. Or, rather, *who* it was.

Duncan waded forward, his pelt melting from his skin as he surfaced. The folds of fur trailed behind him like ink bleeding across the water. He paused when the waves reached his waist, meeting her eyes with an unfathomable look.

A whisper of dread crept up her neck as she realised how alone she was here, out of sight of the careened soulship. Night had fallen across the shore. The seabirds had retreated to their hollowed-out nests in the cliffs. Nothing was around to disturb the water except the two of them.

Isla scrambled back, feet slipping against the polished pebbles. "Stay where you are."

If Duncan was surprised by the tension in her voice, he showed no sign of it. "Why would you say that?"

"You know why." She didn't risk taking another step, but she held her body coiled and ready. "You agreed too easily. That's what gave you away."

"You're talking about your sentinel?" Duncan snorted. "Rest assured, the thought of allowing any human to set foot on our people's bones is abhorrent to me. I only agreed to it because there was no other choice."

"Or because you think it will fail." She took a steadying breath, willing the tremor in her legs to settle. "And when it does, you'll have the excuse to do what you've wanted to do ever since Eimhir brought me to Eileanan Selch. You'll spill my blood across the deck, and you'll take my pelt for yourself."

For a fleeting second, Duncan's impenetrable expression dropped, darkening with quiet fury. Then the calm was back in place, fortified with a smile that didn't reach the corners of his eyes. "*This* is why I call you aineol. Because there are some things you'll never understand."

"I understand better than you think."

"I wish that were true." He sighed. "But this is not the time for me to take insult at your ignorance. If we are to leave on the high tide tomorrow, this may be my only chance to say what needs to be said, though the ancestors know you'll not want to hear it."

Isla stiffened. "Hear what?"

"Eimhir." He spoke her name with a grimace. "If we are to cross the haar, we must leave her behind."

Isla barked out a laugh. "So you can kill me more easily? I have to admit, I didn't think you would be so transparent."

"And I didn't think you would be such a fool." He closed the distance between them until he was towering over her. "You can't tell me you've not seen the signs."

"What are you talking about? What signs?"

He gave her a pitying look. "How many times has she been touched by the haar?"

"You can't possibly believe..." As Isla tried to speak, the words died in her throat. The perpetual shadows lining Eimhir's eyes. The world-sick tiredness of her voice. The chill she couldn't shake.

You can't tell me you've not seen the signs.

"It doesn't mean..." She swallowed, the barbed edges of her words catching. "It's not the mist sickness. She's exhausted. We all are."

"I've watched her. I've long suspected something has taken hold. I know you don't—"

"You *don't* know." Heat rose in her chest. "*I* do. She is my cousin. She has stood by my side since the day I met her, even before she knew what I really was. When her pelt was stolen, when her skin withered with scars of salt, she gave up the one thing that would have saved her because she said it was mine. She has endured worse pain than I could ever imagine, and she survived."

"That doesn't mean she won't succumb to the haar. Any one of us could." Duncan shook his head. "She's not as strong as she once was. I fear she might not survive the crossing. But she won't stay behind unless you ask her to."

"I can't do that. I can't do *this*, not without her." Isla curled her hands into fists. "We promised we would finish this together. I won't leave her behind because you fear she is weak. She is stronger than me, stronger than any of us."

"If you're wrong, you'll only learn it when it's too late to undo your mistake," Duncan said. "There is no turning back from what we're about to sail into."

"I know that. So does Eimhir." She bristled under the measure of his stare. "You're wrong about her, just like you were wrong about me. If you wanted me to trust you, perhaps you should have extended yours to me, like she did."

A pained expression flitted across his face, and he looked away. "Aye, perhaps I should have. I only hope we both don't live to regret that decision."

When Isla headed back along the shore, he didn't try to follow. All she heard was the slap of the sea as he disappeared, leaving her with nothing but the haunting whisper of doubt in the shape of his parting words.

As the sun rose the next morning, so did the tide. Isla watched from the soulship's deck as the turquoise water washed over the shingle, creeping ever closer. When it reached the bone-hewn keel, the ship shifted amongst the pebbles where it was entrenched, yearning to slip free.

For the last few days, the tackles and anchors had held it in place, secure on the shore, forever listing to one side. Now, the lines had been loosed and the ship freed from its restraints. It straightened as the waves caught the curve of its hull and coaxed it towards open waters.

Isla released a breath as the grinding of the pebbles ceased, replaced by the splash of the soulship's prow cutting through the waves. The shore swept away behind them, and out in front, there was only the sea.

"It sails," she said softly.

"It floats," Eimhir corrected, a wry smile dancing on her lips. "In case you forgot, we don't have any sails. The currents will carry us for a wee bit, but we won't get far on them alone. Our only hope is that the sergeant can do what you say, and call the haar to us with his magic."

The mention of the haar summoned an unwelcome shiver to Isla's spine. Last night's conversation with Duncan weighed on her shoulders, ladening her with dread.

"Are you…" The words stuck in her throat, fear thickening around them. "Are you afraid of what we might find there? Afraid of what those mists might do to us?"

"No." Eimhir's voice was firm. "I might have been, once. But I have followed you since the day we first met, caraid. I'll follow you to the end of this too, wherever it takes us."

Her grey eyes were clear and glittering as she held out her forearm. Isla grasped it against her own, trembling as their skin touched. Eimhir's pulse beat against her own veins with the blood they shared, the blood that had brought them together.

A gust of wind swept across the deck, breaking her from her thoughts. It rattled the loose lines and swirled around the mast, mocking the absence of the sails that should have been there to catch it.

She squared her shoulders. The wind was no good to them. It couldn't take them where they needed to go.

From the other side of the soulship's narrow prow, Darce met her gaze, his eyes dark and troubled. He walked over to her and rested his hands agonisingly close to hers.

"I don't know if I can do what you're asking of me," he said quietly. "But if you're ready, I'm willing to try."

She nodded, tight-lipped.

Darce wrapped his hands around the railing. At once, the air changed. The wind whipped up with more spite than before, snarling at her hair. The waves reared higher, foaming and frothing as they crashed against the hull. She felt the sea stirring, restless and hungry.

But all around the soulship, the horizon remained clear. The distant clouds drifted against the dull sky, too far away to threaten rain or storm. No chill permeated the air. No mist crept over the waves. The tides might have answered Darce's call, but the haar remained out of reach.

"It won't work."

Isla spun around, bracing herself for Duncan's hard expression. Instead, she found Angus, his mouth twisting at the corners as he observed from across the deck.

"Why do you say that?" she asked, fighting to keep the irritation out of her voice.

"I don't say anything. *You* did, when you told us of your memories." He loped towards them. "The gun-anam spilled their blood in sacrifice to bring in the haar. So must he."

A hot rush of fury rose in Isla's chest. "If you even *think* about—"

Angus raised his hands. "You call yourself one of us, yet you still can't help but assume the worst, can you? Ancestors help me, I wasn't going to kill him. What good would it do, spoiling this deck with blood that wasn't given willingly?"

"I—" She stepped back, the anger loosening. "I thought…"

"I know what you thought." Angus shook his head. "We're already facing enough without fighting each other. But we'll never reach the soulless realm without paying some kind of price. You should know that better than anyone, after what you've seen in your dreams."

"He's right," Darce said, eyes tired and cheeks hollow. "Whatever magic I possess, it's not enough. This ship, these bones… They need more from me. I can't ask them to do their part if I don't do mine."

He reached into his pocket and brought out a small silver dagger. It took Isla a moment to recognise the markings engraved on the handle, the delicate blade. The last time she'd seen it, it had been in the hand of the selkie in her memories.

"The sgian dubh," she said, her voice barely a breath. "Where did you…"

"Lachlan gave it to me. He'd never admit it, but I think part of him hoped it would find its way back to you." Darce held it out to her. "It is yours, after all."

It was almost weightless in her palm, yet she knew what it carried in the memory of its blade. It belonged to Mara. Before that, it belonged to the ancestors of her pelt, the selkies who only existed in her dreams. The blade was imbued with the blood of those who had come before her, the blood of those who had given their lives for ships like the one she stood on.

She closed her fingers around it. "Where?"

Darce offered her his hand. A scar snaked across his palm, still pink and tender despite the months that had passed. She remembered the glint of his broken sword, the blood welling from the cut as he pressed it to her side and tethered his soul to hers.

When she met his eyes, he nodded.

Before she had time to change her mind, she pressed the sgian dubh against his palm and drew the blade across his skin. He tried to hide the wince, and she tried to ignore it as she drove the steel deep into his flesh. Red droplets streamed across his hand, falling onto the deck with a gentle *tip-tip*. They seeped and spread, trickling underfoot like tiny scarlet rivers against the white bone.

She lifted the blade, and Darce held out his hand. The droplets soon became a puddle, the snaking streams flowing faster.

Then, the deck began to drink.

Isla watched, barely able to breathe, as blood saturated the bone. The ship absorbed the dribbling red rivulets, sucking them into the hollows of the bones it was made from. It was as though it were quenching its thirst after being starved of water, unable to sate itself.

Darce staggered, face pallid and shining with sweat. "I can feel them," he said, rasping. "Every one of them. They're here in the bones they left behind."

Beside her, Eimhir grew tense. Angus shifted uneasily, casting a look towards Duncan.

Duncan stood in immeasurable silence, his arms folded across his pelt. There was no shift in his expression, just the same resolve he always wore.

Then, finally, he spoke. "It's coming."

Isla felt it. Something in the air changed. The icy wind bit her neck. Her arms tingled, hair turning rigid.

She glanced at Darce. The trickle was slowing, stemmed by the frost creeping over his skin. His breath lingered in the dry air. He was paler than she'd ever seen him, ashen-faced and eyes ringed with shadows.

This was what they'd summoned. The deathly touch of the haar.

"The masts," Angus said, voice faint. "Look at them."

Isla tucked the sgian dubh into the folds of her pelt and turned to the towering pillars of bone stretching towards the sky. A drizzle formed, winding around the length of the yards. The mist crawled over the deck, wisping into shapes that fluttered with a non-existent wind.

It was like the vision she'd seen while dreamwalking. Clouds of spray swirled around the soulship, forming sails of fog. The sky disappeared; so too did the horizon. All she could see was the haar closing in.

The soulship rocked gently, restless on the waves. There was no purpose to the way it slipped through the water. She was a navigator with no heading, no course to chart. They were drifting, lost.

Then, something in the air changed. The foul stench of rot and decay clinging to the haar grew stronger. The endless cold burrowed deeper into her bones. They were passing through a barrier she couldn't see, a shifting of the world that leached the colour from her cheeks and the breath from her lungs.

"It's not a place," she murmured. "I could never have found it on any map. It's a state of being. Or the absence of one."

A low groan echoed through the mist, and Eimhir fell to her knees, shoulders convulsing as she choked out a wracking cough.

"Eimhir!" Isla rushed to her side. "I'm here. Try to breathe, slowly now."

A weak, rattling gasp escaped Eimhir's throat, and Isla held her as another cough tore through her, leaving her fighting for air.

"Bloody...damp," Eimhir said through another splutter. "Feels like my lungs are filled with the sea. Tastes like salt...cold..."

The bark of another cough carried through the air, this time from the quarterdeck. One of the scouts was bent double, hair spilling across his face as he struggled through the hacking.

It wasn't just Eimhir. The haar's ghostly touch was leaving its mark on more than half the other selkies on board. Cracked lips and chattering teeth. Suffocating breaths and bloodshot eyes. It spread through them like the sickness it was, hollowing out the warmth left in their bodies.

Eimhir's hand found hers. "Look."

Isla lifted her head, following Eimhir's gaze to the tips of the masts. The fog-sails stretched wide, draping like a pall from the glistening bone. They hung limp and still, with no wind to stir them.

But it wasn't the sails that turned Isla's blood cold. It was the sky.

Night had fallen, but there were no stars. All she could see was a wash of oily colour bleeding beyond the masts, a red so dark and tenebrous she'd never seen anything like it.

She loosened her fingers from Eimhir's and leaned over the gunwale. Below, the sea sat as still as glass, its depths black and opaque. Even with her pelt snug around her shoulders, she couldn't help but shiver at the thought of plunging below the surface.

"We made it." Eimhir's eyes were bright and feverish. "We've crossed the haar."

Isla squeezed a hand around her shoulder and looked across the deck, meeting Duncan's steady gaze. A glittering sheen of frost clung to his pelt, and his lips were a pale, sickly blue. There was no mistaking the warning he held in his eyes.

Aye, they had crossed the haar. And now, there was no turning back.

CHAPTER TWENTY-SEVEN

DARCE

The bloodied rag Darce had used to bind the gash on his hand was frozen to his skin.

He peeled the corner back, wincing as it tugged the wound open again. There was no escaping the unending cold of this place, the traces of decay it left on all it touched. The fish-rot reek in the air, the eerie red gloom closing in, the unnatural stillness of the waves, as if the sea itself had been emptied of all it once held.

The soulless realm.

As he looked around, he realised they hadn't drifted far at all. The distinctive jagged peaks of the Southern Reaches were visible even through the suffocating darkness. But everything had a haze to it, like they'd been cut off from the real world and lost to some ethereal reflection of it.

"The *Jade Dawn* could sail straight past us, and Nishi would never be any the wiser to it," Isla said, moving closer. "That's how our ancestors kept out of the humans' way for so long. They used the haar to slip into this realm until it was safe to return."

"It's difficult to believe they would choose to come to such a place."

"I don't think it was always like this," she said. "The gun-anam in my dreams weren't like the wraiths we've encountered. They came here willingly, carried by the blood and bones of their people until there were no more soulships left to take them."

An involuntary shudder crept up Darce's spine. "What changed?"

"Without the soulships, selkies whose souls were stolen gave themselves to the sea in their despair," Isla said. "Their bones were left to rot in the depths. They had nothing to pass on but their pain, the echoes of the violence they suffered. That's what corrupted the haar. That's what made this place what it is."

Our blood is on your hands, too. Eimhir's words whispered in his ear again, fraught with accusation.

"This didn't start with the Grand Admiral," he said. "This stretches far further than the bounds of one man's lust for vengeance. We hunted them long before we knew what they were. And once we found out, we didn't stop. It will *never* stop, even after Cunningham is gone."

Isla slipped her hand into his. Ever since she'd claimed her pelt, her skin had been cold to the touch. Now, her fingers were like ice.

"I have to believe there's a chance," she said. "A way for both parts of me to exist in this world. A way I won't have to choose one over the other."

"Do you think that's possible?" he asked. "That peace is possible?"

She stilled, her eyes flicking over to where Duncan stood with Eimhir and Angus. "I don't know."

The raw truth of it hung in the air, as sharp as the edge of a blade. Some currents were never meant to converge. If there was a line to be drawn between human and selkie, either he or Isla would have to cross it, or they would be separated forever.

Maybe you are made for waters I cannot follow you to, he'd said to her, once. He'd given her up that day. He'd lost her.

He wasn't sure he had the strength to do it again.

The soulship continued to drift, carried not by wind or current, but by whatever unnatural force governed the haar. Though the blanket of fog retreated over the black, glassy sea, the wisping sails remained. They shimmered against the masts, dancing with droplets of salt water. There might not have been any wind to stir them, but they fluttered nonetheless, their movements odd and erratic.

"Are you doing that?" Isla asked.

Darce shook his head. He'd tried harnessing the strange black waves with his sentinel magic, but the sea spirits were loath to answer. They were unpredictable at the best of times, unconcerned with the whims and desires of humans, but here... It was like he'd been cut off from them entirely. The song in his blood was muted, and when he reached out, all he felt was the abyss.

Isla frowned. "If it's not you, it must be something else. Something is drawing this ship to it."

After some time, the murkiness on the horizon wavered, thinning out to reveal a spit of land protruding from the water. There were no trees, no thickets of knapweed or hawkbit to offer some colour to the shore. Just a barren rock that seemed to be the only harbour for miles.

"Look," Isla said. "Do you see them?"

Darce peered through the darkness. At first, all he saw was a ghostly haze shrouding the island in shadows. Then something stirred, and he caught a glimpse of a familiar wisping shape gliding through the gloom.

The gun-anam.

His hand drifted towards the sword on his belt, but Isla caught his arm. "Not this time. We didn't come here to fight them. We need to put an end to their suffering, not add to it. They're our only hope of ridding the haar of its corruption."

"How do you plan to do that?"

"I don't know, not yet. But I have to go to them." Her jaw tensed as she looked at the shore. "Sometimes I wonder if it wasn't them calling to me all along. That ache in me, the restlessness I felt... I thought by claiming my pelt, living among my people, that it would somehow fade. But it never went away. It pulled me to the wrecks of the soulships. It pulled me here."

She brought them with her, Lachlan said, bitter even in memory. *It all traces back to her.*

Fear wormed through him. Lachlan had been right all along. The wraiths had followed Isla ever since she'd returned to Silveckan, trailing behind her like a ghostly wake. She couldn't escape them—not in Caolaig, not in Arburgh, not out on the wild waters. And now she was here, willingly, in their realm. Because they'd called to her. They *wanted* her here.

"You don't have to do this," he said.

The edge of her lips stretched into a thin, strained line. "If I asked you to stay on the ship, would you listen?"

"I think you know the answer to that." A reluctant smile tugged at his own mouth. "It seems your stubbornness rubbed off on me."

"Oh, you always had plenty of your own. Why do you suppose we clashed so much?" She laughed softly. "That morning in the courtyard... My knuckles bloodied, my pride bruised. It feels like another life, one I'll never be able to get back. Blackwood Estate wasn't home, yet now it's gone, part of me mourns it, maybe even misses it." She shook her head. "I promised Lachlan we'd return, but I could never have kept that promise. Too much has changed."

"Not everything." He closed her icy fingers in his. "I meant what I said when I made the blood oath. I was always yours. I'll follow wherever you go, as long as I'm able to."

She squeezed. "Then let's face this."

The waters around the rocky island ran deep, and the soulship was able to drift close enough for the gangway to bridge the gap to one of the outcroppings. Darce followed the selkies over, glancing down at the black water under the narrow walkway. The surface was so opaque it made it impossible to gauge the depths below it. There could have been another world lurking down there, and none of them would ever know it.

Once his feet hit solid rock, he looked around. The island was eerily quiet. No seabirds mewled over the wind, no crabs scuttled across the stone. It was like a hollow echo of the world they'd come from, the world they'd left behind when they'd passed through the haar. The only sound was a ghostly rustling coming from the gun-anam as they swept aimlessly across the rock, as if carried by a non-existent wind.

One of them drifted towards him. It wore no seal-skull mask, just a swirling cloud of salt and spray where its head should have been. Its blackened bones hung around its ribs like armour, dripping with silt and rotten seaweed.

A hollow rattle came from what should have been its mouth, and as it reached out with one of its silvery tendrils, Darce's throat seized closed. He clawed at his neck as the breath in his lungs turned to spray, filling his chest with ice water. He was drowning, suffocating from the inside.

"Stop." Isla's voice rang out, cutting through the still air like a blade. "Let him go."

Before she'd finished speaking, the pressure on his windpipe loosened, and he fell to his knees, gasping. His throat was raw and frozen, his lungs aching, but the water was gone. All that remained of the gun-anam's attack was the foul taste on his tongue.

He staggered back to his feet. The wraith hadn't moved; it floated in the air in front of him, its incorporeal form wisping across the rocks. It took no notice of him as he retreated, rather it waited, as if for some kind of instruction.

"They know you." Eimhir's voice was low and rasping, but Darce couldn't mistake the tremor of excitement in it. "Your pelt, its memories, the blood of your ancestors... They must recognise it. They must know we've come here to put things right."

Something in the strain of her words gave Darce pause, but before he could dwell on it, a blood-curdling scream tore through the air.

He flinched, the sound piercing through the hollow of his remaining ear. It was an awful, keening wail, wretched and defiant in equal measure, like a wounded animal unable to die.

Angus's face turned white. "I don't know what manner of spirit is capable of making that noise, but I doubt it can mean anything good. We should—"

The scream rattled again, drowning out the rest of his words. An unpleasant shiver crawled over Darce's skin. Whatever was making that sound, it was in terrible pain, and it wanted them to know it. The shrill echo burrowed bone-deep, taking root somewhere he couldn't dig out. He wanted it to stop. He wanted it to—

"No." Eimhir's voice was little more than a breath. Her grey eyes clouded over as she fixed her gaze on something near the edge of the shore. A misty haze lingered around one of the rockpools, writhing like it was in agony.

The wretched scream tore loose again, sending another stab of pain through his head.

"Stay away from it," Duncan said abruptly. "Eimhir, don't go—"

Eimhir paid him no attention. Every step was slow and stuttering, like she was being dragged by something the rest of them couldn't see.

When she reached the rockpool, she stooped low and knelt next to the swirling vapour. Darce couldn't see her face. He only heard the horror-struck scream.

This time, it was coming from Eimhir.

Isla was the first to move. She rushed forward, leaping over one of the rocks and landing at Eimhir's side. When she reached her, she stopped dead, her face ashen.

It wasn't until Darce drew closer that he realised what they were staring at. There in the rockpool was a twisted, wretched creature. It might have been one of the gun-anam, but something was different about its wraithlike form. The spray was restless, the wisping vapour thrashing as if to be free of the bones in its midst. And the bones...

He swallowed, mouth dry. Tides, the bones. They carried the same rot as the rest of the gun-anam, slimy and blackened, dripping with rancid seaweed. But these bones... They weren't big enough to form a cuirass of ribs or a skull-like helm. They were spindly, ill-formed things, so delicate he thought they might disintegrate. These weren't the bones of a grown selkie. This was...

"A bairn." Eimhir's voice was so low, so cold, it sounded like it had risen from the fathoms. She turned to look at them all, tears streaking her face. There was not a word Darce knew to describe the pain contorting her features. It was beyond anguish, beyond grief.

"Is this what became of him?" she whispered. "My wee brother. When my mother surrendered him to the sea, was this the same fate he suffered?"

"Leave it be." Duncan spoke quietly, but Darce didn't mistake the stiffness in his shoulders as he moved towards Eimhir. "No good can come of this. Whatever this creature once was, it's beyond our help."

Eimhir closed her eyes and moaned. The malformed wraith twisted and writhed, turning the air cold.

Do you know what happens to a selkie newborn with no pelt to inherit? she'd asked him once. *They wither and die within months, and each moment they spend without their soul is one of agony.*

Every part of him screamed to look away, but he couldn't tear his eyes from the sight in front of him. The pitiful tangle of mist and bones, the torment on Eimhir's face, the desperation on Isla's as she turned to him for help he could not give.

"We need to put an end to this." Eimhir lifted her head, fixing Isla with a despondent stare. "Only you can do it. You need to make this right."

"We'll find a way." Isla knelt beside her, slipping her hand into hers.

"We'll put an end to their suffering. Once the corruption in the haar is gone—"

"The corruption isn't the problem." Eimhir shot to her feet. "It never was. You *know* what the problem is, caraid. You know what you have to do."

Duncan tensed. Darce glanced at him, his blood cold as he took in the disquiet in his expression. Angus was on edge too, his freckled forehead creased with distress as his gaze flew between them both.

Isla's face fell. "I don't understand."

"No, I don't think you do." A soft chuckle escaped Eimhir's lips. "Or perhaps you don't want to admit it. I can't blame you for that. I know how much this will pain you, how much you'll blame yourself for what must come next. But there's no other choice. They've left us no other choice." A shadow fell across her face as she turned to the tortured wraith. "You want to purge the haar of its corruption and bring back the soulships so our people can pass into this world peacefully like they did before. But none of that matters if the Admiralty is still around to hunt us." She paused, voice hardening. "As long as *humans* are still around."

Isla reeled back like she'd been slapped. "You don't mean that. Eimhir, you can't possibly—"

"Why shouldn't I mean it?" Eimhir rounded on her, eyes flashing wildly. "*Look* at him. Look at what they do to us. I suffered only a taste of it when they stole my pelt, and that agony left a scar that will never fade. But for these creatures, these ancestors of ours... It's endless for them. That violence is all they know. It's what they are."

"We can stop it," Isla said, desperation straining her voice. "Together."

"Aye," Eimhir said. "We can."

Something in the air changed. Darce sensed it like a storm gathering, thick and oppressive. He reached for the tides, praying his magic would stir, but there was no answer. Instead, he slowly brought his hand to rest on the hilt of his cutlass.

He felt Duncan's eyes on him, but the selkie chieftain said nothing.

He just regarded him with an impassive look, then turned back to Isla and Eimhir.

Eimhir stood stiff and unyielding as she stared at Isla. "If we sail the soulship into Arburgh under the cover of the haar, the Admiralty will never see us coming. By the time we emerge from the mists, it will be too late for them to mount any kind of defence." Her eyes shone. "This is our chance, caraid. We can rid Silveckan of the Admiralty once and for all. They won't be able to hunt us anymore. And you...you'll be safe from that bastard who calls himself your father."

Isla stepped back. "It would be slaughter, on both sides. The gun-anam—"

"The gun-anam will follow you. You can give them the vengeance they deserve."

"Stop, Eimhir! Just...stop." Isla buried her hands in her hair. "I know you're hurting. I know you're in pain. But please... This isn't you. This isn't what you wanted when you set out to find Mara's lost pelt. Remember that. Remember who you are."

"Who *I* am?" Eimhir blinked. "What about who you are? You're the last dreamwalker. You're the one who was meant to help our people."

"Not like this. You would unleash a violence so bloody it would leave scars across Silveckan for decades. That kind of violence isn't easily forgotten. It will be answered in kind, and this will all begin anew." Isla reached for her arm. "You know this isn't the way."

"Do I?" Eimhir whispered. "I'm not sure I know anything anymore."

She wrenched her arm away and stepped into the water. For a moment, she hesitated, and Darce almost allowed himself to believe Isla had broken through the despair taking hold of her spirit.

Then she fell backwards, pelt melting over her skin as she disappeared under the still surface.

"Eimhir, no! Where are you—" A choking sob cut through the rest of Isla's words. She snapped her head around, silently begging him for forgiveness. Then she leapt and followed Eimhir into the black sea, leaving nothing behind but the splash of her wake.

Part of him wanted to cry out after her, as she had for Eimhir, but his throat constricted around the futile words. There was nothing he could say that would call her back. Not when it came to Eimhir.

"You have to go after them." He turned to Duncan and Angus, trying to read their stony faces. "Whatever you came here for, you won't succeed without them—*both* of them. Isla needs her. You have to make Eimhir see that."

"I don't think Eimhir is capable of seeing anything more than the bloodlust infecting her." Duncan dropped his head. "I *warned* her. I told her the crossing would be too much for Eimhir."

Angus tensed. "You suspected?" When Duncan didn't answer, he turned to Darce. "Once the mist sickness sets in, nobody can stop it. If that's what has taken root in Eimhir, I fear we're already too late."

"You have to try. Please. Just...bring them back."

The two selkies exchanged a weighted look. Then Duncan gave a tight nod, and they made their way to the edge of the rocks, where the sea lay unnaturally still once more.

Angus took to the water first, his russet-coloured fur spreading over his freckled shoulders as he slipped into his seal form and disappeared into the depths. Duncan waited, his brow heavy.

"I don't envy you, human," he said. "I know what it's like to wait, wondering if this is the time they don't come back. Maybe you'll be spared that today, but it will come. It always does."

He slipped into the water, the glossy fur of his pelt bleeding into the waves. A splash later, and he was gone, leaving Darce with only a dread-filled heart and the foreboding echo of his words.

CHAPTER TWENTY-EIGHT

ISLA

The frantic beating of Isla's seal heart bruised her ribs as she followed the trail of bubbles Eimhir left in her wake. Her whiskers flicked against the current, promising her she was swimming in the right direction. All she could do was trust her body's instincts, sink into the selkie part of her and bury the confusion and fear and heartache that was all too human.

You know what the problem is, caraid. You know what you have to do.

Eimhir's words echoed in the voice of a stranger. They were too cruel to belong to her. She wasn't herself. That wretched wraith had stricken her with grief, pushed her to a place too dark to crawl out of. But Isla could reach her. She'd always been able to reach her.

She kicked with her flippers, shooting through the water with all the speed she could muster. The sea was as black below the surface as it was above. Around her, the darkness was so thick she could see nothing but the trace of bubbles bursting against her snout. If there was any other presence down here, living or spirit, it didn't want to show itself.

Perhaps that was for the best. She already had enough to contend with.

The gun-anam will follow you, Eimhir reminded her. *You can give them the vengeance they deserve.*

Even the layer of blubber under her hide wasn't enough to stave off the chill. She couldn't forget what happened at Blackwood Estate, so long ago it felt like a lifetime. The haar creeping through the halls. The wraiths drifting from room to room, leaving a trail of frost in their wake. The blood-soaked cobbles in the courtyard, suffocated by bodies savaged and flayed.

Not even Arburgh deserved that kind of violence. The capital was home to more than the Admiralty.

She flexed the muscles in her jaw, shifting her grip on the sgian dubh between her teeth. She'd carried the blade in the folds of her pelt ever since she'd used it to spill Darce's blood across the soulship's deck. Now that she knew what it truly was, who it once belonged to, she was loath to leave it behind. It was more than a selkie blade—it was a dreamwalker's blade. It was her responsibility to carry it as Mara once had, as all her ancestors once had.

Ahead, she caught a faint movement: a ripple of fur, the powerful flick of flippers. It was Eimhir. It had to be.

She raced to catch up, following the churn of her wake until a small skerry emerged. Without slowing, she leapt from the water, landing with a thump as her belly hit the sea-soaked stone.

As she rolled over and began shedding her pelt, she saw Eimhir sitting hunched on one of the rocks, already in her human form. Her shoulders were square under the wet, fawn-coloured fur, and she stared at Isla bleakly.

This isn't you, Isla had told her. She wanted it to be true. She *needed* it to be true.

"Please," she said, as soon as her snout gave way to her human lips. "Don't lose sight of what we came here to do, not now we're so close. Let's finish this together like we said we would."

"It is not I who went back on my word."

Isla recoiled. "You think I did? I swore on Mara's memory I would protect our people. That doesn't mean drenching ourselves in more blood, not when we're covered in it enough already."

Eimhir gave a thin smile. "Is it so bad to want the Admiralty to bleed?"

"It's not their blood I'm talking about. If we succumb to that kind of violence, how long will it take for its ripples to turn back on our own people? How many more selkies will pay the price for what we did?" She shook her head. "I have as much reason to want the Admiralty gone as anyone. But if we slaughter a city of innocent people just to strike at our enemies, we'll only end up with more."

Eimhir looked at her, eyes cold. "There are no innocent people. There are only humans."

Her words struck Isla in the hollow of her sternum. A sharp pain tore through her chest, like something straining had pulled too far and snapped. There was no trace of Eimhir's wry humour in the rasp of her voice. No suggestion of the crooked smile at the side of her lips. She was lost, buried beneath something Isla had been unable or unwilling to see.

"The mist sickness." She wrenched the words from her throat, the taste of them like ash on her tongue. "It has you, doesn't it?"

Eimhir stared at her, stone faced and impassive. Then something crumbled, giving way to the stark, awful truth.

"Aye," she murmured. "I'd say it has."

Isla stowed the sgian dubh in her pelt to take Eimhir's hands in her own. Her fingers were cold, her pulse faint. The signs seemed brutally clear now: the bruised purple webbing circling her tired eyes, the deepening hollows in her cheeks, the weight of exhaustion and despair in her voice. The haar had left its mark on her, and Isla hadn't realised until it was too late.

She should have known. She should have seen this.

"There must be something we can do," she said. "We came here to return the mists to what they once were. If we can rid them of this sickness, we can save you, too."

"Ah, caraid, you truly believe that, and I love you for it." A weak smile broke through the pall on Eimhir's face, and for a moment, she seemed like herself again. "I only wish I could believe it. But this despair that has its grip on me... It won't let go. The cold already runs bone-deep, and every day I wake, it tunnels deeper. I feel it hanging over me, like a shadow I can't shake." She pressed her lips together. "I wish I could. I wish—"

Isla wrapped her arms around her and buried a sob into the damp fur of Eimhir's pelt. She didn't know which one of them was trembling more. All she could think about was the pain wracking her heart, the grief flooding her chest. It was happening again. This loss, this wrenching away of the people she loved... How much more could she endure?

Eimhir's arms shifted around her back. The beat of her heart answered her own, echoing with the blood they shared. She was still here. She was alive. As long as that remained true, so did hope.

"I won't give up," Isla said, her voice muffled in the speckled fur. "I'll find a way to save you. I promise."

As she squeezed her, she didn't feel Eimhir's hand slip down her side. All she felt was the irrevocable dread of a mistake she couldn't undo as a familiar blade flashed in Eimhir's palm.

"I'm sorry," Eimhir whispered, and placed a cold, brackish kiss to her forehead.

It happened too quick for Isla to make sense of. The sgian dubh that had been nestled in the folds of her pelt glinted in Eimhir's hand. Something sharp and painful seared down her forearm, and she looked down to see a river of red running from the crook of her elbow to her wrist.

Eimhir had cut her open.

She stared, dazed, at the slick coat of blood covering her arm. It was like looking at someone else's body. Even though the blood trickled warm and wet on her skin. Even though she smelled its coppery tang. It couldn't be hers. If it was, it would mean...

Eimhir's eyes were bright and feverish, tears streaking her skin. "You left me no choice, caraid. Someone had to do it, for our people. It should have been you. I wanted it to be you."

She seized her arm, and Isla cried out in pain. For a moment, she thought she might have seen a flash of regret in Eimhir.

Then Eimhir tightened her grip, smearing the blood over the dappled fur of Isla's pelt. The rippling hues of grey and lavender and midnight blue muddied under a scarlet stain as the blood soaked in and spread. There was too much of it. Isla's head was growing light, her vision blurring.

A wiry pair of arms caught her as she stumbled, lowering her gently to the rock. Something was happening to her pelt. It was peeling away from her, leaving her wretched and bare. It was a distant kind of agony. She wondered if she should feel some sense of shame, lying naked on the stone, but everything seemed so out of reach. The salt water on her lips, the chill of the sea crawling over her skin... It wasn't her. It couldn't be her.

"Eimhir." A gravelly voice rumbled in her ears, muffled by her pounding heart. "By the memories of our ancestors... What have you *done?*"

Someone was kneeling at her side, but she couldn't bring herself to lift her cheek from the cold rock. Raised voices rumbled through the air, the meaningless words washing over her.

A painful pressure clamped down on her arm, followed by a guttural bark and a splash. She twisted her neck to see Duncan leaning over her, his hair dripping across her naked skin as he eased her forearm above her head, hands squeezing around the gash. Blood trickled between his fingers, dripping onto her collarbone, leaving claret spots across her pallid skin.

When she met his eyes, she found only the sting of pity there. "I warned you," he said. "I tried to warn you."

"Make it stop."

"It's too late for that. It's too late for her." His brow creased with deep, disconsolate lines. "You never had anything to fear from me. Not even in my most wretched moments of desperation would I try to take another's soul. Any selkie would have to be broken in spirit, beyond saving, to be driven to such depths."

"She's not lost yet."

"She will be." He looked across the skerry. "It's only a matter of time."

Eimhir stood on the edge of the rock, her hair spilling down her back as she stared out over the water. Even in the dim light, something about her was different. The fur around her shoulders was no longer fawn-coloured and speckled, but a lustrous grey smeared with red.

When she turned, all the traces of remorse Isla imagined were gone. There was only resolve, and the darkness of a gathering storm.

Her vision blurred. She'd lost too much blood. But there was nothing else she needed to see.

As she closed her eyes, she heard Duncan's voice raised in anger, Eimhir's sharp in response. She didn't know what they were saying. It hardly mattered anymore. Her skull was thick and foggy, her mind tired. The clamour grew fainter, fading into the distance, and she slipped gratefully into oblivion.

CHAPTER TWENTY-NINE

DARCE

Darce stalked the shore, the crunch of gravel under his boots scratching the inside of his skull with every step. But he couldn't stop. If he stopped, he might go mad. If he stopped, he might give up entirely.

The soulship floated on the placid waves, the gangway bridging the gap between the island's rocky ridge and the ship's deck. The rest of the selkies stayed on board, waiting for Isla and the others to come back.

What would happen if they didn't?

He rubbed a hand over his face, fighting the urge to empty his lungs and curse the tides. There was nothing he could do. He couldn't follow her. He was alone.

Around him, the island lay dreich and barren, drizzle clinging to the rocks. The gun-anam lingered, but they left him alone, paying him no attention as they drifted past with their wisping tendrils and rattling breaths. It was as if he didn't exist to them, as if *he* were the ghost here.

He reached out in vain, grasping for the barest threads. But again, the tides were silent, and the thrumming in his blood had no call to answer.

Eventually, his weary legs yielded to exhaustion and he sat on the gravel shore, unable to do anything but wait. The black waves had neither encroached nor retreated since they'd arrived. Even the tides were affected by this place.

After what might have been minutes or hours, a stirring of the water tore him from his thoughts, and he looked up to see three figures rise from the sea, their soaking pelts hanging around their shoulders.

Three, he thought, turning cold. *But that would mean…*

Eimhir waded towards him, her expression like stone. She was carrying someone in her arms, their pale skin naked and exposed. A clump of seaweed was tied around a drooping arm, oozing with dark blood.

His heart seized. Tides, no.

It was Isla.

He raced to meet them, boots splashing through the water as he ran. Eimhir tensed, but she said nothing as she gently placed Isla's limp body into his arms. He pressed her close against his chest, shielding her dignity as much as he was able.

Her blood pulsed against his. She was alive.

He carried her to a slab and set her down, whipping off his cloak to wrap it around her naked body. Then he turned to Eimhir, aghast. "What happened? How did she…"

The rest of his words died on his tongue, his mouth dry and stale. There was something different about Eimhir. Something had changed in the rippling tones of her pelt where it sat against her pale skin. It didn't look fawn-brown as it once did. It looked…grey.

"What did you do?" he whispered. As soon as the question left his lips, rage bubbled in his throat. "What the *fuck* did you do?"

If Eimhir answered, he didn't hear it. Blood pounded in his remaining ear, drowning out everything but the roar of his own fury. His sword was in his hand before he realised he'd drawn it, fingers clenching the hilt so tightly he thought it might shatter.

He rushed towards her, blade pointed at the grey folds hanging over her chest. He'd have her heart, or whatever was left of it.

Eimhir didn't flinch. She didn't need to. Before he could get close enough to run his blade through her, the mists closed in. Silvery strands of vapour coiled across his outstretched arm, leaving frozen trails around his wrist. His breath clouded in front of him, then stilled, his lungs seizing as they filled with icy water.

Something wet brushed his cheek, and he forced his head around to see the shadowy face of a gun-anam. Whatever features it might have borne were lost in an ever-shifting haze of spray, but he felt its empty gaze, its rotten breath on his skin.

He parted his lips, but no air came to him. The haar was too thick, the gun-anam's touch too cold. He couldn't escape it. He couldn't—

"Enough."

Eimhir's voice rang through the air, and the gun-anam withdrew, like it had under Isla's command before. Darce dropped to his knees, retching bile and seawater across the rocks. His throat burned, his lungs weak and wanting for air.

He wiped the spittle from his mouth and climbed to his feet. A vein pulsed in Eimhir's temple, and a trickle of blood oozed from her nose. She didn't look like the selkie he remembered. There was no trace of the friend he thought she was—if not to him, then at least to Isla.

"I won't kill you, auld blood," she said. "I know what you mean to her. She deserves the chance to say goodbye."

"You're wearing her pelt. You spilled her blood over her soul so you could take it from her. Did she deserve that, too?" Grief thickened in his throat. "She's going to die, isn't she? She'll become one of those wraiths."

Eimhir cast her eyes over Isla, shrouded under his cloak. "Sometimes I wonder how she did it," she said softly. "How she lived for so long without the soul that should have been hers. A selkie needs the sea. We *are* the sea. A newborn pup with no pelt to inherit will wither and die, like my brother." A shadow fell across her gaunt face. "Yet she survived. I'm not sure if Mara understood that when she ran, or if it was merely the desperation of a dying mother. But Isla lived. The human part of her kept her alive. She never knew what it was to be separated from her soulskin. How could she suffer the loss of something she never had?"

"And now?" Darce asked, voice tight. "Are you saying her human blood might save her again?"

"No." The word rang with excruciating finality. "The moment she claimed her pelt, there was no going back to what she once was. Just as there's no going back for me." Eimhir ran her hands over the blood-stained folds. "I'm sorry, auld blood. I can't even risk giving her my old pelt. She would only try to stop what comes next. But you must know I never wanted to lose her like this. I would rather she fought with the living, instead of becoming one with the haar. But even if she turns to salt and spray, at least she'll be by my side for what is to come. Perhaps that is all I can ask for."

"You mean to go through with this?" Darce said. "After all your talk of peace, you would drag Silveckan into a new age of vengeance?"

"It's the same fucking age," Eimhir said harshly. "Nothing has changed. Nothing will ever change. I didn't see that before, but I do now."

She trudged towards the soulship, grey pelt trailing behind her. Angus stared after her, then followed, his arms laden with a dull bundle of fawn-coloured fur Darce recognised as Eimhir's pelt.

Duncan was the last to leave. He watched them go, then turned to Darce with a sombre gaze. "Here. If you love her like she believes you do, you'll end it before she wakes."

The clang of steel on stone rattled through the air, and a familiar silver blade landed at Darce's feet.

He stooped to pick the sgian dubh off the wet ground, blood running cold as he realised what Duncan meant. The intricate carvings on the handle swirled, making his head spin.

"I can't," he muttered. "I could never—"

When he looked up, Duncan was gone.

He slipped the blade into his pocket and climbed onto the flat slab where he'd laid Isla. The stench of salt and copper filled his nostrils from the seaweed slathered across the bloody gouge down her arm.

Eimhir had done this to her. And he'd let her go.

He wrapped the cloak around Isla's unconscious frame and pulled her into the concave of his chest, shielding her from the drizzle. Apart from the wound to her arm, she looked unharmed. But her pelt was gone. If what he understood about selkies was true, it was only a matter of time before her body followed. It might take weeks, but eventually, her skin would slowly wither and peel, marred with scars of salt. Her sable hair would turn dull and brittle. Her lips would crack until they bled, her organs would waste inside her body.

And he wouldn't be able to do a tides-damned thing about it.

In the distance, the soulship sailed away, carrying Eimhir and the rest of them with it. Darce knew where they were headed. He didn't care. All he could think about was the warning in Duncan's parting words.

If you love her like she believes you do, you'll end it before she wakes.

He pulled the sgian dubh from his pocket, balancing the finely wrought dagger in the palm of his hand. Strange how such a wee blade could have altered the course of so many lives with the blood it had spilled.

Muir had told him the sgian dubh's bearer would protect Isla. But that was before Eimhir used it to carve open her arm and steal her soul.

What kind of purpose was left in it now?

He closed his fingers around the engraved hilt, smothering it in his hand. Perhaps Duncan was right. Perhaps the only thing left to do was protect her from the slow, drawn-out suffering that would surely set in over the coming weeks. He could draw the blade across her throat, swift and painless. It would be over quickly. It would spare her that torment.

The silver edge of the dagger glinted red in his hand, streaked with her blood. Some of the capillary-thin trails were fading, like the steel had drunk them in. Like it wanted more.

Her eyelids fluttered. It was a subtle, involuntary movement, but it was her. She was still fighting, as stubborn as ever.

What else could he do but fight with her?

He slipped the sgian dubh back into the safety of his pocket. Eimhir had taken too much already. He wouldn't let her take what little time they had left.

Leaning forward, he pressed a soft kiss against her forehead and held her close as the eerie red sky flickered, taunting him with the promise of a dawn that would never come.

CHAPTER THIRTY

ISLA

The moment Isla opened her eyes, everything had changed.

It wasn't pain, not quite. Nor was it as simple as grief. It burrowed to a place deeper than the hollows of her bones, deeper than the darkest shadows of her heart. This was loss. Unspeakable, immeasurable loss.

Darce's words washed over her like a wave, but she couldn't take anything in. She only felt the absence of what had once been hers. The rippling grey folds that clung to her like a second skin. The scent of salt and damp fur spilling across her shoulders. The feeling of being whole, of being found.

Now, it was gone. Eimhir had ripped it from her.

That was a loss too. A different kind of loss, one that didn't ache, but stung her heart bloody. *Cousin*, she'd called her. *Caraid*. The echo of her voice rang hollow. It might have been easier if Isla believed it was all a lie, that this betrayal was inevitable. But it wasn't. Eimhir had loved her, and that was the worst part of all.

A day passed, then another. All she wanted to do was sleep, so she didn't need to feel the ache of what had been taken from her. But each time she opened her eyes and found Darce by her side, quiet and patient, some of the fog faded. She forced herself to eat, even if the only pickings were cockles and clams. She found the strength to bathe in the icy black water.

Then, one morning—or whatever passed for morning in this forsaken realm—the haze lifted entirely. The denial holding her together shattered, and all she was left with was the stark truth of what she would soon become.

Gun-anam.

A roar of frustration tore from her throat, jolting Darce awake next to her. He sat bolt upright, hand flying to the sword on his belt.

When he met her gaze, he stilled. "Isla. Tides, I thought—"

"I'm sorry," she whispered, those two words carrying the weight of all the things she couldn't speak of, all the parts too terrible to give voice to.

He pressed his lips to hers. The kiss was all the more painful for how gentle it was, like he was afraid the lightest touch might break her.

A low grumble came from his stomach, and Darce drew back, wincing. The consuming shadow of hunger had already left its mark, hollowing out his cheeks, leaving him pale and gaunt. Handfuls of fallen rainwater and scavenged scraps of shellfish wouldn't be enough to sustain either of them for long.

For her, that might be a blessing.

She reached into the water and plucked an oyster from the half-submerged rock in front of them, the curved shell as large as her palm. The seam tore against her fingertips as she prised it apart, the shell snapping loose to reveal the slippery flesh inside.

When she offered it to Darce, he shook his head. "You first. You haven't eaten today."

"You need it more than I do."

The unspoken implication lingered between them, and she immediately regretted it. The most painful part of what lay ahead was knowing what it would do to him. When the ache of living without her pelt became too much for her to bear, she'd surrender herself to the sea, her soulless body lost to the depths until she rose as one of the gun-anam.

She tilted the shell and slid the oyster into her mouth, the gesture as close to an apology as she could offer. The supple flesh burst as she chewed, releasing a sweet, briny juice across her tongue. There was a time she might have taken some kind of pleasure from the taste, a time she might have savoured the sensation of it slipping down her throat. Now, she just felt empty.

The shell slipped from her hand, clattering against the rock. Her fingers had turned white. She rubbed them together, but she could barely feel her own skin. Whatever warmth was left in her blood, it was slowly abandoning her.

"You're freezing." Darce took her hand in his, but the heat of his palm couldn't bleed any feeling back into her. He rolled her wrist over, then stilled as he found a trail of salt crawling up to her elbow. It was so faint she'd missed the mark it left against her pale skin, but now she'd seen it, it was impossible to ignore.

"It's starting," she said.

Speaking the words felt like a relief, like dropping the weight of the shield she'd been holding to keep the truth at bay. She forced herself to meet Darce's eyes, bracing herself for what she would find there. She didn't want him to look at her wracked with grief and regret. It wasn't what she wanted him to remember, not while she was still herself, still *alive*.

She shifted closer and pressed her lips to his. He yielded to her, his mouth warm and wanting as it parted to meet hers. Her pulse quickened as she leaned in deeper, pushing away every thought in her mind but him. All she could think about was the desperate need rising in her, the desire to drown in the way he was kissing her. The sensation of his hand as it tightened around her waist, separated from her skin by his cloak. His fingers wrapped in her hair, pulling her so close she could barely breathe. The sweet, briny tang of the oyster lingered on her tongue as she explored the taste of him, hungry for more.

He drew back, his cheeks flushed with colour. "Isla, I—"

"Don't stop. Please."

He shook his head. "Not here. Not in this place."

A bitter laugh escaped her throat, too quick to swallow. "There is no other place for us, Darce. This is all we have. And if it is to be our end, I won't let it deny me leaving on my terms." She touched his cheek, tracing his stubble-coated jaw. "I won't let it deny me you."

His brown eyes locked with hers. She saw the conflict on his face, the doubt weighing on his brow. All she wanted to do was reach for the nape of his neck and pull him into her once more. Instead, she waited, her chest rising and falling with each breath.

He leaned closer, taking her head in his hands. "I don't believe there's a force in this world that could deny you, Isla Blackwood. Tides know I've never been able to."

His lips were on hers again, more insistent this time, each kiss deeper and more urgent than the last. She arched into the curve of his chest, then fell against the rock, the folds of the cloak spilling open across her skin. She tore free the fastening around her neck, shivering as the rest of the fabric slid away. Gooseflesh rippled across her body, every naked inch of her trembling with a heady mixture of cold and anticipation.

Darce paused, his eyes darkening as he trailed his gaze over her. Then he followed her down, lips brushing her collarbone as he brought his body on top of hers.

She wanted this. Longer than she'd ever admit to herself. She'd tried to bury it, but it came rushing to the surface, bleeding through her skin, sending flushes through her cheeks, her neck, chasing away the chill.

When his fingers slipped between her thighs, she whimpered, unable to think of anything but the bittersweet ache his touch left her with. Each breath she drew was a gasp Darce was quick to smother, his lips parting again and again, his tongue urgent and yearning like he'd never wanted to taste anything else.

Her hands fumbled with the buckle on his belt, the hem of his shirt. She peeled his damp clothes from his body, taking in the curve of his bare shoulders. She'd had her share of entanglements over the years: stolen moments in cabin sheets, short-lived trysts in different ports. But none of them, sailor or pirate or noble, had belonged to her the way Darce did. None of them had brought the same rush to her heart, the same warmth pooling between her legs.

When he slid into her, she let out a gasp slick with relief. Her mind turned painfully, blissfully blank, filled with nothing but the sensation of him. All she could think about was the way they twisted together, the rubbing of her thighs as she wound her legs around him, the warmth of his breath as his lips traced her neck, the pressure of his hand buried between their winding bodies, bringing her to a place she never wanted to leave.

If she'd lost her soul, she'd found something else tonight, something that rose within her with such wanting, such need, she didn't know how she'd ever survived without it.

Darce released a shaking breath as he slowed, holding his weight above her. Never had she seen him so raw, so exposed. His pale cheeks held a flush, and a sheen of sweat clung to his brow as he brushed his lips over hers. The fleeting touch left her skin tingling, and she looked up to see his eyes glittering as he held her in the heat of his gaze.

"Isla," he murmured again, her name like a promise.

It was enough.

She pulled him beside her, folding into his arms, burying her face against his chest. His hands slid around her curve of her spine, and for a moment, she allowed herself to believe he might be able to hold her until the end. That she might be able to stay in the shelter of him and wait out what was to come.

But when she closed her eyes, all she could smell was the quickening of salt.

It was impossible to tell how much time had passed when she woke. The sky was as dark as ever, aglow with a dim red haze. Darce's sleeping breaths rumbled through the air, disturbing the oppressive silence.

She slipped out from under his arm and climbed to her feet, curling her toes against the rock. The cold didn't burrow as deep as it used to. It was part of her now; she carried it in her blood and bones. Soon, it would spread to the rest of her, until it was too agonising to cling to life anymore.

Looking down, she saw new streaks of salt on her arm, the crystals sinking into her skin like teeth. It would bite deeper soon. The scarring would spread over her flesh and burrow through to her muscles. It would gnaw at her organs and dry her body from the inside out, until she was nothing but a husk.

She knew what the suffering would do to her, what it would do to Darce. There was only one thing she could do to spare them both.

The black waves lapped against the rock as she walked to the edge. Only darkness lurked below the surface, but the depths didn't hold as much fear as they had before. They called to her, promising an end to this. A way out from the pain that would soon consume her.

She slipped in slowly, careful not to make any sound that would rouse Darce. The sea closed around her naked skin, splashing her neck as she swam. She could barely feel her limbs anymore. Her fingers and toes were numb. Her lungs whined with every shallow breath she gulped down. She was fighting a battle with the fathoms, and she was ready to let them win.

In, out. One last taste of air. One last breath let loose from her lips. Then, she let go.

It was strange how easy it was to let herself sink. Part of her thought she'd fight it, that she'd thrash and claw back to the surface. But the moment she emptied her lungs, a calm washed over her. She closed her eyes as the pressure thickened, relentless against her fragile human organs and bones. She had no selkie form to protect her from the sea's unyielding grasp. She'd offered herself to the tides, and they'd taken her.

A heavy fog settled around her head. She must have opened her lungs, but she couldn't recall her final, desperate reach for breath. All she knew was the salt on her lips, the crushing embrace of the sea within her.

Was it over? Was she part of it now?

Something stirred in the darkness. She hadn't opened her eyes, but a hazy shadow wisped into shape in front of her. It twisted and swirled, settling into a form Isla recognised well. Ribs of blackened bone. Trails of mist rippling in the water. A seal-skull mask with vacant, desolate eyes.

Not just any gun-anam. The one haunting her ever since she'd returned to Silveckan.

The wraith tilted its head. *I know you*, it said.

She didn't hear the words, but rather felt them. They resounded deep in her bones in the voice of the sea itself, its tones rising from the depths like they'd always been there. Like she'd carried them with her all this time.

It was impossible. Her pelt was gone. She was drowning—*had* drowned. The depths had claimed her for their own. Yet the feeling of being wrapped in the haze of time and memory was unmistakable.

She was dreamwalking.

The gun-anam reached out with a swirling tendril and slowly lifted its seal-skull mask.

Aye, it said, watery voice rippling with the currents. *It seems you are.*

Isla stilled. Even if there had been air to fill her lungs, she couldn't breathe. All she could do was stare at the familiar features forming in the misty water.

Sea green eyes. Sable hair. A jaw so stubborn it might have been her own.

Mara.

"You," she whispered. "All this time, it's been you?"

The gun-anam—Mara, if it was truly her—gave her a sad, distant look. Her black hair floated in the water like trails of ink bleeding from her crown. There was no light to dance off her pale skin, but it held an eerie glow, like moonlight on chalk.

She sighed, bubbles streaming from her blue lips. *Me? Aye, perhaps. At least, the ghost of me. The echo of the pain and anger I left behind in the world. But who I was before?* She shook her head, stirring the water. *That woman is lost. Only her memory remains.*

"You were at Blackwood Estate." Grief constricted Isla's throat. "They took me in. They loved me like I was their own. And you brought the raiders that slaughtered them."

You cannot blame me for that, not any more than you can blame the sea for swallowing a ship caught in a storm, Mara said. *I am but a fragment of the woman I left behind. A remnant of what once was. You're speaking to a memory trapped in time, nothing more. And that's only possible because you're a dreamwalker.*

"Like you were."

Aye, like I was. Mara gave a thin smile. *You inherited what was once mine. But even before that, I felt you through the water. You were my greatest loss, my deepest regret. More than my soul. More than my life. I followed you for months because I didn't know how not to. Because even the ghost of me knew to search for what I had lost.*

"Then it's my fault." Pain shot through her chest, grief clawing at her heart. "All of it. My father. Blackwood Estate. The gun-anam trailing us. Eimhir... Tides, *Eimhir*—"

Fault? The word echoed from Mara's lips, ringing with the deep tones of the sea. *There can be no fault for the tides rising, for the waves breaking. It is simply the way of things.*

Tears sprang to Isla's eyes, but they refused to spill. The sea held her, keeping her suspended in this dream, caught between life and death.

"I followed you too," she said. "I walked with you through your memories. You showed me things I never could have imagined. I tried to finish what you started." She stared at Mara, this spectre of the mother she'd never known. "There's so much I want to ask. So much I'm afraid of hearing."

A shadow fell across Mara's face. *There are some memories I wish could remain buried, but you deserve to know, no matter how painful the truth might be.*

"The Grand Admiral." Realisation tightened in Isla's chest. "You loved him."

Aye. And I believe he loved me, at least at the start, Mara said. *The man I dragged from the depths was not the same man who hunts you now. And I was young, barely past twenty. When I breathed life back into his lungs, I felt something I never had before. My heart had never known that kind of stirring. I lost myself in him, and in doing so, lost sight of who he was becoming.*

"He took your pelt. He claimed to love you, but he stole your soul."

It was a slow betrayal, one I didn't understand until it was too late, Mara admitted. *At first, the sea was mine to visit as I pleased, though I never returned to Eileanan Selch. Alasdair was human, and such things were forbidden. But as the years went on, his fear of losing me surmounted his love. He told me he was keeping my pelt safe from those who might take it. I don't know if I believed him, but I wanted to. When the salt began to scar my skin, he drew me baths of seawater and fed me urchins and squid from the markets. And every time the agony became too much, he would take me to that island and return my soul to me, just long enough for me to forget why I needed to leave.*

"Duncan told me he found you, once." Isla swallowed. "He said you refused to flee."

I left my people when they needed me most. I couldn't bring myself to go back. Whatever Alasdair Cunningham was, whatever he'd become, he was all I had. Until you. A ghostly smile flitted across her rippling face.

My suffering was my choice. But I could not chain you to that kind of life. You gave me the strength to leave.

A painful wrench caught Isla's heart. "You gave up your pelt to get me away from there. You sacrificed everything for me. But I failed, too. I lost sight of someone I loved. I didn't see how Eimhir was suffering until it was too late. I don't know if I'll ever be able to forgive myself for that."

Nighean. My daughter. Mara reached out a hand. Cold fingers brushed a floating strand of hair, leaving behind a trail of misty vapour. *It is not too late. You gave yourself to the tides, but they are not ready for you yet. There is still a chance for you to do what you came here to do. You can return the haar to what it once was.*

"I lost my pelt, my soul. The haar will claim me like it claimed you."

Not all of your soul is bound to your pelt.

Her words struck Isla's core, reaching a place she'd thought lost. A familiar ache rose, pulsing with each feeble beat of her heart. It was a thread between the fractured parts of her, a thread that hadn't been broken—*couldn't* be broken.

Darce.

He'd pressed his bloodied hands to her side and bound himself to her with a promise. He carried a part of her that Eimhir couldn't take. Nobody could.

His soul will keep the haar from claiming you, Mara said. *He is a sentinel, and his kind are favoured by the sea. They understand the magic of sacrifice like we do. They give themselves, completely and utterly, to another person. That is why the sea grants them her gifts.*

Isla lifted her chin. "The auld blood. That's what connects us to them?"

No, not the auld blood, Mara said. *Though it's little wonder we have forgotten so much of the auld ways, so much of the truth. As the dreamwalkers dwindled, so did our ability to pass on our memories, our histories.*

Isla shivered. "What *is* the truth?"

To understand that, you must first understand how our people came to be, Mara said. *We are not of the sea; we are* the sea. *The first selkie was born of the lifeblood of her waters, the spirit of her tides. The sea imbued her very soul into what we are. She knew what it meant to give up part of herself. To relinquish that which is utterly yours to bring life to another. That gift does not come from our blood, but from our sacrifice.*

"But surely they are one and the same," Isla said. "A pelt can only be passed on with blood spilled in sacrifice."

No, Mara said. *Blood is a symptom of our magic, not the source of it. Somewhere along the way, we forgot that. The auld rituals became twisted, too entwined with killing and death. Our souls still passed on, but we lost our understanding of why.*

A chill fell across Isla's heart. If Mara was speaking the truth, it changed everything she thought she knew, everything Eimhir and Angus and the rest of the selkies believed about their people.

"Then...it wasn't my blood that allowed me to claim your pelt," she said. "It was your sacrifice. It was what you gave up for me."

Mara nodded. *And that is why you still live. We choose who we honour with the gift of our lives, our souls. A sacrifice can only be ours to make. It cannot be taken by force.*

"But Eimhir—"

Eimhir took your blood, took your pelt, but she'll never truly inhabit it. It will haunt her until the day she joins her ancestors in the depths. Mara shook her head. *You are not yet gun-anam. Your soul resides in that pelt, and it is yours to reclaim.*

Isla let the words wash over her. It felt too dangerous to hope. And yet...there it was. A kernel of warmth blooming behind her sternum, where before there was only despair. It wasn't too late. She could stop Eimhir. She could keep her promise to her people.

"The gun-anam," she said. "How do I stop them?"

As only a dreamwalker can, Mara said. *Find them through the memories of our ancestors. Take their suffering into your pelt, make their pain part of you. Without it, they'll be able to return to the sea. They'll be able to rest.*

"And me?"

You will bear it, for as long as you are able to. Then, when the time comes that you cannot carry it anymore, you will pass your pelt to someone willing to take that burden from you. And so our people's pain is shared. It is remembered. Like I was. Like you will be.

Her words should have brought with them a shadow, but for the first time since the water swallowed her, Isla felt a sense of peace. She had a course set. What lay beyond didn't matter.

"I need to go after Eimhir," she said. "Unless there's a way to give the gun-anam peace without my pelt..."

You cannot take on their suffering without knowing it, without knowing them. Only by dreamwalking through the memories in your pelt will you truly understand them. Mara tilted her head, a smile forming across her rippling features. *But you and I share more than our stolen soul. I brought you into this world. You don't need your pelt to know me.*

"I *did* know you," Isla whispered. "I felt you, even when I didn't understand what it was. Every time I looked at the blue line of the horizon. Every time I heard the crash of the waves or smelled the salt in the air."

Blood is not the only thing that binds us, Mara said. *It is not blood, but water, that carries us through this world. It nourishes. It provides. It connects us across land and sea alike. It takes us home.*

Isla let out a choking laugh. "Home. I've spent so many years trying to understand what that means, where I belong. But every time I think I've found the answer, it slips away again."

Where does the wind belong? Mara countered. *Where do the waves call home? You share a soul with the sea herself, and she is a restless spirit. There is no need to carve a place in the world to call your own when you can exist anywhere you choose to go.* She closed her eyes. *It's time for you to leave this dream, leave this ghost of mine to rest.*

Isla's throat constricted. "But I don't have my pelt yet. I can't take away your pain."

Ah, lass. You already have. The depths of Mara's voice quavered. *Long has my spirit searched for you. Now that I've seen you, now that I know my suffering was not in vain, I need nothing more.*

The shape of her rippled, wisps carried off in the currents. The tendrils of her hair bled into a stream of bubbles. Her eyes turned the same colour as the water.

Mara reached out a fading hand and brushed Isla's ribs. Then she cupped her face and pressed a watery kiss against her cheek. *Go, nighean. Take back what is yours, and do for our people what I could not.*

Something pushed between Isla's ankles, forcing her legs wide, and she saw an equine shape forming beneath her. The sea churned, foam forming a thick mane and flowing tail as it grew denser.

A kelpie.

The creature twisted its rippling neck, catching her in its glance with sea green eyes. Bubbles spurted from its nostrils as it gave a gurgling bray and reared up on its hind legs.

Isla grasped for its mane, her elbow knocking against something cold and hard. She stilled when she saw a cuirass of white bone encasing her once-bare chest. Her fingers trembled as she reached a hand to her face and found the edges of a seal-skull mask.

When she turned back, Mara was gone.

The kelpie stirred, restless as the waves. Isla pressed her mouth to the water horse's ear.

"Thank you, màthair," she whispered. "Now, take us home."

CHAPTER THIRTY-ONE
DARCE

Isla had left him.

The thought seemed strangely hollow, like he couldn't bring himself to believe it. Her scent clung to his clothes. The taste of her lingered on his tongue. It was like she was still there, hidden between the beats of his aching heart.

She couldn't be gone. He'd given part of himself to her. If he'd lost her, he'd know.

But there was no denying the stark reality in front of him. The rock was bare and empty. The glittering black water remained unnaturally still. There was no trace of her. She'd left without so much as a whisper.

Grief welled in his chest, and he pushed it away. It would be too easy to give in to despair. Hope was all he had left.

Something stirred against the sky, casting a silhouette against the eerie red glow. A curved wing, a flash of white feathers.

Featherblade. It couldn't be.

The bird circled above, its long neck flitting from side to side like it was searching for something. Darce let out a piercing whistle, but the gannet gave no sign of hearing it. The echo hung limply in the air, like it had come up against a barrier it couldn't breach.

He reached out, grasping for the bird's mind. It *was* Featherblade; he was sure of it. But the gannet's presence was beyond his reach. He was trapped here, lost behind the haar. The soulless realm was a shadow he couldn't escape. He wasn't sure he wanted to, not when Isla still lingered here.

Featherblade circled once more, then peeled away, its huge wings flapping steadily as it disappeared into the distance. Darce sat on the slab, pulling his cloak around him. The fur lining smelled like Isla's skin. He breathed in, trying to ignore the pain. He'd left Lachlan behind. Featherblade couldn't reach him. Isla was gone. For the first time in years, he was alone.

He clasped his arms around his knees and stared at the water. The surface was like polished glass, so still it seemed impossible.

Then, from nowhere, came a ripple.

Darce stiffened. The sea here was unnatural. Whatever was disturbing the water, it was coming from underneath. Maybe the gun-anam were returning. Maybe it was something worse.

The ripples came faster, agitating the surface as they grew. In a matter of seconds, the sea was frothing. He scrambled to his feet, reaching for the handle of the sgian dubh in his pocket.

A roar rang in his ear and the waves leapt high, parting to reveal a huge creature crashing through the spray. It sailed towards him, its hide shimmering with water, its mane thick with foam.

It was a tides-damned kelpie.

The creature towered over him, staring down with ghostly green eyes. Its rippling haunches were formed of nothing but salt and sea. He almost choked on the reek of its brackish breath, the seaweed rot of its mane and tail.

A dread mount, the legends called it. A water horse of ill-omen.

He drew the sgian dubh, then faltered. He'd been so focused on the kelpie he hadn't noticed the creature bore a rider. A rider he knew only too well.

The ribcage armour. The seal-skull mask.

This was the wraith that had been hunting Isla. If it was here and she wasn't...

His hand tightened around the sgian dubh's hilt, but before he could move towards the gun-anam, a watery cry echoed from behind its mask.

"Wait!"

He froze. The gun-anam had never spoken before, not with a voice any human could understand. And the bones of its armour... They were different. No longer black and rotting, but glistening white, like those the soulships were made from.

The gun-anam slipped from the kelpie's back. No vapour trailed in its wake. No mist clung to its shifting form. Instead, he caught a flash of pale skin under the bone armour, a hint of green behind the sockets of the skull mask.

His heart clenched. "Isla?"

Saying her name was too much to bear. If he was wrong, if it wasn't her...

But then she raised a hand to the bone obscuring her face and lifted the mask. Her cheeks were pallid and streaked with salt, but it was her. She'd come back.

He took her face between his hands, tracing his thumbs along her jaw to make sure she was real. Her skin was like ice, turning his fingers numb. She looked like she'd come from the depths themselves.

"I'm all right," she whispered, pressing her lips to his. She tasted like salt, but he welcomed the sting. "I told you once I didn't need an anchor, but I was wrong. Your soul kept the tides from taking me."

"What do you mean?"

"There was part of me Eimhir couldn't take. The part of your soul you gave me." She placed her hands against his chest. "As long as that survives, so will I."

He ripped off his cloak and wrapped it around her. "And Eimhir?"

"I need to find her. I need to reclaim what she took from me."

She settled into his arms, and he looked out over the wet crown of her head towards the horizon. The water settled again, the surface still once more without the kelpie to disturb it. But something else loomed in the darkness, a hazy shadow drifting closer.

"Are those..." Darce released his hold around Isla and stumbled to the edge of the rock. "Are those sails?"

Isla whirled, following his gaze across the water. "Not just any sails. That's the *Jade Dawn*."

"But Nishi left. Why would she..." He trailed off as a familiar shape swooped overhead, letting out a muffled caw.

Featherblade. Somehow, the bird had known to find him.

Isla let out a breath. "We have our way back."

"How?" Darce asked. "Even if we swam out to the ship, even if we could board it, we'd still be trapped in this place, cut off behind the haar. They'd never know we were there."

"Then we summon the haar." Isla gestured at the cuirass of bone she wore around her ribs, the glistening skull she held in her hand. "We don't have a soulship, but we have what they were made from." She swallowed, her throat pulsing. "What *I* was made from."

Darce stilled. "They're hers. Mara's. You found her."

"She found me."

There was more in the depths of her voice than the truth of those few words. Darce heard it all: the wonder, the grief, the longing. But the glint in her eyes spoke louder. She had a course in mind. All he could do was help her reach it.

He drew the sgian dubh from his pocket and pressed the blade against the bandaged gash on his palm. The gauze was soaked red. It wouldn't take much to make him bleed again.

"No." Isla placed her hand over his and moved the dagger away. "You've spilled enough blood on my account."

"But the bones... If they're like those on the soulship, they'll need my blood before I can summon the haar."

"It's not about blood. It never was. Your magic, *our* magic, was born of sacrifice." Isla smiled softly. "These bones know the sacrifices you've made, Darce. They witnessed the night you made your oath to me, the night you shared with me your soul. You don't need to give anything more."

She turned to the kelpie. The dread mount swung its huge head, scattering spray across the rock, then lowered itself to allow her to climb onto its watery back. Its haunches rippled, making Darce feel like he was staring into the sea itself. It seemed impossible that it should be able to carry her, but she sat tall and straight, even as his cloak around her shoulders grew sodden at the ends.

He moved beside her, then swung a leg over the kelpie's back. The horse shifted beneath him, and he quivered at the sensation of icy water around his legs.

"Are you ready?" Isla asked.

Darce drew a long breath and nodded. Then, the kelpie plunged.

The shock of the cold hit him like a blow. Salt stung his eyes. Water rushed in around his missing ear. His lungs burned, threatening to burst if he refused to open them to the sea trying to swallow him.

Not yet, the tides whispered, resonating from the depths. *One day, sentinel, but not yet.*

For days, his magic had lain silent. Now, it sang again, turning his veins as cold as the sea. His blood ran thick with salt. His heart rippled and pulsed like the currents. The sea spirits surrounded him, answering his call.

The kelpie charged, and Darce reached for the haar.

A white haze clouded the water. Silvery tendrils snaked alongside them, mist trailing in their wake. In front, the sea's black gloom turned a murky green.

It was working. They were crossing back.

The water brightened, and the *Jade Dawn's* keel emerged in front of them. The green-stained timber didn't look as hazy now. He could make out the seaweed clinging to the wood, the clusters of barnacles holding fast. The ship was no longer shrouded beyond the edges of the soulless realm. It was there. It was real.

Water rushed up his nostrils as the kelpie changed course, rising towards the surface in a thunder of watery hooves. A glimmer of sunlight broke through in fractures. The crisp sea air waited above.

They breached the surface with a crash, leaping free from the waves on the kelpie's back. The dread mount dissolved underneath them, scattering across the *Jade Dawn's* deck in a silvery shower as they landed.

Darce hit the timber with a thump, gasping for breath. His lungs were burning, but the salty air had never tasted any sweeter.

They'd made it.

The relief was enough to bring a pained laugh to his lips. Then the staccato click of a pistol echoed through his ear, and he looked up to find Nishi advancing.

When she caught sight of him, her eyes widened in disbelief. Then she turned to Isla, taking in the bone armour around her ribs, the pelt that was nowhere to be found.

"I suppose I shouldn't be surprised by anything at this point," she said, lowering her gun. "But was that a *kelpie* you rode out of the mists?"

"Aye, it was." Isla climbed to her feet beside him, pulling the soaking folds of the cloak across her pale, bare skin. "It's a long story, Captain, but I'll happily trade it for some clothes and a dram of whatever liquor you Sea Kith keep in your stores."

Nishi cracked a smile, her lip ring glinting in the sunlight. "It's a deal, Blackwood. Though if the history of our recent meetings is anything to go by, I wager we'll both need more than a fucking dram before the day is out."

The sun had slipped far below the horizon by the time Isla finished recounting everything that had happened, her words punctuated with grief-laden silences and long gulps of the honey-infused whisky Nishi brought up from the *Jade Dawn's* stores. Darce watched as the colour slowly returned to her blue lips and the hollows of her cheeks, but there was no chasing away the lingering marks of Eimhir's betrayal. Trails of salt streaked her skin, scarring her throat and collarbone.

She'd told him it wouldn't kill her, not as long as their bond remained intact. But that wasn't enough to quell the fear of losing her.

"I haven't heard word from the other Sea Kith," Nishi said after Isla had finished. "Featherblade left us for a few days to deliver my message but returned with empty claws the moment we sailed out of the Southern Reaches. That bird knew we had to get back to you."

"I didn't know if Featherblade could sense me on the other side of the haar," Darce said. "For whatever it's worth, I'm sorry we pulled you from your course."

"I'd never ignore a guidebird," Nishi replied. "The tides speak through them, and I'd not be much of a captain if I refused to listen."

As if summoned, Featherblade swooped down from the mast and landed on the gunwale beside Darce. It sized him up with its beady eyes, then jabbed its beak and nipped him on the cheek.

Nishi laughed. "Look at that—it didn't even draw any blood this time."

Featherblade echoed her with a throaty caw, then spread its wings and took off again, soaring high above the *Jade Dawn's* sails. Darce watched it go, unable to muster any of his usual annoyance at the sting left by the gannet's fierce beak. Featherblade had come back for him. He wouldn't forget that.

He took another long sip of the Sea Kith whisky. It burned his throat, but the fire was tempered with the sweetness of the honey, lingering on his tongue long after each mouthful. The warmth chased away the numbness in his limbs, the cold that had clung to him ever since they'd sailed into the haar. It made him feel more like himself again. Made him feel ready for the fight that was coming.

Nishi turned to Isla, her expression growing sombre in the flickering light from the oil lamps. "I don't pretend to understand what it's like for a selkie to suffer. But I know about having something taken from you that you couldn't stand to lose. I owe the Grand Admiral a debt for what he did to Kerr. If you plan to return to Arburgh, I would gladly join your side for the chance to make the bastard pay."

"What about the other Sea Kith?" Darce asked. "I thought you wanted-ed to call them together."

"If Featherblade delivered my message to one of their ships, they'll use their own guidebirds to spread the word," Nishi said. "I asked them for a sea summit on the next new moon. If I survive this, I'll make my case to them there. If I don't... Well, perhaps my death will convince them more than my words ever could."

"If we fail, it's not just the Admiralty your people will have to worry about," Isla said. "Eimhir wants to drown the capital in its own blood. The gun-anam will feast on that kind of violence. The haar will spread across Silveckan and its waters. More selkies will fall to the mist sickness, like Eimhir did. More raids, more retribution, more killing. No one will escape it."

Her words sent a shiver across Darce's skin. Arburgh was a dreich, dismal city at the best of times. He imagined it as the mists rolled in, shrouding the cobbled streets in a thick white haze. Gutters running with the blood of human and selkie alike. Pelts torn, bodies flayed. It seemed like folly to believe they could stop it.

For a moment, he was overcome with a wild urge to run, to abandon the capital and everyone in it for distant shores. Breçhon, perhaps, where his mother's family lived. Or further still to Vesnia, with its lemon groves and volcanic beaches. They didn't have to stay here. They could go anywhere.

He met Isla's gaze. Her sea green eyes glittered with the same fierce determination that had once exasperated him, but now only stirred longing in his heart.

Aye, they could go anywhere. But it would never be home. Not until she was whole again.

"To Arburgh," he said heavily. "And whatever fate the tides are carrying us to."

CHAPTER THIRTY-TWO

ISLA

Isla stood at the prow, the wind snarling at her hair, the roaring spray stinging her skin. She welcomed the lashings of pain. It cut through the numbness that had settled into her bones. It made her feel alive again.

She shifted her feet against the wooden deck, getting accustomed to the boots Nishi had given her. She'd spent months walking barefoot with nothing but the shore and soil beneath her feet. Now, she was clad like a Sea Kith. She wore a lambswool tunic under a long-tailed coat, serpenthide boots that rose to her knees, a leather belt laden with a new pistol and the sgian dubh Darce had pressed back into her hand.

"You should take it," he'd said. "It belongs to you."

It hung by her waist, tucked under the wool of her tunic that hid the white cuirass around her ribs. The Sea Kith were more accepting than most, but the idea of strolling across the deck with bone armour on display for all to see made Isla uneasy. The seal-skull helm she kept in her cabin, next to the bunk she shared with Darce. Each passing night she spent in his arms, their fingers tracing each other's scars, their lips whispering promises between desperate, lingering kisses.

She saw him on the other side of the ship, rolling up a scrap of parchment and attaching it to Featherblade's spindly leg. The gannet gave a disgruntled caw and jabbed its beak towards Darce, but then spread its wings and glided across the choppy waves.

Darce pursed his lips. "It feels strange to be heading back to Arburgh, with what it cost to get out of that wretched place."

He didn't need to say Kerr's name. The loss echoed in the empty spaces between his words. The guilt was etched on his face.

The worst part was knowing it was only the beginning.

Darce's mouth tightened with worry. "Will we reach the capital in time to stop Eimhir? She has a fine head start."

"She won't strike straight away," Isla said. "She'll need to return to the Selkie Isles first and gather the clans. The element of surprise will only carry them so far. They want blood, and for that, they need numbers."

"You wouldn't rather meet her there?"

"We wouldn't get near. Caim is too well protected. It has to be Arburgh."

A fraught silence stretched between them. They both knew what was coming, what they stood to lose. But knowing didn't make it easier. She could taste the truth on her tongue all the same.

The waves leapt high and fierce as she turned to the water. The air was bitter, the wind burning her cheeks. Ahead, a grey drizzle clung to the canopy of clouds.

Arburgh was growing closer. Its dreich shadow chilled her bones.

"I know you mean to stop her, but I also know you mean to save her," Darce said softly. "I won't try to talk you out of it, but..."

"What happens if I can't?" Isla shook her head. "The thought of raising my weapon against her, the thought of striking her down... I can't bear it, Darce. I can't let it come to that."

"She may not give you a choice," he pressed. "The mist sickness has taken hold of her. She's not herself anymore. If you come between her and her need for vengeance..."

"I don't want to think about it."

"But *I* must." He laced his fingers between hers and brought her hand to his mouth, lips brushing over her knuckles. "I don't want to come between you. I know how much you love her. But if it comes down to you or her, I won't stand by and let her kill you. I need you to understand that."

He dropped his hand, but she kept hold of his fingers, feeling the pulse between their skin. "Do you remember what you told me on our first crossing to Arburgh, about the moment the auld blood first awakened in you?"

His face hardened. "That matter with the Vane Company?"

"You said they beat you half to death before the young lass stepped in and took an axe meant for you."

"She died." Darce grimaced. "Why do you ask?"

"It all comes back to what Mara said. We thought our blood gave us our magic, selkie and sentinel alike. But what is blood, if not water? Water blessed by the sea when a sacrifice is made." Isla tilted her head. "I didn't understand at first. What does the sea care for sacrifice? Why should a lost life matter to the tides? But I see it now. It all returns there, doesn't it? By river, by rain, it doesn't matter. The water in our bodies finds its way back to the sea in the end. It's the one constant in this world, the thing connecting us all."

Darce looked unconvinced. "Knowing we'll be reunited in death is not enough reason for me to let it happen. If my powers are a blessing from the sea, then I was given them for a reason. To protect you."

There was a time she might have pushed away his words, fighting to free herself from what they meant. But so much had changed since then. They'd bloodied themselves for each other too many times to deny the way their souls were bound.

"Promise you'll always find your way back to me," she said.

His brow furrowed deeper. "Isla, I—"

A sharp cough cut through the rest of his words, and Isla turned to find Nishi behind them. She nodded to the horizon. "We're not far from the firth. The closer we get, the more we risk running into an Admiralty patrol. It would be handy if we could slip in unseen using that mist of yours."

"It wouldn't work," Isla said. "The haar clings to the bones of the gun-anam, and there aren't enough of them in this armour I'm wearing to shroud an entire ship. We'll have to leave the *Jade Dawn* at sea."

Nishi ground her teeth. "I don't like the idea of leaving my ship and crew behind, but if it means getting the chance to make the Grand Admiral pay for what he did to Kerr, I suppose I have little choice. Rowe can look after things here while I'm gone—she knows the *Jade Dawn* as well as I do. But I don't see how you expect to get into Arburgh without someone noticing. They'll have the docks locked down."

A slow smile crept across Isla's lips. "Well, it's a good thing we happen to know the capital's most notorious smuggler, isn't it?"

"You stink."

Isla glared up from the bottom of the boat, trying to ignore the slimy trail trickling down the side of her face. Her limbs were aching from the cramped compartment they'd been locked in, but that was nothing compared to the reek of gutted fish clinging to her skin and clothes. She'd been buried beneath hundreds of cold, wet carcasses for hours, barely able to breathe. The sight of Muir overdramatically coughing into a handkerchief was doing nothing to raise her spirits.

"Nice to see you too, uncle," she said, swatting away the hand he offered to help her out of the boat. "You couldn't have arranged for something a wee bit less...pungent?"

"Not with the urgency you impressed upon me in your letter." He folded his arms, his weathered brow creasing. "Thanks for that, by the way. Nothing like being ambushed by a gannet the size of a bloody sea eagle when I'm trying to keep a low profile."

Featherblade gave a prideful caw, ruffling its wings as it eyed Muir with a sidelong gaze.

Muir rubbed a hand over his face. "I don't know why you're complaining. I did what you asked, didn't I? You're all here, though what good it will do is beyond me."

Darce climbed out of the boat next, his hair wet with gunge. Nishi followed, shaking a chunk of fish from her tricorne hat.

"Charming place," she remarked. "Between the damp and the cobwebs, I'm not sure which is more welcoming."

"Sea Kith, aye?" Muir cast his gaze over her tattoos. "Didn't think you lot made a habit of coming on land. Starting to wish you'd kept it that way."

"Enough. We're all friends here." Isla looked around the cave. It was different to the one she'd found herself in last time she'd been down here. Darker and narrower, with only a slit of light creeping between the waves and the overhanging rocks. Hardly the ideal place to run a smuggling operation from, but Muir had to keep moving. Even an eel, no matter how slippery, could be caught.

She turned to him, her earlier irritation fading. He was different too. There was a sharpness to him that hadn't been there before. Looking at him now, white braids gathered into a knot, she could almost glimpse the sailor who'd earned his infamy out on the waves all those years ago. The Cirein-cròin himself.

"You seem well," she said.

Muir snorted. "Should bloody hope so. Undermining the Admiralty's operations is busy work. I've not had time for a drink in weeks."

"I mean it, uncle. And I am grateful for you getting us into the city." She swallowed. "I'm grateful for more than I can possibly say."

"Ach, there's no need for any of that," he said gruffly, but his expression softened. "I just wish you hadn't needed to come back. This business with Eimhir, with your pelt... I saw what it did to Mara when she lost her soul. I couldn't—I can't—"

"It won't come to that. There is part of my soul Eimhir couldn't take." She glanced at Darce. "His oath saved me from sharing the same fate as Mara. Now, I have the chance to make things right. But to do that, I'll need your help."

"I've been doing my part to stir up trouble while you've been gone," Muir said. "Sabotaging merchant shipments, spoiling food stores, interfering in repairs. Gathered quite the underground militia along the way. Not that you'd think much of them. They're the usual sorts—cast-offs offs from the Admiralty, bitter and disillusioned, turned to piracy or smuggling or drink. But picking off easy targets isn't the same as a full-scale assault. We don't have the numbers to storm the garrison."

"Storming the garrison won't be necessary. I just need a way in. A chance to warn them about what's coming."

"*Warn* them?" Nishi stiffened. "Didn't we come here to put an end to the Admiralty?"

"If Eimhir and the selkies massacre the capital, there will be no escaping the haar. It will spread until all Silveckan is covered in its mists, and where it goes, violence will follow." Isla met Nishi's eyes. "You'll get your shot at vengeance, Captain. I swear it. But first, we have to evacuate Arburgh."

"And how do you expect to do that?" Muir sent her a sceptical look. "Don't forget, I know Alasdair Cunningham better than any of you. Believe me when I say he's not the kind of man to listen to reason. If you think you can talk him around, you've already lost."

"I don't plan to. The Grand Admiral is not the only Cunningham whose name holds weight in Arburgh. He won't listen, but Blair might." She glanced at Darce. "You told me the lad was not his uncle. I let him go because I wanted to believe it."

Darce folded his arms, his frown deepening. "Letting him go was one thing. Risking everything on him accepting the word of someone he thinks is his enemy... I don't like it, Isla."

"It's worth trying. It has to be." She squeezed her hands into fists. "Eimhir is coming. We can't stop that. But if we clear the city before she strikes, there will be less bloodshed for the gun-anam to feed on. We can contain this violence to Arburgh and save the rest of Silveckan."

All she heard was the wash of the waves lapping at the sea cave's entrance. Nobody wanted to speak. The weight of what lay in front of them was visible in the slump of their shoulders, the bleak shadows behind their eyes. Too much pain and loss, with the promise of more to come.

Eventually, Nishi lifted her chin. "If going in quietly gives us the chance to spare some souls the heartache my own has suffered, I cannot speak against it. As long as our course carries us towards the Grand Admiral, I'll be satisfied."

"I don't think there's any escaping that," Isla said. "I knew our paths would cross again. I only hope this time will be the last."

"And Eimhir?" Darce sent her a pointed look.

"She has something that belongs to me. I mean to take it back." She turned to Muir. "Can you do it? Can you get us into the garrison?"

A slow, satisfied smile stretched across her uncle's face. "Aye, I reckon I can. All I need is a wee bit of help from someone who's always wanted to catch an eel."

CHAPTER THIRTY-THREE

DARCE

As far as plans went, Darce couldn't have conceived of anything worse. Part of him wondered if he might as well walk straight to the gallows and tie the noose himself, for all the difference it would make.

Judging by the look on Isla's face, she was harbouring similar thoughts. Her hood was pulled over her forehead, shrouding her features, but he still noticed her simmering resentment. She'd questioned Muir a hundred times, but in the end, it had changed nothing. For better or worse, they were doing this.

Muir, for his part, seemed to be enjoying the whole thing. He strolled ahead, whistling to himself as he walked the polished cobblestones of the northside streets as easily as he did the filth-strewn paths of the canals. If he had any concerns about being recognised, he didn't show it.

Around the next corner, a familiar townhouse rose into view. The granite façade stretched high, set with rising pillars and hanging baskets bursting with colour. Stained-glass windows glinted like jewels in the mid-afternoon light, and the arched entrance was flanked by two door-men boasting silk finery and a pair of muskets.

Isla glowered at Muir, jerking her hood further over her face. "I can't believe I let you talk me into this. Of all the people… You realise he'll sell us out to the Admiralty the first chance he gets, don't you? That is, if he doesn't kill us first."

"Do you think I'd have brought us here if I thought he could do us any harm?" Muir rolled his eyes. "I've been embedding my people in his business for years. More of the staff here are on my books than his. Believe me when I say we have nothing to fear from Nathair Quinn."

He pushed through the townhouse's gate and marched to the entrance, arms spread wide. "Good afternoon, gentlemen! We're here for an audience with the baron, if you'd be so kind to admit us. I'm afraid I neglected to make an appointment, but I have a feeling he'll clear his schedule once he knows who's calling. It's the Eel, in case you hadn't guessed."

Two sharp clicks rattled through the air as the doormen raised their muskets, levelling the barrels at Muir's head.

Darce shot a glance at Isla, but she shook her head, even as her hand drifted towards the pistol on her belt. Nishi stood behind them, watching the whole scene from beneath the brim of her hat, one eyebrow cocked in amusement.

"Ah good, I see that got your attention," Muir continued, apparently unconcerned about the proximity of lead and black powder to his face. "Better to be escorted in at gunpoint than turned away at the door, I say. Shall we?"

One of the doormen muttered something to the other, then lowered his rifle and disappeared into the townhouse. After a few minutes, he returned. "If you are who you claim to be, you've made the biggest mistake of your miserable life."

"That would be quite the achievement, considering the breadth of those I've made already. Does that mean we're going inside, then?"

The doorman shot him a murderous look. "Weapons first."

"Naturally."

Darce waited as the doormen searched them, digging their hands into his cloak and the seams where his boots met his breeches. One of them baulked at the bone armour under Isla's tunic, but they stepped aside to escort them through the townhouse's lobby into a bright reception room.

There was no sign of Quinn, just a long, empty table with several velvet-trimmed chairs. As soon as the doormen left, Isla sank into one of the chairs, pinching the bridge of her nose. "Tides, it's a wonder you're still alive. I don't know who is the bigger fool—you, for thinking this will work, or me for going along with it."

"Men aren't threatened by fools. Or by drunks. I learned to leverage that a long time ago," Muir said, losing all traces of levity. "For all the wrong I did, all the mistakes I made, falling into disgrace afforded me an anonymity I enjoyed for years. And while the Admiralty overlooked me, I was building something in the shadows. Waiting for the right time to step back into the light."

Something in the edge of his voice prickled Darce's skin. Whoever the Eel had once been, that man was gone. The one in front of him was the Cirein-cròin, with all its serpentine rage and teeth.

Isla seemed to notice the change in him too. "How long have you been planning this, exactly?"

Muir just smiled.

Before any of them could say more, the heavy-set oak doors opened to reveal the smug, satisfied face of Nathair Quinn.

"*You?*"

Darce couldn't help but take some satisfaction at the way the Quinn's slick composure stuttered and slipped as his eyes fell on Muir. A vein pulsed in his temple as his gaze slid to Darce, then Nishi, and finally to Isla, who met his flummoxed stare with a hard smile.

"You're getting careless, Quinn," she said. "Anyone would think you were surprised to see us."

Quinn recovered quickly, chuckling as he walked to the towering drinks cabinet in the corner of the room. He returned with a bottle of wine, uncorking it with practised expertise. "A lesser vintage, I'm afraid. You'll have to forgive me for not wanting to waste a good bottle on a man who helps himself to my cargo."

"Brought my own, as it happens." Muir reached into his pocket and pulled out a tarnished brass flask, keeping his eyes fixed on Quinn as he gulped down a lengthy swig. "Burdock root tea, in case you were wondering. Less of a kick than I'd prefer, but such is the price of gaining the upper hand."

"I'll take your word for it." Quinn turned to Isla with a smirk. "What about you, old friend? Or has your taste for the finer things been replaced with a penchant for salt water and sea scum, given what you've become?"

Darce stiffened, rage coursing through his chest, but Isla placed a hand on his arm. "Let him have his insults. Words are all he has left."

"You think so?" Quinn's smile stretched wider. "I've already sent a runner to the garrison. She left through the porter's exit when you arrived. It won't be long before the Admiralty comes to take you off my hands, and while the four of you swing, I'll be counting the coin they'll pay me for delivering you to the noose."

Muir choked out a mouthful of foul-smelling tea. "A runner?" he asked, wiping his mouth with his sleeve. "Wouldn't happen to be wee Kelsey from the eastside tenements, would it? Aye, she's a runner, all right. I expect she's running right to my watchers on the docks, telling them to be ready to set a match to all those stores of black powder I had smuggled onto that shiny new sloop of yours."

A thick, strangled silence fell around the room.

Quinn paled. "That's not—you couldn't have—"

"Set for Bréchon, isn't it?" Muir bared his teeth in a menacing grin. "Just think, all that expensive wool and fine deerskin going up in flames before you see a penny for it. A bloody waste if you ask me."

Quinn's eyes darted around the room, as if he was waiting for someone to call Muir's bluff. Then he sank into one of the chairs, lips pinched. "I almost had you that time down in the sea caves. Tides, if I'd only been able to see you swing then…"

"Aye, you came close. Only thanks to this careless oaf, mind you." Muir jerked his thumb towards Darce. "But paying off street urchins for access to the gutters of this city is one thing. It's another thing to live in those gutters. To wake up and face the misery of Arburgh's filthy underside day after day, year after year. That kind of resentment, that kind of bitterness… It isn't something that can be bought. But it can be stoked. I know that only too well."

Quinn's fingers tightened around the stem of his wine glass, but he kept measured as he took a sip and met Muir's dark-eyed stare. "Very well. You have the advantage, at least for now. I can only assume your brazen decision to reveal yourself and walk into my home holds some kind of purpose. Care to enlighten me as to what you'd have me do?"

Muir leaned back in his chair, resting his mud-stained boots on the edge of the polished table. "We find ourselves in need of an audience with young Lieutenant Cunningham."

"That shouldn't be difficult to arrange." Quinn steepled his fingers. "I'll send word to Lachlan at once, extending an invitation to him and the lieutenant both."

He was too amenable for Darce to trust a word he said. Quinn was as slippery as a serpent and had the tongue to match. Even now, he could hear the smugness in his voice, like they were playing a game he'd already won.

Muir seemed to have come to the same conclusion. "A generous offer, lad. But I expect they're not the only ones you'd extend an invite to. No, if I let you send word, it's only the Admiralty that will come calling. Instead, why don't you ready one of those carriages of yours and take us to the garrison tonight? You can say you're meeting Lachlan about an urgent matter, and we'll be your ever-faithful staff keeping you safe from the city after dark. You never know the dangers you'll meet in the capital, after all."

The thinly veiled threat was all it took to shatter Quinn's careful veneer. "You really think you'll walk away from this farce? The moment Lachlan sees you, he'll turn you in." He glanced at Isla, lip curled in an ugly sneer. "He knows what you are. He hasn't forgotten what you took from him. How could he? Especially when I was there to remind him that everything he lost, he lost because of what you are."

Isla flinched like she'd been struck, turning ashen at the vitriol in Quinn's words. But she steadied the quake in her jaw and met his eyes with a defiant stare. "You've been outplayed, Quinn. A wiser man would concede, but maybe I gave you too much credit all these years."

"Or perhaps you haven't given me enough." Quinn's expression smoothed over again, and he gave a thin smile. "If you wish to hasten your own downfall, who am I to stand in your way? I'll take you to the garrison. If nothing else, I'll enjoy bearing witness to the happy reunion. Lachlan will be *so* pleased to see you, I'm certain."

"The only thing you'll be bearing witness to is your merchant fleet going up in flames if you sell us out," Muir said with a grunt. "Something to keep in mind, dear baron. Now, kindly fetch us a carriage. We have some business with the Admiralty to attend."

The rattling of wooden wheels over the cobbled streets did nothing to ease the tension in Darce's shoulders. As the garrison rose into view, its grim walls tall and foreboding, he couldn't help the feeling that something was off. Muir might have outmanoeuvred Quinn this time, but that didn't mean the game was over. He only hoped whatever hand Quinn was holding wasn't enough to bring all of them down.

They passed through the checkpoint without incident, Quinn playing his part under threat from the blade Muir held at his side. None of the guards looked closely at the baron's staff—they had no reason to. Quinn was a regular visitor around these parts, it seemed, and not even the Grand Admiral would have expected them to return to the place they'd fought so desperately to escape from.

Darce pulled aside the gauze netting draped across the carriage window, trailing his eyes over the garrison's featureless walls, the shite-stained cobbles, the Admiralty banner flying from the ramparts. For months, this place had been his prison. Now, if he wasn't careful, it might well be his end.

"Twenty-five years since I last set foot here," Muir said, a shadow falling across his face. "Leaving might have been the last time I did something good in this world."

The carriage came to a stop, and Darce peered out the window to find the granite façade of the barracks before them. "We're here."

"Perhaps I should go first," Quinn said. "I am no stranger to the officers' quarters, and you'll arouse less suspicion as part of my entourage."

Muir snorted. "Aye, right. You'll sit here with the Sea Kith captain and her pistol, so you won't be able to stick your nose where it doesn't belong." He glanced at Nishi. "Don't let him move. Don't let him talk, either. He has a habit of using that silver tongue of his to get what he wants."

"I know how to cut out a tongue," Nishi said. "The Grand Admiral gave me a personal demonstration when he took Kerr's." She flicked a dagger into her hand. "If he tries anything that will get in the way of me seeing that bastard pay, he'll lose more than that."

The cloak of night was already falling by the time Darce climbed out of the carriage. Braziers flickered on the stone walls of the barracks, casting shadows everywhere he looked. If this went wrong, if Blair called for their arrest...

He met Isla's eyes. She knew the danger as well as he did.

They ducked under the arch at the barracks' entrance and crept into the narrow halls, Darce leading the way to Lachlan's quarters. The corridors were empty, but that stroke of fortune wasn't enough to chase away the dread coiled in his stomach. Every step brought them closer to something they couldn't turn back from.

"He has to listen," Isla murmured, as if she'd heard him. "He has to understand."

Something in the strain of her voice told him it wasn't the lieutenant she was talking about.

When they came to the end of the corridor, Darce pressed his ear against the mahogany doors and was met with the muffled rumble of two familiar voices. Even if he couldn't make out the words, he knew who they belonged to.

He turned to Isla, wondering if she was aware of the colour draining from her cheeks, or the way her hand drifted towards the sgian dubh tucked into her belt. Not even when she'd faced down the Grand Admiral had she trembled so much. For the first time Darce could remember, she looked afraid.

She met his eyes, then nodded.

The doors creaked as he pushed them open and entered the room. The hushed voices fell quiet, and he found himself face to face with the disbelieving features of Lachlan and Blair.

"Galbraith?" Lachlan managed. "What are you doing here? How did you..."

He trailed off, turning grey as his eyes fell on something beyond Darce's shoulder.

Isla emerged from the shadows of the corridor, a weak smile tugging at the corners of her mouth.

"Hello, wee brother," she said. "It's time we had a talk."

CHAPTER THIRTY-FOUR

ISLA

Lachlan's face was already pale, but now it lost the little colour it had left and turned to stone.

She'd prepared herself for how much it would hurt, but there was no bracing against that kind of bitterness, that kind of pain. It struck her somewhere between the ribs, pushing through bone and muscle and sinew to reach the very heart of her. He was looking at her through the eyes of a stranger.

No, it was worse than that. A stranger would have no reason to hate her.

"You shouldn't be here," he said.

His voice carried more than the weight of his words. She heard the pain lacing it, the anger simmering under the surface. She knew it was close to breaking, and all she wanted to do was make it stop, for both their sakes.

"There is so much I wish I could say to you," she said, half whispering. "So much I want to explain, if only you would listen. But we don't have time."

His eyes fell over the cloak around her shoulders. "Your pelt.

It's…missing."

He was sharp. He'd always been sharp—more than she'd given him credit for. It wasn't the worst way she'd failed him, but it was one of them.

She swallowed. "Aye, it is. Eimhir…Eimhir has it."

Lachlan's chin jolted up, eyes burning with something that might have been vindication. But there was more than that. Whether it was a flicker of fear or a shadow of grief, she couldn't be certain.

Before she could search his expression for anything more, the look was gone, replaced with flint once more. "I'm giving you one chance to get out of here before we call for officers. I suggest you take it before anyone else gets hurt."

Isla didn't miss his eyes flitting to the scar crawling up the side of Darce's head. To the missing ear—the ear he'd taken with the blade that now hung by her belt.

She slid the sgian dubh into the palm of her hand. The shining silver blade glistened with claret stains, its grooves forever marked with the blood it had spilled.

"You held this to my throat once," she said, "only to let me go with my life. You slid it across the cobbles to my outstretched hand when Finlay was about to kill me. You used it to scatter a gun-anam trying to freeze the breath in my lungs. It hasn't forgotten what you've done to protect me. Neither have I."

Lachlan's face twisted. "It should never have come to me. It wasn't mine. I thought it was, but it was a lie. Just like you."

"I didn't know."

"That only makes it worse. You didn't know, and you chose them anyway." He looked away. "You need to leave. There are some things I can't protect you from."

"Not yet," Isla said. "Not before you hear what I have to say."

"I don't *care* what you have to say. I—"

A low chuckle echoed from the corridor. "You should listen to your sister."

"She's not my—" Lachlan peered behind her. "Tides, that can't be... *Muir?* You're supposed to be dead."

"Is that disappointment I hear in your tone, you insolent wee wretch?" Muir stalked into the room, a grim smile quirking at the corner of his mouth. "You didn't do much of a job in looking for me, right enough. I suppose it was convenient for you to believe your traitorous uncle was lost to the bowels of the canals. Cleared the way for you to cosy up with the Admiralty." His eyes darted over to Blair. "The Grand Admiral's nephew, no less? Of all the bloody people..."

An angry flush coloured Lachlan's cheeks. "You don't know what you're talking about."

"*Please.*" The word clawed at Isla's throat, its edges ragged with desperation. "We haven't the time for this, not with what's coming. I didn't come here to cause you any more suffering. I came to prevent it."

Blair had been silent, watching the barbed exchanges with an impenetrable expression. Now, he met her gaze. "What's coming? You mean your selkie friends, no doubt."

Friends. *Caraid.* The memory of Eimhir's voice was a blow, rattling her to the bone. It was a reminder of all she'd lost, all Eimhir had taken from her. Grief welled in her throat, but she swallowed it down. She couldn't let it take hold of her. There would be time to mourn later, if only they succeeded.

She lifted her chin and looked at Blair. He was her cousin as much as Eimhir, no matter how she wanted to deny the blood they shared. He hadn't called for the guards, not yet. Perhaps there was a chance she could reach him.

"You've seen the mists," she said.

It wasn't a question, but Blair nodded anyway. "Aye, and the wraiths that lurk inside. From what I gather, it's you and your kind that draw them out."

"It's *violence* that draws them out, and that violence is as much yours as it is ours." Isla took a steadying breath. "The haar acts as a crossing into the soulless realm, the place those wraiths are condemned to suffer. It keeps our world from theirs, but when humans and selkies meet in violence, when we spill each other's blood, the barrier weakens. The crossing opens. And all their wretched pain and wrath comes forth."

Blair's eyes were like steel. "So all we have to do to stop the mists is stop killing selkie raiders? How convenient."

"It's too late for that. Violence will fall on Arburgh no matter what we do," Isla said. "The haar is coming. Eimhir is coming."

She didn't want to look at Lachlan, but his gaze was hot on her skin. When she met his eyes, she found no sense of victory there, hollow or not. Only resentment.

"You trusted her," he said, voice brittle with accusation. "How did this happen?"

She forced a smile. "It wouldn't be the first time I let someone I love slip away under my own watch, would it?"

He flinched, and she turned back to Blair. "The haar carries within it a sickness. It infects selkies with the same despair as the gun-anam, driving them to bloodlust and vengeance. That is what has taken hold of Eimhir. That is why she...why she did what she did."

"And what does she mean to do now?" Blair asked coldly.

You left me no choice, caraid. Someone had to do it, for our people.

"She means to attack," Isla said, pushing the memory aside. "She means to show Arburgh a kind of violence the capital has never seen, a violence even the haar can't contain. That amount of blood, that amount of death..." She swallowed. "The mists will spread across Silveckan and all its waters. The soulless realm will bleed into our own, and the gun-anam will feast on the killing that follows until all that's left are ghosts."

Blair's face took on a pale sheen. "It would be folly. Think of how many of her own people would die."

"She's not thinking clearly," Isla said. "The mist sickness is driving her. Eimhir believes she's giving the gun-anam their vengeance, that this will lay their tortured spirits to rest. But the more the haar spreads, the more selkies it will infect. More raids, more killing, more stolen pelts, more gun-anam. The cycle will go on and on."

"But you believe you can stop it." Lachlan's voice cut through the room, sharp as a blade. "You wouldn't have come here otherwise."

His gaze carried a challenge she was half-afraid to meet, but she lifted her chin. "The gun-anam are restless spirits—selkies who returned to the water without their souls, who could not become part of the sea they were born from. They surrendered themselves to the depths, their bodies dissolving into salt and spray, their bones rotting black." She touched the fabric of her tunic, fingers brushing the armour underneath. "They cannot be killed, but they can be given peace. *I* can give them peace. But to do that, I need my pelt."

"That's what this is all about?" Blair shot her a contemptuous look. "You just want our help defeating Eimhir after she stole from you."

"No," Isla said. "That burden falls on me alone. I want your help in evacuating the capital."

Blair choked out a disbelieving laugh. "That's all, is it? You think it's some easy task, convincing some ten thousand people to leave all they own behind?"

"Better that than be slaughtered," Muir said dryly.

"Who's to say they'd be slaughtered?" Blair shot back. "The *Vanguard of the Firth* did not come across its name by accident. If the selkies come, we'll drive them away."

"You won't see them coming until their blades are already at your throat, and by then, it will be too late. Even for the *Vanguard*." Darce moved beside her, eyes flitting between Blair and Lachlan. "You've both seen what happens when the mists come. You know how quickly the Admiralty's finest sentinels can be struck down by those wraiths. Think what kind of devastation they could bring about with a selkie armada. If we do nothing, Arburgh *will* fall, and the rest of Silveckan soon after."

"What do you expect him to do, Galbraith?" Lachlan demanded. "He is not the Grand Admiral."

"No, he's not. And when you told me that, I believed you." Darce turned back to Blair, holding him in the measure of his gaze. "Lachlan thinks you're a better man than your uncle. I'm asking you to prove it."

A muscle in Blair's jaw twitched, but he said nothing as he stared back. A terrible weight filled the room, leaving no space for anything but suffocating tension. There was nothing Isla could do, no words she could say. Everything hung on what Blair decided.

He exchanged a glance with Lachlan, uncertainty flickering in his eyes. "This would be a coup in all but name. What would you do, if you were in my shoes? If someone you thought was the enemy asked you to stand against your own blood?"

Lachlan blanched, and Isla turned away, unable to bear what she might see on his face. The wound between them was as raw as ever, ripped open too many times. They'd never had a chance to let it heal. Perhaps they never would.

"I would..." Lachlan hesitated. "I—"

The click of approaching boots echoed in the corridor, cutting him off. He shot a look at Blair, then reached towards his belt.

It took Isla a moment to recognise the pistol he pointed at her head. All she could see was the gullet of its barrel. Then she noticed the polished mahogany stock, the pearlescent gleam of the handle. It wasn't just any pistol. It was the one she'd shot the Grand Admiral with. It was hers.

"We're really going to do this again?" she asked gently.

The last time Lachlan held her at the end of a weapon, his hands had been trembling. Now, they were steady, his resolve absolute. There was no doubt in his eyes as they darted to the corridor, waiting for the footsteps to reach them.

She didn't need to see who was coming. The shiver scuttling down her spine told her all she needed to know.

"Isla."

She quailed at the familiar voice, the way it pretended to lay claim to her. Underneath the softness was a steel that promised no mercy.

The Grand Admiral approached slowly, a company of officers trailing in his wake. His features were weary, bearing the cost of the death that had nearly snatched him weeks before: skin so pale it was almost translucent, spidery black veins crawling underneath, eyes so bloodshot she could barely see their whites. And there, in the crook of his neck, was the ugly scar where Darce had plunged the sgian dubh.

It should have killed him. But in his gaze, she saw no sign of frailty, no weakness—only the same rage that had smothered him in its hold ever since Mara left him.

"You came back," he said gently.

She shifted her hands inside the sleeves of her cloak. The sgian dubh's handle was agonisingly close to her fingertips. She imagined Mara calling, urging her to draw the blade and end it all.

"They surrendered themselves," Lachlan said, his hand unwavering around the pistol. "They agreed to lay down their weapons for the chance to come to terms."

She wanted to rage against the lie, to tear it down with a scream and the flash of her dagger. But she saw the way Cunningham's gaze fell over Darce, and finally Muir. His face hardened, and Isla realised the mistake she'd made in bringing her uncle here.

"Please," she said. "Spare them. It's me you want. Listen to what I came here to say, and let them go."

He brought his eyes to rest on her, then froze. "No...*no.*" He traced the slope of her shoulders, expression twisting into something inhuman.

"It's gone," he whispered. "Those tides-forsaken creatures took it from you." His hands were around her arms, fingers digging into her flesh. "Where are they, child? Tell me where their islands lie, and I swear on your mother's memory I will not rest until I return to you what is yours. They'll *bleed* for what they've done."

Isla forced herself to look him in the eye. "It's not them who will bleed. They're coming here. The mists will hide them until it's too late. And when the fighting starts, the wraiths will follow. You must evacuate the city, or Arburgh will be lost."

"The capital will never fall to those creatures. Not as long as I have but a single ship left to command. If they come, the Admiralty will meet them." He smoothed a loose strand of her hair with a tender touch. "You see now the monsters they truly are. All I wanted to do was protect you from them, as I failed to protect Mara."

Behind, Muir snorted. "The only person Mara ever needed protecting from was you, Alasdair. For so many years to have passed without you being able to admit it... Tides, I wonder how I ever thought I knew you."

Cunningham fixed Muir with an unforgiving stare. "I might say the same about you. My first sentinel, my oldest friend, and the blade that stabbed me in the back not once, but twice. There is no amount of pain I could possibly wring from you to make up for what you took from me. But that doesn't mean I won't try." He signalled to the officers. "Take him to the garrison prison, and the sergeant too. They'll both answer for their treason."

Muir lunged in front of Isla, putting himself between her and Cunningham. The two men stood nose to nose, unblinking as they stared each other down.

Cunningham was the first to speak, his voice dangerously soft. "You will not stand between me and my daughter another time."

"See, that's where you're mistaken. I'm not standing between you and your daughter." Muir gave a tight smile. "I'm standing between you and my fucking niece."

He struck faster than Isla could draw breath, knuckles crashing into Cunningham's face. Blood splattered across the floor as Cunningham reeled back, lip torn and eyes wild. Before he had time to gather himself, Muir was on him again, throwing his weight behind another punch. Her uncle hadn't reached for his pistol or one of the fishknives on his belt; the blows were all fists and fury, raining on Cunningham without quarter.

"She was never yours," he grunted. "Neither of them were."

He brought his fist back again, but before he could land another blow, Lachlan hooked his crutch around his arm and pulled him away. Admiralty officers rushed in, knocking Muir to the floor as they scrambled to clamp irons around his bloodied hands. They grabbed Darce too, wrestling his cutlass from him and forcing him onto his knees.

Isla stumbled back. The sgian dubh on her belt would do her no good against half a dozen Admiralty officers. She was out of options. The only chance she had left...was *him*.

Cunningham staggered to his feet, nose crooked and streaming with blood. He stared at Muir with fury, shoulders heaving through ragged breaths.

"Please." Isla forced herself to step towards him. "This city will soon be under attack, and when the mists come, the gun-anam will follow. We don't have time for this."

She might have been a ghost, for all her presence stirred him. Cunningham's attention—his *hatred*—was fixed firmly on Muir.

"I agree," he murmured, then gave a cold smile. "He'll hang tonight."

The echo of drums rang around the stern-faced buildings surrounding Gallowgate's dismal square. Isla tried to block out the sharp, staccato bursts, but they filled her ears with the rhythm of an inevitable march towards what was coming.

Her throat was hoarse from pleading, but all her attempts were met with stony silence. The Grand Admiral would not change his mind, not even for her. Muir had taken too much from him.

A breeze swirled around the square, ruffling her cloak. She followed the gust of wind, watching it skitter through the bustle of bodies and stir the length of rope hanging in wait.

Beside her, Muir gave a heavy sigh. "It's rather an ignominious end, after everything. All these years fighting in the shadows, yet I'm fated to leave this world in front of half the tides-damned city, with twitching feet and loosed bowels, no doubt."

"You're not leaving anywhere," Isla hissed. "Stop talking like that."

Muir held up his wrists, the shackles clinking. "You want me to run? I'm not likely to get very far in these, am I?"

"We'll get you out of this. We have to."

"No, you don't." The humour faded from Muir's voice. "There's more at stake here than the life of a washed-up old seadog who lost himself in a bottle. You can save more than me tonight. But only if you live. Only if you get that pelt of yours back."

She shook her head. "I'm not giving up on you."

"You're a stubborn bloody mare."

"And you're a crabbit arse." A smile pulled at her lips despite the wrench in her heart. "But I wouldn't change it for the world, uncle."

Muir looked away, throat bobbing as he swallowed. The weathered lines on his dark brown skin suddenly seemed deeper, like time had caught up with him in these last precious moments they'd been given to say their goodbyes. His sailor's braids spilled over his shoulders in seafoam white as he lifted his chin towards the darkening sky.

"There are a lot of things I'd change, if I could," he said quietly. "A lot of regrets. But the best thing I ever did was getting you out of there. Mara, Cat, Cormick... They'd be proud of you, lass. Like I am."

Isla's chest tightened. "I don't want you to—"

"It's time to go." Blair appeared at her side, brow heavy. "I need to take you back to the dais."

If there was a note of apology in his voice, she didn't want to hear it. She shook him off as he tried to take her arm, and instead reached for Muir's shackled hands. His knuckles were split and bloodied from where he'd hit Cunningham.

I'm standing between you and my fucking niece.

"Just a moment." A new voice cut through the air, coming from behind Blair. "I wouldn't want to miss the chance to get the last word, after all."

Isla snapped her head up. There in front of her, with his perfectly coiffed hair and a satisfied smile, was Nathair Quinn.

"You..." she said, shaking. "It was *you* who tipped off the Grand Admiral. You who sent him to Lachlan's quarters. But how did you get away from—" Her stomach lurched. "Where is Nishi?"

Quinn chuckled. "You continue to disappoint me, Isla. Did you think you caught me so unaware? My merchant scouts spotted the Sea Kith ship the moment you returned to capital waters. As for its captain, well, all I had to do was open the carriage window and point her towards the spire of smoke rising across the firth. If she hurries, perhaps she'll reach her precious ship before it's nothing more than charred timber and pirate bones."

Isla lunged, a snarl rising in her throat, but Blair stepped between them. She tried to push past, but he held her firmly, his eyes like steel as he shot a glance at Quinn. "You shouldn't be here."

"It's a public execution." Quinn shrugged. "And considering I was the one who delivered this piece of canal scum to your uncle, I'd say I have more right than most to watch this unfold."

Muir gave a coarse laugh. "I hope the show is worth the abject poverty you're shortly about to find yourself in, *baron*. Earning the favour of the Grand Admiral won't be enough to keep that pretty title of yours when your merchant stock goes up in smoke."

"Do you suppose your lackeys will be so eager to follow your orders when they see you hanging from the gallows?" Quinn shot back. "They'll stand down as soon as your feet stop twitching, unless they wish to join you rotting in a gibbet where you rightfully belong." He smoothed the velvet lapels of his coat, then turned to Isla with a fixed smile. "Give your brother my regards when you see him. It brings me such joy when I can do him a favour in exchange for the friendship he's shown me."

Rage bubbled in her chest, but before she could say anything, Blair ushered her away. His grip tightened around her arm as he guided her through the crowd, his face pale with anger. "That man is a snake. Lachlan had nothing to do with any of this."

"Are you certain of that?" Isla couldn't help the bitterness lacing her tongue. "He and Quinn are—"

"I'm sure," Blair said curtly. "You might not believe it, but if there's one thing I know about your brother, it's that there's nothing he wouldn't do for his family. No matter what it might cost him."

Something in his voice turned her cold, but he kept his eyes firmly ahead as he guided her through the restless crowd. Ahead, the Grand Admiral stood on the raised dais in full regalia, surveying the gallows with an austere look.

Isla scanned the throng of Admiralty officers in front of the platform, picking through their tartan bonnets and jewel-toned cloaks. There was no sign of Lachlan's golden hair. No flash of tawny eyes.

Her heart stilled. "Blair, where is he?"

He didn't answer.

The steps to the dais rose in front of her, and she stumbled up, legs shaking. Cunningham waited with an expression that might have been contrition or disappointment—the hard-edged lines etched in his face betrayed little beyond the callousness of the man.

"He was never truly your uncle," he said. "He stole you while you were still in your mother's womb. He lied to you from the day you were born. If I could spare you this, I would. But there are some treasons no man can forgive."

Isla looked at him coolly. "I know too well there are some things beyond forgiveness."

Cunningham turned back to the gallows, jaw tight. The executioner led Muir to the trapdoors, the noose swaying in the wind above them. In a few minutes, the doors would spring open. The rope would catch. And Muir...

Tears thickened in her throat. She couldn't lose anyone else. It was too much for her heart to bear.

The night sky glittered with stars. It was so clear and crisp she could see her own breath. The only sound was the echo of the execution drums, rattling out a rhythm that would soon be cut short with the drop of the doors.

Across the square, Muir lifted his chin and met her eyes. There was no fear in his gaze, no regret. Just the grim acceptance of a battle fought and lost.

"Please," Isla said. "Please, don't…"

Something stirred in the crowd. At first, it was a ripple of bodies and hushed whispers. Then it grew, until the bustle parted like the tide retreating from shore. A hooded figure was moving towards the gallows. A figure with a long, loping gait, followed by the scrape of a wooden crutch on cobbles.

The hood fell, and her stomach dropped.

Lachlan.

He was almost at the trapdoors by the time the executioner noticed. By then, it was already too late.

It happened quickly. A glint of mother-of-pearl in the moonlight, a spark of flint and cloud of black powder, the spurt of blood from the executioner's leg.

The murmuring from the crowd grew to a roar that drowned out the gunshot ringing through her ears. In the moment it had taken Lachlan to pull the trigger of his pistol—*her* pistol—Gallowgate erupted into a surging, furious chaos.

Blair stared at the gallows with an agonised expression.

There's nothing he wouldn't do for his family. No matter what it might cost him.

He knew, she realised. He knew what Lachlan was planning, and he'd done nothing to stop it.

"What is this?" Cunningham's face twisted with anger. "Is he such a fool as to think he'll get away with—"

He broke off, a shadow falling across his expression. Isla followed his gaze to the gallows, her heart stopping as another cloaked figure climbed onto the platform.

A flash of steel winked from under the woollen folds, and Darce stood tall, holding a gleaming longsword.

His eyes met hers. Then he turned to Muir, slicing the sword through the rope raised around his neck.

Muir sank to the platform and Darce followed, fumbling with some kind of tool against the irons clamped around Muir's wrists. The shackles fell with a dull thunk, and Muir was free. Darce stood by his side, helping him to his feet. If she could only reach them…

She slipped her hand into her cloak, reaching for where the sgian dubh hung on her belt, hidden beside her seal-skull mask. They had a chance to get out of here with their lives. She had to take it, even if it meant leaving Arburgh to its fate. There was nothing more she could do for the capital.

As she readied herself to move, another gust of wind caught her cloak. Something in the air changed. This wind wasn't the usual breeze chasing through the city's streets. It carried the chill of the sea, its breath on her neck, its teeth scraping against her skin.

She cast her eyes skywards. The stars were disappearing, snuffed out by clouds. She pressed her fingers to her cheeks and found her skin dewy from the moisture clinging to the air, a drizzle threatening to turn into something more.

On the wooden carcass of the gallows, Darce stilled. He slowly turned his head, eyes telling her what she already knew.

It was too late.

The sound was distant at first—a muffled drumming in her ears. Then it grew louder, hammering off the cobbles as it approached.

Rain.

All at once, the skies opened, and a torrential downpour fell on the square. The crowd surged, bodies jostling as they fought to find shelter.

Voices rose in fear and panic, drowned out by the hammering rain and the low rumble of approaching thunder. There was no escaping this storm; it was already upon them.

"They're coming, aren't they?" The Grand Admiral was watching her, eyes steely.

"I warned you," she said, anger rising in her chest. "This rain will run red tonight, and it will be your fault."

"That may well be true. But it will not be our blood." He turned to the Admiralty officers surrounding the dais. "Take us to the *Vanguard*. We'll meet these creatures in the firth. They will not set foot in this city."

"It's too late for that," Isla snapped. "Haven't you listened to anything I've told you? Their soulship is likely already moored at the docks, hidden from sight beyond the haar. The moment the mists roll in, they'll be..."

Horror constricted her throat. She couldn't see the gallows. The other side of the square disappeared, shrouded by a drizzle growing denser by the minute. A drizzle thick with swirling fog, carrying the stench of salt and rot.

Then the screaming started.

"No," she whispered.

In front of the dais, the Admiralty officers rippled and parted, a hushed cry of terror spreading between them. Someone was crawling from the scattering crowd, pulling themselves across the cobbles with a low, strained moan. A smear of blood trailed in their wake, and as they crept closer, Isla saw where it was coming from: a ripped sapphire tunic, split down the middle to reveal flayed muscle and sinew.

It was the Admiralty executioner.

Bile rose in her throat. It had already begun.

Cunningham stiffened. "To the *Vanguard*."

"No!" She threw off the arms reaching for her. "Not while they're still out there. Muir and Darce... Lachlan..."

Beside her, Blair turned grey. "We have to do something. If those creatures are already in the city—"

Cunningham rounded on him before Isla could move, grabbing the collar of his coat with a white-knuckled fist. "I made myself perfectly clear. Now, get my daughter to the *Vanguard*."

The Admiralty officers closed in, seizing her arms. She thrashed against them, but even the latent selkie strength in her muscles wasn't enough to break free. They packed around her until she could see nothing but a wall of jewel-toned cloaks ushering her to safety.

"Blair," she cried out. "Blair, *please*. Lachlan is out there too."

If he heard her, he gave no answer.

CHAPTER THIRTY-FIVE

DARCE

All Darce could taste was the coppery tang of blood.

The handle of the Admiralty longsword he'd stolen was slick between his fingers, the blade crimson. The selkie whose neck it had cleaved through was lying at his feet, blood spilling onto the cobbles from the stump that had once held the creature's head.

One swing was all it had taken to separate it from its body.

Around him, screams filled the air. They were muffled, but there was no mistaking the terror in them. The streets of Arburgh were no longer safe. The stench of death already hung in the air: the filth of loosed bowels, the metallic reek of blood. Not even the relentless rain would be enough to wash it away, not if this horror continued.

It had all happened so quickly. One moment, he was prying apart the irons clamped around Muir's wrists. The next, he looked up to find the haar rolling in. The mist clung to the buildings like a shroud, spreading across the square until he could see nothing past the length of his sword.

The dais was gone. So was Isla.

"Galbraith, we have to get out of here." Lachlan's face was pale. One of his hands wrapped around the mahogany handle of the pistol, while the other gripped his crutch with shaking fingers.

It had been difficult to believe his eyes when the younger Blackwood had marched into the garrison prison barely an hour before. At first, Darce thought he'd simply come to say goodbye. But there had been no regret in Lachlan's gaze, no hesitancy in his voice as he brandished a release warrant with none other than Blair Cunningham's seal. He'd sprung him from his cell and brought him to help save Muir.

Lachlan had come through. Darce only hoped it wasn't too late.

He found Muir leaning against one of the walls. Another selkie lay at his feet, head twisted at an unnatural angle.

"Bloody waste," Muir muttered, casting his eyes over the dirt-streaked pelt across the selkie's limp shoulders. "How many more of them will lose their lives tonight for this madness?"

"Eimhir doesn't care about that. Not anymore." Darce glanced around the square. The haar obscured the surrounding buildings, but he could still hear the battle: clashing steel, tortured screams, wet flesh and spilled blood. Lachlan was right. It was time to move.

"We need to find Isla," he said. "Nishi too. I didn't see her in the cells."

"Your Sea Kith friend went to save her ship. Or what's left of it, at least." Muir grimaced. "Seems I underestimated Nathair Quinn after all. He knew we were coming, and he laid a trap we were only too willing to walk into. As for Isla... To find her, we need to find Alasdair. He won't let her out of his sight."

"Do you think they returned to the garrison?"

Muir shrugged. "It's as good a place as any to look. Likely to be swarming with Admiralty, mind you."

"The Admiralty has bigger concerns than the three of us." Already Darce felt the chill in his lungs, the air turning frosty. The haar was unrelenting as it spread through the winding alleys and narrow steps. Shadows stirred in its midst, releasing the foul stench of rot and salt into the air.

It wasn't just the selkies. The gun-anam were here.

He followed Muir and Lachlan out of the square. Rain pelted down from the storm clouds, turning the streets into rivers awash with water and blood and filth. He picked his way around fallen bodies, unable to keep his eyes from lingering on the violence marking them. Flesh flayed to ribbons, exposing bone and sinew underneath. Seafoam dribbling from blue lips. Waxy, pallid skin and bloated tissue. It was more than he could stomach, but he couldn't look away.

Overhead, a stifled caw fought through the mist. Featherblade was somewhere above them, flitting over the streets. Darce sensed the outline of the gannet through the incessant rain, his magic showing him what his eyes couldn't see.

"Find her," he murmured. "Help me get back to her."

He felt a tug of understanding as their minds brushed. Then Featherblade peeled away, its rattling cries fading into the clouds.

By the time they reached the north side of the Admiralty Bridge, Darce's hands had gone numb around the handle of his sword. Each breath squeezed his throat, filling his lungs with ice and water from the frigid air.

He turned to the others. Muir's white braids were frozen solid, sliding over his broad shoulders. Lachlan had taken on a ghostly pallor, his fingers stiff around his crutch. Every minute, the haar thickened, breathing its rot into the air. Before long, it would consume the entire city.

Then, it would spread to the rest of Silveckan.

Darce shook his head, trying to push the thought from his mind. Through the gloom ahead came the clang of steel and the crash of spray, and he readied his blade.

Out of the mist, a selkie sprang towards him, axe dripping with blood. Darce barely had time to bring his arms up to parry the blow. His elbows rattled, and he stumbled back, pushing the selkie out the way as he fought to regain his balance.

Muir slipped around the other side of the selkie, swinging a scavenged Admiralty cutlass to slice at the creature's shoulder. The sandy, speckled fur split open with a gush of blood.

The selkie snarled and rounded on Muir, axe scattering droplets of rain as he whirled it high. But before the creature could let it fall, Darce plunged his sword into his back. The blade crunched as it pushed through the selkie's ribs, tearing through muscle and flesh until it slid out the other side. He pulled it out in a swift, fluid stroke, and the selkie fell to the ground.

"More of them," Lachlan said. "Up ahead, look."

Darce followed his gaze along the cobbled street. All he could see through the haze was the blur of fur and the flash of jewel-toned capes. Admiralty and selkie, locked in bloody violence.

"Leave them," Muir said. "We can't do anything here that won't lead to more death."

He was right. There would be no victors in the bloodshed that had fallen across Arburgh. All they could do now was survive.

"Sergeant!"

A cry pierced the air, and a figure came stumbling out of the mist. Darce raised his sword, searching the girl's matted hair and dirt-stained cheeks for a sign of recognition. It wasn't until he saw the gleam of the twin stiletto daggers that he realised who she was.

"It's Rhona," Mhairi choked out. "One of those wraiths—"

Darce saw her limp figure lying across the cobbles. Her brown hair was plastered across her pale skin, her eyes wide in terror at the gun-anam drifting towards her. Wisping tendrils snaked around her throat, turning her face blue, drawing water from her spluttering mouth. She thrashed against the ground, the inked muscles of her forearms flexing as she tried to twist her fingers into a ward.

The tides, if they were listening at all, didn't answer. Her hand fell to the cobbles, and the gun-anam drew a shimmering blade from the mist.

Darce moved without thinking. He was vaguely aware of the clatter of steel as his longsword fell, but he didn't remember releasing his hands. All he could focus on was the magic calling to him with the furious roar of the sea.

He spread his arms, reaching with everything his sentinel powers had given him. The rain lashed down, stinging his cheeks, clinging to his soaking hair. The thrum of each droplet battered off the cobbles like a rhythm inside his veins. His blood turned cold, surging with the churn of the tides.

Rain swirled around him, filling his head with the sound of crashing waves. Then he released the torrent straight at the gun-anam.

The funnel of rain slammed into the wraith. The creature's wisping form scattered, its blade dissolving into silvery vapour that fell across Rhona's face in harmless droplets. She sucked in a wheezing gasp and hauled herself onto her elbows, eyes bloodshot as she blinked away the salt.

When her gaze met his, she gave a low, disbelieving laugh. "Sergeant Galbraith. Ye have a fine way of showing up whenever things turn to shite."

Mhairi rushed over to help her to her feet. Rhona looped an arm around her shoulder and allowed herself to lean on her captain's smaller frame as she limped doggedly towards them. Her lips were cracked, her eyes shadowed with dark circles, but she quirked her mouth into a wry smile.

"Seem to remember telling ye I'd not hesitate in doing my duty if our paths crossed again," she said. "A wiser man might've kept walking."

"You let us go with our lives last time we met. It's only right I returned the favour."

"Well, I cannae say I'm not grateful. Even if it's only a stay of execution." Rhona winced as she pressed a hand to her ribs. "The skinchangers are everywhere. I don't know how they got into the city unnoticed, but they've no been shy in letting us ken they're here. Everywhere we turn, we see more flayed bodies. Not all o' them dead, either. Poor bastards."

Mhairi shuddered. "At least the selkies can be killed. Those wraiths... How are we supposed to fight such things?"

"You can't," Muir said bluntly. "We warned your Grand Admiral this was coming, but he wouldn't listen. It's too late for the capital. You'd do well to get out while you can, though how far you'll get before the mists follow is anyone's guess."

Lachlan stiffened. "That's it, then? We're going to leave all these people to their fate?"

"What else would you have us do?" Darce said. "We tried. The only person who can stop the haar is Isla, and she has no hope unless she gets her pelt back."

"Even if we can't stop the mist, we can buy people time," Lachlan shot back. "I believed you when you said you were here to evacuate the city. Did you mean it, or was it all about Isla again?"

"Tides *take* you, Lachlan!" Darce wheeled on him. "You think it's easy for me to walk these streets and see the reminders of what we brought here? I know the kind of violence Arburgh will drown in tonight. But short of knocking on every damn door and dragging folk from their beds, there's nothing we can do about it."

Mhairi exchanged a glance with Rhona. "That's not entirely true. The capital bell would rouse them."

"The capital bell?" Lachlan frowned. "I thought the Admiralty rang that to put the city under lockdown. People need to *leave* Arburgh, not hunker down."

"There are two bells," Rhona said, a pensive look falling across her face. "The second has never been rung—never had reason to be rung. Its toll signifies only one thing... Arburgh has fallen."

Her words hung in the air, giving voice to something none of them wanted to admit. The capital was lost. The bloodied bodies of its people lined the cobbled streets. Every minute, the haar swallowed more of the city as human and selkie fell.

The soulless realm will bleed into our own, Isla had warned them. *And the gun-anam will feast on the killing that follows until all that's left are ghosts.*

"Would people know what it meant?" Lachlan asked, turning to Mhairi. "Would they leave?"

It was Rhona who answered. "Aye," she said, voice strained. "At least, those who could."

She looked away, jaw clenched. Darce opened his mouth to question her, but before he could speak, Lachlan stepped in front of him with an uncompromising expression. "That bell *must* toll, Galbraith. Whatever you think of the Admiralty, the rest of the people in this city don't deserve what's coming."

"I know," Darce said. "But if we lose Isla, it's not just Arburgh that will suffer. Eimhir wants to shroud all of Silveckan in the haar. Your sister is the only one who can stop her."

Mhairi jerked her head up, eyes sharp. "Is that true, Sergeant?" When Darce nodded, she pressed her mouth into a tight line, like she was fighting against what she wanted to say.

Rhona sighed. "It's treason to tell ye this, but your lass is likely on the *Vanguard* by now. That's where the Grand Admiral was headed when he left Gallowgate."

"The *Vanguard?*" Darce's stomach turned cold. He didn't want to see that ship again, much less set foot on it. The thought of its black sails, its blood-soaked timber, the restless spirits of all the souls slaughtered on its deck... It brought back memories he didn't want to return to.

But if Isla was there, he had no choice.

When he lifted his head, Lachlan was staring at him. "Go to her. I'll take care of the bell. This city's blood is on my hands, too. I played my part in bringing those creatures here, just like she did." He shook his head bitterly. "You wonder why I can't forgive her, Galbraith? How could I, when I can't forgive myself? I should have tried harder to rebuild what was broken between us. Maybe that would have been enough to make her listen. Instead, I pushed her right to them."

Muir scoffed. "You give yourself too much credit, lad. She didn't choose to help Eimhir to spite you. She chose to help Eimhir because something in her soul knew it was the right thing to do. Isla is more stubborn than the barnacles on a ship's arse when she sets her mind to something. She gets it from—"

"Don't," Lachlan said. "I don't want to hear about whoever—"

"Cat," Muir finished, smacking the back of his head. "Aye, that's right. The mother you share, and don't you bloody forget it. She was my sister, remember? From the moment my father brought her home from that workhouse to the day she died. I didn't need to share her blood to know she was family. Neither should you." He ignored Lachlan's scowl and turned to Darce with a sombre nod. "I'll go with him to the garrison. If tides be kind, everyone will be too busy pissing their breeches at the raiders to worry about guarding the bell tower. We'll meet you at the docks after. Make sure you have my niece back when we find you."

"We'll come with ye, Sergeant," Rhona said, glancing at Mhairi. "You'll never reach the *Vanguard* on your own, not with the docks crawling with skinchangers."

Something in the weight of her brow gave Darce pause. Too many times he'd seen a shadow cross her face, speaking of some unknown dread, some burden he couldn't quite place. Now, it etched deeper than ever, turning her features hard beyond their years.

"What is it?" he asked quietly. "What else is there you're not telling me?"

She shook her head, lips pursed.

In the distance, another muffled scream tore through the wind. They were out of time.

He placed a firm hand around Lachlan's shoulder. "I'll send Featherblade to guide you back to us." He paused, tightening his grip. "Swear to me you *will* come back to us. I have precious little family left in my life to bear the thought of losing a brother."

Lachlan gave a weak smile and clapped his hand over Darce's forearm. "I'll do my best, Sergeant. You taught me well, after all."

"Everything I could."

"Then trust it will be enough." He dropped his arm and arched an eyebrow at Muir. "I hope you can wield that cutlass like you did in the auld days, uncle."

Muir barked out a laugh. "You'll see soon enough, you cocky wee gobshite."

Darce watched them go, the rain battering down until it engulfed them. Around him, the city screamed. All he could hear were the echoes of a war he was too late to stop.

He turned to Rhona, finding the same desolation in her own dark gaze. "To the *Vanguard?*" she asked.

"Aye," Darce replied.

And whatever awaited them there.

CHAPTER THIRTY-SIX

ISLA

The docks were quiet. *Too* quiet.

Isla shrugged off the officer gripping her arm as she climbed onto the gangway, the soles of her boots sliding on the slippery surface. Even without her pelt, she held no fear of falling into the tumultuous waves chopping below. If the tides decided to claim her, their grasp couldn't be worse than the chains the Grand Admiral was determined to bind her with.

The *Vanguard's* towering masts were all but invisible as she edged forward. The haar closed in, burning her throat with the sting of salt. She felt its touch against her cheeks, its otherworldly chill biting her skin. It shrouded the ship in a ghostly pall, so dense that not a shadow stirred within.

She stepped onto the deck with a shiver. Her pelt was gone, but part of her was still selkie. She knew the spirits that clung to the timber, the lives cut short here. The wood below her feet had gorged itself on the blood of her people.

It was a graveyard. A monster built on the slaughter of selkies.

A fierce gust whipped up around her neck. No sound stirred but the spiteful whistling of the wind, the low groaning of the masts.

"Where is everyone?" she asked.

Her words disappeared into the mist, muffled by the dampness hanging in the air. Beside her, the Grand Admiral's steely eyes narrowed as he peered across the deck. "I left enough crew to get us underway at haste if the need arose. They should be here."

"They're not."

She stepped forward hesitantly. Something wasn't right here. She felt it in the weight of the air.

The tip of her boot hit something soft, and she looked down into the lifeless eyes of a fallen officer.

She realised at once what had killed him. Horror clung to his expression, frozen in his slack features. The teal trim of his cloak was stained crimson. If she rolled him over, she'd find his skin flayed to strips of flesh, his muscles bloodied and exposed to the salty air.

Perhaps he deserved it. Few who served on the *Vanguard of the Firth* could claim innocence to the horrors committed in the Admiralty's name. But that didn't make it any easier to witness.

Cunningham drew close, his breath hanging in the icy air between them. "Beasts. Every one of them."

"Even Mara?" Isla turned to face him. "Even me?"

A muscle in his jaw twitched as he appraised the officer's unmoving corpse. "They mean to cut down our greatest weapon. But the *Vanguard* can survive the loss of a few deckhands. My sentinels will fill our sails, no matter what it costs them."

Isla shuddered. She knew the kind of magic he could call on. The fact he was standing on the *Vanguard's* deck when he should have been rotting in an unmourned grave was proof enough of that.

The wind stirred again, and the mists parted, offering her a glimpse across the firth's waters. Something glinted in the middle of the river's gaping mouth. She might have mistaken it for the moon's pale reflection, had the sky not been shrouded in storm clouds.

It was the soulship. The anam-long.

She barely had time to trail her eyes over its glistening masts, its wisping sails, before the haar closed in again. But there was no mistaking what she saw. It had entered the firth like a ghost, cloaked by the mist. No Admiralty scouts would have seen it coming. The city never stood a chance.

The Grand Admiral stilled. "We're not alone."

There was no fear in his voice, only a coldness that trickled into Isla's bones. She moved her hand towards her belt, where the sgian dubh rested. The dagger was a comfort, despite its diminutive size. It had kept her alive all her life.

A muffled yell cut through the mist. Isla spun around, but she couldn't see anything past the wall of the haar. The *Vanguard* was so huge that the other side of the deck was beyond what she could glean through the dense fog.

"Caldwell!" Another voice rose from further down the ship, then devolved into a strangled scream.

The sentinels were being picked off. Something was hunting them, something that could slip between realms and strike without warning. Something—or some*one*—had been watching, waiting for them to step into this trap.

The Grand Admiral reached for his cutlass, loosening the sword from its sheath. He shot a warning glance at Blair. "The *Serpent's Wake* and *Tempest's Thrall* are moored alongside us. Empty those ships of every sentinel and bring them here."

Blair nodded, his face pale as he hurried away and disappeared into the haar.

If his sentinels fell, the Grand Admiral was vulnerable, Isla realised. Only their sacrifice could bring him back from death.

The thought sent a frantic rush through her. She could be free of him. All she had to do was survive this.

"I knew you would come back to this ship."

A cold voice cut through the haar, as sharp as the salt in the air. It was a voice Isla recognised well. But where it once held the familiarity of someone she knew, someone she *loved*, it sounded now like a stranger.

"I've waited a long time for this," Eimhir continued. "Ever since I was a bairn, I was told it would be my fate to take back what you stole from us all those years ago. And now I have it, all that's left is to see you pay the rest of your debt."

Eimhir stepped forward, a shadow in the mist. There was no warmth in her eyes, only the reflection of the storm.

Isla's gaze fell on the pelt around her shoulders. The grey folds that once belonged to her now hung around Eimhir's arms. It felt *wrong*. Part of her still existed there, whether Eimhir wanted to admit it or not.

No matter what she said, it wasn't hers. It never would be.

Eimhir locked eyes with her, then froze. It was like the rest of the ship had melted into the mists, leaving nothing but the two of them balanced on the tip of a blade.

"I didn't expect to see you here," Eimhir said. "I thought the sea would have called you home."

"It did." Isla pulled the cord of her cloak, casting it from her shoulders to let it fall on the rain-soaked deck. Underneath, the cuirass of bone glistened as white as the soulship, caging her ribs in its armour.

"What you did left its mark on me," she said, rolling up the sleeves of her tunic to reveal the salt scars streaked across her skin. "But when I sought the depths, they were not yet ready to take me. The soul I thought I'd lost is mine to reclaim." She shook her head, bitterness rising in her throat. "I offered it to you freely. If only you'd taken it then, this might never have come to pass. But there is no amount of blood you could spill from my body to make that pelt your own, not when it was taken unwillingly."

Eimhir blanched. "I never wanted it. Not until there was no other choice."

"Aye, I know." Tears pricked the corner of Isla's eyes. "And I'm as much to blame for that as you are."

Eimhir shifted her gaze back to the Grand Admiral. "And now you stand at the side of the monster who started all this. The man who stripped Mara of her pelt, who denied you your birthright. Is *this* what you call family?"

A cruel smile curled across Cunningham's lips. "You have something that belongs to me, selkie. If there are debts to pay, I will recover mine with your blood."

His knuckles tightened around the ebony handle of his pistol. Before Isla could do anything, he raised his arm and fired a shot straight at Eimhir.

"No!"

The scream tore loose from her throat as the air crackled with lead. Eimhir whirled away, lips contorting into a snarl as the shot clipped her shoulder, sending blood splattering across the deck. She pressed a pale hand to her pelt—*Isla's* pelt—her fingers wet and red.

Cunningham reached for his cutlass, but Isla grabbed his arm. "I won't let you hurt her."

"Don't be a fool." Cunningham pushed her off. "You think these creatures will show you mercy? You're not one of them. You never were."

"She is my family."

"*I* am your family." He rounded on her. "I will not let them take you from me. I swear it on Mara's memory."

Rage fluttered in Isla's chest. "You have no right to speak her name, not after what you did to her, what you're *still doing* to her people. If she were here, she would—"

"Get back!" Cunningham shoved her, the bone armour bruising her sternum as she stumbled and fell to the deck. She rolled over in time to see Eimhir leaping through the mist, axe raised and face twisted in fury.

Cunningham met the blow with his cutlass, staggering under the weight of Eimhir's vicious strike. No sooner had he shaken her off than she was on him again, sweeping her axe towards him with two hands. The edge scythed through the air, scattering raindrops as the storm continued to batter down.

Isla hauled herself to her feet as Eimhir charged at Cunningham with a roar. There was no rhythm or reason behind any of her blows—the axe was an instrument of her rage, as wild and frenzied as the fury in her eyes. She struck at Cunningham relentlessly, hammering down on him again and again.

Eimhir would soon tire, Isla realised with a burst of fear. She wasn't thinking about how to win. The only thing driving her was the mist sickness, the bloodlust wrapping her in its unforgiving hold. All Cunningham had to do was fend her off long enough for exhaustion to set in, and he'd find an opening to strike.

Thunder rumbled from the black clouds above, and the sky lit up with a blinding flash. The storm was getting worse. Every second, the rain lashed down with more fury than before, stinging her skin and soaking her to the bone. The haar was thicker than ever, creeping across the waves. Before long, it would claim Arburgh entirely. Between the bloodshed and the storm, the city would be washed away. The only way to stop it was to stop Eimhir.

Stop Eimhir. That was why she'd come here, wasn't it?

The thought chilled her. If Eimhir fell, she could take her pelt back. She could take control of the haar and put an end to the violence. All it would take was a betrayal beyond anything she could imagine, an act that would leave a scar that would never heal.

She wrapped her fingers around the sgian dubh. Eimhir's pale cheeks flushed as she swung her axe, sucking in breaths between blows. It was easier for Cunningham to parry them now the force behind them had weakened. He watched Eimhir carefully, his footsteps steady as he drew her with him.

Without warning, Cunningham moved back, and Eimhir stormed into the space he'd left behind.

She didn't see the trap.

Cunningham whirled out of reach, ducking under Eimhir's axe as it sliced through the air. In the same movement, he swept his cutlass high, blade flashing through the rain.

There was a cry, then the *thunk* of iron against timber. Eimhir's axe clattered to the deck, and she wheeled away, clutching a bloodied arm.

She looked up with hate in her eyes, the fur of her pelt smeared with red. "I'll kill you."

"I doubt that." Cunningham's voice was soft, no less threatening for how quiet it was. "Whatever you think you've managed to achieve here, it will end with your death. My fleet will scour Silveckan's waters until every remaining selkie is slain. This will be the last time your kind threatens my city."

He advanced, cutlass outstretched. Blood trickled down the edge of the blade, mingling with the rain. Isla tightened her numb fingers around the sgian dubh, ignoring the way her body was shaking.

It will end with your death, Cunningham had told Eimhir.

All Isla had to do was let it happen.

"No," she whispered.

Her legs moved of their own accord, boots splashing through the rain. She wrenched the sgian dubh from her belt, twisting the dagger in her palm as she rushed forward. There was no time for doubt. All that mattered was not letting this chance slip.

Cunningham was facing away from her, his blade advancing on Eimhir. He didn't turn until the last second. The only thing Isla saw was the whites of his eyes before she sank the sgian dubh's blade into his heart.

For a moment, there was only silence. It was like the storm itself held its breath while Cunningham teetered on his feet. Then he fell, collapsing to the deck with a dull thump, blood blooming around the hilt of the dagger buried in his chest.

Eimhir snatched her axe from the ground and scrambled away, staring between Isla and the fallen body of the Grand Admiral. Blood poured from the wound in her shoulder and the gash along her arm. She was hurt, but she was alive.

Isla leaned over Cunningham's lifeless frame. She snatched the sgian dubh from his chest, the crimson stain seeping through the brocade of his tunic. A gurgle rose from his throat, then died. All she could see in the dull blue-grey of his eyes was the reflection of the swirling clouds above.

He was gone. It was over.

She turned to Eimhir, who was watching her with a wary expression. "Is this not enough for you, cousin? I chose you. *You* are my family. Please, put an end to this horror, for both our sakes. Let's finish this together, as we were meant to."

Eimhir's shoulders loosened, but her face was as stony as ever. "It's too late for that."

"You don't believe that. I know you don't." Isla stepped cautiously towards her, the dagger warm in her hand as she tucked it into her belt. "Nobody else needs to suffer. I can give the gun-anam the peace they deserve. We can stop the mist sickness, stop the haar from spreading. All you need to do is give me my pelt back."

"It doesn't belong to you, not anymore." Eimhir lifted her chin, eyes glittering. "The Grand Admiral was right. You're not one of us. You never were."

Isla shook her head, tears thickening in her throat. "You'd never say that. It's the mist sickness talking."

"Why can't it be both?" She gave a humourless smile. "You had the chance to do what was right for our people, and you refused. You forced me into a choice I never wanted to make. You can't ask me to take it back."

Above, the thunder let loose another roar. Then something cut through the scream of the storm—a low, sombre knell that resounded in Isla's ears with an echo of dread.

The capital bell.

As soon as the thought struck her, she pushed it away. She'd heard the bell toll before. She remembered its brassy clang, the warning with which it reverberated across the city. This was different. Each distant peal was full of mourning—a lament for something beyond hope, something that wasn't coming back.

It was over. Arburgh was lost.

She turned back to Eimhir, searching for a flicker of the woman she once knew. Her cousin. Her *friend*. "I failed you."

Eimhir moved to the gunwale. The wind whipped her ragged blonde hair and ruffled the grey folds of the stolen pelt around her shoulders. All that was left in her eyes was the cold glint of vengeance.

"You should leave Silveckan while you still can," Eimhir said. "All I can offer you is the chance to escape what's coming. Sail away from here, Isla, and never look back."

"I can't do that."

"Then I'm sorry. Truly, I am." Eimhir climbed onto the edge of the ship. A fork of lightning flashed across the sky, casting her face in shadows.

There was no trace of her cousin left. Only the suffering left behind.

"It will haunt you," Isla whispered. "What you've taken from me... What you've done."

A bleak, ghostly smile curled at the corner of Eimhir's lips. "Oh, caraid. It already does."

The waves crashed against the *Vanguard's* hull, and Eimhir leapt to meet them.

CHAPTER THIRTY-SEVEN

DARCE

Darce ran over the rain-soaked cobbles, lungs burning. All he could hear was his frantic breathing.

Until the death knell tolled.

The bell sent an ache to his bones. Lachlan and Muir must have reached the garrison, but the sound of their success brought no relief. It was only a reminder of how they'd failed.

Beside him, Rhona exchanged a glance with Mhairi. "It's done, then. The capital has met its end tonight."

"Aye, it has," Mhairi said. "But not its people. That bell will give them the chance to escape with their lives."

"Which is more than can be said for us." Rhona shot him a pointed look. "I hope your selkie lass can do what ye say she can, Sergeant. If these mists aren't stopped..."

"I know." Darce gritted his teeth. "But first we have to find her."

The docks stretched in front of them, their sprawling jetties and seaweed-strewn mooring lines lost to the gloom of the haar. Each ship was a murky shadow, timber groaning as they bucked and rolled, agitated by the storm. Somewhere among them was the *Vanguard of the Firth*.

Somewhere among them was Isla.

"This way," Rhona said. "The aft gangway should be a wee bit further. Keep an eye out for—"

She stuttered to a halt, expression darkening. At the foot of the long wooden gangway was the lean-limbed frame of a young man clad in a familiar russet-coloured pelt.

Rhona readied her arms, hands winding into the shape of a ward, but Darce stopped her. "Give me a moment."

"Ye want to *talk* to that thing?" Rhona glared at him. "Have ye lost all your wits?"

"There's been enough blood spilled tonight. I'd rather not add to it if there's another way." He pushed past, ignoring her protests as he approached the foot of the gangway. The selkie was hunched over, but when he looked up, Darce saw a glimmer of recognition in his eyes.

"Auld blood," Angus said, then coughed. "Eimhir thought you'd be by Isla's side, if she made it this far."

"That's my intention."

"Then you've failed." Angus straightened, revealing a nasty gash across his torso. He pressed his hand against the wound, grimacing through the pain. "I might have caught the wrong end of a blade, but that won't stop me. You're not getting on this ship."

Darce flexed his fingers. "Bold words from a man already bleeding."

"The young Admiralty pup took me by surprise. He got away. I won't make the same mistake with his uncle."

Darce stiffened. Blair was here. Or at least, he had been. "I'm not here for the Grand Admiral. I'm here for Isla."

"If she's with him, she made her choice." Angus gave a pained shrug. "Eimhir told me to guard this ship. Until she's done what she came here to do, here I'll stand."

"Impressive loyalty. Shame it was bought with a stolen soul."

Angus drew his lip back in a snarl. "Don't. It was I who bound Isla's wounds with seaweed to stop her bleeding. I helped carry her back to you.

I did all I could to save her life, but her soul was already forfeit. There was no undoing what Eimhir had done."

"That's it?" Darce demanded. "After what Eimhir did, you'd still follow her?"

"It's *because* of what she did that we must follow her." Angus turned away, jaw tight. "Aye, she is lost. She did something that should be unthinkable to any clear-minded selkie. But whatever she has become, she's fighting for us. She's the *only* one fighting for us. If my people are to survive, it will be thanks to Eimhir."

Darce felt Rhona stir at his back. The sentinel magic in his veins hummed, promising to answer if he called on it. Every passing second was like the closing of a door, sealing off the hope of ending this without blood.

Angus stood between him and Isla. He didn't have a choice.

He let out a breath as the magic rushed through him.

"Wait." Angus tilted his head, eyes darting towards the water. "Ah, there she is."

Darce paused, but all he heard through the ragged mess of his missing ear was the storm raging around him.

Then he felt it. The surging in his blood, the rush of magic... It wasn't just Angus. More auld blood had been spilled. He sensed its trail across the *Vanguard's* deck, trickling over the gunwale into the waves.

"It's done." Angus pulled the russet folds of his pelt across his pale chest and shuffled to the edge of the jetty. "I need not die tonight after all. I'm glad. There is blood more deserving of being spilled than yours and mine."

Darce frowned. "What do you—"

His words died in the air as Angus leapt into the frothing waves.

Darce stared at the water, then turned towards the *Vanguard's* looming hull. The gangway disappeared halfway up the huge side of the ship, swallowed by the mist. There was no way of knowing what he'd be walking into when he climbed it.

It's done, Angus had said.

Darce didn't want to think about what that might mean.

The rain pelted against the plank, splashing his ankles as he climbed. Every precarious step carried him deeper into the haar, closer to what was waiting for him on the *Vanguard*.

When at last he reached the top of the gangway, all he could see was a wall of white. The mist clung to the masts and swirled along the deck. There was no sign of the crew. There was no sign of anyone.

He ignored Rhona calling behind him and pressed through the mist. It parted in front of him, bleeding out of his way as he walked.

"Isla."

Her name left his lips a moment before he saw her, like he'd somehow breathed her into being. She stood at the gunwale, her salt-scarred arms spread wide as she stared down at the water.

When she turned to him, her green eyes were shining. "I couldn't do it. I didn't *want* to do it."

His hands found the curve of her jaw, and he held her as she trembled. "I know."

"What happens next? What's left for us to do now that I've failed?" She shook her head. "I thought I could bring her back, but she was already beyond my reach. And now, so is my pelt."

"We'll find another way to—"

"There is no other way." She squeezed her eyes shut, pulling away. "This was our only chance, and we lost it. *I* lost it."

The faint lines of her brow furrowed with a pain he couldn't imagine. Faint trails of salt glistened across her skin, mingling with the tear-stained streaks on her pale cheeks.

When at last she opened her eyes again, he saw only defeat. "We can't stay here," she said. "We need to leave Arburgh. Find calmer waters, at least for a while."

Darce glanced at the *Vanguard's* towering masts. "There aren't enough of us to rig and sail a ship this size."

"No," Isla said. "We'll have to find another."

He followed her gaze across the water. Through the mist, he could make out a shimmering, ghostly silhouette.

A chill prickled his skin. "You mean to take the soulship."

"You can see it?" Isla pressed a hand against the selkie bones she wore as armour. "It's still in the soulless realm. But when I wear these bones, the barrier between those worlds seems thinner. They let me see beyond the haar. Perhaps the blood oath allows you to see it too. In any case, that ship is our only chance of getting out of here. It needs no crew, only your magic."

"I doubt your old selkie friends are likely to let us sail away with their ship without a fight. But if that's where we're headed, it's best we leave before..." He trailed off, unease twisting his stomach. "The Grand Admiral, is he—"

"Dead." Isla's voice was flat as she clenched the dagger in her hand. The blade was stained, droplets of blood trickling down to the hilt. "I put it through his heart."

"Where is he?"

She flitted her gaze towards the starboard side of the deck, eyes clouding over. "See for yourself, if you want to make sure. I can't bring myself to look at him, not even in death. But be quick. Blair was here too, and he'll likely be back before long. I'd rather not be here when he sees what I've done."

Darce squeezed her hand, then slowly edged through the mist to the far side of the ship. Even with Isla's words ringing in his head, he couldn't believe it. Not until he saw for himself.

The mists thinned, and the timber underfoot glistened with red. There, in a pool of his own blood, lay Alasdair Cunningham. His body was limp and lifeless, his eyes blank and glassy as they stared at the sky. Not a breath stirred from his chest.

He was gone, just like Isla said.

"She did it, then."

Darce spun around to find Rhona at his shoulder. She stared at Cunningham, an unfathomable expression etched on her face.

"It's over, Rho." Mhairi appeared at her side, slipping her hand into her sentinel's. "He has no power over us anymore. We can leave the capital. We can go anywhere we want."

"Aye," Rhona said.

There was no relief in the low tone of her voice, no relaxing of the tension in her shoulders. Instead, a shadow fell across her eyes.

"Mhairi's right," Darce said gently. "Whatever he did to you, whatever he threatened you with, it doesn't matter anymore. He's gone."

Rhona's lips pulled into a pained line, and she squeezed her hands until her knuckles turned white. Then she released a breath, and the anguish vanished, replaced with an unflinching resolve.

Darce had seen that look before, but not in her.

"No. Rhona, *no!*"

It was too late. As he reached for her, she whirled away, drawing her sword from her scabbard in one fluid motion. Mhairi's eyes widened with a flicker of realisation that lingered in the air, drawing out every agonising second of the betrayal rushing towards her ribs.

All he heard was a wet, feeble squelch. Rhona's blade was buried in Mhairi's stomach, its hilt pressing against her ribs. The two women's faces were close enough for a breath to pass between them, for a whisper Darce couldn't hear. Then Rhona pulled the sword free and Mhairi fell to the deck, blood pouring from her stomach.

Darce's mouth ran dry. "Tides take you... What did you *do?*"

"Only what was asked of me. What I had to do." Rhona dropped to her knees, pressing her palms into Mhairi's blood. Already it was mingling with the Grand Admiral's, slipping into the rivulets running across the stained timber.

She lifted her hands, twisting her fingers into wards. Magic thrummed in the air, and Darce's own blood quivered in response. This wasn't what the tides intended when they granted their gifts. This perverted everything a sentinel should be.

"Stop." He drew the longsword from his hip, hands shaking around the hilt. "I won't let you do this. I won't let you bring him back."

"You can't undo this, Sergeant. The price has already been paid. The tides will protect him until he rises again." She cast him a sideways look. "You should leave. Your selkie lass, too. Neither of ye want to be here when the tides send him back."

A huge wave crashed against the *Vanguard's* hull, as if the sea itself echoed her warning. Already he sensed the change in the air, the chill running through his veins. It was sentinel magic like he'd never felt before, a distortion of what he was. What he thought *Rhona* was.

"She was your captain," he said, hardly able to utter the words through the horror. "How could you... How could anyone..."

"Ye think I wanted this?" Rhona's dark eyes flashed with anger. "Ye think *any* of us serve him willingly? He took my sister, Sergeant. He has her somewhere I can never hope to find."

"So you bought her freedom with your captain's life?"

"Her freedom?" She looked at him bleakly. "He'll never release her. He'll never release any of them, lest they expose him for what he is. But if he dies, so does she. So does *everyone* else he's taken from his sentinels. His orders will outlive him. He made it that way, so we're all hostage to his survival. You should know that as well as anyone."

Darce shuddered. The echo of Muir's warning rang in his head. *If you had to choose, you would break.*

"I wouldn't," he said, so low he could barely hear his own voice. "I would never..."

Rhona curled her lips into a pained smile. "I hope for your sake you never have to find out. As for me..." She bowed her head, brushing a hand over Mhairi's pallid forehead. "I ken the truth of it now. Maybe I always did. There's nae going back after what I've done. But there's nae living with it, either."

With a jolt of horror, he saw the gleam of a stiletto dagger in her hand.

He lurched towards her, but only grasped empty air as she spun the blade and thrust it squarely into her sternum.

"Tides *take* you, Rhona!" Even as he roared, he knew it was too late. The dagger was buried deep in her chest, wet and glistening. The only sound she made was a faint wheeze as she fell over Mhairi's crumpled body, her inked arm coming to rest over her fallen captain.

"Darce? What's happen—" Isla stumbled through the mist, eyes widening as she took in the bloody sight in front of her. "No... She can't have. Tell me she didn't..."

"She did." Darce wrenched his gaze from Rhona's lifeless features. "We have to leave. Before he—"

"Don't say it. I know." Her cheeks turned pallid. "I'll never escape him. Not as long as he has a sentinel left to spill their blood for him."

"That's not true. Not as long as *I'm* left alive. If you need a wild wind to keep you out of his grasp, I'll carry you wherever you need to go."

She swallowed. "I should never have left you behind. I won't make that mistake again."

The low, mournful toll of the capital bell boomed through the mist, sending a quake through the *Vanguard's* deck.

Darce cast his eyes to the sky, knowing he'd see nothing through the haar but still waiting, still hoping. If Lachlan and Muir made it out of the garrison alive, Featherblade would find them. He'd lead them here.

"It's time to go." Darce pulled her to the gangway. The docks waited for them below, as silent as when he'd arrived. A damp cloud of fog smothered every sound apart from the dismal tolling of the bell.

The minutes drew out as they ran, each stretching longer than the last. Rain pelted down, crashing off the slate roofs of the towering dockside buildings. It seemed like there would be no end to the storm, that the darkness swallowing Arburgh was there to stay.

A guttural shriek rattled through the air, and Featherblade swooped over them, white wings trailing vapour. A moment later, footsteps thudded through the mist, followed by the familiar scrape of a crutch.

Relief swelled in Darce's chest. Muir's coat was torn down the front, and the bottom of Lachlan's crutch was smeared with red, but they didn't bear any grave wounds.

He wrapped Lachlan in a one-armed embrace. "Glad you made it, little laird. I assume you got the job done, if the wailing of that bell is anything to go by."

"A bloody racket, isn't it?" Lachlan gave a wry smile, then quickly sobered. "But the city... Hundreds of bodies line the streets, human and selkie alike. The gutters are awash with blood. The bell might save some, but it's too late for so many."

"You did what you could. We all did."

Beside him, Isla stared at the cobbles, her jaw twitching.

Lachlan seemed to catch something in her expression. "What happened here? Is the Grand Admiral—"

"We need to leave," Darce said. "I'll explain once we've put enough distance between us and this wretched port."

"Not that way," Muir said, as Darce started towards the eastern docks. "We came from there. The young lieutenant is heading this way with a company of captains and sentinels from the other ships."

"Blair?" He glanced at Lachlan, who baulked at his name. "Surely he'll—"

"You're right, Galbraith. We need to leave." Lachlan's voice was even, but there was no mistaking the strain in his words as he started along the jetty.

Darce caught up with him. "He helped you get me out of that prison cell. He knew you were planning to save Muir."

"Drop it, Galbraith." Lachlan pressed his mouth into a tight line. "I made my choice. I knew the position I was putting him in. The consequences of that are mine to bear. Let's get out of here while we can."

Isla came up behind them, avoiding her brother's eyes. "We need to get out on the water. There's a ship in the firth that's ours to claim, if we can reach it."

"I have a small skiff moored nearby," Muir said. "It won't do us any good in the open sea, but it will be enough to get us up the firth."

Lachlan craned his neck for a final look at the haar swallowing the docks behind them. From the mist came raised voices and the clarion call of an Admiralty sea horn. It wouldn't be long until Blair and his forces were upon them.

Darce placed a hand on Lachlan's shoulder and urged him onwards, following the fading footprints of Isla and Muir as they rushed ahead through the rain.

Muir's skiff was waiting for them on the waves, its hull rocking. They piled into it, and Darce took a seat beside Muir as they scrambled to bring the oars to bear.

Even when the seaweed-encrusted rope was cast loose and the skiff peeled away from the jetty, Darce couldn't bring himself to release the breath he was holding. After all they'd lost, it seemed too much to hope for that they might escape this night with their lives.

Featherblade landed on the prow, letting out a throaty caw as it shuffled its wings. As the skiff passed through the haar, the air thickened with mist, seizing Darce's lungs. He tasted the familiar reek of rot and ruin, as foul as the last time he'd crossed into the soulless realm. His fingers were numb, barely able to clutch the oar as he heaved with all the strength he had left.

"What's...happening?" Lachlan choked. Beside him, Muir shuddered, his sailor's braids glittering with frost.

"There." Isla pointed into the fog ahead. "The anam-long. The soul-ship."

Its masts rose out of the haar, carrying silvery sails of vapour. Darce felt its song through the waves, carried from the bones holding it together and the blood spilled on its deck.

"It's calling us," he murmured, half to himself. "It wants us to take it."

Lachlan cast a wary glance towards the hull. "Not that this will come as much of a surprise to anyone, but I *really* don't like this."

"There's no reason to be afraid," Isla said softly.

"I never said I was afraid. Leave it to you to assume the worst of—"

"Enough," Muir said. "Whatever quarrel you two have with each other, you can settle it once we're out of the Admiralty's grasp. Until then, try to stop being such a gobby wee shite."

Lachlan glowered at his uncle, but said nothing. They sat in silence as the soulship's hull loomed closer. The waves battered and raged against it so fiercely it seemed the bone might splinter, but the ship held steady.

As they approached, something glimmered from the deck above, and a wisping, silvery thread unfurled, making no splash as it met the waves. It hung there, shifting in the mist, so patient it was like it was waiting for them.

"You were right," Isla said. "It *knows* us. It knows what we're here for."

"You can't be serious." Lachlan shot them an incredulous look. "You want to board? It's obviously a trap."

"I don't think so." Isla reached for the silvery vapour. At first, her fingers passed through it. Then it shimmered with thousands of droplets of salt water, and she wound her hand around it like it was a length of rope.

Darce watched as she hauled herself up, hand after hand, ankles hugging the misty rope for balance as she pushed herself higher.

As soon as there was enough space between them, he followed. The vapour was cold against his hands, so slippery he thought it might glide through his grip and send him plummeting to the icy water below. But somehow, it held firm, carrying his weight by some kind of magic he couldn't understand, not even with his sentinel gifts.

He hauled himself over the gunwale, waiting for Lachlan to follow behind him, crutch looped through his elbow. Muir was last to clamber onto the deck, stooping to catch his breath.

The ship was deserted. No sound stirred the deck apart from the gusting wind and hammer of rain. The billowing sails hung limp and unmoving, unaffected by the storm.

Something wasn't right. The selkies wouldn't have abandoned the soulship, not when it was so precious to them.

Muir's expression mirrored his thoughts. "I don't like this, Isla. There's something unnatural about this ship. And even if it's hidden beyond the haar as you say, I don't believe the selkies would have left it unguarded."

"We didn't."

Darce spun around, hand flying to his sword. Across the deck stood a lone selkie in a black pelt.

Duncan. One of the chieftains of the Selkie Isles.

He cast his gaze over them, stopping when he came to Isla. His brow furrowed at the bone armour around her ribs. "Is that..." His deep, gravelly voice ground to a halt. "Ancestors, it's hers, isn't it?"

Isla peeled back the sodden folds of her cloak to reveal the seal-skull helm hanging on her belt. "After what Eimhir took from me, I was ready to surrender myself to the tides. But it wasn't the depths waiting for me, it was Mara." She looked down at the empty eyes of the skull. "Or at least, the memory of her. She sent me back. She gave me her bones so I might cross the haar, so I might finish what I started."

Duncan fixed her with a measured look. "And what is that?"

"What it always was." She lifted her head. "I gave you my word that I would protect our people. I intend to keep that promise, even if it means protecting them from Eimhir. The path she's chosen will only lead to more blood."

"Not all of it ours."

"How much are you willing to see spilled?" Isla shook her head. "I thought you were waiting for the chance to take my pelt from me, but I was wrong. I didn't see the truth in your heart until it was too late. Please, don't make the same mistake."

"It is not your heart I doubt, aineol. I know the loyalty it commands." Duncan flicked his eyes towards Darce. "But our people deserve someone who'll fight for them above all else."

"Even if that means their end?" Isla retorted. "Eimhir is driven by the mist sickness, by her hunger for vengeance. That will only bring ruin."

"You believe there's another way?" Duncan's voice was weary. "What would you have me do?"

"He's stalling," Lachlan said sharply. "We need to get away from Arburgh before more of them return. End this, and let us get underway."

Isla's gaze settled on Duncan. "I would have you help me, but asking that of you is futile. Instead, I would have you help yourself. You cannot fight the four of us and live. Leave now, so we might be spared more needless killing tonight."

"Fight you?" A wry smile twisted Duncan's mouth. "You still don't understand, do you? You're Mara's wee girl. You were never in any danger from me."

He stalked over to the gunwale, placing his hands against the bone as he looked over the edge. "I won't stop you taking this ship. Mara led you to it for a reason. I believe that. But my place is with my people, whatever their fate."

Around his shoulders, his ink-black pelt shifted, the fur melting over his skin.

"She never got the chance to prove me wrong," he said. "I hope you do."

The rest of his pelt spread over his body, and then he was gone, leaving nothing behind but a splash echoing with years of regret.

Darce turned to Isla. She stared at the empty space Duncan had left behind, the weight of her brow tired and heavy. Her hand drifted towards the seal-skull mask hanging from her belt, the bone carrying an eerie sheen in the non-existent light. As her fingers brushed it, her expression grew rigid.

"I don't know what to do," she said. "Where can we possibly go from here?"

Darce's throat closed, tight and painful. What could he say? There was no hope to offer her, nothing he could tell her that would chase away the bleak shadow behind her eyes.

It was Lachlan who answered. He tucked his crutch into the crook of his arm and lifted his chin, meeting Isla's gaze with the reminder of a promise.

"Home," he said. "We go home."

CHAPTER THIRTY-EIGHT

ISLA

Isla had sailed away from Arburgh a dozen times or more, each journey stirring a different kind of emotion in her as she left: relief, frustration, sorrow. This time was different. This time, for the first time, there was no going back.

As the soulship slipped through the mist, the cries of the fallen capital followed. Long after the shoreline disappeared into the depths of fog, she heard the dismal toll of the bell ringing with the city's screams. Their wake was awash with all they'd left behind, all they'd failed to do. No matter how far they sailed, they'd never escape it.

With the storm behind them, the night sky was clear and crisp, bright with the near-full moon. Darce filled the silvery sails with his sentinel magic, carrying them from the soulless realm into the living world once more. The wound around his missing ear had burst open again, but he didn't seem to notice the trickle of blood running down his neck. His eyes were focused on the horizon as he twisted his fingers into wards, calling the wind and waves to his command.

His gaze found hers, dark and sombre. It carried the weight of everything that had passed between them, everything that lay ahead. But if a storm was coming for them, it was one they'd sail into together this time.

For now, at least, that was enough.

They'd only made it a few miles clear of the firth when they came upon the carcass of the *Jade Dawn*. The ship was smouldering, its once-vibrant sails withered and burnt to ash. The green-stained timber of its hull was charred and black, crumbling into the waves like dust. As they drew closer, Isla saw the molten bones of one of the crew strung up against the mast. The poor bastard had been metres from the water that might have saved him, unable to reach it. Unable to do anything but burn in the blaze that had taken the ship.

"I thought it might have been one of Quinn's bluffs," Darce said, voice dull. "I hoped..."

The rest of his words drifted into the wind. Hope was beyond any of them now.

Bile rose hot and angry in the back of Isla's throat. Tides take Nathair Quinn. Tides take the cowards in the Admiralty who'd set upon the *Jade Dawn* with pitch and fire, too gutless to board a Sea Kith ship.

She stared numbly ahead as they passed, unable to wrench her eyes from the devastation. Featherblade circled the smoking wreck, its shrill cries alternating between outrage and despair. It wasn't until the gannet landed on a piece of driftwood, opening its beak to release a blood-curdling caw, that Isla realised it had been searching for something.

Or some*one*.

Nishi was barely breathing when they pulled her from the water. Her fingers were raw from clinging onto a scrap of driftwood, a splinter of the *Jade Dawn* that had kept her above the waves. The residue from the blaze coated her skin in ash and grime.

Then Isla rolled her over and saw the burns.

She wanted to scream. The left side of Nishi's face was blistered and bloody, ravaged by flames. It didn't seem possible that she was alive. Even with the shallow rise and fall of her chest, the strained wheeze of her smoke-thick breaths, Isla didn't dare believe it.

Not until one of Nishi's copper eyes opened, shining with the reflection of fire.

"Too late." Nishi's voice was faint and rasping, every word strained to the barest of threads. "I was too late."

Her bruised eyelid closed again as she let out a low moan wracked with pain.

Isla glanced up at Darce. "Can you do anything?"

"I can try." He knelt beside her, coaxing his hands into wards to draw a shimmering stream of droplets from the sea. They hung in the air, glistening like rain, before he eased them towards Nishi's skin.

The captain hissed in protest as the salt cleansed her burns. Then, whether it was to pain or exhaustion, she gave way, slumping into unconsciousness.

"I'll keep an eye on her," Darce said. "I owe her that."

Isla pushed herself to her feet as he drew another glittering trail of water and pressed the droplets' cool touch to Nishi's raw skin. Her legs felt like lead as she stalked to the stern and looked out over the soulship's wake. All they were leaving behind was death and ruin. She saw that as clearly as she saw the spires of smoke rising from the *Jade Dawn's* blackened remains. Even when the wreckage faded into the horizon, she couldn't tear her eyes away.

The loss. The *failure*.

A shiver tore across her skin, raising the hairs on her arms. It wasn't the cold of night or the bite of the wind; the chill of such things didn't burrow as deep as it once had. This was something different, a whisper at the nape of her neck warning the worst was to come.

"You once made me a promise we'd return home together. I never imagined it would be like this."

Lachlan stood behind her, his gaze lost somewhere in the darkness. He hauled himself forward, the rosewood foot of his crutch lightly scraping against the deck as he joined her.

"Neither did I," she said, the words catching in her throat.

The silence between them was a raw, ugly thing. All she wanted to do was shatter it, but to do that would be to risk shattering whatever this was between them. It was the closest she'd been to him since he'd released the sgian dubh from her throat and let her go all those months ago. His hair was longer now, tied back in Admiralty fashion. His face was leaner and harder. But his expression was exactly how she remembered it the last time she left him.

"I need to know," he said, voice straining. His knuckles whitened as he gripped the gunwale with both hands, eyes steadily avoiding hers. "Our home...our family... Was it you who drew those wraiths there? Is it you they've been hunting all this time?"

Her hand drifted to the bone armour, fingers brushing the smooth surface of the cuirass around her ribs, the curved helm of the seal-skull mask hanging at her waist. The whisper of Mara's words echoed in her ears.

I followed you for months because I didn't know how not to. Because even the ghost of me knew to search for what I had lost.

She swallowed the lie burning the tip of her tongue. Lachlan deserved the truth. She would have done anything to protect him, but she couldn't protect him from this.

"Aye," she said, the admission sharp in her throat. "It was me they were looking for. They've called to me ever since I can remember. And when I didn't come to them, they came for me. *I* did this. I brought them to Blackwood Estate. Everything that has happened since then..." She bowed her head, unable to keep the tears from spilling. "If I'd never come back—"

"But you did."

All she heard in his voice was a cold, cutting pain. It drove straight to her heart, drawing another wracking sob from her chest. She could barely bring herself to look at him, but something inside her forced her to lift her chin.

His gaze was fixed on the horizon. There was a time she'd have known what was simmering under the surface. Now, his bleak features were impossible to read and more distant than she could bear.

"You did come back," he said again. "But it wasn't of your own accord, was it? She brought you back. My—*our* mother."

Isla froze. Her hand, as if by instinct or memory, searched for a pocket in a cloak she no longer wore, grasping for a tattered letter long lost.

Come home, my child. Allow me to give you the gift I have kept from you for too long, before it is too late for us both.

She could never have ignored those words. Even if she'd returned too late to understand. Even if it had meant...

Lachlan's eyes glittered. "She brought you back. I don't want to believe her final act was a mistake. If I believe that...I..."

"Please." She choked out the word, reaching for him at the same time. "I need to—"

He shifted away, pain flashing across his face as he braced himself on his crutch. "I'm sorry," he said. "I can't. Not now."

She dropped her arm, chest turning cold. "I..."

"Just...not now, Isla." He shook his head. "Not never, but not now."

She opened her mouth, but there were no words she could summon that would bring him back. Not before he was ready. All she could do was bear the pain as he walked away, leaving her with nothing but the wind for company.

No, that wasn't true. Something else stirred inside her, buried under the grief and guilt wrapping around her fractured heart.

Not now, he'd said. *Not never, but not now.*

The rift between them was as wide as it had ever been. But far as it stretched, it held something more than the fear of the abyss.

For now, finally, she could see her brother waiting on the other side.

It was difficult for Isla to believe more than half the year had passed since she'd last set foot on these shores. Caolaig was waiting for them as if they'd only just left. The small fishing village lay nestled at the foot of the towering limestone cliffs, its bay sheltered from the worst of the open waters. Small boats bobbed on the waves, eager to be loosed from their moorings and taken to sea.

Nobody would be coming for them.

They sailed into the bay, skirting around the sea stacks rising from the surf. The pillars glistened in the morning light, guiding them towards the lone jetty. There was a time they might have found another ship there for company, but not anymore. No ships came to Caolaig now.

The moment Isla stepped off the gangway onto the wooden jetty, a shiver danced across the nape of her neck. The shore was washed clean of blood, but Caolaig still bore the scars of what had been done to it. She felt it in the dead air, the unnatural silence clinging to the cobbled streets. Next to the old fishmarket, the bones of someone she'd once known lay propped against a wooden crate. A flash of colour caught her eye—a sudden movement from a yellow-green pincer belonging to the crab making its home in the skeleton's hollows and crevices.

She turned away, swallowing the grief before it drowned her. There were no witnesses to the violence that had befallen the village. None but her, Lachlan and Darce. Coming back seemed wrong, as if their presence threatened to disturb whatever peace the wretched remains of this place had found for its ghosts.

"We should stop by the doctor's old place," she said, wincing at how sharply her words carried through the air. "We might find some salves to help Nishi's burns."

"Aye," Muir replied. "We'll do that. But she's safe enough on the ship, and I need to…" His eyes trailed up the craggy face of the cliffs, where Blackwood Estate loomed above them.

"We'll go together," Lachlan said. "All of us."

He glanced at Isla, his expression unreadable. It might have been a peace offering or a rebuke, a reminder of all the times she *hadn't* been there.

But she was here now.

The cliffside path rose from the rear of the village, winding to the rocky summit above. As she climbed, Isla drew in ragged breaths, her shoulders laden with a weight only she could feel. It bore down on her, bruising her heart with the ache of it.

Perhaps this was a mistake. The last time she'd come back here…

"Look." Darce gestured to something up ahead. "Do you see it?"

The sky was overcast, smothering the morning light as if dusk were upon them. But through the gloom, she could make out a strange glow on the path ahead. A flicker of ethereal light, floating up and down like it was on a string.

She stilled. She'd seen this before. She knew what it was, what it *meant*.

A will-o'-the-wisp.

She stepped forward, ignoring Muir's look of alarm and Lachlan's protestations. The wisp looked the same as the night she'd returned all those months ago, when it had hovered over the waves like a beacon guiding her home. Her heart had filled with dread, then. She knew the Silvish tales about the ghost lights, and what the presence of one meant.

A soul extinguished. A life lost. Lady Catriona had drifted out to meet her that night, when Isla arrived too late to say goodbye.

The wisp's gentle light wavered, and it floated further up the path, casting its ghostly glow across the stones. Isla followed, her chest tight with something deeper than grief, stronger than sorrow.

Her mother, her *human* mother, was here, lighting the way home.

"She did bring me back," she said, turning to Lachlan. "And you were right. It wasn't a mistake."

He met her gaze, the wisp's light reflecting in his tawny eyes. "Then we have to make it worth something. We have to put right what happened here."

"We will." She swallowed. "If the haar spreads, it will only stir echoes of the violence that fell upon this place. I won't let it get that far. We *can't* let it get that far. Our family deserves to rest."

A shadow of grief flashed across Lachlan's face. For a moment, he looked on the cusp of saying something, and she braced herself for the sting that was certain to follow. Then it was gone, and he trudged up the path in silence, crutch scraping through the loose stones.

The wisp followed, its soft glow spilling across the steps he left behind.

Isla faced the horizon. A veil of low-hanging clouds clung to the grey waves, bleeding the line between sky and sea. Somewhere out there, Eimhir had her pelt. Its absence was written on the salt scars stinging her skin, the incessant chill running through her veins.

But it was not lost. It was still out there, waiting for her to reclaim it.

"Isla?" Darce took her hand. For once, she could feel his warmth through the numbness of her fingers. "Lachlan and Muir have gone ahead. If you're ready, we should go too."

The final twist of the steep, craggy path lay ahead, winding towards the iron gates at the entrance of Blackwood Estate. Towards the home that once felt like a cage, all because she'd been missing a part of herself she didn't know existed.

In the other direction, the cliff fell away to the churning sea and jagged rocks below. The soulship waited patiently at the jetty, its white masts glistening in the dim light.

For the first time she could remember, the sea was silent. There was no tugging in her heart, no ache in her bones calling her to find it. Everything she needed was right here.

"Aye," she said. "I think I am."

AFTERWORD

First of all, thank you for reading! I hope you had a great time with *Mists of Memory*, and it means a lot that you've taken a chance on an indie book - your support means so much. Before you go, I would greatly appreciate it if you could help other people discover this series by leaving a review or rating on Amazon or Goodreads.

Reviews, particularly on Amazon, are so important for independent authors and helps more books like this get written, so any kind of feedback, whether it's a written review or a quick star rating, is much appreciated!

The Sea of Souls Saga concludes with *Tides of Torment*.

You can keep up to date with future releases by visiting **ncscrimgeour.com** and signing up for my newsletter, or by following me on Instagram, TikTok and X at **@scrimscribes**.

Also by N. C. Scrimgeour

A dying planet. A desperate mission. A crew facing impossible odds. Humanity's last hope lies with them...

Time is running out for the people of New Pallas. Nobody knows that better than Alvera Renata, a tenacious captain determined to scout past the stars with nothing but a handpicked crew and a promise: to find a new home for humanity.

But when a perilous journey across dark space leads to first contact with a galactic civilisation on the brink of war, Alvera soon realises keeping her word might not be as easy as she thought.

Her only hope lies with the secrets of the ancient alien waystations scattered across the galaxy. The mysterious technology could be the key to humanity's survival...or bring unwanted attention from the long forgotten beings who built them...

<u>The Waystations Trilogy</u>
Those Left Behind
Those Once Forgotten
Those Who Resist